THE
RETURN
New Path

THE RETURN
New Path

LM MORSE

CITIOFBOOKS, INC.
3736 Eubank NE Suite A1
Albuquerque, NM 87111-3579
www.citiofbooks.com
Hotline: 1 (877) 389-2759
Fax: 1 (505) 930-7244

Ordering Information:
Quantity sales. Special discounts are available on quantity purchases by corporations, associations, and others. For details, contact the publisher at the address above.

Printed in the United States of America.

ISBN-13:   Softcover   979-8-90124-016-8
                        eBook   979-8-90124-017-5

Library of Congress Control Number:

A very special thanks go out again to my old friends and to my new friends from "Creeksquad". (You know who you are!) I truly appreciate all of your support!

"Where is she?" THEY demand. THEIR voices coming from multiple directions at the same time.

"We don't know!" Several of the group tell them as they all look east-southeast; following the direction where all of the critters are staring.

"That is an unsatisfactory answer!" one of THEM growls.

"Yeah well, no shit! But that's all we've got right now." Riley growls back.

"FIND HER!"

I listen to that exchange as I pick myself up off the ground. Apparently, I'm still getting some things from the others, but they're not getting anything from me? *Hot damn!* That's both good and bad, but I'm okay with that, for now. But right this very minute? I've got other concerns. See, I'm standing on the side of some road. To the right are some houses and a fairly clear road, to the left are a few businesses and probably the start of a downtown area. I have no idea where I am, but I do know that there are other things, including people out here and being found on the road wearing… not much… is more than likely going to get me into some serious trouble. I turn to look for a relatively decent hiding place but then feel a powerful blow to the back of my head, then…

I wake up, covered in furry, feathered and scaly bodies. Nothing new there, but I'm not sure what's going on. I feel… not as refreshed or as rested as I usually do. As a matter of fact, I feel like shit! Like I've been beaten up and like my skin is too tight. You know, like when you get a sunburn? I can also still hear the song "Eye of the Storm" by Pop Evil rattling around in my head and I can "see" some scenes from my really weird... dreams? See... when I say weird, I mean waaayyy out there. In some of the dreams, I don't even think... well, you tell me what you think.

For example, the first thing I see and feel... well... it's like I'm in our/my strange place, but not in a body or maybe trapped in someone else's body? See? Weird right? Anyway, I feel like I've travelled a really long way but whenever or wherever I stopped, I ended up kind of eaves dropping on a few people, some of which I've never seen before. If this is real, then I'm guessing that this is important so... this is what I witnessed.

I saw a woman sit up and practically yell "NO! Oh no! Why? Why is did this have to happen now?" After the woman sat up, she pulled her hair back and grabbed a tarot deck and started shuffling the cards.

"Hey Becki, what's wrong? Oh, and why do I feel like someone just punched me in my chest? That and why are you up so early and have your cards out?" A man with overly large eyes and maybe even some feathers mixed in with his white hair asks as he rubs his beaky nose after rubbing his chest. He watches what the woman is doing intently. But at first he seemed more confused than concerned.

"Jim, oh Jim... did you feel that too?" Becki asked while still shuffling her cards.

"Well, I sure felt something. What the hell was it?" Jim asked while scanning his surroundings.

"Well... my guides were showing me something... in a dream? Oh, and if you felt it too... then I guess that means we're both on the right path. Oh! My guides are yelling at me to check the cards, now!" Becki finished shuffling her cards and laid them out while Jim watched quietly. "Oh... this is bad. But..." Becki said while placing the cards in a strange configuration on the ground in front of her.

"What is it? What's happening now?" Jim asked as he watched Becki and her cards.

"You know that group I've been telling you about? The ones my guides are saying that we need to find? Well, the… nexus… of that group just had her heart ripped out! Oh shit… sorry. No, not …physically but… that must've been what we felt. That shit really hurt, didn't it? Okay so now? Everything seems dark. Or I think there's something dark covering? or maybe blocking the…no, her… light? I don't know." Becki stops there and turns over a couple more cards and starts again with, "Okay, so now my cards and guides are telling me that at least the bulk of her group will keep going, but it's going to be hard on them… without her… for a little while. Oh! And we need to get a move on too. Well now… this is weird, everything is telling me that we need to go to… Oklahoma?" Becki flips over a couple more cards then, "Oh, okay, I see. After we get there, we're going to have to find a place to hold up for a little bit. Maybe for a couple days. Oh, and see here? The cards are saying that we need to leave here, this place and… the sooner the better. It's not safe here anymore." Becki told Jim while wiping tears from her face.

"Well, your spirit guides and cards haven't been wrong so far, so you know that I'm in. But… what happened to the… what did you call her? The nexus?" Jim asked as he continued to make periodic scans of the surrounding landscape.

"Well, okay… so, it's like this… everyone has choices, right? Yeah, we all know that, but sometimes… sometimes we make the wrong ones. Even though, at the time, the option we choose seems like the best… or the easiest? Or the one that causes the least amount of drama, or whatever. The worst part? Something like this has happened in the past?… and it seems like nothing was learned… from those mistakes. Does that make any sense? Anyway… Jim, could you come over here and give me a hand? I think we really need to put some good vibes out into the universe. We also need to focus on righting wrongs and maybe… and maybe that the belief that love is enough? You know, anything that can help make some good come out of this fucking mess?" Becki said with a tired laugh and started shuffling her cards again.

"Oh, yeah sure! You know me, I'll always help you, any way I can. After all the help you've given me since we first met, what? Almost three weeks ago? Man… it feels longer… and just like yesterday." Jim said with a laugh and Becki joined in after swatting at him.

There's a strong bond between those two, I can feel it. Then they sat still for a few minutes, holding hands over the cards that she'd spread out in a different configuration and placed face down.

After a quick fast forward, like when you skip over the advertisements on your DVR? Becki told Jim "Okay, that should do it, for now. Thank you. Now, as to why Oklahoma. Okay, so my guides talked to me a little bit while we were sending out all of those good vibes. They themselves are unsure about why there, but they did tell me that there's something coming this way that we really don't want to meet, so we need to hit the road within the hour or so." She said that with a shudder and Jim looked thoughtful for a moment then told her that he's been seeing signs of some things even stranger than him moving away, so whatever it is, if it's scaring the odd and unusual, then yeah, they need to go and wake up everyone. As Becki was starting to gather up her cards, a couple more practically flew out of the deck and landed with the others. Becki stopped and studied what was there then said "Well shit… I know you've heard me talk about tower moments and… what happened to the nexus was… bad, in more ways than even my guides can see at the moment. I really wish that I could help, but it's up to them… or up to her to… find a new path. Hopefully one that brings everyone back together again." Then she packed up her cards and searched the horizon before giving Jim a long look.

"Now, let's worry about us for right now. I'll start the coffee while you roust everyone else. Yeah, we at least have time enough for that, but not much more." Then they shared a smile while she put her cards into a beautiful wooden box. Jim moved off after giving her a wink and telling her that he was on it. I'm not sure what the slightly mean laugh was about as he walked off to wake up the others as Becki put some coffee pots by the fire. She had a faraway look on her face and then she started talking.

At first, I thought she was talking to her guides, but maybe it was to me? But no, her lips aren't moving so… are these her thoughts? If so, I sure hope this new ability isn't permanent. Anyway, if these were her thoughts, then this is what she was thinking.

I think it started out with what's happened and everything she's been through, over the past few weeks. Magic, real magic coming back into existence, has been both wonderful and terrifying for everyone, not just her but… actually having her spirit guides sort of manifest themselves has been a mind-blowing and an amazing addition to her life on top of being an absolute life saver on multiple occasions. Having her tarot cards help in clarifying some things for her has been a brilliant addition as well. It's the part about having to deal with some people, some personalities… that's been an absolute nightmare. Oh, she's well aware that people will only change when, and if, they want to, and that nothing and no one can force them to do it. That's something she continues to be upset about. Oh, she knows that everyone everywhere has lost so much but even when her guides keep telling her that she needs to stop wasting her time and energy on certain individuals? That makes her mad as hell, and it's a hard pill for her to swallow. No, she's not actually hoping her guides and cards are wrong, but she's still not willing to leave anyone behind, or at least not yet. She's even been told, multiple times, to pick her battles better. Trying, or still trying when no one wants to listen or just doesn't care about anything other than their own needs and wants is draining and really bad for everyone's mental health. Hers included, plus it's really pulling everyone down so… she's reached the point that she's seriously considering how to cut a few of her folks loose, but she just can't do it in a mean way. Yet.

Then I'm on the move again, but when I stop, I recognize several individuals. I also feel a little bit better, as if just laying here, remembering, is helping me get back to… myself?

Anyway… I watched as Walter woke up crying and rubbing his chest. I think it was the Thunderbird and the mustangs caterwauling that actually woke him. That noise was loud and strangely haunting. I watched as he went out to them and listened as he talked to them. He stood quietly with them and touched each one as they all stood looking to the southeast. He doesn't seem all that surprised when they tell him that they're going to be leaving soon and that they want him to come with them. But just like with Becki, I think I hear his thoughts. When that shit starts again? I want to get the hell out of Dodge, but no… I'm… stuck? Well, I don't know, it's not like I'm moving under my own steam anyway so… I get to witness what he's thinking about.

At first, he was wondering if the Thunderbird and the mustangs actually sleep or if they just stop. That thought made him laugh because I'm sure he's had that thought many times over the past three weeks or so. Then he jumps around to the fact that he's never been more than one hundred miles from the place of his birth, but now the mustangs and Wakinyan want him to leave not only his home state, but to go a thousand or more miles away. That thought fills him with concern, but then again, he just can't imagine his new life or… any life really… without the manifestations of his late wife and her love in it. Losing her was hard, but he'd had time to prepare due to her cancer diagnosis, but the way she was actually taken from him and what she had done to the Thunderbird, Wakinyan, and the mustangs with her dying wish? No, he just can't picture his life without them, but this time, it feels more… final? Then he laughed as he jumped to the thought about all the times that his late wife had planned a vacation somewhere exotic or just far away, but… they'd never gone on any of them. He then took a good look at his new "children" as he and the rest of his new group calls them. The mustangs had started out as slender metal sculptures and now they've all "fleshed out" due to all of the bad things that they've hunted, killed and "eaten". He's still unsure of how all of that works, but… it's magic, so he reminds himself to just stop wondering. Then he thinks about the time, a week ago when he'd followed his "kids" hunting something that had ended up in northwest Arkansas, at Crystal Bridges, the art museum up there. That's when he realized that not only are the mustangs filling out, but now they've started choosing their gender as well. He'd found several of them in the museum and one seemed enraptured by a WWII poster of Rosie the Riveter. So that's how Rosie picked her gender and her name. *(That's so cool!)*

I'm pretty sure I laughed at how he remembered that a couple days later, in a music store, two had walked out as (Steely) Dan and (Iron) Maiden. (Iron) Mike's no brainer and the other three are still on the lookout for their new identities. Wakinyan just picked her name out herself, something about wanting to keep different parts of different names and cultures alive.

I personally think that we could all have some fun helping the other three out with finding names for them and I'm really happy to see how well they're all doing, but then I'm whisked away, again. And yes, I'm definitely feeling better.

When I stop again, I can't help but to smile. The General is definitely smaller than he was when I last saw him and he seems able to move around a lot better as well. But his thoughts are rather heavy, if that's what I'm getting from him. *Greeaaat.*

Charles Levin Parnell. General Charles L. Parnell. The General. So many names… but he's happiest with the last one, just the General. Something small, which he… is not. Oh, he's nowhere near as big as he was but… it's just not the size, or even the shape that he really wants or… needs now. Since magic changed him and his tortoise, he's faced many hardships and suffered from his share of problems and especially doubts but… the one thing he has never doubted was the new path that his life is now on. According to him that's all thanks to a bunch of irreverent, snarky, clueless, happy, loving people that kind of blundered into his refuge less than a week after this whole mess started. Those people blew his mind when they accepted him in his new form with absolutely no hesitation and they even helped him and his people out because… they thought they could. *(That's Lee's gift.)* Those people, even then, had no doubts about their path, their mission, though they didn't know what it really was… at the time. And now, even though the core of their mission has changed drastically since they started, they still continue on. At first it was just to reach a certain location, but by the time they'd reached Y City, they were already well on their way to perfecting their new calling. To spread hope, to protect the innocent and to help in starting to rebuild a better new world. All of that without asking for anything in return. Well… except for people to step up, *(that's Doris, no doubt about it.)* But once people see what that group's doing, it really motivated everyone else. Who would've thought that just the simple offer to help and the offer of friendship would blossom into what they all now have? Clear roads, for the most part, and thriving communities where once there were traps, pain, suffering and death. Speaking of pain, that's what woke him up but… because of the shape he's in, he couldn't even reach the spot that hurt, so he just started rubbing his bottom shell on a curb. His size, even though much smaller than before, is really pissing him off. He wants to be able to go places again and be able to personally help, to do the jobs that he's asking others to do. But most of all, he wants that irreverent group to get back together again, but he feels like it'll take some time. In a way he wishes that he could take her (my?) pain away. Mainly by saddling everyone with more monikers and more duties. The schmuck thinks it's funny that he's been able to get away with so much for so long. But… now he's worried. He feels something is coming, something that's going to need most of this ever-expanding group, no, family to handle. Or at least something that we all need to face… together.

His thoughts would've made me blush if I could have and I wish I could give the big galoot a hug or a swift kick in the ass but suddenly I'm on the move again.

I'm lying on the ground, warm because of all of the furry and feathered things on or around me. There are a couple scaly things here that are enjoying the warmth too but seriously, I'm not sure how I feel about those dreams… or visions, or whatever they are. I'm also almost positive that at some point songs like "Thunderstruck" and "Hell's Bells" along with many others had been blasting, either in my head or… out of me? Like what happens with Drew? *Ha! It's not like any of this shit isn't weird enough as it is though, right?*

"Uuhhh lady? So, are you… are you okay now? If so… can I have my dogs back?" asks a young man. Luckily, while he was asking his question, all of the critters had moved enough so that when I sat up in surprise, no one went flying. But the dogs in question did stay pressed up against me, telling me that everything is fine. I give both of them ear rubs as a thank you then look more closely at the guy.

"Oh! Uhh, yeah, sure. Thanks for letting me borrow Chet and Daisy… I think."

"Oh! That's… no problem, but… Hey! How'd you know their names?" he asks as his eyebrows disappear into his shaggy hairline.

"Oh uhh, they just told me their names." I say with a shrug. Then I get a better look around. The sky to the west is very bright and I can see that several buildings are on fire. I stiffly get to my feet and the young guy and I watch as the closest building to us that's on fire caves in on itself. I look around again and realize that I'm wearing some of my regular clothes and my armor. Both the shirt and the cargo pants are a bit worse for wear, (kind of like how I feel), since both the pants and shirt have got quite a few new rips and holes in them. Then I see my sword stuck in the ground a few inches away, it's well within arm's reach and next to it is a bag that I recognize. *Uh oh. What the fuck?*

"Holy shit! Uhh… what happened?" I ask him as several other people slowly approach us and most of the wild critters calmly scamper off. The hold out is a hummingbird, lizard and some type of bug combo. It's so cute, kind of like a teeny tiny dragon. It hovers around my head before landing in my hair. The folks approaching are looking mostly at me and my new buddy than at the town that's on fire.

"What?" an older man says, like he's unsure of my question.

"Are you kidding me?" a woman says.

"What? Are you going to say you don't remember?" another man sneers at me.

"Well, I'm sorry, but no… I don't remember. I don't even know where I am." I say with a shrug. I mean, my paltry problems seem so small compared to what's going on here, right?

An older woman steps forward, points back towards the town and says "You… you did this. Some of it before you… rescued us, some during the rescues but… mainly the rest after you'd found us a safe place to hide. Thank you for that, by the way. You know, you do seem… a lot different, than you were before. Why is that?"

While the woman was talking, very lightly, in the background in my head, I hear my darkness laughing and singing along with "Thunderstruck." *Oh shit?* Well, if they can't handle the truth, then that's not my problem.

"Well, I guess I had a kind of… dissociative episode? My uhhh… my alter ego came out to play." I say with another shrug.

"Huh? Well, I for one am extremely glad that that's what happened. Quite frankly… I don't think most of us would've made it much longer… if you hadn't come along when you did. Those assholes were getting worse by the day. Yeah, I truly believe that it was only a matter of time before they got too bored or… called away, then… they would've killed what's left of us." the first older man says as he steps forward and sticks his hand out for me to shake.

"Lucas! How can you say that? She might've killed your son!" the sneering guy says.

"Bah! You know exactly how I can say that. Anything else out of your mouth better not be any more of that bullshit. My wife and I raised my boy right, but what he started doing? Especially there at the end? That shit wasn't anywhere close to being right, and y'all know it. Yeah, I get that he fell in with the wrong crowd here, but I honestly believe he enjoyed watching me, his mother and his wife being... treated badly, being beaten and abused. So, no. After seeing the fanatical smile on his face when some of that was going on? He was no longer my son... he was just another asshole to me. And you have absolutely no idea how hard that is to say or how glad I am that his mother and wife are no longer with us now, and do you want to know why? No? Well, I'm going to tell you anyway... it's because before they were killed in that "accident", can you believe that they were blaming themselves for his atrocious behavior? Can you believe that horse shit? They tried many times to get him to see reason or to change his ways, we all did but... he simply refused. I hate to say this but... I think... I think he may have had something to do with their deaths. I hope like hell that he didn't, but I'm... I'm just not sure. So, no... I'm glad that this woman came along when she did." Lucas says, even though he had a few tears running down his face. *Holy shit! What the fuck is going on around here? What did I miss? Better yet, what the fuck did I do?*

As I shake his hand, I also tell him how sorry I am for all of his losses, and I mean it... to all of them... including this town. He nods and mutters a thank you. Two other women approach and there are a hand full of kids between them, none of them are older than maybe ten years old. A few of the smaller ones are either being carried or holding hands with someone bigger.

Now I know earlier that I had felt like hammered shit and still kind of do, emotionally, but these poor folks look way worse than I feel. "When was the last time any of you had anything to eat?" I ask, seeing how skinny the kids and people are looking.

"Actually, we finished a big meal a little while ago. We ate and then we watched over you while you… slept? At a… safe distance, of course. Thank you for that, by the way." One of the women holding one of the kids says while I'm still looking over the group again. *Huh?* The look on my face must have clued a few of the adults in because they laugh nervously and tell me that I may have burned down a good chunk of their town, but I left a building that had a small stockpile of food and stuff alone and got them all to it when I wasn't too busy. I guess it's a good thing my darkness can be rational. And apparently helpful. Jeez… I don't know why I'm trying to rationalize this; my dark side is still me, not an entirely different person. Right? Though the way she just laughed at me does make me wonder. *WTF?*

"Oh, uuhhh, my name is Lara by the way. So uuhhh… can you tell me a little bit about what's going on here? If it's too difficult, I'll understand." I ask as I relax a bit. Lucas relaxes almost immediately after I do then backs up and leans against a tree and starts his/their tale. "It all started three days after the orange fog came rolling in. A group of "God's Soldiers" came into town. At first, we welcomed them! With open arms! Then the next day they supposedly scared off something bad. We all thought that maybe, just maybe, that they actually were sent from heaven. But then… they stopped being helpful… stopped being "godly". They took what they wanted… including people… and made us feel like we weren't giving enough. Then… things got worse. See, in the very beginning, some of our friends and neighbors eagerly joined them, but most went missing or went to shit not long after joining. For some reason… the ones that joined the soldiers turned… on everyone. Like my own son did, practically overnight." He stopped there to wipe more tears from his face but then went on with "Now, you have to understand something… the main man, the leader of these

"God's soldiers" is a minister that some of us know from a few towns over. So, it was really easy to just let him and his followers waltz right in, no questions asked. But by God, we were suckered! You know… even though I personally witnessed some of those folks decent into… evil… I still don't understand it!" he stops there and wipes away a few more tears then continues with, "I would dearly love to blame everything on the fog, I really would but… deep down I know that I can't. People will be people after all, and people with power? Yeah, you get it." *Huh.* I think Lucas' new gift is something along the lines of seeing the truth of things. That might explain why he's so relaxed with me now and not casting suspicious looks at me like a few of the others still are.

"Oh, hey yeah! Some of them folks went kinda crazy and… I'm just about positive that they got some of their "games" from movies and TV." Another man says but then nods to Lucas who takes up their story again.

According to Lucas, the "games" started out as a way to alleviate some of the "soldiers" boredom, that they started out acting like gladiators or something, you know, beating the shit out of each other, but that caused a lot of dissension in the ranks so it was decided that they would "incorporate" the townsfolk that were useless to them or were causing issues. When that happened, most of the townsfolk that were left here knew beyond a shadow of a doubt that there wasn't anything "holy" about any of the soldiers and they all just wanted out but just couldn't do it, they couldn't leave. At some point the leader came back into town with something… and after that, no one put up a fuss anymore. It was like everyone had been brainwashed and they just let bad things happen. It seems no one interfered with any of the shenanigans that were going on. Then more people went missing and the "live" hunts started. That's where I apparently came into the picture. Lucas was being hunted and had a pretty good hiding place. He said that he saw me pop up out of nowhere, but so did the assholes that were hunting him. He then tells me that he's sorry for not stepping in to help me, but I wave his apology away. Not because I'm truly okay with what he'd done but because while he was giving that portion of his tale… it was like I could see some of that happening. I think my crystals are giving me a brief playback of the moment I stumbled out of our/my strange place and they're letting me relive it, only in fast forward. My darkness starts growling and then giggling in the background. *Holy shit!* Honestly, I also can't blame him for not helping me because he'd just said that no one interfered, but I can tell that he's fighting that… compulsion? Even now? *Huh.*

"So uuhhh… where did you come from?" Lucas asks, but I think he can tell that there's a lot going on with me at the moment because it takes me a few seconds to answer.

"Okay, so… uhhh, believe it or not, but… I really don't know. Where is here, by the way?" I ask.

"Really?" the young guy asks with a surprised laugh.

"Oh, in that case… I'd like to welcome you to the friendly little town of Butler, Alabama." Lucas says with a small snarky chuckle. *Oooooh shiiittt!*

I take another look around at the mostly destroyed town and slump my shoulders as I sigh. Oh, of course it is. Well… now it really does look like all of my dreams have gone up in flames… one quite literally. Typical, right? Well… fuck it. You know what? I'm not a quitter, so maybe… maybe it's time for a new dream. Will I miss my original one? Hell yes. I probably always will but… again, fuck it. This is just a setback, and I can't, I won't let this change what I want for myself… and for my family. There's no way. That's just not me. Sooo… since I'm in Alabama… Butler, Alabama no less… I might as well have a look around, you know? Looks like I need to scope out a new place, but first I really need to apologize to everyone here.

"Again, I'd like to apologize for… destroying your town. Buuuttt… what I'm not going to apologize for is… taking out the folks that were a threat to me… and to you. Look, this may sound… harsh, but you've got to know that when this group was done with you, they'd probably move on to another place and do this kind of shit to other innocent people, right?"

"Oh no, we do know that. Remember when I said that the leader is a minister? From a few towns over? I overheard my… son… talking to some of the other soldiers and shit like this is already happening. Everywhere they go, as a matter of fact." Lucas says, but he looks really angry. *Good!*

"Oh! I overheard some of them sons of beeswax laughing about what they'd done to a couple other places and something about the mutated people. I didn't catch a lot of that part but… I know that they did take off with a bunch of folks from here, some of which… no longer look completely human. I'm Sandra, by the way." the older woman keeping an eye on the kids says.

"So, what are we going to do now? We obviously can't stay here. And… if I'm being completely honest here, I'm terrified of what's out there and I'm not… not much of a fighter. I'm sorry… but, you know what? I'm willing to learn, if that's what it takes." a younger woman who'd come up behind the kids says. Well shit, she's got a point. Except for a few of the men, none of these folks look like they're trained for any outdoor activities, let alone hunting and… being hunted.

"Are you out of your mind? Now you look here, we can't run. They'll find us! I say that we all stay here and blame this whole mess on her! It's her fault anyway! Pastor Ansdale… he'll understand! He'll know that none of this was our fault! I'm sure of it!" the belligerent guy says. *Really? Is this guy delulu or what?*

"Excuse me sir… but are you fuckin' kiddin' me right now?" the guy with the dogs says. *Ha! I really like this guy.* He reminds me a little of David, only an older and maybe a softer version.

"Bobby! You watch your language with me!" the delulu guys says.

"You know what? Fuck. You. Todd. You're not in charge and you're not dating my mom anymore… especially since you Let her get taken off by those assholes. To wherever they've taken everybody else. I still can't believe you did that! What kind of man are you anyway? You never once stood up to any of them and you never stood up for any of us! You just rolled over and…" Bobby stops his rant after Lucas and another man put their hands on his shoulders. *Fanfuckintastic! I get to start a new list!* Finding and possibly rescuing the missing is now right under finding a new, safe place. But first…

"You know what? If you want to stay here and blame me for all of this? Go for it. As a matter of fact, please do. Because I sure as shit don't want you anywhere near me. Got it? You never know, I might go… crazy again… only this time, I'll be aiming at you." I say but I can feel my darkness giving Todd a nasty smile. Being the stand up kinda guy Todd seems to be, he turns tail and runs away. *Ha!*

"Good riddance to bad rubbish." another woman says after winking at Sandra.

"You got that right, but… he's going to be a problem, if he can. I'm Roger." another man says after sharing a concerned look with Lucas.

"Well, what's he gonna do? She done blew up all the weapons and stuff and there ain't nothin' left to drive around here and oh, all of those guy's radios are gone too. So, what's he gonna do, use smoke signals?" another man says with a bark of laughter.

"Nah. She already done that and ain't nobody answerin'." a maybe ten-year-old boy says as he points to the still burning town. I walk over and give the little boy a high five for that comment. He's not wrong after all, but jeezus, I've got to get these folks out of here.

"Are all of the vehicles around here really destroyed? Oh, and are all the bad guys… gone?" I ask, trying not to say anything that might upset the kids.

"No, you didn't get them all. You missed the ones that left right before you showed up, something about securing another town. I'm afraid of what that means for those people." Sandra says. One guy thumps another guy in the chest and points.

These two look enough alike that they could possibly be twins, but the other one starts nodding his head and says "Oh, well... you know? There might be a couple buses at the school... but I'm not sure if they run. Them guys took all the batteries outta just about everythin' to power their radio room."

Well now, I've got this very familiar bag laying close by, so now I'm wondering not just how I got it and the clothes I'm wearing, but what else might be in the bag. I don't care that these new people think I'm weird when I laugh and sit down in front of the bag and open it up like a Christmas present. Oh, and I kinda hope Casey doesn't mind because it's his military duffle bag that I've got. As I open the bag, I see a couple more shirts and pants, plus underwear and socks! *Hot damn!* But under all of that it's like I've hit the jackpot! I find quite a few gizmos from the Brainy Bunch! Four of the ones for starting vehicles, two to power a couple houses and two that work on really big buildings and oh! a couple things I've only been briefly briefed on but helped to put together, not to mention a radio. I push all of that aside for now and come up with a gun, ammo, a couple different sized jars of goop, and a few snacks. The homemade IED's give me some concerns, but I recognize Perky's designs so I know that they're harmless, for now. *Holy shit! What did I do and why can't I remember?*

"Alright folks! How fast can y'all pack up everything that... I didn't burn, food wise and... anything else you might need? Oh, and how far away are the buses?" I ask excitedly. From the looks on everyone else's faces, it seems that my excitement might be catching.

"Hey! How 'bout this? Half of us stay here with the kids and pack things up while the rest go with you to check out the buses. It would be a whole lot faster that way; don't ya think? Oh, and I'm Jamal and this is Jalen." the only one to talk so far says. And yeah, I think that's pretty smart.

The Butler folks split up while I repack my bag and then I'm going to check out the bus situation with Bobby and his dogs, Lucas, Roger, Liz, Jalen and Jamal. They all take the lead and we go past a lot of things that apparently, I'm responsible for damaging. I cringe as I look at the devastation. *Holy shit.* At the next corner, right past downtown, they all start to slow down, so I guess we're getting close. But nooooo."I can't believe you burned this building." Lucas says, sounding funny. *Uh oh.*

"Ohhhh… I can… feel them…" Liz says, sounding like she's had a few too many. I stop with everyone else and then I turn to get a really good look at Lucas and Liz, but everyone else has almost the same blank looks on their faces too.

"Okay, so what's so special about a florist shop?" I ask.

"Pastor Ansdale brought them here when he came back… the second time." Roger slurs.

"Brought what back?" I ask as I start rummaging around in my bag for a jar of goop. Then I throw caution to the wind and open myself up a little. Wowzers! There's definitely something here… and it's not good. *Ugggg.*

"They brought everyone left here in town to see them." Jamal says as he starts to sway. *Crap on a cracker!*

"I think I hear them calling." Jalen mumbles, or at least I think that's what he said. I personally don't "hear" them, but I do feel something and whatever it is does something to my crystals… I think.

See, all of a sudden, I can see and hear something that I recognize. I think what I'm experiencing is from… Jones' perspective? It started out with "FIND HER!" coming from a voice I recognize, and it's one of the last things I heard before I tuned out everyone back in Arkansas. The next part is completely new. Is this some of what I've obviously missed?

"Hey! **YOU** guys are supposed to be everywhere, so why don't or why can't **YOU** find her?" David yelled in the direction of the voice. Alex came up and put his hand on David's shoulder and asked him to calm down. After taking a couple deep breaths David then said "She'll be back. She always comes back. Right?" while looking at a lot of other people that are standing around.

"Yeah. She does always come back. But… I don't think she'll appreciate it if she sees all of us out here waiting for her. I know she's going to be pissed off that we witnessed that… that dick move… that was just perpetrated on her. So how about we give her a little space? Okay?" Casey said, but he doesn't look like he means it. He actually looks… worried? But mostly just pissed off.

"Casey? I just want you to know that I kind of hate it when you're smart. It completely ruins your rep as a schmuck." Helen said while giving Casey a wink, but she looks worried too, but he nods at her like he understands something that she's not saying. If that makes any sense.

"A dick move? Really? And I suppose you'd know all about those?" Doris snarked.

"Hey! I may be a guy, but I have never, and I mean never… done anything like that. I'll swear on anything you've got! Guys? Have any of you ever pulled anything like that?" Casey asked, looking truly offended.

"Uhh… The worst I've ever done is ghost someone. But, I mean, we both knew it was a one and done type of thing. Does that count?" Doug said with a shrug.

"Oh, ummm… I stood someone up once. But… I mean, I didn't have her number or anything so I… I couldn't call her to cancel." Ox said while Lynx was giving him a seriously dirty look.

"Oh yeah? And why would you do something like that?" Lynx asked with her arms crossed and her claws coming out.

"Oh well see uhhh… that was the day I met you." Ox said as he started to scrunch down on himself. Lynx's claws disappeared and she walked up and gave him a kiss.

"Well then… I'm not saying that that's okay, but it's okay with me." Lynx said with a sexy smile aimed at Ox. *Blech.*

"Well, I've had my share of hit it and quit it moments but they were mutual, ya know?" Pit Bull said with a shrug.

"I've gotten my share of phone numbers and never called any of them. Would that be considered a dick move?" Dozer asked.

"Yeah, maybe. But how many of those numbers were 867-5309?" Sonny asked with a smirk. Quite a few folks chuckled at that, and it seemed as if the heavy weight was lifting off everyone.

"Holy ssh… Alex, remind me to never take any romantic advice from any of those guys. Okay?" David said and there were a lot more chuckles as most of the group went back to their trailers.

"If she's not back in a couple hours… then we might as well continue on with what we were doing. That way… when she does show back up, we can all pretend that we didn't witness that… what we did. I think that might help her the most." Alex said to the vanguard and a few of the others that were still standing around. Then Drew went rigid. A song came out of him, and it was kind of ominous.

"What was that?" was asked by just about everyone.

"I think that's pretty obvious; the song is called "The Dam" by Daughtry, I think, so… something must have really set her off and she's… she's about to blow." Casey said and everyone there started nodding and talking but Drew had a very concentrated look on his face, even after the song ended.

"But hey, wait! At the end of that song she had a pretty big "oh shit" moment. What do you think that means?" he asked but no one said anything. From the looks on their faces, I'm guessing that they're afraid of what that might mean, and so am I. Then I see a few people come and go in fast forward really quicky and then Drew goes rigid again. The song that came out of him this time was… definitely disturbing, to say the least.

Casey sighed as his shoulders slumped and everyone turned to look at him after the song ended.

"The name of that song is "Raven" by Peyton Parrish. It's… well shit… if that's what she's going through right now, then things might be worse than we thought. Drew, was that all you got from her? Can you get anything else?" Casey asked looking very concerned.

"No, or at least not right now. I didn't even know that I could do that or know that song but… what does it mean?" Drew asked while panting and giving Casey really good eye contact.

"It's… I think… she and her darkness are fighting but…" Casey started silently.

"Well… look, let's not go borrowing trouble. Okay? So… let's meet back here in a couple hours." Riley said while he and a couple of the other guys were trying really hard to hide their concerns, especially because of the look on Casey's face.

Then I'm back on the street with the Butler people. The squeaky-hissy noise from my new friend hiding in my hair snapped me out of whatever that was, but I really don't think all that much time has passed because the others are all still just standing there, staring at the flower shop and kind of swaying.

"We have to save them." Bobby slurs but his dogs are blocking him from moving forward and growling at the mostly burnt store front. I finish pulling out a jar of goop, open it and run a thickly covered finger down the side of his face. Within a few seconds he starts to shake his head and blink rapidly. I watch him but I'm also wondering about what the hell just happened to me. But... I just don't have time to deal with that... weird shit... right now.

"Hey, why'd we stop here?" he asks as he quickly snaps out of whatever trance he was in. He looks at me and I point at all of the others still being affected.

"Holy shit! What's wrong with them? Wait! Was I like that too?" he asks and I nod.

"Really? So uuhhh... how come I'm not like them now?" he asks and I point to his face and smirk.

He reaches up to check his face and says "What? Did you hit me or somethin'?" but then his fingers find the goop. My smirk gets bigger at the look on his face. "Uuggg! What the fu... what is this? Holy shit! What'd you do? Hack up a big ol' luggie on me?" he asks as he wipes the excess off on his pants.

I laugh and tell him no, but then Jamal starts forward and Bobby watches as I get another finger full of goop and put a big smear down the side of Jamal's face. Then I just go ahead and do that to the others. We watch as they come out of their trances and then Bobby asks me if that's what it was like with him and I just nod. Everyone there looks at Bobby as he tries to explain what just happened to them. None of them look very happy.

"So... what's so special about this flower shop?" I ask.

"Gawd dammit! I cain't believe I forgot about this fuckin' place!" Jamal says angrily.

"Again... what's so special about this place?" I ask louder.

"Oh! I remember! The soldiers forced us to come here... at least once, for sure, but..." Roger says but it looks like he's struggling with something. "I… I remember thinking… that they were scary as hell but… also kinda pretty?" Liz says as she puts her head on Roger's shoulder.

"Uuhhh… hello? What is it about this place?" I ask again but I already know that there's something nasty inside that needs to be dealt with.

"Yeah, they're… creepy. Pastor Ansdale… he talked to them and… and made sure they were… always kept… comfortably cold?" Bobby says while seeming to struggle with his own memories.

"That's right! I heard him say something to one of his soldiers about how they better keep them cold when… when not in use?" Lucas says.

"So… let me get this straight. The bad guys brought everyone here to see something and you were all exposed to it. How did you feel when you left here?" I ask, but I think I already know the answer to that question. They don't remember and… I'm going to bet that this is where the compulsion to be nothing but compliant came from. Maybe even the compulsion not to… feel too much? Is that even possible? I mean, these folks should be a lot more… emotional? than they are. Or maybe I'm just wondering about myself. Either way, the Butler folks all look at each other, then at me. I think they're figuring out that something is way out of whack here too.

Well, since my darkness missed these things, I guess it's up to me to make sure that whatever this is can't be used against anyone else. It's already caused enough problems. So, I head for the broken door and go inside.

"Hey, wait!" several yell as they all follow me into the building.

"We can't be in here! Those things are dangerous! Look at what they did to us!" Lucas says and the others nod. I just turn and look at them with my eyebrows raised.

"Oh yeah? Well... I'm dangerous too." Then I turn back and walk further in. In the back of the store, the only thing I find is the walk in cold room door. I pull out my sword and open the door slowly. Inside the cold room the atmosphere immediately turns misty due to the temperature change, but nothing comes rushing out at me, so I just stand there, letting the mist clear. Then I see... them. *Yikes! Holy shit! Okay sooo...You know how some orchids look kind of alien? Well...* multiply it. Three very freaky looking plants are the only things in the cold room and they're swaying back and forth, kind of like a snake does. Each has a brilliant blood red flower with black veins running through it at the top of the stalk, kind of like a head but I'm not seeing a "face", and short stubby limbs, like arms. The stalk and arms are covered in nasty looking thorns. I take a step closer to them and they all lean in my direction. As I open myself up, I can feel that they're all full of magic. Some of it seems to have been stolen, but most of it's their own. *Imagine that! A big bad that's not actually big, and powerful to boot!* I bet just one of these little beasties has enough juice to change Stanley, Oscar and maybe even Megan! And now they're all mine. *Mwahaha!* I turn to look at the folks in the doorway to see if they're being affected by the plants but they're just staring, in awe, I think.

"You said that they brought these things here, right? So how many more do you think they have?" I ask, but I'm thinking about how many more folks can be helped by these things. Roger just shakes his head and the others shrug. *Yeah, that would've been too easy.*

"You're not afraid of them? Well... I am. Just looking at them is givin' me the heebie-jeebies!" Jamal says and several of the others give a shudder.

"Well, I'm not going to lie to you, these things are obviously very dangerous... but I think I know how to contain them. Do you see those containers over there? Could someone bring them to me, please?" I ask. The contraptions look like a reconfigured hard sided golf bag case crossed with that thing at the bank that you use at the drive thru. Only made out of buckets and heavy-duty plexiglass. One of the containers looks like it's built for two of the plants, so after digging around in my bag and putting on my armored gloves, I grab two and shove both nasties into that container. I can feel where the thorns are really trying to get through, but they can't. *Nanna nanna boo boo!* The last plant tries to play keep away then it tries to stab me, so I'm not as careful as I should've been when cramming it into the other container.

"These fuckers are a handful, no doubt, but if they're enjoying the dark and cold? Let's see how they like the dry and hot." I say with a mean smile. I think they heard and understood me because they stopped scratching on the glass. I don't believe for a second that I've scared them… yet.

"Uuhhh, not to be rude here but… why didn't you just use your sword to kill them?" Lucas asks and the others nod.

"I still might if they give us any more trouble but… I have a plan on how to… use them… to help other people and things. Right now, they can't hurt any of you, so y'all are safe from them. Plus, the more we take from good ole Pastor Ansdale and his soldiers, the less he has and the less terror he can inflict on others. Killing these things now would actually serve no purpose. Does that make any sense?" I ask.

"As long as I don't have to take care of them, you can do whatever you want with them." Roger says. Lucas looks thoughtful for a moment then nods his head.

"You sure they're safe? That we are? Well… Okay then." Jamal says as he and Jalen grab the containers by their handles and walk outside with them. I guess that's their way of saying that we need to get a move on.

Back out on the street I ask the group a few more questions about Pastor Ansdale, like if he's into exotic plants. No, he isn't, but apparently his wife is. Ooooh? So maybe that's why there's a human feel to those things. But was that intentional or… Then I wonder what else he uses them for besides mind control. Oh, and what does he do with the stolen magic?

Maybe I'll ask him, or maybe my darkness will. Either way, the rest of the group stops and gives me a look because of my snort and my not so nice chuckle. I just shrug and tell them that I'd had a bad thought. I think they're starting to understand me, a little. The group doesn't talk much as we make our way a few more streets over to the school. Maybe because they're still afraid of running into any remaining soldiers? But I can tell that there's nothing out here. No other people, except for Todd, no animals anymore, nothing. It's like we're now in a dead zone. No pun intended. Then I feel Drew trying to make contact with me and the music from "Mission Impossible" starts rattling around in my head. The others stop again and look at me. *Ha!* I guess they're wondering where the music's coming from. I just laugh as I push Drew away and keep walking, but the song "I'm Working Bitch" by Ashnikko starts up. I know that I didn't pick that song but I think my darkness did. *Ha!*

"So, Lucas… you said you were being hunted when you first saw me, right? So, what hit me?" I ask as my new little friend finds a new spot on my shoulder and hanging onto my ear, it's tail flicking with the beat of the still softly playing music.

"Huh? Oh! They hit you with a bean bag from a riot gun. See, on most of their hunts… they liked to incapacitate or knock out their "prey" first." he says with a look of disgust.

"What? Oh yeah sure, that's like… so sporting of them." I snark. Then I ask "So… are the guys that did that to me… did I… kill them all?"

"Well now… I don't uuhhh, I don't rightly know since I didn't actually see any of the bodies or anything, but… after they grabbed you and took you back to the garage they liked to "work" out of… at first, I thought the screaming was coming from you. Then it got really quiet. Then the garage… exploded! I uhh, I felt really bad for you but…it served them right! I mean it wouldn't have surprised me any if they did actually blow themselves up, it was a garage after all. Lots of flammable things were in there and I've seen them smoking around there, a lot.

But… when I saw you again, much later that day, I was totally shocked! I mean… it was you but… you looked… different and… scary… and you were sneaking around, so I… I left you alone. I mean, after the explosion, I realized that everyone knew that I was supposed to be the target that night and since the garage and the guys in it were gone and I was still walking around? Yeah, no. So, I stayed hidden. If anyone had seen me, that wouldn't have gone well for me, you know? Also… during that the time, I thought about just leaving but… the stories that some of the soldiers told us, about what's out there?" he points out into the distance. "I'll admit that I was, and still am… kind of terrified, but… is everything really that bad out there? Or were lying to us, to scare us into staying put? I mean… you made it here." The others in this group all nod their heads and stare at me. *Awww shit.*

"You know what? I've run into other people who thought something very similar, about being afraid of what's out there. And like you… they were rescued from pretty dire circumstances. Now let me ask you this… how much worse could it be out there, when you're being kidnapped, hunted and killed in your own town?"

I know that's harsh, and I'm not going to apologize for it. We've been dealing with this shit for over a month now and they've already faced death here, so getting them to be willing to leave shouldn't be too big of a stretch. They're all stronger than they know, they just need to see it. Getting them to embrace what's to come might take a bit, but if they stick with me, willingly, then hopefully it'll be a fairly smooth transition. The transition from being victims to… I hate to use the term vigilantes, but… Avengers and Guardians have already been used, so how about we use… just the righter of wrongs? *Eewww, no.* Or hell, just survivors. I know, it doesn't have as good ring to it but…

"Look, things can only get better if we stick and work together, so how about it? Do you want to learn how to survive out there? And how I made it this far?" I ask.

I know, I'm trying to sell them on this, hard, because… I have a feeling. I let them think over what I've said as we continue along until we finally reach the school. Well would you look at that. *Hot damn!* There are three buses, and even though one looks like it's been used for target practice, a lot, at least we now might have transportation. Unfortunately, they're locked up behind a big chain link fence with concertina wire across the top. My sword can easily take care of the lock and chain. Hell, it can take care of the fence too, but I think they need to see if they can do this on their own. While we're all standing around waiting, Liz asks if she can go into the school and grab a few books. I smile and tell her that the old world may have ended, but education is still important. I laugh as she, Roger and Lucas head inside discussing which books they need to grab. Bobby hangs with Jamal and Jalen while I ask if the gym has a shower. I'd seen what I look like, wild hair and who knows what smudged across my face. Pretty scary, even to me.

While in the shower I feel a couple small nudges so I guess Drew is trying to get in touch again, which I ignore, but dammit! So… I end up sending back "I'm Alright" by Kenny Loggins but then Drew sends back "What I've Done" by Linkin Park. That song plays as I look at myself in the mirror while putting my hair up in its usual style. I guess that's his way of saying that I need to forgive myself, for what I've done in and to this town and… I will, eventually.

Even after taking a bit of time in the shower, I still beat Liz, Roger and Lucas out of the school. Then I just can't take watching the others trying to get in to where the buses are anymore, so I walk over and cut the chain with my sword.

"Hey! How long were you gonna let us struggle with this?" Jamal asks with a shocked look then a laugh.

"Oh, about this long." I say with a smile. All three of the guys smile kind of bashfully but then Jamal and Jalen strut through the now open gate and immediately start to check out the better-looking buses. I laugh when I get a good look at the shot-up bus and the guys look at me. I tell them that I've actually seen a van in worse shape than this and that it's still in use. They just shake their heads but then after a minute or two they tell me that it's like they suspected, none of the buses have batteries in them. I rummage around in my bag and sort through the gizmos that I've got. I think Jalen would've ripped them out of my hands if he wasn't still kind of afraid of me. I just put them down on the ground and try to remember what each one does and how to make them work. Once I remember which ones go in the vehicles, I have to ask the guys to show me where the alternators are. Clip a wire to this thingamabob then clip a wire to this doohickey. *Voila!*

"Okay guys, who wants to start this bad boy up?" I ask, but all three are completely engrossed; two with just looking at the unused gizmos and Jalen practically laying on top of the bus's engine looking at where and how I'd connected the wires. Bobby snaps out of his staring contest with whichever one he was fixated on to happily hop into the bus and then he asks how he's supposed to start it with no keys. Jamal walks over and hands him a screwdriver and then tells him to stick it into the key slot and see it that helps. The bus starts up with a smoky cough, but it does start and stays running as Bobby jumps out and continues to jump around for a moment, his dogs jumping along with him. So, I pick up another gizmo and go to the other bus, Jalen is practically attached to my back as he watches me attach this new gizmo. Jamal pulls out another screwdriver from somewhere and he climbs in and starts that bus up too. I step back and Jalen turns to me and… smiles. Roger, Liz and Lucas come up with a ton of books and they stop at the look on Jalen's face. From the looks on everyone's faces, I don't think many people have actually seen his smile before, or at least not very often. It's one of those smiles that when you see it, you just have to smile too. It's kind of like watching the sun come out from behind a big dark cloud, and even I feel lighter because of it. *Wow!*

"Well, I'll be damned. Would you look at that! I guess things really are looking up for us. If that's the case… you know what? I'm not afraid to leave here anymore. As a matter of fact, I can't wait to get the hell out of here! So, let's get this stuff on board and go pick up the others!" Lucas says with a happy yell.

After just sliding the boxes of books and other supplies, along with the nasty plants, into the back of the buses, we all clamber in and off we go.

_On the way back, Bobby takes over from Lucas's story and I just… find it amazing. According to him, not too much time later, after taking out the four guys from the garage, he, Jalen and Jamal had been able to slink away from some other bad guys questioning them when I caused another… disturbance? Anyway, some of the bad guys left in a hurry because they got a call on their radios. Bobby said that after that, any time they saw any of the bad guys they all looked scared and/or pissed off. Also, Bobby, Jalen and Jamal accidentally ran into Lucas right after their close call and the four of them went about trying to follow me, discreetly. No one knows how I blew up two buildings or how I brought down two more that night. And even though most of the residents that had been locked up were now loose, none of the bad guys paid any attention to them because they were too busy looking for me. The next day, most of the bad guys were holed up in the courthouse, but then it went up with such a blast that it broke most of the windows for a couple of blocks. Over the next day and a half, if there were any stragglers, the guys watched as I picked them off whenever they came out of wherever they were hiding. *Daaammnn!* I don't remember doing any of that… or seeing any bodies.

"Wait! Are you telling me that I did all of that in two days?" I ask, dumbfounded.

"What? No. Technically, it took you three days… and nights." Bobby says with a shit eating grin. *Holy shit!* I'm stunned!

"Wait, you didn't know?" Liz asks, surprised. Yeah, I'm surprised too. Believe me!

"Uhhhh… No?" I manage to squeak out but then we're pulling up next to a slightly scorched building with a very large pile of stuff stacked by the front door. Sandra steps out first, then the kids come rushing out yelling, laughing and clapping as we get off the buses. *Oh shit!*

First things first. "Hello again! I uuuh… I know this might sound strange, but could I get everyone to line up… please? On our way to get the buses we came across some… things that might have some… side effects… that aren't very nice. But I just so happen to have something with me that can… protect you from them." I say, then cringe. *Jeez, I'm not very good at this. Shit.* Luckily, Bobby steps up and laughs at my delivery and tells everyone that it's going to be okay. He tells everyone that he and everyone that went with me to get the buses have already had the treatment and that it doesn't hurt. Not even a little bit. That part made the kids laugh. Then it was my turn to laugh, especially at the horrified looks on everyone's faces as I pull out a jar of goop. I open the jar, stick my finger in and give Bobby another smear.

"Oh! Eeewwww! Twice? That's nasty! Oh! But see? It really doesn't hurt!" he says with a laugh as he tries to wipe it off, looking disgusted. I give him a cheesy grin and tell him to consider this a booster. Lucas steps up and takes my still goop covered finger and rubs a bit of the stuff on his bristly cheeks and chin. By this time, the kids are all laughing again and are more than happy to get gooped. The small girl with her thumb in her mouth comes up and points to herself, so I goop her first, but very gently. She removes her thumb and smiles at me and then waves at my tiny friend. After my shower and combing my hair it reattached itself to my ear. I hear it hum; I think in pleasure? The little girl then walks calmly back to the others. The last three adults still look a bit wary, but after seeing that nothing bad is happening to anyone, they step forward for their turn.

"What is that sh… stuff?" A woman named Marybeth asks while curling her lip and pointing at the jar.

"We just call it goop. It would probably be better if we just leave it at that." I smirk.

"Who is the we? What does it do?" Sandra asks as she checks out the jar and its contents.

"Well, as you might've guessed, it's magic, but it actually helps keep other things with magic from… clouding your mind. Oh, I know that it looks really nasty, I'll give you that, but it does work. I've seen it and experienced it. The "we" part is my friends, no, my family." I say with a laugh.

"To prove her story is true, what do any of you remember about Jackson's Flower Shop?" Liz asks. At her question, everyone shudders, and Sandra mentions some freaky looking plants, and everyone shudders again.

"Yeah, okay, but before being gooped, most of us didn't even remember that much. Do you see where this is going?" Roger asks.

"I feel like we're missing a lot of things… it's because of those plants, right?" a man named Henry asks.

"Yep! Now come on! Let's get this sh… stuff loaded into the buses and get the fuh… get out of Dodge!" Jamal says as walks by. All of the adults laugh at his good try at not cussing in front of the kids. I have a feeling that I'm not going to be as good as he's trying to be. Scratch that, I know that I'm absofuckinglutely going to suck at it. And quite frankly, I don't give a flying fuck. If all they ever come across are some vulgar words, for the rest of their lives? Then they'll have lived wonderful lives, indeed.

"Are fucking kidding me? Do you have those creepy plants? Here? Why?" Marybeth says in a harsh whisper.

"Well, mainly because… do you really want the bad guys to have them when they come back here? To be able to use them somewhere else? On other people? Besides, I know how I can use them for a worthy cause and… I've got a feeling." I say with a shrug.

"As long as I don't have to see or deal with them, I'm okay with this. Come on Marybeth, she's right. We're keeping Ansdale and his goons from having them and now they can't be used against anyone else." Henry says and Sandra agrees with him.

"Fine, but you can't expect me to be happy about this." Marybeth says. I can understand her feelings, but eventually, I'm going to have to tell her about our "waste not, want not" philosophy. *Ha!*

Twenty minutes later, all seventeen of us are on the road. Before we leave, I make sure to ask everyone if they know of anyone that might be left here in Butler. I even include asking about folks pets. That's when I learn that the bad guys, before the plants got to everyone, those assholes thought it was fun to kill someone's pet in front of everyone and telling them that someone else they love would be next, just to keep them in line. My darkness is whispering to me that she'd had fun taking care of the perpetrators of that disgusting display of power. I wonder about Bobby and his dogs but then remember that when Chet and Daisy were laying with me, they told me that Bobby and his mom had kept them hidden, even from Todd. *Good for them.*I tell everyone that we're going to be heading south, but we make sure, because I'm sure Todd's watching, to leave town by going west first.

Now, I can't give the soldiers too much credit, since they didn't actually clear the roads, lazy bastards, but at least they made a usable path for a while. Also, having Bobby and Jamal as my navigators is interesting, especially when they wanted to know why we were going south. They don't get my I snicker, but I don't think it'll take them long to realize that when I get a feeling, they should just go with it.

 After leaving Butler, the roads are marginally clear as we pass through several small towns. Red Springs, Hodgewood and Toxie, to me, feel completely empty, I don't even sense any animals. Several people comment when we have to stop and move a couple cars farther apart so that we can pass through the gap that from what little they can see it looks to them like everything just up and left the area. Maybe they did, but my question is, did they leave on their own or was it because of the soldiers? But the farther we get from Toxie, the more things I feel. Mainly regular animals, but there are a few new beings roaming around out there too.

While cruising down Highway 17, I get a kick out of all the squealing and screaming due to my driving. I keep having to remind myself that these folks are new to being out and on the road, and most, if not all, can't really see much due to the orange fog. To me, most of the time I forget that it's there since I really don't see it much anymore. Now, if my bus is loud, I can only imagine what the other bus sounds like because Jalen is doing a fantastic job of keeping up with me. *Bwahaha!* Then we have to stop right before Gilbertown. It appears that the soldiers haven't made it this far. Me, being me, and incredibly paranoid, I decide that we only need to move what we have to in order to get by and then we move everything back where we found it. Just in case, ya know? Plus, I'm having another feeling. When I tell this new group that we're doing it this way to cover our six, I nearly smack myself. Yeah, I've definitely been spending too much time listening to police and military jargon. *Ha! Oops, I did it again! Bwahaha!*

Anyway, after entering the town, I decide to pull into the Piggly Wiggly parking lot with Jalen seconds behind. I'd recently been informed that everyone needs to pee, or worse, and we all need to stretch our legs a bit. Apparently, I've made a few people extremely tense with my driving skills. I'm pretty sure my fam is going to get a big kick out of the fact that I've literally scared the shit out of a bunch of people with just my driving. *Ha!* The plus side of this is that we get to see if this place had been picked over. From what we've encountered on the road so far, I seriously doubt it.

Once inside the store, the place is practically pristine, if a little smelly due to the rotting produce. The bugs flying around the store get my little friend's attention and off it goes, to pig out, I'm sure. So, everyone hits the restrooms and for those out first it's time to do a little "shopping". Now, this being the deep south, even the Piggly Wiggly has a hunting section, so everyone is picking out a few new things to wear. I get the honor of helping four-year-old Emily pick out the perfect pink camo print outfit. In reality, she doesn't give me much of a choice, but I enjoy my time with her anyway. While everyone else is going up and down every isle, I find a Rand McNally, then find exactly where we are and start plotting a course. Then it's time to take our haul out to the buses. After putting a ton of stuff in the back of both buses I turn and see something. Something that I just have to have. When I start walking toward it, I'm followed by everybody. They all stand back and watch me as I walk around it and check the tires. Why, I have no idea but I've seen my guys do that, a lot.

"So, are you going to find the owner and make them an offer?" Marybeth asks then smirks.

"No, but I am going to drive it like I stole it. Because… let's face it, that's pretty much what I'm about to do." I say with a huge grin.

"This thing? You like this thing?" Henry asks with a shocked look on his face.

"Well… I could really do without the confederate flag on the back glass and the paint job sucks, but I'm really diggin' the rest." I say with a laugh.

"Where'd you say you was from again?" Jamal asks while I watch as he and Jalen go over the outside of it much more thoroughly than I did.

"I don't think we ever got that far, but I'm recently from Arkansas. So, Jalen, is this thing up for a long trip? Maybe a little off roading? Will the winch work to pull, say, a bus out of a ditch or something?" I ask as Jalen approaches and opens the driver's side door. He gives the interior a cursory check but then pops the hood. After a minute or two of checking things under the hood he nods his head, but Jamal laughs and says that there are no keys and a screwdriver won't work. I dig around in my bag and pull out another gizmo. Jalen snatches it out of my hand and checks it out. Once he hands it back to me, reluctantly, I spend a minute trying to figuring out where this new type of gizmo goes. After I get it where I'm pretty sure it's supposed to go Jalen nods to Jamal who hops in and starts up the truck. *Fanfuckingtastic!* I'm now the newest… operator… of this jacked up, supped up, 4x4 redneck special. *Yeehaw!* "Now that that's settled, just know that whoever rides with me is on push duty. And while we're moving cars and things, everyone, please stay in or really close to your bus, in case something nasty is roaming around. Speaking of something nasty, I think we should go. Not to frighten anyone but… we're being watched, and I have a feeling that the short ones are looking like easy pickin's, if you get my drift." I barely finish that statement before everyone starts herding the kids to their bus. I was kinda joking, but maybe not really? I mean, we are being watched but I don't feel anything other than curiosity. Except… I think one of **THEM** is somewhere close by and I'd rather not deal with that bullshit right now. But yeah, as for the rest, we've definitely seen a few signs of violence, and sometimes hunger does override caution. I'm just glad no one has asked why we haven't seen any bodies. Yeah, I know, but they'll learn all about that, in time.

Before we're able to truly leave Gilbertown, we have to stop for gas. I really don't miss those days, so I guess the Brainy Bunch has really spoiled us. Luckily, Henry, Jamal and Jalen know how to turn on the pumps and we fill everything up, plus a few gas cans that the convenient store had on hand. We also swipe a bunch of drinks and snacks because I see the guys looking longingly at the beer, so I tell them to go ahead and get it. Hell, I'll drink a few with them, maybe even tonight. I feel the need for a few after what happened in the Piggly Wiggly.

See, while everyone was filling their grocery carts, I got another "update" from my crystals. It was definitely Jones' perspective. It started out, I guess, the same morning that I didn't return. Some time had passed, and everyone was up already and they'd gotten back to clearing the bridge. Jones was upset, they all were, I could feel it. He was talking to the group, and he even went so far as to comment that he thought that I might be upset with everyone if they just gave up or quit. That they needed to continue on with our "mission" until I returned. He even threw out a Star Trek reference. (I wouldn't be upset with anyone, and he knows it. Who taught him how to pull a guilt trip? I'm going to have to have a talk with him, that's for sure.) Anyway… this is what happened.

The group had started on finishing the bridge, but they ran into an issue that none of us noticed the day before. The trucks that were wrecked on both sides of the bridge were wrecked at almost the same location. We also missed that the ones heading west had a lot of damage to their trailers. Not to mention there's a forty-foot section on both sides of the bridge itself that has some serious structural damage. That news didn't go over very well.

"Well, this certainly sucks ass." Doris commented.

"It kinda looks like something massive manifested on the bridge or came up from the river and crossed the bridge. If you look here, you can see that the damage is in an almost straight diagonal line. There are quite a few places where you can see the river through the holes in the pavement. I'm sorry guys, but I don't see a way to get across this without leaving our transports and walking for a while." Perky said as he and a few others rejoined the group, looking morose.

"Seriously? Fuck! We can't leave our rides. We need them! How the hell are we supposed to carry all of our stuff? We seriously need to keep… uhhhh… at least half of what we've got!" James said, shocked.

"Can we… I don't know, take everything out? To make the RV's lighter?" Kabir asked. No.

"Can we patch the road?" Melissa asked. Maybe? But…

"What we need is a crane or something to hoist everything across the sketchy section." Mark said. Pit Bull laughed and gave Mark a pat on the back after checking his pockets and telling him that he was fresh out of cranes. A long pole, sure. A crane, nope. The laughter and whatnot from that broke the tension a little bit.

"Fuck me. Okay… So, I hate to say this, but I'm going to go to pothead central to see if they have anything that might help us, if the compound doesn't have anything." Nate said morosely. Everyone chuckled at his downtrodden look. I remember that the day before, the stoners had hit him up for some constipation relief, and even though everyone laughed about it, it didn't make his day, at all.

"That's actually not a bad idea, I'll even come with you." Alex said trying to hide his smirk.

"Yeah, no reason to do something stupid just yet." Zee said as he went to catch up with Nate and Alex. The rest of the group went back to moving things and marking off where the damage started, until Drew started yelling.

"Hey! Hey! Holy shit! Mom! Guys! She was just here! I just ran into her, but then she just… disappeared!"

"What?" was yelled by most as they ran to where Drew was, which was by where they'd parked our rides.

"WHAT?" and **"Where did she go?"** was growled by the voices that followed everyone to where Drew was.

"How the fuck should I know! But I did just see her! Hey! Aren't **YOU** guys supposed to be everywhere? I mean… Why haven't **YOU** found out where she is yet?" Drew said as he turned to where the voices were coming from. It appeared that he was hoping to start a fight.

"Drew, please… tell us everything." Lee said after putting his arm around his son. But Drew was so worked up, so angry, and so scared? that the song "Walk this Way" came out. After he took a deep breath, he started again.

"I was walking this way, and I saw her come out of her RV. She had a bag with her, one of the military ones… and her sword." At that point, several people started peppering him with questions, but he held up his hands.

"Look, when I called out her name… shit… when she looked at me… I think I… I peed a little. I mean, it was her but… fuck… she… she looked… different. Like…" The song "Cold as Ice" came blaring out.

Riley shuddered and said "Oh fuck! I know that look, very well. It's her darkness. I think her darkness is still in control."

"Oh shit. That's not good." I hear several people say.

"Wait! When you saw her, you said she had a bag and her sword, right? Did you notice anything else?" Dozer asked.

"Like what?" Drew asked while pacing around. Casey went up and put a hand on his shoulder, maybe as a way to help ground or calm him while the former SEAL's have fallen back on other ways of communicating. They must think something really bad is about to happen and they don't want to alarm everyone. (This way of thinking surprises Jones.)

"Well… I mean… she was wearing cargo pants, boots and a long sleeve shirt. I could tell that she had at least an amour shirt on under the long sleeves because I could see it. How does any of that help?"

"Well, it gives us a better glimpse into what she might be up to. And it seems to me that she might be gearing up… to go to war." Casey said sadly.

"What? No way! You think that she's going to go and… kill him?… for hurting her?" Tarina said, seeming shocked. "What?" and "No way!" were said multiple times by multiple people.

"No! She would never go after him. So… so it has to be someone else. But who?" David asked.

"Well, whoever she's after, they better run as far and as fast as they can, that's all I'm saying." Riley said with a nasty ratty smile.

"You don't think it's us, do you?" Clark asked, then smacked himself on the head. That did save a lot of other people from doing it to him and took some of the sting out of his question. *(What a dork.)*

"No, seriously. If her darkness is in the driver's seat, shouldn't we all be… I don't know… still afraid of her?" Lynx asked. *(Really?)*

"No. Absolutely not. Look, there's still a fight going on with her as to who's going to be in charge, but Lara… well… she Will Never let her darkness do anything… to us. The perfect opportunity just presented itself with all of us being occupied with other things and with Drew and… nothing happened to us or to him. I think we all need to believe that Lara wouldn't… Ever… allow that to happen." Casey said, but he looked very thoughtful and determined. *(Hhmmm?)*

"Alright, so I hate to be indelicate here, but we need to know what else she took so that we can get a better idea of what she's up to." Perky said very seriously. David said that he'd go with him to look in my cabin, seeing as how he shares closet and drawer space with me. Dozer and Sonny stopped in the doorway of the RV then asked everyone else to go and see if they could find anything else that might be missing. Riley laughingly said it looked like someone had stepped on an anthill, the way everyone turned and went off to check out things.

David yelled out that a pair of steel toe boots, and a pair of sneakers are missing, along with a couple t-shirts and two of his long sleeve shirts. He absolutely refused to go through my underwear drawer. Helen tells everyone that several prepackaged snack bags and a few jars of goop are missing from her inventory, and even though David points out that my shields are still here, for some reason Sonny still seems concerned about all the items that are missing. Once back outside, Sonny turns to Drew but he seemed stumped by whatever he was wanting to say or know.

"When she was here… did you feel her… at all?" Jones asked instead; I think as his way of turning the subject to something else.

"No… not a first. Oh, but when I first made eye contact with her… holy shit, her eyes… that's when… Uummm yeah. I can feel her now, but I think… I think she's doing something to block me."

"That might be another reason why you came away unscathed. Look, her darkness may be in control, for now, but you and some of us now have a deeper connection to her than the rest. The question is, will that be enough to… perhaps break through the blockage? Just enough to see what she's up to?" Jones asked.

"If Drew is up for it, I'd like to give him a hand or maybe help give him a boost." Casey said with a mischievous yet determined look on his face.

"Oh, I'm up for it." Drew said. But yeah, it doesn't take a rocket scientist to figure out that they're up to something.

"Casey, ever since you and Lara helped Drew, it would come as no surprise to find out that the two of you now have a stronger connection to her than even she knows about." Jones said, looking thoughtful. *(Oh yeah? Well, I do now!)*

"Okay, so how the fuck are we supposed to get to her? Or through to her?" Drew asked. Casey put a hand on Drew's shoulder and told him to "follow" his lead. Everyone was wondering what they were doing but then both went rigid and then AC/DC's "Thunderstruck" came blasting out of them.

"Holy shit! Now that's a song to go to war to." Doris said and everyone there agreed with her. The whole song played, with an extended beginning before Drew and Casey, got control of it.

"Well, that's it, I'm relieved. I mean, hey! It's not us that's having a seriously fucked up day. Because guarendamnedteed, if that's how Casey and Drew are interpreting how she's feeling? Someone's totally fucked." Pit Bull said with a snort and then a belly laugh.

"You know, if we still had news stations broadcasting, I'd be channel surfing right now, trying to find out where there's a late breaking news story about a massive disturbance." Ox said with a belly laugh of his own. Most everyone else joined in, even though there was a slightly grim undertone to it.

"So. You still do not know where she is?" the horrendously ominous voice that everyone recognized asked.

Everyone either jumped or twitched at the question.

"No, we don't. But keep **YOUR** ears open. I'm sure one of **YOU** will be hearing about something, very soon." Riley snarked.

"WE have been closely monitoring all communications since WE realized that she was gone from here." Another familiar voice said.

"That's great! Then what?" David asked, but there was no answer. After that, David said that since there's nothing that anyone can do... but wait, that is, they might as well get back to work. And figure out what to do about the damn bridge.

Now, after watching that "playback" it appeared that none of my new group noticed anything off about me. Was it just like before? How much time did that take? How the fuck is any of this possible? Yeah, yeah, it's magic and I should just stop asking. I get it. But still!

Anyway, after leaving the convenience store, on the outskirts of town, I see something and I'm definitely making a mental note of it. Dwayne's

Electrical and Hardware. The building is huge and looks undisturbed. Maybe I can come back here at some point and maybe bring the Brainy Bunch with me. Or let Jalen and Jamal loose in there. Who knows?

Maybe fifteen miles down the road, I can suddenly feel of a bunch of people up ahead so I warn everyone in the truck that I'm stopping for a few minutes. They're confused, but they really have no choice. Yet. *Ha!*

We find the people, or at least where the people are. They've barricaded themselves in the Choctaw Elementary School, just off the highway. After stopping and trying to get them to talk to us, all we get in return is a warning shot. Now, I know that it would be so easy to just say "Fuck you too" and leave, but I can sort of feel their fear and I know I hear a couple kids crying. So, I rope my new crew into helping me as I revert to one of my/our original missions.

"Now, I know that we just practically wiped out the Piggly Wiggly, but these folks… I think they need some of this stuff more than we do. Besides… we can always get more, while they all seem to be too afraid to even open the doors. And maybe they have a very good reason to be that way, but… there are kids in there and maybe us giving them a hand and them seeing the kids with us will change some things around for them. So… who's going to help me, help them?" I ask.

Even though we still have guns pointed at us, everyone gets out and we start pulling out bags and boxes full of food and other stuff. Boxes with canned meats like tuna and chicken, boxes of soups, some powdered milk, boxes that have pasta and sauces in them. Cereals, canned fruits and vegetable and a couple boxes that have… I do a double take. Someone must have wiped out the entire snack cake section! Now, I would swear that I'd heard Marybeth, Liz and Sandra tell everyone to pick only the "good for you" stuff and to leave the junk alone. No one says a word when I leave a couple boxes full of that stuff with the others, then I wish those folks well. I do warn them about the "Soldiers of God" and then we all get back into our rides and we leave them in peace.

"Seems to me that you've done something like that before." Liz says not too long after we get going again.

"Oh, so now you're wanting to hear some of my story? Well, okay, that's fair. To answer your question, yes. Me and my group have done things like what we just did back at the school before. Many times. Most of us, my very original group… we all worked together, or at least at the same place. A couple days after the orange fog started, we met up again and of course we multiplied due to having family members and other friends joining us. Some of the crew that left Fort Smith with us were brand new to all of us as well. Before we left though, we stayed in my neighborhood for a little bit and checked it over really well, but I knew that I had to leave. I had to get to someone, no matter what. The others decided to join me, and we left Fort Smith and headed south, clearing the roads as we went. At Y City, we met some more folks and helped them out. Some of my very original group decided to stay in Y City to wait on other friends and family, but the rest of us kept going, with a few new additions. The next place we came to had some… seriously fucked up stuff going on and we… put a stop to it. It also helped all of us become… closer? Anyway, we lost a few people and gained a few more individuals to our crew after that. No, no one died. Oh, but one guy did leave because he just didn't like us. His name is Perry, and we weren't sad to see him leave but he did give us something to laugh about and we've been laughing about it ever since.

The rest, they just… the road life and what we're finding? It's not for them. Which is fine too really, and also lucky because we keep finding really bad shit and… really bad people. But we've also found some really great people and, well… we call them new beings. Now you have to understand that my very original group… we already had quite a few new beings traveling with us, so we've never had any problems accepting… anything.

So, from Fort Smith to Y City and from there we worked our way across the entire state of Arkansas, helping where we could and kicking ass when it was needed. Growing our ranks even as we left some behind because they felt that they were better suited to stay wherever it was to help other folks out. But as you can imagine, it took us a while." I finish with a smirk.

"Wow! That's… that's just incredible! But how did you end up in Butler? And where's the rest of your group?" Liz asks but at that exact moment, I feel Drew trying to make contact with me again and my darkness seems to be having a tough time of pushing him away. Then the song "I Will Not Bow" by Breaking Benjamin begins to rattle around in my head. From the strange and shocked looks on everyone else's face, they hear it too. *Well shit.*

"Well now… that's… not something I want to talk about right now. But I will say this, my original plan was actually to come to Butler, to meet up with… someone. Unfortunately… like your town, that dream has gone up in flames too." I say as the song continues to play and as my darkness washes through me, trying to smother the pain that that statement causes. It did help some, but it couldn't stop a tear or two from rolling down my cheeks. I don't care that everyone in the truck is staring at me, but I'm glad that no one says anything until we come upon a six-car pileup. By the time we're done clearing just enough of that to get through, my darkness has settled down and I guess she's gone back to waiting. I know that while we're working, those that heard part of my story share with the others what I'd told them, and I'm okay with that too. Saves me from repeating myself, I guess.

Back on the road, I pick up sort of where I left off with, "So, you wanted to know how I ended up in Butler, right? Well, the only answer I have for that, at the moment is… it was magic. No, I'm not making light of this, I promise you. I was in no shape whatsoever to actually come to or be in Butler. But once I got there, well… apparently, I ran into some trouble. Oh, yeah, by the way, I'm a trouble magnet, just thought you should know that. Ask anyone in my group, they'll tell you. Anyway, even though I was having… an issue? That doesn't… or didn't… stop me from trying to make things right. Personally, I find that to be a good thing, you know? Knowing that my personal problems *(demon?)* didn't... or maybe won't... interfere with what my group laughingly calls our "New Calling". The last time I was with my group, we were getting ready to cross the Mississippi River at Lake Village. Now, believe me or not, I really don't give a shit, but my group... my family and I are... special. What I mean by that is... well... we kind of thrive on our new calling. Scratch that... we absofuckinglutely thrive on it. Together, we're a... functioning dysfunctional mess." I have to stop there because I'm laughing too hard to continue. By the time I get my giggles under control, I restart with "While what I just said is certainly true, we're also very tight, very close. When we're together... we can tackle just about anything, and we usually do. We've helped too many to name or count. But here's the thing, we're trying to make... I guess you could call them safe zones or safe havens, for those willing to work for it, along with trying to make a better future. The places that we've helped set up or helped get back on their feet? They're going to make it... they are making it.

This world will never be like it used to be... I mean, how could it, right? Now? Now we've got super intelligent animals and people that can change their forms or have already turned into a completely new form. Good plants and bad. We've got magic! How cool is that? Now don't get me wrong here, some of the new beings and some of the people with power are... they're fucking terrifying! But, if they're using their new gifts and whatnot to hurt people, hurt other things? Well then... they've got to go. Period. I mean, come on. I don't need to tell y'all that. You've seen it, lived it. Lived through it. So... in a nutshell, that's what my family and I do. We help when and where we can and we... take out the trash when needed." I finish.

The truck is silent for close to a minute before Roger snorts out a laugh, then Bobby cracks up. Liz is trying to play it cool but then she starts to giggle. I just let them get it all out of their systems, but I can't hide my smirk. *Ha! If they only knew. Holy shit! if they only knew how much I left out. But dammit! I don't think they're ready for the doomsday shit just yet.*

"Thanks for that. I mean it. I know that you left a shit ton of stuff out but… thank you. For helping us. Oh! How I wish my mom was here. Ha! She would probably threaten to wash all our mouths out with soap, but she'd also be the first person to volunteer to help you with just about anything." Bobby says with pride then laughs again.

"Yes. Thank you for helping us and… for showing us that it's not all bad. Yes, definitely, thank you for showing us that there are still good people out here. People who are willing to give a helping hand and ask for nothing in return. I don't think it would've ever occurred to us to stop and offer to help those people… I'm sad to say." Roger says looking thoughtful.

"Alright, look, you don't need to keep thanking me. It's okay. I get it. Oh, and Bobby? Speaking of your mom… once I find a safe place for all of you, my plan is to find out where the shithead soldiers have taken everyone and… get them out. To get all of the hostages or whatever you want to call them out and away from whatever mess that's going on with those nutjob soldiers. With or without my family. I'm just not sure about that part yet. I've still got a few things to work out first."

"Are you serious? Hot damn! I'm in! I'll do anything I can to help you! Just say the word! Fuck yes! I'm all over that!" Bobby says excitedly.

"Bobby… I think we're all in, but we've got the little kids to look after and… I'm not sure that all of us are going to be effective… fighters?" Liz says, but now I'm having another déjà vu moment. Does any of this sound familiar?

"Oh, well then, that's okay. Uhhh… those that can't fight… they can… uhhh… what can they do?" Bobby asks.

I laugh and tell him that we call the folks that don't or don't like to get into the thick of things "support staff" and we all laugh at that. Then we have to stop and get out to move a few abandoned cars and trucks. The four of us plus Lucas, Jamal and Jalen have picked up a pretty good rhythm already, but while we're clearing enough space to squeeze by, I get another "update" from my crystals. It's another glimpse of what had happened, mainly from Jones' point of view again.

It started out with Jones and a few others walking up the bridge. In the distance I can see that the jack-knifed trucks have been moved but then I see that yeah, there's a serious amount of damage to the road itself. From the way Jones feels, he knows that this mess had absolutely nothing to do with me. I mean, I know that I'm responsible for what happened to Butler, so me being totally innocent of the bridge damage is still a relief to me. Jones, Ox, Bulldog, Dozer, Pit Bull, Perky and Mark carefully maneuver to the other side of the damaged area and start to move vehicles from that section but then they had to stop because they'd come upon more damage.

"Hey! Check this shit out! I can see the river through a couple of these new holes!" Ox yelled. The other guys go to where Ox is, and they follow and uncover several more holes.

"Wow! Now I'm seriously wondering what the hell did this!" Pit Bull said.

"Is it me, or do these holes actually look kinda like footprints?" Dozer said. The guys move a few more vehicles and then they can see that Dozer is right. They really do resemble footprints.

"Can we drive around these spots if we can get past the other damage?" Ox asked.

"If we can get our rides over that other section? Maybe. But there's no way with the trailers attached. Not enough room to maneuver." Perky said with a look of calculation on his face.

"Well fuck." Came from a very unexpected source.

"What?" Everyone said as they all turned to stare at Jones. *(I'll admit that I thought the same!)*

"Dude! You just dropped the F bomb!" Mark said with a laugh.

"Well, yes. I did. You know what? Now I understand why so many of you all use such foul language, and so often. Sometimes... no other comment fits and... it's strangely satisfying." Jones said and shrugged.

I could feel a smile spread across my face but then I can tell that someone had silently passed on the fact that Jones had just cussed by the way the guys all burst out in laughter. Then Casey and Riley came up at a run and clapped Jones on the shoulders before they went and checked out the newly uncovered holes.

"I have a question, though I don't believe that any of us will have an answer." Jones said. Casey, Riley, Dozer and Perky look up from their inspection and turn their attention to Jones.

"All right big guy, what's on your mind?" Riley asked.

"Well... I'm wondering about **THEM**. What I mean is... when **THEY** said that things were going to be getting harder, did **THEY** mean just for us... or for **THEM** too?" Jones said.

"I don't know, but... that's a damn good question. Maybe... maybe **THEY'LL** even be willing to answer it, if **THEY** even let us ask it." Casey said and shrugged. Then Jones let that line of questions go and asked if the smaller holes could be filled with something temporarily. When everyone asked why he shrugged and said that maybe with some holes filled perhaps that at least the motorcycles could make it through to the other side. I'm glad that everyone there was so supportive of his suggestion.

After a few minutes of consultation while a few of the others went back to moving vehicles Perky took off saying that he thinks that if they packed the smaller holes with the something and then slapped a piece of plywood or something over it, it might hold up good enough to drive over, at least a few times. When he left to go get his supplies he had a big smile on his face. A quick fast forward and everyone's heads popped up and they all took off running, again.

I'm glad I don't get motion sickness because Jones' crystal was bouncing around as he ran back to where all of our vehicles were parked. He stopped near where Perky was backing away from his trailer and like everyone else, he was asking what was wrong.

"Someone's been in there! The place is a wreck! Oh! Oh shit!" Perky said then went back into his trailer. Then "Shit! Some of my IED's are missing!" he yelled.

"Holy shitballs! You don't think any of the stoners got ahold of them, do you?" Casey asked with a bark of laughter. Perky and everyone else couldn't contain their laughter and their horror of that thought. Then Perky said "If the stoners had been in here, then their smell would surely still be lingering. Wouldn't it? Ha! No, seriously, look… I know I said this place is a wreck, but it's really not. Yes, some things have been moved around, but it seems more like a… targeted search." Then Brandi showed up and pushed Perky out of the way so that she could check things over. Another fast forward and Brandi's out of their trailer and she confirmed that twelve IED's were missing along with some ammo.

"Holy shit dude! Why in the hell are you ridin' around with twelve IED's?" Bulldog asked, looking horrified.

"Well… uuhhh… I actually have a lot more than that. But hey! That's beside the point! Someone has taken them! Not only that, but… it's twelve of the ones that the Brainy Bunch helped me with." Perky finished after listening to what Brandi had to say, but he'd scrunched down, like he knew he was about to get yelled at.

"Well fuck a duck! Dude! How much damage can one of those things do?" Catherine asked, kind of outraged.

"Well now, that's just the thing! We never got to test them out but… well… we're guessing that just one could level a building. Easy."

"Did Lara know about them?" Parker asked looking shocked and scared.

"Well yeah. She even helped me make some of them while we were on gizmo duty, as she called it. What? No! You think she came back here and grabbed some? For what?"

"Did you miss the last time we tried to make contact with her? She's fucking someone's world up!" Doris said while throwing her arms up in the air.

"Drew… I think it's time for us to try to make contact with her again." Casey said, but he didn't look happy about it.

"Okay, I'm willing but… I'm also afraid to try again, ya know?" Drew said.

"Oh yeah, I get it. I'm a little on the leery side myself." Casey said quietly to Drew. I could almost hear the call that went out because everyone that was out and about came back in a hurry. While Jones and the rest were waiting for everyone to return Casey, Riley, Jones, Drew, Doris and Tarina had set up a big sturdy table that apparently Drew is going to be laying on. After a bit of dithering Drew finally laid down and Casey had everyone put a hand somewhere on Drew. The PPE's, Megan, Bane, the coyotes, the ponies, all of our personal pets, the wormholes and Ginger were touching and, in some cases, looked like they were supporting the folks touching Drew.

As everyone was getting settled Drew popped off with "Whoever has their hands near my uuuhh… lap… please keep your hands off my junk. Just sayin'." Most everyone there laughed, and he was hit several times, once quite hard by his mother, but then Boo and The Baby hopped onto the table and then made themselves comfortable on his lap.

"Oh, hey Drew, looks like you're getting some pussy after all." Ox said. He was hit by anyone that could reach him, but everyone was laughing. Then Drew closed his eyes. At first, nothing seemed to happen, then he started to shake. Casey looked like he was holding Drew down by how tight his grip on Drew's shoulder was. Then the song "Popular Monster" by Falling In Reverse started blaring. From the looks on everyone's faces; I don't think anyone was having a good time. I don't know what they were getting but it made a couple of people cry while others fell to their knees. But no one lost contact with either Drew or the person they were next to. Then it looked like most everyone was… released? Since most immediately dropped to the ground. *(The look of relief on most of my family's faces? I don't think an "I'm sorry" is going to cut it.)*

"What the hell just happened?" Nate asked.

"I think Boo and The Baby are responsible for that. I think they started shielding as many of us as they could." Jones said while panting and snorting.

Ferret said from his spot on the ground "Good gawd almighty! Drew… hey man… I'm sorry for givin' you shit. I didn't know how hard this was for you."

"Do you think, because we were all connected, do you think that's why that was so strong? Or why it… hurt?" Tarina asked looking very shaken.

"What? D'you mean I ain't havin' a heart attack?" Pit Bull asked as he sat up with a little help from Molina.

"You'd have to have a heart for that you old dog. Oh! And why are you furry?" Luna asked as she was leaning on George. The levity, as usual, was very inappropriate. *(Yay! It's not just me. Ha!)* Pit Bull wasn't the only one who had sprouted fur either. Megan popped off with something along the lines of now she knows why everyone said that I'm the scary one. Whatever they just did caused the shifters to at least partially shift, and it's also apparently given Megan a small boost with her communication skills. It hurt watching my friends, my family go through whatever that was but… I'm just not ready to come… back. Yet. Then Doris asked Nate to check on Drew since he was so still, and Dozer noticed that Casey was still hanging on to Drew and that neither was responding to anyone.

Nate checked their pulses and pupils then said that as far as he could tell, everything was fine. Then both Drew and Casey's eyes popped open. Drew sat up in a rush, but Casey never lost contact with him or the look of concentration on his face. My girls crawled off Drew's lap but settled in again between him and Casey.

Tears streaking both of their faces Drew said "I just saw her… she just blew up a building. Wherever she is… she's beyond pissed. Or at least her darkness is. When I first made contact with her, I think I surprised the shit out of her. She was busy, you know? I mean… well… the best way I can describe it is… well… Okay, so it's like when your phone rings while you're in the middle of having sex. I mean, you automatically stop, right? Then you look at the phone and maybe even throw it across the room. But when you try to get back to what you were doing… your uhhh… your rhythm's off. You know what I'm saying? I guess when I made contact with her, that got her off her rhythm, so she cut me off and… kicked me out."

"Drew!" both Helen and Doris yelled at the same time while everyone else laughed.

"Oh come on! Can you really tell me that that's never happened to you? Anyway, I think I've made a… small hole in her shield? Actually, I think Casey's the one that made it."

"I think her darkness is… using violence to… drown out her pain? Or at least I'm pretty sure that's what's happening." Casey said while panting.

"Yeah, but it's not as bad as it sounds, because I saw something else. I saw some scared people… She was freeing those people from somewhere." Drew went on to say.

"Phew, okay. I'm… I think we should all take that to mean that she's not just killing people indiscriminately. That's… that's a very good sign as far as I'm concerned." Casey said with a smile, then he slumped.

"I caught a little bit of that and… it also felt like she was… having fun? It was almost like she was playing cat and mouse with whoever she's after." Riley said in his squeaky rat voice.

"Did any of you get how careless she's being with her safety?" Jones asked.

"No, I didn't get that at all, but I did pick up that she's… worried? About the nice people?" David said as he stood up and changed back to human.

"Of course! She's worried that she might hurt the wrong people! That's really good, right? We all know that she wouldn't do that so… can we like, send to her…" Tarina started.

"Send to her our… our absolute belief that she'll do the right thing." Alex finished for her. I guess that's what they did when they were all quiet and had their eyes closed, but from Drew or… it might've been Casey, but whoever it was, they sent the song "Eye of the Storm" by Pop Evil.

"Now that that's done, did anyone see anything to tell us where she is?" Alex asked while the song was playing from everyone there and for the second time.

"Does this mean that you still do not know where she is?" a deep growly voice asked making everyone jump.

"Look! She's blowing shit up and burning shit down! That should make it easier for one of **YOU** to find her! So get off our backs about it!"

David yelled in the direction of the voice and Alex and Jones put their hands on his shoulders.

Then Alex said "Seriously, we promise **YOU** that if we find her, we'll let **YOU** know. Can **YOU** say the same thing?" What happened next was… incredible!

"Yes… WE can do that." A very familiar and scary voice said. Then the show ended.

I can still hear the song as I open my eyes, only to discover that Liz, Lucas, Roger and Bobby are all standing in front of me, staring. Oh, and little Emily is attached to my leg and my little buddy is pinching my ear.

"So… where did you go?" Lucas asks me with a concerned look on his face.

"Did I go somewhere?" I ask as I pick up Emily and give her a hug and she gets my buddy to stop pinching me with a gentle touch.

"Not physically, but you were staring off into space for a minute or two and then Emily came out of the bus and started hugging your leg. Then you just seemed to snap back." Liz says.

"Oh yeah, don't forget about the music coming out of her. Again." Roger says with a snort.

"That's so cool by the way." Bobby says with a big grin.

"Well… I don't know what to tell you… I think I was getting a message? Or something. See… I got a… glimpse… of what my family are, or were, going through. I don't know how else to describe it." I say with a shrug.

"I'd like to hear more about that, but not right now. Right now, I just want to know if you're good to go." Lucas says as he takes Emily from my arms.

"Yeah, I think I am. For the moment anyway." I say with another shrug. He looks me in the eyes and after a few seconds he nods his head. Then we get back on the road.

We get my new ride and the buses through what we'd cleared then move a few cars or trucks back to where they were so that we cover our trail a couple more times all the way to Highway 84. We turn left on 84 and take it east for a while, leaving a fairly clear path for now, before stopping at Bobby Dahlberg's Fish Camp, for the night. I know that we can't or shouldn't keep going and it feels safe enough.

So, after making sure that the camp's empty and nothing around is too interested in us, we use the camps showers and then kitchen facilities to make dinner. Everyone's starting to relax more, and the kids are really enjoying playing on the playground equipment. Then it's time for a campfire and smores. After the smores are wiped out, but before Lucas can ask the questions that I know that he has for me, my new group and I get a big surprise. My new group gets an unexpected, but small look at my far-off family.

I say unexpected, but that's a massive understatement. I don't know exactly what happening, but daaamn! They must have really cranked up the magic, and I think, maybe, four-year-old Emily has something to do with what happens on our side. I know Drew has made contact with… my darkness and I before, and I know that all I have to do is turn on the radio in my bag, but I really haven't wanted to make "real" contact because I'm having too good of a time practicing avoidance at the moment. But it looks like that's not going to work anymore. *Shit.* See, I feel something, or someone trying to grab my attention. Drew and Casey. I can feel them worming their way in and that causes me to go rigid, but then Emily crawls into my lap and wipes her recently sucked thumb on me and… *Holy shit!* It's like a hole opens up in my personal shield and then over our firepit. The song "Heathens" by Twenty One Pilots, comes blaring out. Then I can see my family. It's… amazing! And better than any Skype call, that's for sure.

"Drew! Knock that shit off! Jeez…how would you like it if I poked you that hard?" I yell over the song.

"Oh shit! Sorry! I'm sorry! I didn't realize that that was going to happen! There, is that better?" Drew asks as the power, the magic, smooths out to a much calmer level and the hole steadies.

"Oh, fuck that! Where are you? How are you? Who's that with you?" Tarina, Doris, Riley and David yell at just about the same time.

"Long story. I'm okay. I'm… getting there, you know? How are you doing this?" I ask. *Jeez. Gaslighting much?*

"Well, once we found out your general location, Boo and The Baby wanted to try something, so here we are." David says with a laugh and a wave.

"Now get your ass back here!" Mark yells.

"Ooooh, look! New people! Hey new people!" a couple of the bikers say as they pop up around those that we can clearly see. *What a bunch of goofballs.* My new group looks at my family in wonder, then the kids start waving and laughing at the goofy antics going on.

"Look, I'm glad that we could do this but… Drew and Casey are getting paler by the second and Jones and Ginger are starting to sway, so let's cut this off quick!" I say, feeling quite concerned, yet a bit annoyed. The connection ends with a snap and a bunch of people yelling threats at me. But… I'm not kidding. Drew and Casey were losing color as I watched, and Jones and Ginger look like tall grass blowing in the wind. Poor Boo looks like she'd bitten into a power cord, her fur sticking out in every direction and The Baby, The Baby looks like she's shrunk since the last time I saw her. But… dammit! Do I feel bad about staying AWOL? Yes. Of course I do. I also feel bad about what they're going through, because of me. But I'm just not ready to go back. I've got this new group to get up to speed and secured. But the song "Better Days" by Staind starts rattling around in my head, then out of me and I'm almost positive that my fam is getting it too.

Everyone here, almost immediately after the song ends, starts asking me questions, after finally closing their mouths. The kids want to know about one critter or another and the adults are asking something, but I just can't make any sense of it, so I hold up my hands and tell them one at a time. Then I point to someone.

"Holy shit! That was fu… uumm… that was awesome!" Bobby says in lieu of a question.

"If someone told me about something like that? I would never believe it." Roger says in awe.

"Now… now I can see why you laughed when you said that you all are a functioning dysfunctional family." Liz says with a laugh.

"No shit? I still can't believe how different everybody was. Even them animal things. How big is that chicken anyways?" Jamal asks in wonder.

"Okay, so let's start there. The big chicken is Ginger. She's at least ten feet tall. She can fly, but her landings are… well… they still suck. She's also a great actress and a very fierce warrior, so don't fuck with her. I've seen her kill things, including people." I say with pride in my feathered friend and just in case he was thinking about trying to fry her up.

"Now I don't usually cuss, but this time… I'm going to go with… Holy shit! Now… I'll admit that some of your friends… no, your family… they sounded scary to me when you talked about them before. But now? Now I can't wait to actually meet them all!" Sandra says with a look of wonder on her face. Then the kids start in again, wanting to know if they'll be able to pet whoever it is that they're talking about. I just laugh and tell everyone to calm down. I then tell the kids that if they want to pet someone, they need to ask for permission first. That seems to satisfy everyone, for the moment.

"So, they're friendly but… also incredibly dangerous. Just like you, right? Yes… I can see that, but I've just got to know… what was that thing… no, sorry, that new being? At the bottom of the table?" Marybeth asks.

"That my friends… is Molina. She's what we call a wormole. Part worm, part mole." I say with a laugh.

"Forget about her! What was the big purple thing in the back? I'm sorry, but I'm afraid that… that new being is going to give me nightmares!" Henry says with a strange look on his face. Part fear, part wonder and part horror, probably.

"That's Stanley and yeah, he's a sight to see; I'll give you that. You see, five other people and Stanley got caught up in someone's magic. They all turned into One Eyed One Horned Flying Purple People Eaters. Or PPEs for short." I say with a fond smile.

"Do they? Eat people that is?" Henry asks, shocked.

"Well…Yes. Now look, you have to understand… they don't do it to be mean. At first, they did it in order to protect a bunch of people. Elderly people at that. And… because they were hungry." I say with a shrug. "Really? Aren't you afraid that they'll turn on you?" Henry asks in wonder.

"No. I'm not worried about that at all. But let me ask you something. Would you turn on any of your friends or on this group here?"

"What? No! Of course not! Oh, okay. I see what you're doing. I'll uuuh… I'll try to keep that in mind from now on. Sorry." Henry says while nodding his head. The rest of the adults start nodding along with him. Good! I think it's really starting to sink in for them.

"Well… on that note, I think it's time to turn in for the evening. That way we can get an early start in the morning. Right?" Marybeth says but she still seems to be in a kind of shock, just like everyone else is from seeing my family, live and in person. Sort of. I also think all of the adults are going to be thinking about everything that I've said and everything that they've seen. It's a lot, I know, but they're handling everything thrown at them, including by me, really well, despite the circumstances.

I get lucky and have a small cabin all to myself. *Ha!* I don't believe that for a second, but that's okay. I'm still new and I'm definitely a really wild card sooo… Plus, I'm not really alone. I've got my little buddy and the nasty ass plants with me. They're so awful that my little buddy keeps hissing at them and has even made a few flyby's just to pee on them. And that gives me an idea. So I drop some ice in a goop jar before adding it to their buckets. After that I crawl into bed and realize that this is the emptiest my bed has been in weeks. What ever am I going to do with all this extra room? I laugh and spread out of course.
Then I roll over.

Day 37

Fuck! I know exactly where I am, and I really don't want to have to deal with this shit right now! I sit up and look around and off to my right is a crumbling wall, so I crawl toward it, then duck behind it. Dammit! I can feel him, not too far away. Whatever the fuck Drew and the rest did, they must have unblocked something. It's like they ripped off the band aid that I'd put on my... whatever. Now that it's gone... I can feel things... and Joe, again. Stronger than before. *Well shit.* Yeah, no. I'm not going to face him, at least not right now. Especially since my darkness is ready and waiting in the wings to come out and rain down hell. Or at least that's what it feels like to me. So, after a quick peek and seeing that his back is toward me, I take off running, and I hate running. Both physically and... well... you know. I like to face things and deal with them head on, but... I don't trust myself... or my darkness. I run for at least ten minutes, so I stop and look around. Nothing looks familiar so I open myself up. *Huh? Holy shit!* I passed my group! *Hell!* I passed Y City! That means I've got to be somewhere in Texas! *Wow! How fucking freaky is that, right?*

I wander around for a bit and then something catches my attention, so I follow the weird feeling. I find myself approaching a small farm with chickens, ducks, goats, cows and a pony scattered around the yard but... whatever I'm after is in the neat little house. I open the door and just walk in. There are several cats in the house, cats that I absolutely adore because they're all Devon Rex, like The Baby. In the master bedroom I find an older couple laying in their bed. Now, from what I saw, all of the animals look very well cared for, but the people don't look like their doing all that well.

Then the woman in the bed sits up and even though her eyes are still closed, it's like she knows that I'm here.

"Of course I know you're here. I've been calling to you for days! And now you've finally come! It's about damn time too! Look, I'll make this quick, I'm… well… I'm dying." She says and even though her eyes have never opened, it's like she still can see the look of shock on my face because she laughs at me.

"No, not right this second, silly, but soon enough. When I go… you'll feel it. Now… I'm going to ask you for a really big favor. I'm asking you to take care of my babies. You see, every animal here is one of my children. I can feel that you're a good person so I'm asking you to come here and get all my babies and to take them someplace safe. You see, my husband won't be able to handle them after I'm gone, and I need to make sure that they're taken care of. Can you do this for me?" *Can I? Fuck it, yes, I can.*

"If you feel that I'm a good choice, then yes, I'll do this for you. My name is Lara, by the way." "Hello Lara, I'm Sophia. Well, now that that's taken care of, I'll get back to what I was doing. I'm just so tired. Oh wait! First I need to tell you a few things. The first thing is that I'm still trying to find good homes around here for some of my babies, so if any are missing, don't be too alarmed. Secondly, I'm also glad that you came in the way you did; I can tell that all of my babies will have your scent now and they'll go with you with no problems. Oh! And thirdly, before I forget… can you feel what's happening? between us? right now? I know that this is very different from what and how you're used to doing things but, can you feel that difference? Good, because now you can do this. This is my other gift to you. There's a ton of people and things out there that can call out, but very, very few that can answer. That's what I've given you. You're going to help so many, I can tell, but first you need to find a way to access this strange place that's… been made for you? … on your own. You have a strong connection to this place, but that's been… damaged? Well, that sucks. Yeah sorry but you're just going to have to find a way to access this place some other way. It's very important. Yeah, yeah, I know that I've given you a lot to think about and I'm sorry for dropping this on you in such a chaotic way. Ha! What I really wish is that I could give you an operator's manual or something, but I've been learning as I go too. You'll figure it out… eventually. 'G'night now." Sophia says then lays back down and the power that I felt… dissipated. The "talk" we just had looks like it took a lot out of her, because I'd swear that she appears smaller and paler than she had been. I'm also floored by what she said, what she's dropped on me and what I now feel. *Daaamn!* Sophia is powerful! But I don't think she's been able to use her powers much, or even all of them. From the look of this bedroom and the rest of the house that I've seen, it appears that she's been sick for a really long time. Anyway, as I'm leaving, I see a cat sitting on the back of the couch and it's looking at me. I walk over to it, and it head butts my hand.

"Me Peanut. Will wait for you. Come soon." she says before jumping off the couch and disappearing into Sophia's bedroom. None of the other cats raise their heads or even move, and I'm floored that she talked to me. *This is fanfuckingtastic!* I really wish we had more time, that way I could ask Sophia a ton of questions, but she's so fragile and even though that makes me incredibly sad… I know that she's right. I do need to get back and I will figure this shit out… eventually. *Ha!* It's just more flying by the seat of my pants shit. I should probably get a new tattoo that says SNAFU… since that's how my life's been working out so far.

Once outside I walk around all of the other animals but none of them move or even notice me, but I'm sure that what Sophia said is correct, that they'll know me when I come back. Then I turn and start running back toward the fish camp. I was going to say home, but I can't go back to my family just yet, no matter how much I miss them. Also, have a mentioned that I hate running? The strangest thing is that when I'm fairly close to where my family is, I swear I hear the song "Leave a Light On" by Papa Roach. And… I don't think it's the first time I've heard it either.

I make it back to the fish camp and come stumbling out just outside my cabin door. I think I'm at least getting the hang of coming out of our…

no, scratch that… my place, close to where I intend to be. Then after Gilly, short for Gilligan, finishes fluttering around my head, I turn in. If you're wondering who that is, well… what else am I supposed to name my little buddy? Right?

This time when I fall asleep and dream, I'm pretty sure it's not really dreams but more from my crystals, at least as far as my fam goes, because it's still Jones' perspective. But I think someone else is pushing for me to see this. It had to be sometime after the first day, when I didn't come back, because everyone was still visibly pissed off and worried. Plus, there was a ton of stuff stacked up on the bridge. Also, not everyone was there, some of the SEAL guys appear to be missing and so's Stanley.

Drew was back on the table telling everyone that he'd gotten a feeling and that he needed to try again. Boo and The Baby were in their places on his lap and I guess he immediately made contact with my darkness. The song "The Dead Don't Die" by Shinedown came rolling out and the tone may have been kind of bad but the atmosphere? didn't seem as bad, or as frantic and angry as the last time I heard and saw something like this. Oh, and I think that other people can see more of what's going on by the looks on their faces. Then the comments and a few chuckles started.

"Did anyone get a good look at the courthouse?" Parker asked after he whistled.

"You mean the big building peeking out of all of that smoke? Yeah, couldn't miss it. I'm not sure but… I think I did see a couple of the letters." Pit Bull said while rubbing his bristly chin.

"I'm pretty sure the middle word is County, but the smoke was obscuring the rest." Tarina said blinking rapidly.

"Okay, so we know she's still fucking someone's world up, but is that song a true representation of how she's feeling?" Doris asked. It took Drew a few seconds and a bunch of face contortions then he sucked in a big breath and the song "Jekyll and Hyde" by Five Finger Death Punch came rolling out.

"Holy shitballs… Okay, that's…Ha! Okay so… I'm going to guess that she's still in a battle with her darkness, but… I'm also going to say that I'm pretty sure that she's winning. Don't ask me why I said that, but… I'm going to steal a page out of her book and say that I've got a feeling." Casey said with another laugh then patted Drew on his shoulder. After the patting, Drew seemed to slump a little while everyone else groaned.

"That was a… you… did good Drew. Was it me or did that time seem easier too?" Riley asked.

"Drew, that wasn't just a good job, that was… fucking amazing! Riley just doesn't know how to give compliments." Parker said with a laugh. Drew laughed along with everyone else as he wiped the sweat off his face. "Uhhh, guys? I think… I think I just had a eureka moment." Jones said and everyone turned to look at him.

"Alright big guy, what've you got for us?" Casey asked.

"Well… we've got those sheets of metal, and we know that they bend when we try to use them to cover the holes so… what if we stuff the holes full of Justine's rope stuff? If the holes are full, then the sheets should work. Right?"

"You know what? That might just work! But only for the smaller holes. I don't think that… uummm… no matter how much of her rope stuff we stick in the big holes, I just don't think it could hold up the RV's. The holes might get bigger with that much weight put on the edges of them. But hey! That's definitely something to try!" Parker said while it looked like he was doing calculations in his head.

"If the guys would get back to us, or when they finally show back up, they'll be surprised to see at least most of our stuff waiting for them." Ox said with a laugh. Jones' solution seemed to have lightened everyone's mood.

"Oh yeah, only having to find new RV's is going to be easier than trying to find replacements for everything else." Helen said with a smile.

"So how are we going to do this?" Alex asked.

"First, we need to fill a few holes in a fairly straight line. Oh! And we can use the rope stuff to connect some of the rebar or other supports to make it so there's less give. Then try bringing over the empty trucks. If they make it with no problems, then we'll try the empty cargo trucks. If everything is still fairly good after that, then the ambulances and the bigger refrigerated trucks." Parker said as he was walking around trying to figure out the path that they were going to need.

"Then we get to start refilling them. Yay." David said morosely. Brandi gave him a swat but then smiled at him.

"You know… If this works out… you realize that Perky and the other guys are going to be pissed. Right?" Brandi said.

"Oh! No doubt! They're so used to blowing shit up that fixing things is not really at the top of their to do list." Parker said with a laugh.

"That's certainly true, but I think there's more to it than that. See… their "box" is still so ordinary, while our solutions are not only outside the box but…" Casey started to say but then even he was at a loss for words.

"Magical and bizarre?" Catherine asked with a laugh.

"Yeah, that just about says it all, right there." Riley said while nodding his head.

"Okay, I see what you're trying to say. Uhhh… something along the lines of… or the fact that… we've been at this shit a lot longer than they have and… we're already used to looking as far outside of the box as possible. And that… they need to start doing that too." Alex said with a smile and everyone there laughed..

"Well, come on gang. Let's see if Jones' idea is just the ticket for this problem. If he's right and this does work? Then they'll see for themselves that their thinking in linear lines isn't going to cut it anymore, that they need to add a few new curves." Nate said. I think he's had a few moments like that himself from the look on his face. Several other people notice the look and laughed at him. (I remember when Dr. Hathaway said that he's into science, not science fiction, but now he's been forced into being into both, since they've pretty much melded into each other.)

"So, it's unanimous then." Radio said with a clap.

"What are you talking about?" several asked.

"Oh, just the fact that we all think Perky and the other guys are smart and capable of just about anything but... since there's just not a "conventional" solution for this, we're going to have to get them to change their ways." Radio finished with a laugh. That set everyone else off and they went to work on Jones' idea.

Then I'm whisked away and I'm back to watching Walter again. Some man walked up to him and yelled "Walter! What the hell man! What's going on? First, they go crazy a few days ago, but you said they were fine. Now they're at it again! In the middle of the night! Again!" (I'm not sure if I like this guy. He seems ... you know what? He's not my problem. I have enough of those already.) Another guy came up and laughed then said that it wasn't as bad this time but then asked what had gotten into them. Walter was silently communing with the mustangs and Wakinyan then turned to the men and answered the question.

"The last time? They were upset because someone hurt a friend of ours. This time? I think they're wanting us to do a dance? They need our help in calling something... no, calling someone in."

(I really didn't like the way the guy scoffed at Walter and the others.) But then after getting a good look at Walter and the other guy, I realized that they weren't too thrilled with him either. *Good!* I'm not worried about Wakinyan and the mustangs; they can handle themselves and this asshole if they need too. Then the other guy told Walter that he'd found the house that Walter wanted him to. That he'd met several people, and they'd told him to go to Y City and to talk to someone there. He then told Walter that some of the people that he'd talked to were in the process of packing up and heading that way themselves. The guy then told Walter that he'd been shocked at how friendly and helpful everyone he'd talked to had been. Walter laughed at him and told him that he's met me twice, and that it didn't surprise him at all, especially if the people he'd talked to actually know me. And even though most of this conversation was light, I can tell that Walter is suffering from some heavy thoughts. Thoughts about what his charges are thinking of doing. Oh, he knows that Wakinyan, Rosie and the others have done an amazing job helping people and quite a few new things around where they are and they've killed off a lot of things that were bad for everyone and everything around them, but... the thought of leaving is still frightening to him. No, scratch that, it's beyond terrifying, but he knows that he'll leave with them. He also knows that some of his new people will go with him. Especially Grace. Wakinyan and the mustangs are partially responsible for his diehard followers and... his new girlfriend? *Hot Damn!* Grace can do things with wind, and she's able to communicate with Wakinyan almost as well as he can. When they first met, after his "kids" took care of a problem with the almost cow sized vultures that were causing havoc and killing people in Grace's small community, she told him that Wakinyan and the others told her that they like her and she even has his late wife's approval. She had no idea what that meant at the time, but it made him nervous and happy at the same time.

Then I'm whisked away again, but this time I just wake up, still in bed. So, after my cowardly behavior, my trip to meet Sophia and seeing a little of what's going on with Walter and my fam, I still feel pretty rested, but as usual I'm up well before the sun. So, after a shower and checking on the plants, which do seem to be in a much better mood this morning, I walk down to the dock. I stand there and breathe in the cool damp air and open my senses up while thinking over everything that I saw and did last night. There are plenty of animals and bugs around, but there are a couple other things too. I felt them last night while we were sitting around the campfire. It's the closest one I'm interested in right now, it's not sinister or aggressive, or at least not yet. But I've got a feeling, so I head back into my cabin and put on my boots and grab my sword. After coming back outside I head off to the left, but after maybe a dozen yards I hear footsteps behind me. Whoever it is, they're not trying to sneak up on me, that's for sure, so I stop and wait. Bobby, Lucas, Liz, Roger, Sandra, Jamal and Jalen stop when they reach me. "Uhhh, morning. So uuhhh, since you've got your sword with you… does that mean you're hunting something or making sure that nothing is hunting us?" Lucas asks quite nervously.

"I don't know yet. I can tell you that something's out here, and it's watched us, is watching us. Right now. At this point… I'm just planning on having a chat with whoever it is. Y'all can come if you'd like but… don't freak out. Or freak out silently, you understand? Oh… and if I tell you to run? You run. Got it?" I say and they all nod. *Jeezus. This should be interesting.* After I turn and start walking again a few flashlights turn on as they follow me quietly. I'm kind of feeling like a mother goose with all her babies following her, but we don't go more than a dozen yards before I turn more to the right, heading more towards the water, and then I see her. *Good Gawd!* She is one big, scary looking bitch, let me tell you! But as with a lot of things, looks can be deceiving. Sometimes.

Alright… imagine, if you will, a six-foot tarantula. I'm not sure but I think she might be part Chilean Rose. Anyway, scary right? Now mix in some Emperor scorpion. You know, those big black suckers? Yeah… them. Okay, so mix the two together, but remember, over six feet tall and maybe about that long. Her hairy legs and body are that pretty dusty rose color, but her pinchers and tail are shiny black, and huge! She's actually hanging horizontal to the ground, in front a strange web, and she has a massive egg sack off to her left. From behind me come several startled squeaks. I think they came from Jamal, and maybe Jalen, but after that everyone's deathly silent. The flashlight beams still dance a bit as I take a few more steps toward her and I can already tell that she's not all arachnid. How do I know this? Well, it's magic, plus at least two of her multitude of eyes are human shaped… and blue. *Ohhhh maaannn.*

"Hi." *Really smooth, I know.*

"Are… are you insane?" the new being asks, I think she's surprised.

"No, but I do have my moments." I answer with a smile.

"Yeah, no doubt." She snorts, I think.

"I'm Lara. And you are?…"

"A freak! A monster and a killer! You should get as far away from me as you can! While you still can!"

"Really? Well, truth be told… I'm a freak… and a killer too."

"No! You don't understand!"

"Okay then. So, explain it to me." I say as I lean against a tree close to her.

"NO! Get away from me! Don't make me come down there and kill you!" she yells at me.

"Oh yeah? You know what? I dare you to come down here." I could feel everyone behind me freaking out and tensing up, getting ready to run. But hey! At least they're still quiet about everything. That's a plus, right?

"You must have a death wish. Well… so be it. No one can say I didn't give you a chance!" she says as she drops to the ground and starts toward me. When she's within a foot of me, I stand up straight and take a big step forward. If that wasn't unexpected enough, I did the most unexpected thing I could think of, I put my arms out and hugged what

I could of her. I hugged her as tight as I could. After the first few startled seconds, her huge pinchers slowly close around me and… she hugs me back as best as she can. Am I afraid that she's going to take a big bite out of me? No. See, the closer we got to each other, the more I could feel how lonely she is, how alone she feels and how much she hates those feelings… and herself. Then I put my belief of how beautiful she is into my hug, and I inadvertently broadcast it. The song "You Are So Beautiful" by Joe Cocker came out of me very softly as well. *Ha!*. After the song ends, she takes a step back and those big blue human eyes have tears running down her furry face. I think a couple of her other eyes do too, but that's okay. I have a few of my own going on, but I also have a huge smile on my face.

"So, are you going to tell me your name now? But hey! I've got to tell you… I've already killed one spider lady named Charlotte, so please don't use that one."

"What? Really? Ha! No, my name is Natalie, but everyone calls me Nat."

"Hi Nat."

"Oh, uumm… hi. You uuhhh… you do know that I could've killed you, right?"

"Uhh yeah. You can still try… if you want to but… can you feel me?"

"Yessss…" she says, looking perplexed, I think.

"Okay, so what do you feel?"

"Well… now I know for sure that you're fucking insane."

"Why?" I bark out and laugh.

"Because! Because I can feel your… your acceptance? Of me? And that you truly do think… you think that I'm beautiful!" she wails.

"So? What's wrong with that?"

"Well… just look at me! I'm a monster! No one in their right mind would think I'm beautiful or… or just accept me… the way you are!"

"Oh yeah? Okay, so let's give this a try." I say as I walk up to her and put my forehead against her head and with the help of my crystals… I "pour out" my first meeting with David. I feel David, my connection to him is growing stronger, and I ask him to give us his perspective on our first meeting. Nat takes it all in and cries some more. Huge tears flow from all of her eyes, and by the time she finishes crying, she's surrounded by the feel of my love for David and his love for me. And now our love for her. *Oh shit! What the hell did I just do? Oh, and who do I blame for this new wrinkle?* Well… I'm going to guess that this is because of Ajay and his Naga shit.

"What did she just do?"

"WE have witnessed something like this from her before, but not like this. Not firsthand."

"Ahhh, now WE know why WE follow her."

"If nothing else, WE find this marginally impressive."

"Sentimental rubbish."

"Perhaps, but WE were asked to watch."

I can still feel David and he's fading fast. It's like I'm becoming some type of vampire, sucking energy, or magic from him, but Jones is there to catch him, and he'll be fine after he wakes up from this. I can feel Casey too. He's wanting to know how I am and the more I try to push him away, the harder he holds on, so I finally tell him that I'm okay, that I'm getting there, but the song "Pieces of Me" plays out while I'm still trying to get him to leave it at just that. *Dammit!* He's also getting stronger with this shit!

Nat has quit crying and is staring at me as I'm having my struggles, but I ignore her questioning look. I do finally call everyone behind me to come forward so that I can introduce them to Nat. There isn't a dry face when I look at them, and no one seems to mind. *I'm not going to ask what they witnessed because I… just don't want to know.* After the introductions, Bobby is brave enough to ask Nat if he can give her a hug too, which she shyly accepts. Then, mainly because I think she's still in shock, I coax her into to giving us a bit of her tale.

So, Nat and her boyfriend live in Tuscaloosa where they both go to college. She doesn't say his name, so I'm guessing that that's still a touchy subject for her. *That's okay, I've got one of those too.* Anyway, her boyfriend is really into exotic pets. That's where the tarantula and the scorpion come in. Once Nat found out that she was pregnant, she told him that some of his more exotic *(I'm guessing the more poisonous)* pets had to go, or she was leaving. They were actually having that argument again, for the umpteenth time the morning the orange fog started. They were so busy arguing that they didn't notice it. But during the argument, Nat gave him an ultimatum. She told him that he was going to have to choose. "Dumb Fucker", her words, told her that he couldn't choose between them, that he loved all three of them equally. The next thing she knew, he was lying on the floor with her new tail rammed through his chest, her new pinchers pulling his arms off and something from his stomach area was in her new mouth. And if that wasn't bad enough, not only was she pregnant, but the spider and the scorpion were just about to start laying their eggs.

"After seeing what I'd done and… what I now looked like, I ran away. I've been chased a few times and somehow, I ended up here. Then… last week I started feeling weird and I ended up… making my egg sack." Nat said while looking back at her humongous egg sack attached to her big, strange web strung between three trees. Then she continued with "The first time I stopped running, when I was someplace quiet, I felt the other two, the scorpion and the tarantula, kind of fighting? For the top spot? But I knew… I Knew that I had to stay in control. Especially since I really don't remember what all happened while I was running. I knew, somehow, that I had to stay in control or what happened to Dumb

Fucker would happen again, so I... I managed to keep at least most of my... human sensibilities? And if that's not freaky enough, I now know just about everything that the spider and the scorpion know about their bodies and how to hunt like them. But... you see... sometimes, when they hunt, I kind of let them take over... but that's all! The rest of the time, it's me. I swear!"

"Oh, my dear, I'm so sorry that this has happened to you... and I'm even sorrier for the way I reacted to seeing you. Can you ever forgive me?" Sandra asks as she walks up to Nat and gently gives her a hug. Nat shoots wild eyes my way, but I shrug at her in response. "No. Because there's nothing to forgive you for. I know that I'm... scary." Nat says but she's muffled by Sandra's hug.

Sandra steps back and says "Why yes, you most certainly are but... you're also very lovely and lovable. Please, don't ever doubt that. I'd... I'd really like it if we can be friends." hope shining in her eyes. Nat looks back at me and asks if my insanity is contagious and I just laugh and tell her the only thing I can. Probably. We all laugh at that but... I'm just glad that it's only been my insanity that might be contagious and not say... my boom chicka wow wow moments, from before. Then I clamp down on those thoughts because for some reason that makes my darkness stir. A lot. Like she's ready to come forward to help me if I need it. But I think I'm good, for now.

"So... do you have any idea, or know if the other two know what's going on with your egg sack?" Liz asks while looking at it but not getting too close.

"Nope, not a fucking clue. That's one of the many things about this that's killing me! See, I was really looking forward to being a mom, ya know? Mine left when I was three. See... my dad is an amazing guy, really, but... every one of his girlfriends turned out to be a cunt. They'd come in all nice and helpful, but then it would go to shit really fast. They weren't just mean to me either! Once they got mean, my dad would kick them to the curb. My dad is a really great guy, but his taste in women sucks donkey balls." *Jeezus... her language is worse than mine! I like it and Doris is going to love her!*

"Is your dad still alive?" Jamal asks.

"Yeah, or he was as of ten days ago or so. I'm not sure of my days anymore. I went by our house, but I obviously couldn't go in. I did overhear him and a couple of his buddies talking about heading for the military base. If anyone can hold out, it's the military... right?"

"Well... I know quite a few military guys that now have some type of magical issues going on, but I hope you're right, that they can hold out but... without taking things out on their own. You get what I'm saying here?"

"Oh shit... I never even considered that. I wonder how they're handling those things."

"The guys that I know? Pretty fucking awesome! But... there have been challenges." I shrug.

"I hate to change the subject, but the sun's coming up, so we better get back." Lucas says so I turn and look at Nat.

"Come on girlfriend, grab your sack and let's go."

"What? Are you nuts? No... we've already established that... but seriously! There's no way! I can't go with you! Look at meeee! I'll scare the shit out of... everyone! No. It's better if I stay here. But I do... I do want to thank you. All of you. This has been fabulous... but let's get fuckin' real here. I'm not someone... or something that should be around... normal people."

"Oh, come on. Get over yourself already. Look..." I say but then I just walk up to her and put my forehead against her head, again. This time I show her the rest of my friends, my family. All of them. I also let her see that she's not getting rid of me, that she's not someone that I can just abandon. That I will not abandon her, ever. She's a part of my family now. Whether she likes it or not. *Ha!* I don't even need the Naga woo woo shit for this one.

"But… but… I don't want to scare the kids! And who the fuck knows what my babies are going to be like! They might be monsters that eat people!" she ends in a wail.

"Well, technically, you're a monster… and you eat people, sooooo. Hey! Maybe your babies can learn to be different? To be more like you are now?" Roger says with a kind smile.

"You all are seriously fucked in the head! But… I guess I am too because… I really want to go with you." she says and then sags.

"Look, we'll take it slow. If the kids get scared, then they get scared. They're kids, they'll come around. Besides… this is a new world, and we need to start teaching them about it. We've all been kind of sheltered for too long." Sandra says. Yeah, these new folks are really starting to get it, and I'm excited and thrilled to see it. So, we all head back to the camp. Eight people and an eight-legged new friend with her own baggage traveling through the woods. What could possibly go wrong? *Mwahaha!*

As soon as some people, Chet, and Daisy see us coming out of the woods, they start for us. As soon as they see Nat? They stop dead in their tracks, mouths hanging open. But not little Emily, she doesn't stop until she's wrapped around my legs giving me the universal sign for "up".

"Good morning star shine. Did you sleep well?" I ask as I pick her up and settle her on my hip. She nods with her head on my shoulder and then points at Nat. No one else has moved so much as an inch.

"Emily, I'd like to introduce you to a new friend of mine. Her name is Nat. Can you say hello to her? It would mean an awful lot to her if you did." I say, and I can hear and tell that a lot is going on around me, but I just don't give a shit. This… this is important!

Emily has yet to take her eyes off of Nat but then she takes her thumb out of her mouth and says shyly "Hi Nat. You look weally soft... can I pets you?" I feel my eyes start to burn at that innocent question. I can't tell you how happy that question makes me or the fact that I now know that she really was paying attention to my warning last night about asking for permission before touching.

Nat's blue eyes shed a couple more tears before she says "I think I would like that, very much. And thank you so much for asking." I take a couple steps closer, and Emily runs her hand down part of one of Nat's legs. They both giggle and claim that it tickles. So, several other people and I start stroking Nat's legs while the dogs give her a good sniffing. Because we were doing it, several other kids come forward and ask if they can pet Nat after them saying "hi" and giving her their names. After a couple of minutes, everyone has come over and all introduce themselves and ask to pet Nat. Yes, there are still a lot of strange looks aimed my way, but I think that everyone here now can feel that... yes, they see a monster but... her insides don't match what they see on the outside. Or... at least that's what I hope is going on.

I have no doubt that Marybeth and Henry have about a zillion questions, but no one stops me as I head back to my cabin to pack up my stuff and the plants. But as I open the door, not only am I greeted by an angry Gilligan, but my crystals give me another glimpse of what's happening to my family. It's definitely Jones' perspective, it's also closer to now and... I see what he's writing. *Ha! OMG!*

Jones started out writing that they were on the outskirts of Greenville getting ready to leave but then David started swaying and he fell... except he's using really flowery language. Then he snorted and crossed that out. He shook his head, and he mumbled to himself that he's blaming Helen for his out of character prose due to the "trashy romances" that she'd let him read. I didn't catch everything that he'd written but I did get one line. The line was... (I rushed over and scooped David up like a swooning maiden, then cradled him to my chest.) *OMG! Bwahahaha!*

Anyway, David told everyone that I'd made contact with him and that I had needed his help with something. Apparently, Casey had rushed up and had grabbed David's hand when he went down. He was then able to tell everyone a little of what was going on while David was losing consciousness. When David woke up, he was able to "share" a bit of what had happened with everyone there. (Well… that's new. I guess I'm still able to share some of my new abilities with the fam even though I'm not physically with them. That's cool and… scary as hell, all at the same time.) *Mwahaha!*

Jones then goes on to write that he's glad that I'm the one reaching out, but he's suspicious? He thinks Casey is holding something back? From everyone? I think Jones might be right, but I don't think it's anything bad. Then I'm back in my cabin doorway.

We've almost packed up everything and we're planning on leaving after breakfast, but as Liz and Sandra are finishing up the cooking, Marybeth is brave enough to approach me and gets up in my face. "Are you insane?" she demands in a hiss. *Is that the question of the day?* I don't answer her, but I do keep major eye contact. After I didn't answer, she continues her hissy comments with "What was all that talk about keeping the kids safe? How are we supposed to do that when you bring in a… a monster? That you just met no less? And you're allowing it to travel with us?" I respond to her comments in a not very nice way. I open the door to my darkness, and she comes really close to the surface. Marybeth sucks in a quick breath and steps away from me because of my "new" look and takes another one when I smile. Then it's my turn to invade her personal space as I step up to her. She cringes and tries to make herself smaller. "Look, Nat is my friend. For fuck's sake… you saw her with those kids! She would never do anything to hurt them… or you. She will protect every one of us as fiercely as she protects her egg sack. You watch. Believe me…she's a good one. But… if push comes to shove, I'll take her and anyone who wants to go with me and leave you here. The choice is yours." Was that mean? Maybe. Was it needed? Probably. Let's face it, I'm definitely not Alex. He would've handled this much better, or at least more diplomatically. Me? I'm starting to feel a time crunch so I'm just not going to sugarcoat anything. Take it or leave it. Now, don't get me wrong here, I like Marybeth. She's a very nice lady. But I also know that she's been thrust into the part of playing the mother figure to a gaggle of kids that aren't even hers. For about a month now she's done everything she possibly could for them, including giving up what little food she got to make sure that none of them went hungry. So, I get that she's extremely protective, I do but… but I also know that she doesn't want to be the "mother" figure. That's her wife's thing. She told me yesterday, while we were unloading things for the folks at the school that about three days after the soldiers came to town, she and her wife Kris were handed a couple kids to take care of. She and Kris discussed it, and they made a promise to each other. The promise being that no matter what happens to either of them, the kids came first. Then Kris was taken. Marybeth doesn't even know what type of magic Kris might have started exhibiting. I also know, beyond a shadow of a doubt, that Marybeth will be staying with us, but I do believe that she needed this "Come to Jesus" meeting in order for her to get beyond her all-encompassing fear for her wife and her feelings of utter helplessness. That's not a very good magical gift but that's all I'm getting from her. Because now… now she knows that there's someone, or several someone's, who are going to do everything in their power to find out what happened to those that were taken, and if possible, get them all back. I ask my darkness to fade into the background while Marybeth gets her thoughts and feelings under control.

Finally, she says "I'm sorry. I know that doesn't mean very much, but… I am. I don't… I don't know what's wrong with me."

"Well… I accept your apology. And I think I know what's wrong. I can feel it. You're so afraid for Kris, and the others, that you think that if you can't control the situation, or whatever… then you'll never have what it takes to protect anyone. That's bullshit, you've been doing great for weeks now. But look… I'm not a child and I'm… more than you'll ever be able to handle so… let me handle this. I'm way more experienced with shit like this and… you know, deep in your bones, that I'm going to find out what happened to her, and get her back, to you, if I can."

"Yes… yes you will. I truly believe that but… just know that if… that if she's gone, and there's proof? I'll… I think I'll be okay. But I have to know! This not knowing is tearing me apart! Making me do incredibly stupid things. Like… going after you." she says with a watery smile.

"I get it. I really do. So, are we good?"

"Yeah. Yeah, we're good. Again, I'm sorry." she finishes and wipes away her tears.

"Good, I'm glad. I guess reality is finally starting to set in, huh?"

"Yeah, but… you mean something else, don't you?"

"Ha! Yes and no. What I mean is that… a lot of things are different now, right? Okay, so think of it this way… our parents raised us to handle a world that… no longer exists. So… we can't raise any kids the way we were raised. That's doing them a very big disservice and we want them to survive, right? So, let's start now, okay? Tell you what… on the ride, why don't you make it a point to talk to Nat. Once you do? I bet you won't see a monster anymore. I'll even go so far as to say that y'all will become very good friends." She gives me such a skeptical look that I laugh, but then I add "Oh! I bet she's going to be a tremendous help to you with watching the kids from now on too." Yeah, her look is still a bit doubtful, but I know she's thinking about it. As we're walking back to the buses, we run into Sandra, and she stops me. Marybeth continues on with a new look of determination on her face, so I turn to Sandra.

"That's not the way I would've handled that situation, but… I'm beginning to understand why you do things the way you do." then she walks away nodding her head. *Huh? Maybe my insanity really is contagious.* Then I go back to my cabin and finish packing up my meager belongings and the plants. The plants are actually being very nice today and they still have a shit ton of power. I wonder if the goop really did help something with them and this is why they're feeling and acting different. Might as well give them another dose, it certainly can't hurt, right?

As I'm packing them up, I wonder what they were originally like and what they were meant to be, or who they're a part of. If they're part of the good reverend Ansdale's wife, I wonder what happened and what changed her so much. But enough of that, I've got to get my stuff and them out to the redneck special and we need to get on the road.

After we finally get on the road, we aren't traveling very fast due to a lot of derelict vehicles left everywhere, but then we have to stop completely at a bridge spanning an extremely overflowing river. A very damaged bridge. As most of us adults are standing there looking at this new mess, even I'm stumped, and also suffering from a bit of déjà vu. *Damn!* We could all see sections of concrete missing from a couple of the support pylons and a few potholes from hell on the bridge's tarmac itself. A few of the support cables are broken and a couple look a bit wonky too.

"Does anyone know if there's a different bridge around here?" I ask.

"No. But even if we did, we'd still have to cross that one and it might be in worse shape than this one." Lucas says as he's checking out my map. *Well fuck.*

"I think we're going to have to go on foot, carefully. We can always pick up new rides and come back for some of our stuff, later." I hate to say that, but it's definitely the safest way.

"Uuhhh, Lara?" Nat says.

"Yeah?" I and everyone else turn to look at Nat.

"Well, I was just wondering… you do know that spider silk is stronger than steel, right?"

"Yes, actually I did know that but… Wait! Are you saying that you can fix the bridge?"

"Maybe. Not the whole bridge but... Actually, I'd like to give it a try. With some help... I think I can make it safe enough for us to cross with what we've got. I mean, it won't be pretty, but I think it'll hold up."

"If you think you can make it safe enough for us to cross... go for it. I'll help any way I can." I say. Lucas, Bobby, Jamal and Jalen jump at the chance to help too.

"Thank you. I really mean that. Oh! While I'm working, could someone keep an eye on my egg sack?" All of the kids eagerly volunteer to stand guard, but I laugh to myself because really, where is it going to go and what's it going to do? From what I've heard, Nat has the thing plastered to the ceiling of the bus and so far, no one is even remotely interested in touching it. Watching it, yes. I'm told that it's kind of mesmerizing, like watching the waves at the beach. How freaky is that? But as I look at Nat, she seems so very happy, to have everyone accepting her and willing to give her a "hand" when needed. After Nat spends a couple minutes inspecting the bridge she confirms that it's bad but not that bad, and she asks us if we can search the riverbank for some rocks or concrete. She needs that for the potholes and it should help with the pylons. She's just going to use her webs for the support cables. I have a bad thought, and my snort gets several folks attention.

"What?"

"Well, after you fix the problem areas, could you... could you make it look bad? Or the fixes uuhhh... make them look like random webs being strung up willy nilly?"

"Yeah sure. But why?"

"It might scare anyone coming behind us. Maybe make them think twice about crossing this bridge." The evil chuckles that follow my reasoning are absolutely fabulous.

"You know... after we get across, I can run a couple lines so that if anyone follows us, it'll cut through the roof of their car."

"Well, uuuuhh…" I have to stop there because my darkness is jumping up and down yelling "Do it! Do it!" I'm almost inclined to agree, but…

"What if they're not in a car, or they're nice people, or even some of my people? Sorry but that's a no go for me. So how about this… can you run a couple lines about three inches off the ground? That way it'll take out their tires and wheels. That'll slow anyone down, right? And not decapitate anyone by accident?" My idea causes a bunch more evil chuckles and laughs, but no one is against it. But first, it's time to fix up the damn bridge.

As some of us are down on the bank looking for concrete or just big rocks, Henry comments something about should we trust Nat's webs to fix things. Bobby jumps in and says that if Nat's willing to risk her egg sack, our lives are probably safe. I would've given him a hug, but my arms are full. He may be a few years older than David, but I can see them becoming good friends. Then I get another flash back from my crystals.

It's Jones' perspective again but also from before the last scenes, I think. See Jones was staring off to the east and pacing. Luna came up and clapped him on his back and told him not to worry and that the guys would come back. He told her that he knows they will, but he might be experiencing a case of my excessive worrying. She laughed at him and told him that sometimes I do seem to be a worry wart. *(I'd like to be mad with both of them, but I can't because they're right. So, sue me.)* Anyway… apparently, they sent some of the guys not only all the way across the bridge, but maybe as far as the casino to look for new rides for us. I guess that the fixes that they came up with were good enough for the motorcycles and maybe a few of our other rides but not for the RV's. *(I hope David was the one to remove the vials of blood from our fridge and hid them.)*

I know that they'd made it as far as Greenville and that's quite a distance past the casino so no… not all of these "flashbacks" are in chronological order. Anyway, Jones and everyone else were mainly just milling around when they heard a very familiar voice.

"WE may have had a sighting." After everyone jumped a bunch of questions were asked, Another voice replied, **"WE may have seen her in a place called... Alabama."**

"Oh! Uuhhh... Alabama is a pretty big place. Can **YOU** narrow that down a little bit?" Alex asked, looking perplexed.

"No" said another familiar voice.

"No. WE were not paying that much attention to the surroundings or the... survivors." Another familiar voice said.

"The abundance of... edibles took center focus." Said another regular, though he did sound kind of disgusted. Whether it was from talking to my fam or the **OTHER's** behavior I can't tell.

"Huh? But... I thought **YOU** were looking for her. Why would... Ohhhh." David said.

"Yes. WE are quite irritated by OUR behavior." Said our main ominous follower.

"Quick! Drew, get out the maps and check around the area of, I'm going to guess somewhere near Butler. Do **YOU** think **YOU** could point out where she was last seen?" Alex asks but there's no more communication from **THEM.**

Drew had gotten a map, spread it out and asked if anyone knew where Butler was. Alex, Lee and Doris point right to it. Drew then stared intently at the spot on the map. I guess he was trying to make contact with me. Then it looked like someone grabbed his face and pushed him away, but then the song "I Am the Fire" came flowing out of him.

"Well, I take it you made contact." Casey said with a strange look and a bunch of others smirk at his tone and the song choice. Drew shakes his head and tells everyone that he couldn't get too close, that my darkness had sensed him and pushed him away. The Baby and Boo came up and told him that they'd help when he tries to do that again later. To me, it seemed that the girls might be up to something. Then a bunch of different RV's came up the newly cleared side of the bridge and there was a bunch of cheering going on.

Then I'm back, still hanging onto a big rock. When I look around, no one seems to have noticed my "pause". So, it's back to work for me. *Yay.* We have lunch before the bridge is done to Nat's satisfaction. While we're working Nat fills us in on a little bit more about her life, from before.

Nat was in Tuscaloosa going to the university there. She was actually supposed to receive her master's degree in engineering this month. Also, she told us a little about how she became the top consciousness.

"After I'd turned into this I… I guess I talked to Rosie, the tarantula and Stella, the scorpion. At one point I made the decision to become the top dog and a monster to beat all monsters. By that I mean… I can now make my webs razor sharp. That helps with hunting and keeping things that have hunted me away. I can also make my webs super sticky, that helps a lot too. But… those two traits aren't really natural, by the way but… apparently it's really coming in handy now. Not just my webbing but I do believe my degree is coming in handy too. Who would've ever thought that? I'm still finding all of this fucking crazy!" she laughs like a loon after that and I think I get where she's coming from.

"Nat? If you're still trying to scare us away, you can fuckin' forget it." Jamal says with a laugh.

Bobby puts in his own two cents with "Yeah! We're friends now! I couldn't give a flying fuck how scary you may look to everyone else, to me you're just… Nat. My friend." while holding a big piece of concrete in place while she wrapped a bunch of webbing around it to "glue" it in place. I clap him on the back as I walk past him and think to myself that his mother is really going to kill me because he's been picking up cuss words and phrases from both me and Nat. *Oh well.* To tell you how much we've come to accept her, none of us even blinked an eye when she makes us our own special harness' to help her with the underside of the bridge. Of course, the kids set up a fuss because we're getting to swing, and they aren't. *Ha!* So then she takes a few minutes and makes them several swings between some trees and in between the buses. That keeps them out of trouble for a little while and gives Marybeth and Sandra a bit of a break from trying to keep them all close. Then it's time to cross the bridge. I've got to say, she'd make an absolute fortune doing webs for Halloween decorations. The bridge still looks scary as hell because of the damage it's received, but add in Nat's webs? Yeah, no one in their right mind would just blithely cross this thing. And after moving the abandoned vehicles back to where they had been makes it look ten times worse, if that's even possible. Nat did an amazing job of camouflaging her patchwork and even though there's a lot of crunching while going over the potholes, no one's nervous or scared because we all know that there's absolutely no way that she would hurt any of us or endanger her egg sack. Then she has a lot of fun running her trap webs while we all wait patiently on the eastbound side of the bridge. Once she's done I think we've actually managed to wear her out.

We make it a pretty good distance away from the bridge and decided to stop on the far western side of Coffeeville for the night. It's getting late and most of us rock movers are tired, so we check out an abandoned motel about five miles from town. The kids immediately head for the playground after it's been declared safe while the rest of us enjoy a good stretch. I pull out the plants and take them out of their boxes to enjoy a bit of late afternoon sun when Nat comes up to get a good look at them for the first time.

"What the actual fuck are those things?"

"I'm not 100% sure but I do know that these ladies are what the good reverend Ansdale and his asshole soldiers are using to control people."

"No shit?"

"Oh yeah, no shit. We looked like mindless zombies before we got "treated" by Lara." Bobby says with a laugh, though he and some others still give the plants a leery look. I laugh and tell everyone that they're actually now asking for our help, or at least I think that's what they're trying to tell me. Even though they're powerful beings in their own right, something was done to change them into how they used to be, behavior wise that is.

"Yeah, okay but… what are they?" Nat asks while the rest of the adults come closer to hear.

"I think each of them is a… piece of Ansdale's wife."

"What?"

"No way!"

"How? Or should I say why is she like this now?"

"If I had to guess, she was probably too powerful to control when she was whole, and once someone chopped her up… the smaller parts?" I couldn't finish because I'm just guessing but… it feels kind of right, or at least close.

"But why would… how did they…?"

"If someone now has power, or magic over plants… the cut-up pieces could be repotted?" Sandra says while thinking hard about this and Lucas nods his head because I think he's seeing at least a little bit of the truth in this conjecture.

So, after making sure that we're going to be safe for the evening and eating soup and sandwiches for dinner, we all watch the kids playing for a little while longer before we all decide to turn in. I know I'm tired and I think I'm out as soon as my head hits the pillow, but then I roll over and I can feel it.

Day 38

I can feel him. *FUCK!* I can't run because he's right behind me, pressed up tight. I feel my darkness rising up like a tidal wave as his arm comes across me and he tucks me into him tighter. It feels so good, but I know that it won't last. Just as I'm about to let the bitch out, he says all husky and sexy, "Hhmmmm… I've missed you." Even my darkness pauses at that, and then his hand is on the move as he runs it down my stomach and into my undies. *OMFG!* Then he… he bites me between my neck and shoulder and tries to find his way into me. If my undies weren't in the way, he'd have slammed into me! *WTF?* No foreplay? Just going for the gold? I wish I could say that I was mad enough to stop him right there, or that I felt nothing, but nooo. Even my darkness is stymied by his behavior. But OMG! Everything he's doing feels so powerful and… amazing! Then, after a couple more tries, it's like he finally realizes what he's doing and then… he stops. He goes completely still for a few seconds before he pulls his teeth out of my neck, then rolls over and sits up. I just lay there feeling empty and kind of used, again. My darkness is up and ready to pounce.

"Dammit! You need to stop invading my dreams! I can't keep doing this!" he says after rubbing his hands over his face a few times.

As I roll over and sit up, I feel my darkness trying to blanket me, but no matter how hard she tries, it can't stop the stabbing pain that his words cause. I didn't do this! He's the one doing it! He's the one reaching out to me!

I stand up and wipe at the wound on my shoulder and look at the blood and spit on my hand. Then… I want to slap him with my messy hand but, I just wiped it on his cheek, even though he's yet to look me in the face.

"I…" there are so many things that I want to say, so many things I should say, but… I don't. Instead, I turn and walk away, the song "All I Had Left" by LethalCulture runs through my head, playing softly. My darkness is screaming at me; she wants payback but… she's just going to have to be as unsatisfied as I am. I hope he is too, but I can tell at least Drew and a few others just got an eye full of me getting fucked over… again. *Shit!* Whatever he did definitely screwed up our connection, I can't seem to stop… anything from being passed between us. All I know is that I've got to get away, so I start walking, I'm just not in the mood to run. No, let me rephrase that. I'm Not going to be running from him… anymore.

I walk for a long while and I feel something, so I head in that direction, following a call. I'm not dressed for visiting… anyone, but you know what? I just don't give a shit. I stop in a parking lot in front of a motel, similar to the one we're staying in actually, and it looks empty. I blink and the next thing I see is a woman sitting at a small table. I recognize her, but I know we've never actually met. It's Becki and she motions me over to take a seat opposite her. On the table between us several tarot decks appear. She takes two decks off the table which leaves three but… when I look at her, her eyes are closed. I feel a lot of sadness coming from her, but I also feel a great sense of peace. So, I sit and wait for whatever she wants me to know, or whatever it is that brought us here. She just sits, facing my direction for a few seconds before using her T-shirt to wipe away her tears. If I'm crying, I can't feel it… I can barely feel anything at the moment but since I decided to answer this "call" my darkness feels fairly calm and like me… curious too. After another few seconds, she wipes her hands on her shirt, pulls her flowing dread locks back and rotates her head and neck and runs her hands over her decks of cards.

"Hi, I'm Becki. I'd like to help you, if I can. Will you let me pull some cards for you?" she asks.

"Sure. Why not." I say but my voice sounds strange, even to my own ears. Then she picks up the three decks of cards and gives each of them a shuffle.

"Well… okay then. Uhhh… as you can see, there are three decks in front of you, so would you place your right hand on each deck, please?" I shrug and place my right hand on each deck, but I'd forgotten about the blood still on my hand so as soon as I touch each deck, it's really weird. It seems like the cards are getting a taste of my magic, or at least that's what it feels like. My darkness doesn't seem to mind and neither do I because what I feel after that is a different magic that feels… warm and inviting. After touching all three decks I finally tell her my name. "Oh, I know who you are. Or should I say, my guides have told me some things about you and that I'll eventually find you, or you us. I'm not sure yet. I'm slowly making my way across the country, from Utah." Then she shuffles the decks again then places them in the center of the table. She runs her hand over all three and picks the deck on the far right and turns over the top card. She studies it for a few seconds, even though her eyes are still closed.

"The moon upright here represents things that are hidden… but those things need to come into the light. Hmmm… my guides are now telling me that that's how you got here, by using a… hidden way? A new path? Since you weren't here before and now you are or… am I here? This is so confusing." she says, but as I look at her and start to answer her question, I realize that I can't because I just don't know and if this is anything like my meeting with Sophia, the best I can do is just go with it. I also wonder if either of them remembers any of this when they wake up. Anyway.

"The truth is… I don't know. But let me ask you something… are you dreaming?" I ask but she immediately turns over the top card on the middle deck. It's the moon again, but this time it's in reverse.

"Oh! The hidden path is… hiding from you. No… not hiding but… being hidden! Yes! Someone that you care a great deal about has done something to hide the way… the way in… from you. I see… jealousy but… I also see… love. Uummm yeah, his love for you was warped by how he was previously… kept? I'm sorry but I don't understand any of this, but I think you do. Something about him not feeling love from those that were supposed to love him? But he felt it… from you? You were kind to him and then you… took him in? Gave him a real home? Gave him others to love and to love him? Yes, I see… he was loved by many, but he was damaged from his past and… he wanted to keep you to himself. So, that's the jealousy. Ah! I got it. Oh, and some others have fought with him about this… because of this but… he's stubborn. Oh! The natural way into your hidden place is blocked… by something that he's done! But he… he had a little help and now… now he can no longer fix what's been done!"

Yeah, Chance did something all right, but he had help? I wonder… who could or would have done that? Then she turns over the top card on the left. It's the moon again, but back in the upright position. "Ah! Someone else that loves you… that's fought with him over this… is or… has made you a… back door! Or at least that's what my guides are guessing. You will or can use this new door. Or you have used this door but don't remember? What the fuck? Anyway… it's a difficult way to go even though there's already a part of you that can get in and out with ease because of? … Holy shit! I don't understand this at all, and I don't think you do either. Sorry, this is such a fucking mess. Oh, but to answer your question, yes, I'm dreaming this. But I feel that you've experienced something like this before?" I think she's waiting for me to answer, so I do.

"Yes, I recently met a very nice lady from Texas. I would've loved to ask her a million questions about this shit, but she's not doing very well, and I didn't want to overtax her. Does that make sense?"

"Oh! Yes, that actually does. Oh, hey, my guides are now telling me that you usually enter this place when you dream. NO! Oh, sorry, when someone else dreams, Wow! Holy shit! Oh, ummm, shit. Okay so… uummm… Hey! Time to change the topic! Did you know that meditation and dreaming are closely related? I know that this seems way out there but bear with me here. Maybe… maybe in order for you to be able to access your hidden place on your "own"? using the backdoor that's been… made for you… instead of dreaming, could you try to meditate? See, once you get in here… on your own… you'll actually be making it so that you can open the new "door" and access this place at any time? Oh! Holy shit! You've got to try this! My guides are now telling me that when you can come in here, on your own and under your own power, you'll be helping and maybe saving a lot of people. Including me and my group. Oh shit! I'm so sorry to drop that on you. I don't think I was supposed to say that… or to figure it out, really. Anyway, I hope I was able to help you." Becki concludes with a laugh, but then she seems sad again.

"Actually, you've been a help, I think but… what's got you sad again?"

"Just thinking about free will and not seeing or… you know… ignoring the signs. Being manipulated and… not realizing it or just letting it happen. You know, the usual. Anyway, I just want you to know that I've tried to help people in the past and they… they just wouldn't listen. I don't know what I could've done differently. Or even if they're okay. Some people just refuse to see the signs, or they don't listen to their hearts. They'd rather listen to and take bad advice from others than be seen doing what their heart wants. Not many people listen to their inner selves… but you have. So, I'm feeling sorry for all of the ones that have refused to what? … To grow? To change? There are so many of them out there. And unfortunately, there always will be. That's free will.

Anyway, it's been really nice to finally meet you, sort of, and I can't wait to do it for real. Ha! That sounds so fucking weird, doesn't it?"

"Yeah well, I'm used to weird. Weird and I are best buds, or better yet, we're family." I say with a small laugh, but I hope she knows that I'm not kidding about being super close to weird shit. I'm including myself in there too. As she laughs along with me, poof! She disappears. See! Weirdness! But Becki did give me some insight on what Chance has done and what someone is trying to fix? So… it looks like I'm going to have to try meditation. I'm game to give it a try but I wonder if it'll work. But right now, I need to get back. Plus, I keep hearing the song "Call Me" by Blondie, but it's mainly just that refrain. It's like my fam is all singing that one part over and over again. I'm not up to dealing with them in person yet, but I can at least stop by and see what's got their panties in a twist. Right?

The closer I get to where the rest of my family is, the louder the call is, and let me tell you, some of my family can't carry a tune in a bucket. I think my ears may start to bleed if this racket keeps up, so I yell "ENOUGH!" The silence after that? It's like coming out of a concert and your head is still ringing. I'm not sure if I'm just hearing impaired now or if the call is still bouncing off things softly in some far-off corner of this place, like an echo. This is definitely something new and I hope Drew doesn't have to or just doesn't ever do this again.

So, I stop close to where there are a bunch of people standing by a fence. Casey's head jerks up and he looks in the direction I'm coming from so he walks my way. I stop but he keeps getting closer before he stops too, but he's not quite in front of me.

"Look… I know you're here, or sorta here, somewhere. I think. How the hell…? Yeah, yeah, it's magic and who the fuck knows! I got it. But seriously… I know you're going through some… shit, again but… we really need your help here. If you're really here that is."

"Can you hear me?" I ask, but as soon as the words are out of my mouth, he turns his head closer to where I am. *Wow! This is so cool! Or not. I'm not sure yet.*

"Holy shitballs! Yeah, but you sound weird though. Sorry. But look, we had to call you because these new beings are… we can't seem to get through to them and we don't want to hurt them. It's the exact opposite, you know? They're hurt, scared and really pissed off but… they're not something that we want or need to put down. You know? Anyway, we've been trying for hours to get them to even listen to us, and we've tried to get them to accept us, but they just won't. Isn't that what you do? Or how you do it? Yeah, yeah, stick to the problem. So… can you give us a hand here?" he asks. I can feel him trying something, but I ignore it.

"I think so. Let me get a better look at what you've got here." I say as I walk closer to the fence and then go in through the gate. I'm not sure what they saw when I did that. But then… I'm sorry but I can't stop the laugh that pops out. Someone must have really liked all of those dinosaur movies.

"Are those emu… emuraptors? And dino… dinocows? Oh, have you classified them or renamed any of them yet?" I ask in wonder while giggling. The blends or just the changes are amazingly good and work really well.

"No, we haven't done that completely, yet, because we can't see everything. This fence is the closest that anyone has gotten so far. Just FYI, some of these guys are pretty good at aiming their shit and letting it fly… our way. We do know that there's a lot of other things in there, but like I said, they won't let us see everything. I'll pass on the emuraptor (snort) but the dinocows were already named… exactly that." Casey says with a laugh.

So, I walk closer and I talk to the critters that I can see and even though they can't see me, I know that they can feel me and my intentions. What they tell me… what's been done to them… pisses me off and my darkness is just beneath the surface again, ready to go after the bad guys. I struggle to remain calm as I let these new beings know that none of my folks will ever do anything like that to them or let anyone else do that either. I pass that on to them but they're still so leery that I ask Casey to see if any of our regular pets and critters are willing to come in and meet these new beings. They might be able to help smooth the way and Casey passes that on. Soon Ken and Tammy come up with Ringo, George and a few of our normal pets along with Molina and Rumpy. Loretta and Reba join them at the gate. I tell Casey that he, Riley, Daivd, Jones, Ken and Tammy need to come in slowly and project more of their animal than human sides at first. But once these new beings accept them, they need to get Nate in here to put hands on a few of the more seriously injured of these guys. That might really kick start the process of acceptance and the healing will be both physically and emotionally. As those that I'd named come in slowly I tell Casey that Riley needs to rat out a bit more and Jones and David say that they thought they heard me say that. If they did, this'll make things easier because I have a few things to pass on to my folks and I think Casey is going to be too pissed off to give a word for word playback. But then Lynx, Ox and Ferret run up dragging Drew with them. They keep him kind of hidden between them and Casey puts a hand on Drew's shoulder. After that? I can feel the bonds opening up a little more. Okay, so this'll work too.

"Okay guys, I'm sure you know that these new beings were created, but they were created by someone who really loves them… and they love him in return. Whoever it is that's been hurting these new beings… they hurt their creator too. As a matter of fact, these guys are protecting their creator… or no… they're guarding … Aww shit. They're guarding his body. Fuck. That's another reason why they don't want any of y'all to come in here. They think you're going to do something bad to their creators body. Shit. Okay, so I'm letting them know that that will never happen. I'm sorry guys, but if you feel the need to hand over some of those assholes? I think some of these guys might not only enjoy killing them, but it might also help you with building a better bond with them.

But first, could someone get Bane and bring him in here?" "Bane? You want to let Bane loose? In there? With them? Are you crazy?" Riley asks and a few other people gasp in shock but then chuckle.

"He's a menace!" Lynx says with a shocked laugh.

"He's a loose cannon." Ox snorts.

"Yeah, he is, but… he's not mean, and we do put up with his antics. Including him playing turd hockey." Tammy says with a sigh and a laugh. Turd hockey? What?

"Oh shit. I think I see what Lara's going for here." Casey says with a groaning laugh. So, the next thing I see is Ginger and the other ponies coming up with Bane on a… leash?

"Is that some of Justine's web stuff?" I ask with a shocked laugh.

"Yeah. It's the only thing he hasn't been able to chew through. Hey, don't be mad but… we had to have some way to keep him close and fairly contained!" Ken says with a shrug.

"He's been having way too many "squirrel" moments." David says with a snorting laugh.

"Yeah. We all pretty much agree that he's got a big dose of ADHD." Casey says with a frustrated sounding sigh. I'm glad he can't see the smile on my face, but I do tell him that I completely understand. Stanley and Oscar land not too long after that and they take over holding the leash. At least it's long enough for him to get a good distance away from everyone and he's still be able to fly a little bit. Bane, being Bane, just barrels toward the new beings, but first he comes up to where I am and rubs against me. I'm shocked and also hoping that he didn't just remove me from my place, but he didn't. *Phew!* The new beings are of course leery of Bane, but he just walks up and starts sniffing them, then Molina and Rumpy waddle past me after giving me a rub as well. I get a quick rub from the Fab 4 and Reba and Loretta body check me as they move past. All of our critters move in and greet the new dinocows and emuraptors like they're long-lost friends. As all of that's going on the others get closer to where I'm standing, Casey asks if the critters can see me.

"I have no fucking clue, but I don't think so. I know that they can feel me, better than you can, apparently, so... But that's for another day, right now it's time for me to get back."

"I'm glad you answered our call and I'm glad that you're... you again." Lynx says as she starts heading closer to the critters, all nonchalant.

"Don't stay gone too long, okay?" Ox says as he rushes to catch up with Lynx.

"I know you've got a lot on your plate right now but... we miss you" Jones says as he walks past.

"I miss you... mom." David says with a laugh as he walks towards the new beings but he's not fooling me.

"I miss you too you know." Casey says.

"I know. I miss you... all of you too but I'm... I'm trying... to get my shit together. And I will, I promise. Oh! And if things work out, y'all might want to stay prepared."

"Prepared? For what?"

"To maybe join me... in here."

"In here? You mean... where you are right now?"

"Yep." I say and I see his Adam's apple bob as he swallows nervously. Then he gives me a cheeky grin.

"Oh! I think Ginger's going to see them first but... be prepared to start dealing with her and a few... chickendactyls." I say with a laugh. That causes Casey to stumble and look back my way with a look of shock and maybe wonder on his face, but then I walk away. I can only imagine the look on his face when he sees the raccoonosaurs? saber tooth squirrels (which were a real thing once), turkeyranadons?, aramatrodons? And a few other things that I'm going to have to think really hard about. I'm also going to have to let them deal with all of that, I've got other shit to take care of. Starting with learning how to meditate. But seriously, I'm beyond curious on how my fam ended up where they are now and how they're all doing. Maybe I'll get an update soon? Anyway, I make it back to my hotel room and come out just inside the door. I scare the shit out of Gilligan and even the plants become extra spiky. I laugh quietly and apologize to them then hit the bed after making sure everyone has forgiven me.

Day 39

I must have slept some because when I wake up, it's barely sunrise. After a shower and taking care of the plants and with Gilligan now firmly attached to my ear, I exit my room and run smack dab into Nat, who's now stationed across my door.

"Holy shit! Damn girlfriend! I didn't realize just how hairy you are!" I say into her cephalothorax. (Thank Jones for knowing that.)

"Huh. You look like shit. Are you okay?" she asks after coming down out of her… I think her defensive posture?

"Well, I'm as good as I'm going to get at the moment. What are you doing?" I ask as I push on one of her legs to get past her.

"Guarding your door. Obviously. I could tell that at one point last night, you weren't in there, so I was going to ask you where you went when you got back. When I heard your shower turn on, I found that strange since I know that there's no other way into your room except this door. Care to explain?" she says while giving me a bunch of hairy eyeballs.

"No, not really. I mean… I would if I could, but… just chalk it up to magic." I say with a sigh.

"It isn't just magic that's made you feel so… down. What the fuck happened last night?" she asks, but as I try to think of a way to explain… anything… to her, she takes a step away from me because my darkness has come up and she wants to lay it all out, in her own way.

"What the fuck is that?" she asks after locking every eye on me.

"Oh. That's just me. Or the darker side of me." I say as I try to get my darkness to calm down.

"I've heard a few of the others talking about this. They met her before they met you, right?"

"Yeah, I guess you could say that." I say as we reach Liz, Roger, Lucas, Sandra and Bobby.

"Morning! We're out here wondering how you want to handle going through Coffeeville." Sandra says as Lucas folds up our map to show this area only.

"That and we're taking bets on if we'll actually go through Coffeeville or find another way around." Lucas says with a laugh. At this point I really miss my family, especially the coyotes and their ability to ghost through and report back. This is almost as bad as starting from scratch, since these folks are so far behind. But hey! It's not their fault and I shouldn't even consider taking my bad mood out on them, so I take a deep breath in and consider our options.

"Well look… we don't know what's going on in Coffeeville. What we do know is that no one has been around here for a while because of the bridge so… we're going to have to be really careful. As a matter of fact, fuck it, we're going to drive straight through, if we can. That way we can check things out. I'll lead and if I find a good place to pull over, that's when we'll stop to discuss what we saw while driving through. We have no way of knowing if any of the people we see are "good" or if they're working with Reverend asshole, I mean Reverend Ansdale. Not to mention what some might do if they see Nat. So maybe we should black out some of the windows on the buses so that no one can see in. Sound like a plan?" I say and I get head nods from everyone. This tells me that these folks are starting to get on the same page as I am as far as our groups security goes. *Fanfuckingtastic!*

So, after eating a quick breakfast and putting up some of the kids artwork to black out the buses windows, we hit the road. Having to move quite a few wrecks and things, it takes us a while to get to town. We enter through the southwest side and well… it's inhabited but… the people we do see? Let's just say that the hairs on the back of my neck are standing straight up. What's worse is that I don't see anything that could be causing this reaction. Yet. I also don't see any vehicles that look like they can be driven. So how did these people get here and why are they staying? We pull over just east of town at an abandoned gas station and everyone gets out to stretch and talk about what they saw and to ask why I had Jamal and Jalen to park in an inverted V. It took them a few minutes but then the light bulbs start coming on. Then a few of the adults are practically begging to go back into town to check a few things out. Yes, most of the stores that we saw were at least heavily damaged, if not completely flattened, but the biggest parking lot had a bunch of makeshift booths set up in it. To me it looked like a long, jumbled flea market or swap meet mixed with a homeless camp. I'm not thrilled about this, but it's decided that Bobby, Liz, Roger, Lucas and I get go to check a few things out and if everything is kosher, or kosher enough, then everyone but Nat will get to go back to town to see what's going on with the townsfolk. *Fuck. I have a bad feeling about this.*

The first red flag for me came from the folks that approached us as we got out to see what there is to see. They asked a few questions that we could answer but they really didn't seem surprised and even commented on the direction we came in from. I mean, as far as we could tell, no one has used that bridge for a couple of weeks, at least. Then a couple of these new folks easily volunteer that they'd heard of the "soldiers" and were actually refugees from towns farther north that have been taken over by them. *Ding! Ding! Ding! The alarm bells are a ringing!* But luckily, I'm not the only one hearing them. Lucas and Bobby keep shooting me strange looks while Roger and Liz almost seem a little unsure. I'm glad to see that some of these folks are really starting to think about the groups security first. I hate to use the term soft, because they're not, maybe unseasoned would be better, but they're learning, quickly.

Maybe I'm the way I am due to my former job. Or maybe because I now hang out with so many cops and military people. Either way, I'm just glad that some of my new group are really beginning to understand the dangers. But dangers or not Liz and Roger have gotten out the list of things that were asked for and are ready to do a little shopping and swapping while Lucas, Bobby and I continue to chat up the "refugees". At first these folks just wanted to swap stories, though I'm really only interested in any information on where the soldiers have taken the stolen people. A couple refugees do mention that they witnessed a few of their acquaintances being kidnapped but they have no idea of where they were taken off to. Now to me, kidnapping means ransom and as far as I can tell, the soldiers aren't after anything like that, so what exactly are they after? And for some strange reason, none of these folks seem… diverse enough? Power wise? I mean, we see a couple new beings and people with new gifts? But seriously, I doubt that the good Reverend and his shitheads are very interested in the two very flamboyant fairy boys… that as far as I can tell only have enough power to spread around the personal glitter extravaganza that surrounds them like a rainbow cloud every time they flap their wings. I'm going to bet that the majority of their power is wasted on their sparkly fairy dust crap and there's not even a lot of that. *Dammit!* I wish I could talk telepathically with my new group! If I could, I wouldn't constantly be trying to get their attention! Fine… it's not like I have a problem with being rude. *Ha!*

"Oh, hey Liz? Roger? Could I have a word before you wander off?" I say with the fakest smile I can muster. Believe me, it's better than what I really want to do.

"Oh, yeah sure!" Liz says all bubbly as she and Roger come over to me. Luckily, Lucas and Bobby are nosey enough to wander over too.

"I know you know that something's really off here, so when you're swapping stories and whatnot, keep your ears open for anything interesting and don't go anywhere out of sight from anyone."

"Are you serious? These people are refugees! They wouldn't do anything bad to us, would they?"

"Are you sure about that? I mean, we were all "controlled" at one point in time. What if they really aren't true refugees?" Lucas says, looking sad.

"Oh yeah! Think about it! If you really were on the run like these folks say they are, would you be advertising it?" Bobby says, looking kind of proud of himself. I can't help but smile at him.

"Bobby nailed it. These folks seem nice enough, but they just aren't… afraid enough? Not if they were treated as badly as y'all were. Get it?"

"Well shit. I thought you were just being mean or…paranoid. This sucks, but maybe you're right." Liz says.

"If that's the case, that guy over there was telling me about a bookstore that we need to go to, to pick up some of those how to live off the land, off grid and other survival manuals. He was saying something about making an appointment to get in to see someone." Roger says.

"And you didn't think that was suspicious?" Lucas asks incredulously. I just smirk.

"This new way of living is going to take a lot of getting used to. Dammit!" Liz says with a slump to her shoulders.

"Wait! I know this is going to sound weird, after everything we've just talked about, but go ahead and make that appointment." I say because, well… I've got a feeling.

"But… what if it's a trap?" Bobby asks.

"Oh, I'm pretty sure it is." Lucas says while looking directly at me.

"You want us to just walk right into a trap? Are you crazy?" Liz asks in a hissy whisper.

"Haven't we already been through this? Yes, I'm certifiable. But… think about it… we have an advantage." I say with my darkness peeking out through my smile.

"Uuhh… how's that?" Roger asks after a shudder.

"Well, we've got goop so y'all are immune to the plants now. Right? The question is, are the folks in the bookstore immune?"

"Oh! No shit? I wouldn't have thought of that." Bobby says but then he smiles a slightly evil smile.

"Huh. I guess this just proves, yet again, that you're way more than just a pretty face with a sword." Lucas says with a laugh. Liz and Roger giggle a little as they go off to make us an appointment. When they come back, they have directions and tell us that we've still got over an hour to kill before we have to be at the bookstore where they're handing out the how to guides. So, we head back to the rest of our group to fill them in. Everyone but Nat wants to go back to check things out. Our warnings are taken seriously, but they want to go anyway. Against my better judgement and Sanda's promise to keep an eye on everyone, I agree. My main worry is the kids inadvertently saying something, but while I'm talking to the kids, Emily comes up and wants to be picked up, so I do. When I get back on topic with the kids, Emily takes her thumb out of her mouth and wipes her wet thumb on me, and I feel a huge zing of magic. *Wow! This kid has got some juice!* Why the hell no one noticed that she's a walking booster I can't imagine. Or maybe it's because she's so young? That doesn't feel right either, but for whatever reason, she boosts my desire for everyone not to say anything that would give us away or to get us into any trouble. From the look on everyone's faces, her boost definitely got my message across. *Holy shit!*

So, after spending a few minutes with Nat, it's time for us to go back for our appointment. Liz, Roger, Lucas, Bobby and I walk a couple of parking lots over from the bookstore and then we get in line behind two other groups. The first group in line comes across as… junkies looking for a score but knowing that there are cops around… to me. Their paranoia is off the charts but they're here soooo. The three women and guy are all dirty but… for some reason, these folks really appear to actually like each other and seem kind of dependent on each other. They're all super twitchy and two women keep looking at each other, like someone used to have something that would help them out but they don't have it anymore, and now they're all a bit lost. Like something critical is missing. Super weird.

The group directly in front of us are just soooo not prepared to live off the grid or practice any type of survival techniques. Prada shoes, Gucci belts and bags, Rolex watches, things like that. They keep flashing their bling at us and it takes a lot for me just to only roll my eyes. I can also tell that these folks didn't steal any of their useless shit, they all practically scream "Look at me!" and "My daddy's rich" or "I like spending other people's money on unnecessary shit." They also seem to be too shallow for anything else. *Oops, my bad. I'm being mean and judgmental here but… I think you all know what I'm talking about.* I'm trying here, really hard, but after another pose from one of the women, I snort a laugh. I play it off that the group that has just come up behind us said something funny. Luckily these new folks play along because they're now staring at the "elite" group and shaking their heads in wonderment too. The door to the book shop opens up and the tweaker group is ushered in. I turn my full attention to the group behind me and strike up a conversation with them.

In less than five minutes, I've made a few new friends and the tweakers come out. We all know instantly that something's very wrong. See, when the tweakers come out, they're acting… normal! The rest of my group and the folks behind us see this and *Ding! Ding!* Alarm bells are going off for all of us. Hopefully this will cure Liz and Roger from giving me any more shit about my "paranoia". But the group behind us stiffens up and I think they're preparing to leave but… I have to stop them. "Please, could you guys stay here and maybe run off any other people if they come up while we're in there?"

"What? Why should we do that?" a guy asks.

"Look, if the Gucci crew come out acting differently, I think I know what's going on. When we go in, nothing is going to happen to us but… we're going put a stop whatever's going on in there. Can we count on you to have our backs? If you do, I promise to let y'all in on some things." I say. Well, it's more like pleading, but…

"I'll do it." Another guy says and his group turns to stare at him, but he doesn't appear to be moving from his statement. Then the rest of them nod at us. *Fanfuckingtastic!*

"Alright gang. If anyone in there asks you to do something, do y'all think you can act kinda… blank? Then do what they say? I'm betting there's something in there that we've dealt with before and the bad guys are using it to find the type of people they like to… possess." I say quietly to my four compatriots.

"What? Well shit. I… can try." Liz whispers back while Roger closes his eyes, maybe in prayer, but then he nods. Lucas and Bobby both have big grins on their faces. *This is awesome!* Then in less time than it took the tweakers the door opens, and the Gucci crew come out acting not nearly as stuck up as before. They also appear to be sporting a lot less bling than before too. *Ha!* Then it's our turn to enter.

The Book Nook is a really nice little used bookstore, but we can see where some of the big shelves have been rearranged. The first person we see when we come all the way in is a really big man. I think he might just be the muscle, then a woman that would've fit right in with the last group is sitting at a desk, sporting some new bling if I'm not mistaken. She's sitting with another musclebound guy standing behind her. That guy makes a hand gesture, and I can feel that another plant has been unleashed or uncovered. The seated woman waits a few seconds then tells us to take a seat. I'm not the best actress, but I think we all play our parts perfectly as we all have a seat, and I put my bag with one of our plants in it at my feet. I can then feel Uno, our plant, doing something with their plant, some type of dominance thing? Whatever it is, Uno's easily winning. I can also tell that the other plant is… afraid? because there's another or stronger plant so close. Weird, right? I mean, our three co-exist nicely and even work together. Why is this different? *Jinkies! A new mystery!*

Anyway, as Uno and the other plant ramp up whatever they were doing, the only people that are affected by it is the three people we can see, and it's scary watching their facial expressions flick from one thing to the next, like a slide show, but I don't think they have enough time to actually feel what their faces were showing. We all have to look away after a few seconds because watching their eyes go in and out of focus and constantly changing is making, at least me, nauseous. I get up and I'm preparing to go looking for the other plant but first I take Uno out of my bag and put her on the desk. I think because I touch her, she gets a boost because after that, I don't feel anything from the other plant and Uno started happily swaying in her pot. I'm pretty sure that's her version of a victory dance. I'm still a bit lost as to how they work but last night all three reached out and tried their best to talk to me. The more we talked, the more… human*ish*? … they started to come across as. I now know for a fact that they were made by and a part of someone and then cut up by another, but they don't remember what or why that happened, just a little bit of the pain and then it was over. They do remember that they've been forced to steal magic and that's made them all very angry and hard to control. Because of that they've somehow been zapped, and they were put under the same type of compulsion to only obey commands given to them. But… since being with us and gooped, they're now free from that and in the process of developing their own personalities. None of them seem to mind the names I've been calling them since they can't remember any other names to begin with. I'm happy the goop has helped to release them from the compulsion that was controlling them and now they're having a good time learning and… growing?... with us?

At first, trying to communicate with them gave me a headache, but since they've all been released and they've all agreed to help us, the headaches aren't as bad and have almost stopped. Unfortunately, I now know that I can't use them to help any of my friends because… they're now my friends too. But that doesn't mean I can't use say… the one that Uno now has control over, especially if it can't or won't become more amiable, like our three. *Mwahaha!*

Once Uno lets me know that she's got complete control of the other plant I have the two men sit down and go looking for this new plant. I find it and another well-dressed woman towards the back of the store and grab the plant and have the woman follow me and sit with her cohorts. After plopping the new plant on the desk next to Uno, we can all tell that there's a lot of differences. The new plant is more barrel or bush shaped compared to Uno's slightly more humanish shape and not anywhere near as exotic looking or even as aminated as she is. The color difference is obvious too since Uno and the other two are a very vibrant green with their brilliant red and black flower heads compared to this one's muddy and dull green and very small dull whitish flower now trying to hide in the middle of the bush.

"What does this plant do?" Liz asks while getting a closer look at it and one of the women answers her.

"This one can locate and control people and other things, especially if they have power."

"What happens to the people or other things after that?" Bobby asks.

"If the individual has enough power or has something that we can use, then we take immediate control of them and then tell them a time and place to go to. It's the next location that does the culling and pick-ups. If our picks are adequate, then they're shipped off to somewhere else. If not?…" the woman shrugs her shoulders. *What a Bitch!* I'm glad I'm not the only one getting pissed off by her answers.

"So, who controls you?" Lucas asks while his face is turning redder by the second.

"You do… at this time." She answers with a nonchalant shrug.

"Okay, so who had control before us?" Roger asks, kind of exasperated.

"An emissary of the good Reverend Ansdale." She replies kind of robotically. *Ha! I bet these assholes don't even know who's pulling their strings! How sick is this shit?*

"Roger? Would you be so kind as to invite the other group in? Please? I think they need to see and hear some of this shit for themselves. Liz? Could you get some goop ready as well? Thanks." I say as I'm thinking a million things at once and moving the "bad plant" a bit farther away from Uno, who keeps whacking it with one of her limbs. After jumping into action, Roger opens the door and invites the next group in. I'm glad they stayed and are willing to marginally trust me. Once all four are in the building and complaining about Liz smearing goop on them Roger shows them farther in and they get a good look at who used to be running this operation. Then they get a good look at the plants. The looks of horror on their faces speaks volumes.

"So, I take it y'all have seen something like these before." I say as I watch them prepare themselves for a fight. But since none of my group have moved and the bad guys are still seated on the floor, the big guy that said he'd watch the door for us decides to answer.

"Seen 'em? Yeah. Seen what they can do to people? You bet your ass. But… how is it that we're not, ya know… zombified yet?" he asks. Lucas, Bobby, Roger and I point at the jar of goop still in Liz's hands.

"That nasty lookin' shit is an antidote or something? How'd you come by that?" the only woman in the new group asks.

"Well now… that's a long story but it works on other things besides the plants, or so I've heard. We're just glad it works for us." Lucas says with a laugh.

"So you've seen these things in action huh? I guess that means that y'all escaped. My question is, where from?" I ask with a friendly smile but I'm not really expecting an answer.

"You really expect us to answer that? We barely made it out! There's no way I'm goin' back!" another man says as he looks around, I suppose he's looking for a way out.

"I ain't tellin' you shit!" the big burly guy in the back says as he clenches his big fists and stands in a boxer type stance.

"Hey! That's just it! I don't want you to go back, I just want to know where you were and if there's any more people stuck there!" I say with my hands up, then "Look… I'm planning a… jail break, if you will. Everyone and everything needs to be freed from that place… and any other place that's like it out there! What happened to you and to a whole shit ton of other people, and new beings, is wrong and… I plan on putting a stop to it."

"You can't be serious! Them places are guarded by some seriously nasty people and … things, not to mention that they have a bunch of those fucking plants! There's no way you'll be able to pull off a jail break or rescue or whatever you want to call it. We almost didn't make it out!" the leader guy says.

"Look… us getting out was sheer luck! If that massive storm that came through almost two weeks ago hadn't happened? We wouldn't be here!" the woman says.

"So y'all think I'm nuts for wanting to rescue all of the hostages… or prisoners? That's fine. You don't think I can pull something like that off? That's fine too. Just give me a location. Any location. I'm not asking any of you to go with me. As a matter of fact, I think y'all should get as far away from here as you can get. But remember one thing. Shit like this is happening all over the place. Maybe not with the same group… even though it appears that assholes like them are spreading like a virus.

Look… I've run into a couple groups doing similar things before. One group was in the process of trying to start a breeding program that would create a new master race, or so they thought. Another group didn't care about that kind of stuff; they were catching people just to kill and eat. Now… think about that." I say with a sigh.

"Wait! They was eatin' people? Are you fuckin' kiddin' me?" the burly dude asks while turning green.

"Yeah, well they were killing people to feed to other people who they then kidnapped to… you know… repeat the process." I say with a shrug.

"So uuhhh… so what happened to them?" the woman asks.

"Well, when we found out about it? We put a stop to it."

"Just like that? I'm sorry but… y'all don't look like much to me." The leader says.

"Oh! Oh, it wasn't us that was with her. It was her other group, her family." Liz says. *Awww, that's so sweet!*

"Dude! If you could see them? Holy shit! Then… then you wouldn't have any doubts. None." Bobby says in awe and then he blushes at me. *He's really a good kid.*

"Oh yeah. You should see them! They're some really badass… folks, let me tell you." Lucas says with a look of wonder and a fond smile.

"Yeah well… I get it. We don't look like much to you but seriously… she is. She rescued us! All on her own! She wiped out a bunch of soldiers and our town!" Roger says, getting angry in my defense.

"Oh yeah? What town was that?" the burly dude asks while the other all start to look… hopeful? Like they're starting to reconsider their outlook on this situation?

"Butler." Liz says with pride.

"No shit! We've heard of Butler. Well, more like we overheard some talk about Butler." the woman says in shock.

"Oh yeah! See, the day before yesterday, as we was hidin' way northwest of here, we overheard a bunch of them soldiers talkin' about Butler bein' a total loss. Oh hey! Them soldiers know that some folks made it out of that town and… if that's you? Well, they're lookin' for you. I mean… they have a serious hard on, wanting to get you." burly guy says. I'm going to go out on a limb here and say it was good ole Todd that squealed on us. Probably to save his own hide. *What a dickdwad.*

"Yeah! But they couldn't figure out where you went. From what we overheard, they don't think y'all were able to cross the river anywhere around here so they're concentrating their efforts more to the northwest." The leader says with a very considering look. The rest of my group follows my lead when I just smile at him.

"Oh? Did you happen to hear how many are out looking for us?" Lucas asks with a saccharine sweet smile, but I can tell that he knows that Todd turned on our group and he's pissed off about it. Bobby finally gets it and he has a mean yet scared look on his face while Roger and Liz are just starting to look a little scared.

"About a hundred, maybe a hundred fifty guys." Burly guy says while it looks like he's trying to calculate the odds of us making it this far and I think he's also wondering if we're really as good as we say. "How did you get this far?" the burly guy asks, and I get the impression that these folks aren't going to be a danger to us. As a matter of fact, I'm pretty sure they're going to join us. "Well let's see, oh, we crossed a bridge that no one in their right mind would even consider trying. I doubt anyone will see the repair work that was done. All anyone can really see are a bunch of freaky spiders webs and that'll probably scare the shit out of everyone. That and we made it seem that no one has used that bridge since it was damaged." I say with a laugh. Nat is going to laugh her ass off when she hears about this. But…

"You didn't happen to hear if the soldiers have done anything outside Gilbertown, did you?"

"Ha! From what we heard, the only thing that happened to them for miles surrounding Gilbertown was that they were under almost constant attack! They said something about not being able to stop anywhere around there until they hit highway 84. Why?" the leader asks with a smirk.

"Under constant attack? By what?" Liz asks.

"Don't know. It musta been scary for 'em because they talked about tryin' to get help to come out and clean house in that area." The burly dude says with a shrug.

"Clean house? How are they going to do that?" Bobby asks, looking concerned.

"Do they have an... extermination team or something?" Roger asks.

"Yeah, they do. Or they have something like that anyways. Sometimes, they just use the plants to brainwash everything and then they use the people and things with power to take out anything that they can't keep under their control." The woman says, looking scared.

"Is it me, or are they, I don't know... attempting to become something like the new Roman Empire or something?" Lucas asks.

"Oh shit. Hey! You might be on to something there." The other guys says and the rest of them think about this situation and then they all start nodding. To me, it really doesn't matter what Reverend asshole, I mean Ansdale, and his crew are trying to accomplish, they need to be stopped because of how they're going about it. Slavery and murder? Yeah... nope. But dammit! I'm going to need a lot more help. I know that Bobby's going to volunteer and a few others, but... it's not going to be enough.

"See? Whether you realize it or not, you've given me something to work with. Now I just need some locations where the prisoners are being kept. Can y'all help me out with that?" I ask as I'm running a few scenarios through my head. My darkness is having a blast showing me how some of them are going to be completely disastrous. *Fuck.* Things aren't looking all that good.

"Sure, I'll tell you what I know but first… where did you get that plant?" the leader asks.

"Well, the bushy one was here with these fine people, the other one we took from Butler." Lucas says, but he's giving the leader a strange look.

"Really? Well… did you know that no one is supposed to be able to handle those things without Reverend Ansdale's approval and uuhhh… something else, but I don't know what that is." The leader says then shrugs.

"Oh! Oh shit! Now that you mention that I do remember… from before… that only certain people could handle the bad plants, but uhhh… why does that matter?" Bobby asks. *Huh?*

"Do you have any idea of how the good Rev got them?" I ask, confused by Bobby's claim.

"I think I heard that his wife was somehow involved. Why?" the woman asks.

"Uh huh, I'm going to say it was something way worse than that." I mutter and Uno starts to bob up and down and waving her limb like arms.

"Whatcha mean?" burly guy asks while giving Uno a strange look.

"Oh, I have no doubt that the Rev's wife was involved. Actually, I'm pretty sure that a part of her is in each of the pretty plants. Or more specifically, what's left of her is in the pretty plants."

"Do what now?" several ask in shock.

"Okay, so supposedly all of the pretty plants look similar right? If we're able to get all of them together, we might have the Rev's wife… or at least most of her. I think Uno was trying to tell me that someone made some newer plants that are magically manipulated cuttings from the originals and I'm pretty sure that most of these barrel shaped ones are newer still and have absolutely none of the Rev's wife in them, at all." "No fuckin' way" and "they split her up?" is said multiple times by multiple people.

"Yeah, I'm afraid so. Look… there's a little bit of something human in each of the pretty ones, the originals."

"You can tell that? Ah!.. You've been dealing with… Uno for a while now. Well, I've got to say that she has changed, a lot, since you got her. She used to be really nasty." Lucas says and Uno waves at him and he gives her a little finger wave back. The others continue to stare at me, and I think they're trying to figure out how I know so much.

"From what Uno has tried to tell me, I think there should only be… maybe… seven original plants? So, we need to find the others." "Holy shit! Seven? Look, we've actually seen way more plants than that." The woman says.

"How come there's so many and… different types now?" Liz asks.

"Well, I've met several people that have a magical gift that involves plants so… it seems someone's figured out how to get a bunch of cuttings off the originals or maybe they've whittled down a couple of the originals to make a bunch of these new plants. These new plants, the bushy looking ones, are the ones that the Rev and his crew have complete control over somehow and then they're using those plants to control everything else."

"That's… that's diabolical!" Roger says.

"No. That's evil with a capital E." burly guy says.

"Oh, and let's not forget that it's very Christian of them too." Liz snarks.

"So let me get this straight… you're planning a jailbreak and you're also planning on taking off with every plant you come across. Why?" the leader asks.

"The jailbreak because… nothing deserves to be used like this… and the plant removal because that's going to make it really hard to control what prisoners they have left." Lucas answers with a thoughtful expression on his face. *Hot damn! He's really getting it!*

"Okay, that's all well and good but… what are you going to do with these assholes?" the leader asks as he points at the bad guys that haven't made a single sound in quite some time. I know that they're listening, but it's not like they're going to be passing on any secrets.

"Oh, you know. Find out what they know and then cut them loose." I say with a shrug.

"Cut them loose? Are you fuckin' crazy?" the woman asks, shocked.

"What? As soon as they get out of here, they're going to run back to the soldiers and tell them about you! Not to mention that they'll tell them about us!" the leader says.

"Am I fucking crazy? Probably. I mean, I do get asked that question… a lot. But… I didn't say where I was going to let these guys loose… at." I say as my darkness comes roaring up. I guess everyone felt it because everyone took a step back and even the plants leaned away from me. *Ooops!*

 "Holy shit! Are you sure you're one of the good guys? Because… damn!… the look you just had and what I just felt was anything but good." The leader says with a shudder.

"Oh, no. No… she's definitely one of the good guys. Believe me. It's just that she's… also incredibly scary… sometimes." Liz says as she gives me a nervous smile and a shiver.

"If you say so, but… Okay, so just to ease my mind here… where exactly are you planning to let them loose at?" the other guy asks.

"Well… I haven't quite made up my mind on that yet. But uuhh… you do realize that there are now a lot of things out there that uuhhh… eat people, right?" I ask.

"Oh, yeah. We met us a few of them things back in…" burly guy starts with a shrug. I get it, he's still not 100% sure and I'm okay with that. For now.

"Really? Okay, let me ask you something about that. The ones you saw, were they mean about it? Or were they just hungry?"

"If you're askin' me… I'd say they was… mostly hangry." Burly guy says with a grim chuckle and the others with him nod.

"Now that I understand. And I think you do too. Look… if these assholes, during the course of our conversation, tell us that they've done nothing but follow orders, then I'll let them go somewhere that uuhh… has a few things that might find them tasty running around. But at least they'll have a fighting chance… and I'm sure that's more than they've given any of their victims. But! If they've done anything that's beyond shitty… you know, torture and shit like that? Then I'm personally going to hand them over to anything that wants to eat them. I might even stay to watch." I say and I can feel that it was my darkness talking through me, but the smile was all mine. Everyone shivers again but no one has any objections to my plan. I guess we're all on the same page here. Jack's going to shit a brick at my plan, but I think the General will back me up. If I even tell them about this.

"But first, we need to know everything that they know." Lucas says, giving me a nod.

"Oh shit! Wait! I think I hear some people outside." Roger says as he takes a peek out the blinds covering the door then, "Oh shit! Uummm…

there's a small group out there and they look really anxious." he stage whispers as he jerks the blinds closed again.

"What do we do with them?" Liz asks.

"Well shit. Okay, uummm… does anyone know anything about this stuff?" I ask as I pick up a small stack of "how to live off grid" pamphlets and fliers.

"Well yeah. I probably know most of it, but I couldn't remember anything about water filtration, so that's why we're here." burly guy says after a quick glance at the material.

"Great! Then you can go out there and hand this stuff out. Maybe make it look like you're bored with this place and if anyone has a question, answer it the best you can without too much detail." I say with a slightly nasty chuckle. He looks at the goons on the floor and then at his leader who smiles a mean smile and nods.

"You think this is going to work?" burly guy asks his leader.

"Ben, it better work. If it doesn't work, then we'll know that there's a lot of spies around here. So go ahead, we'll be fine until you get back. I'm Larry, that's Ben and this is Wendy and Eddie." Larry the leader says after ushering Ben out the door and pointing out who's who.

"Oh! Hey hi! I'm Bobby and this is Lucas, Liz, Roger and Lara. It's nice to meet y'all." Bobby says as he proudly points to each of us. He's probably lived his entire life in Butler, and he's known everyone for forever, so meeting a bunch of new people is a new experience for him. I think him jumping in and making the introductions is very brave and sweet. He needs a little work, but he'll get better at this, I'm sure. The happy look on his face is enough for me.

While Ben's outside handing out pamphlets and answering questions, I have the bad guys tell us what they know, and we start with what they actually do and how they got involved in this shit. The two women came from very well to do families in Demopolis, that's where the Rev and his top goon squad have moved to for the time being. The two men were just plucked from the ranks of "soldiers" because they're big and look intimidating. The soldiers now control the west central part of the state. Tuscaloosa, Birmingham and Montgomery are on their list to take control of, but they don't have enough of the "right" kind of soldiers to pull that off. That's why they're searching everywhere and taking over everything that they can; to swell their ranks. By any means necessary. *Fuckers!*

According to one of the women, in the beginning, the soldiers just moved in and took over but then if any of the townsfolk protested, they got introduced to the plants, which made them much more "manageable". But since that took time and in the end they ended up doing that anyway, now they just start with the plants. Supposedly, without anyone being able to think for themselves, it's easier for the soldiers to keep a lid on things. (More like easier for the soldiers to do as they please.) *Assholes!* Then they bring in some of the newer plants and use them to locate anything that has a decent amount of magic or power. That's why they're here, to find anything that may have slipped through their original net. Plus, now that it's been confirmed that Mobile is gone, anything with power that got out might be heading this way. With only the smaller cities and towns left, it's becoming easier for them to ramp up their campaign and swell their ranks. Also, if this small group of assholes manages to round up enough escapees or find enough things with power, then she thinks that they'll get to move to a much better location. *I don't think so!* In the past week or so, they've found a few magical people and things, and their plant has been used to implant the suggestion to hang around Coffeeville until it's time for them to go to a different place and meet another group. This bitch is actually hoping that what they've gotten ahold of so far will get them out of this shithole. *Well now… Mwahahaha!* At my evil laugh, everyone looks at me and I share my nasty thought with them.

"If these guys find this shithole bad… the next one they might come out of is going to be soooo much worse!" Larry, Lucas, Wendy and Eddie get it right away and try really hard not to join me with their own evil laughs, but they can't do it. The rest get it right after that and Liz tells me that I'm awful while cackling like a loon. When Ben comes back in, he wants to know why everyone is laughing and Larry tells him between his own chuckles. Ben walks over to me and gives me a high five but then asks what we've learned so far, so Wendy tells him that she'll fill him in later. But… I still have a few questions left. The other woman picks up where their story left off and tell us that once the "new recruits" are met at their next destination, they're given an "interview" and subjected to yet another plant. If they're magical enough and "pass" that exam, then they're shipped off for training. If they don't pass? Most are shipped off to somewhere else and kept for other things.

"What kind of other things?" a few ask. Well… according to these fucktards, they're used for medical experimentation and maybe even breeding, but she doesn't know that for sure. The ones that aren't picked, sometimes they have their memories wiped and are free to go on their merry way but in the beginning, they were probably just killed. These bitches are just so cavalier about this whole thing that I have to get them to stop talking or me and my darkness might just strangle both of them with our bare hands!

"Holy shit! Fuck the Romans, this is more like…" Eddie starts but he doesn't need to finish, we all know where he's going with this. *Goose steppin' morons.*

"Gawd damn! I know that the Klan has some really deep roots down here… but shit! Even they're not this sick." Ben says. One of the big guys tells us that Reverend Ansdale is from Linden, but Lucas and the others already knew that, but the guy thinks there might be some type of camp near there, but he was pretty sure of a "holding center" outside Dixon Mills and a "training camp" somewhere near Uniontown, maybe.

He's unsure about anything else since he's not privy to that kind of information because he's just muscle.

"Holy shit! That's a lot of ground to cover." Eddie says.

"No shit! Especially since it's controlled and being patrolled by who knows how many soldiers." Wendy says, looking really angry.

"Yeah, it is. It doesn't matter which place I hit first either, because once I do, all the others are going to go on high alert. Hmmm… the best option I can think of right now is to hit the "training center" first. That way they'll lose a bunch of their heavy hitters right off the bat." I say as I'm going through other scenarios in my head.

"Are you out of your cotton-pickin' mind?" Wendy asks looking from me to everyone else.

"Ha! No shit! What happens if they turn their heavy hitters loose on you?" Larry asks.

"Well, that's a distinct possibility but… what if I can get my plants to kick their plants asses? If that happens, then their heavy hitters won't be under mind control anymore. No one would be."

"They still might turn on you anyway. Look, if they come out of the… compulsion? they're under, they're going to be pissed off and just looking for someone to take it out on." Larry says.

"True but… maybe, once they're free… maybe they'll see what I'm doing and decide to join me for a little mayhem and destruction? But… I'll settle for everything just getting the hell out of Dodge. Once they're free, they're free. I'm not going to force them to do anything. That's like trading one fucked up situation for another. Nope. Not my style. I only take volunteers." I say and everyone is quiet for a moment

"Well, that's it then. I don't know about them, but I'm willin' to help ya." Ben says after looking at all of the folks in his group, all of which nod at him.

"I'm game too, but first… what did you mean when you talked about your plants kicking their plants asses?" Larry asks.

"Yeah, didn't you say something about the fat one being useless?" Eddie asks.

"How many of those things do you have?" Ben asks. I wiggle three fingers while smiling.

"Three? You have three plants? Originals? How?" Wendy, Eddie, Ben and Larry say almost simultaneously.

"Yes, we have three." Bobby says, looking smug.

"Holy shit! How? Oh, and how do you know that you're not being controlled right now? That we all aren't?" Eddie asks looking fearful.

"Oh well, I'm absolutely positive that I'm not being controlled, and neither are you. Believe it or not but… I've had a lot of… let's call them conversations with Uno here and the other two and… huh. Think of it this way… here you are, in a room with two of them… do you feel like anyone, or anything is trying influence you? Make you do anything that you feel uncomfortable with? Do you feel like you're not in control of yourself? Am I forcing you to answer any of my questions?" I ask but I can tell the new folks are seriously thinking about it.

"Nah, I don't feel nothin' like that. Nothin' like before even but… hang on a sec, I hear somethin' outside. Be right back." Ben says as he slips out the door again.

"Well, it's no wonder the soldiers are really intent on finding you, I mean, not only did you escape, but you've taken off with three plants and wiped out a bunch of their soldiers." Wendy says in wonder.

"Lara, I hate to bring up a sore subject with you but, I think these folks need to know." Lucas says while giving me really good eye contact. I get it and I just nod at him to go ahead.

"It's like this… Lara isn't from Butler, like the rest of us so… it's not like she escaped. She… just rescued us. But in the process of rescuing us, she did manage to wipe out the soldiers and destroy most of the town. Alone." Lucas says. Wendy, Eddie and Larry give me another once over, probably wondering how the hell I managed that. My darkness kind of purrs at that. *Greeeaaat.* Ben slips back in and tells us that some of the locals are wanting to know why the bookstore is closed but he told them that the others were moving on and he was with the new replacement team and that they need to go over a few things and that it might be a few days before they see anyone or the store opens again. That's smart thinking on his part but I think all of us can tell that he's pissed off that some of the locals might be in on this shit. But then he tells us that he thinks that most of the locals really don't know what's going on. *Huh.*

"Hey! I've got a question. Really, what was that stuff Liz put on us when we came in?" Wendy asks, I think as a way to change the subject.

"Oh that? We actually do call it goop. You really don't want to know where it came from but… just know that it blocks mind control powers from being used against you. It's even helped release people from being… under thrall? And from being slowly consumed? I think that's what was going on, anyway. Look… I don't know how else to put it." I say with a shrug.

"What?" a few ask anyway.

"Okay, so you say that that stuff has really helped people, right?" Eddie asks.

"Oh, definitely."

"So where are they now?" Larry asks.

"Well… most are in the process of building new lives for themselves back home and a few are traveling with the rest of my family."

"The rest of your family? Where are they?" Ben asks.

"Somewhere in Mississippi right now."

"Mississippi? How the fuck did that happen?" Ben asks while the others look flabbergasted.

"Well we uhh… we got separated." I hedge a bit.

"And you ended up in Butler? How the hell did that happen?" Larry asks.

"It was… an accident… and magic, so let's leave it at that." I say but I think they can all feel my darkness is on the rise again, so they all back off a bit. It could also be due to Liz motioning for everyone to drop it. She knows that I'm still not ready to share that part of my story, especially with strangers.

"Well, if the rest of your family's still in Mississippi, then we've got plenty of time to plan our next steps." Larry says with a grim chuckle. Maybe, but I don't think so. So, it's back to questioning the bad guys. They tell us where the brainwashed folks are supposed to meet the next group of assholes and when. Then they fill us in on a few other things and none of it's good. At all.

Dammit! Oh, how I wish Casey, David, Riley, Jones or Ajay was here. Hell, I'd even take Kabir's help right about now. *Jeezus.* I don't want these assholes dead, or at least not yet, but fuckin' A man… I want them to hurt! I'd love to kick the shit out of them, but I don't trust… myself or my darkness. At the moment. But then I get an idea. Now… most people would Not consider it a good one, but… I like it and so does my darkness. Make of that what you will, I don't give a shit.

"So, in a nutshell here, everyone that these fools have brainwashed is going to end up in West Bend some time tomorrow morning. But as of right now, the town should be empty. So… who wants to go there with me to set up an ambush for the next group of assholes that show up and "free" the brainwashed?" I ask and there were a couple people that had big grins on their faces at my question. *Fanfuckingtastic!*

"Oh, and how are we supposed to do that?" Eddie asks, but then he sees the nasty smile on Larry's face and then he gets it.

"We're going to pretend to be the bad guys for the brainwashed and take out the real bad guys when they show up, right?" Eddie asks and we all continue to smile, not very nice smiles.

"Wait! Whoever's comin' is gonna to have a couple plants with 'em, right? So how are we supposed to fight that much mind control?" Ben asks, since he missed a bit of pertinent information. So, Wendy fills him in on a few things that he's missed.

"Alright, I can get behind this, but I've got a couple more questions. How long does this goop stuff last? Will we still be covered by tomorrow or are we going to need to reapply? Also, if we need to reapply, are you sure you have enough?" Eddie asks but he seems excited. But before I answer any more questions we decide to get out of the bookstore and find a safer place to plan.

Larry, Ben, Lucas and Bobby go to pick up our ride and the bad guys conveyance while Liz, Wendy, Eddie and I go through all the papers that the bad guys have. As far as we can tell, the list of names and descriptions of the folks and other things they're having go to West Bend is the only thing they have and it's not that many. Oh, and it looks like the Gucci crew didn't make the list. *Ha!* No maps, no directions to other places and nothing on who else is doing this same job in other locations.

"This is it? This isn't very much to go on, is it?" Liz asks while I shake my head in frustration. I turn back to the bad guys and ask if they'd made any copies or if they have a radio or some other way to pass on any of their information. They tell us that it's just the list we now have and they usually hand that over to whoever shows up and asks for it.

"Then how does anyone know if someone's escaped or whatever?" Eddie asks but the bad guys have no answer to that.

"Maybe these guys have handlers too? They don't seem like the sharpest tools in the shed, and I doubt that the good Rev is really this trusting with his powerful… artifacts." I say, then I turn to Uno and ask her what she's gotten from this new plant. Yes, I do get some funny looks at this, but I'm used to that by now, ya know? As I try to piece together what Uno is telling me, I also pass that on to Wendy, Eddie and Liz. Uno is still not quite up to human communication, but from what I gather she lets me know that it's the plant that keeps all the pertinent information and that when the "new recruits" are picked up, the plant goes with them to inform Reverend Ansdale or whoever has a "seed" whatever it knows. Oh wow! It's like this new plant is another type of living recorder. So, these guys were going to be getting a new plant? Huh, and they're not supposed to know about that or be able to tell the difference? Yeah, I don't think anyone in the Revs camp is trusted, at all. But how is it that this muscle guy knows?

"The plants? Really? How, or more importantly, why? Why are they doing this?" Wendy and Liz ask.

"The seed, or seeds or whatever they are. That's how the bad guys control the plants and make them control everything else. Uno, would being near a seed affect you?" I ask but she tells me that she, Dos and Tres are pretty sure that my dosing them with goop is what's given them their separate thoughts, separate identities and she's pretty sure that none of the seeds or any of the other plants will ever have any influence over them, ever again. She tells me that she and the other two are almost positive that the goop is what's released them from their former commands and that they refuse to go back to that type of life. Spending time with me has also helped them communicate a lot better and they're somehow starting to find more of the human parts of themselves, if that makes any sense. They're still not able to remember much, but they are seriously pissed off about what's been going on. When I ask her if gooping this new plant would help it any she informs me no. This plant and others like it are just too far removed from her so those plants really don't have anything to them other than their directives. When everyone asked what that meant, I try to come up with a better analogy, I think.

"Okay, so this is going old school here but does anyone remember the movie "Multiplicity"? A guy was cloned and then his clone was cloned etcetera. Each generation of the clones was different and something was lost with each cloning. But that doesn't seem to matter to the Rev. These things are being manufactured just to obey orders, they have very little to nothing of the originals in them anymore, just some of their abilities."

"So, it's like a breeding program? Like trying to make the biggest and meanest new dog breed?" Eddie asks.

"Uuhhh… sorta?" I say with a shrug but personally, I'm thrilled to pieces to hear that these new plants are not worth saving. Even though it's a corruption of the originals and they've got their ability to siphon and store magic, I'm overjoyed with the fact that I can use these nasties for my friends. *Mwahaha!* I'm no longer willing to even consider sacrificing one of our three to help out Megan, Tony, Stanley and Oscar. I'm also super happy that our three have turned over a new leaf and are more than willing to help us out with their… demented clones. *Damn, I wish the fam was here to groan over that one. Ha!* Oh, and my devious little mind is starting to come up with some really good ideas but then we hear a couple horns honking outside. Time to go!

We have the bad guys lay down in the back of my truck and our new friends get in their big black Escalade (of course) and follow us back to where we'd left Nat and the remaining bus. Yes, I do indeed hit every bump I can, including going over a curb or two. Sue me. Once we get back, I'm glad to see that everyone else is back safe and after introducing these new folks to everyone but Nat, who's still in her bus with her egg sack but listening in, I drop a bomb on the rest of my new group.

"Alright folks, so here's the deal. Around nine am tomorrow, some heavily influenced people and maybe a few other things, are going to show up in West Bend and either be killed or taken off somewhere to become pawns in the Rev's war or whatever it is he's got going on. I plan on being there to stop that shit and maybe find out where they're taking everyone." Can you believe that that caused a stir? Jeez, it's like I'm back with my fam. *Ha!*

"Look, this is our first solid lead and our best opportunity to start really hitting the soldiers back hard and where it hurts them the most. By taking their plants. The fewer of those things they have, the less control they can keep and use against other people. Oh, and there's another plus… the bushy plant that we now have? It has no redeeming qualities and no… personality. According to Uno, it will never get one, it wasn't made that way. That means I can use all of that type of plant, at some point, to help some others." I say.

"Wait! What exactly do you mean, you can use them to help others?" Larry asks.

"Oh, we don't know because we haven't seen her do it yet, but we've seen some folks that she says she's helped." Lucas says before I get a chance to answer. It's a good answer but I'm not sure that it's going to be enough. Aaaand, I'm right.

"Helped how and how are you going to use the plants?" Larry almost demands.

"Okay, so the thing with these plants is that they can store stolen power or magic, right? I know of a way to release that stuff and focus it on people and other things that… need it. To help them. For example, I've helped people with their magical… change. Have you seen anyone who's changed into something else and can't get back? Well, I've been able to help them change back to normal and now they can change… at will." I stop there and shrug because now I'm not so sure I can do this on my own. *Well shit.* Oh, and I'm pretty sure everyone that knows about Nat is wondering if I can do that for her too, but I really don't think so. Call it a hunch, but I think that when she and the spider and the scorpion vied for supremacy, she didn't try to change her body, she was just too busy fighting to see who would be in charge of them mentally. If… and I mean if, I could change her back to her original body, I'm not sure she'd do it because her baby was involved and I'm absolutely positive that I can't put that back. Besides, I really don't think the other two sentient beings would survive the full human change and I know she's not willing to sacrifice them. I'm also pretty sure that with Millie… if she doesn't change, neither will Jasper. Rosa and Becca might after their babies are born, but then again, maybe not. But having Oscar and Stanley being able to change at will? That'll help the species, I guess, but that's another can of worms that will have to be looked at in the future. Now I'll admit that I'm guessing about some of this, but it feels right.

"Now back to the issue at hand. I don't expect any of you to go with me and I'm not going to let them take me off anywhere, or for them… to leave at all, actually. So, having said all of that… you know that it might get nasty, right? I know I've told the Butler group that for me… the bad guys have got to go. Yes, it appears that most, if not all, of the bad guys are being controlled, but I'm pretty sure that the more ardent of a follower they are, then I think that proves that they were willing participants in this… corruption?... to begin with. Their being controlled just ensures that they stay in line and so that they really can't pass on secret squirrel shit or think about taking over or something. So yeah, nothing and no one is really safe from them so… they need to be dealt with… harshly."

"Oh, we know that… I know it but… I just don't want you doing what you're planning to… I don't want it to… to make you harder? Like you were before or… or more like them? I don't… I don't know how else to say it." Sandra says with a shrug.

"What? Oh, I think I get what you're trying to say but… seriously, I'm not going to kill them if that's what you're worried about. No. Well… at least not personally. See… I'm thinking about letting whatever's following us have them."

Yeah… "Oh!" is said… a lot but while I was saying all of that, Nat has opened the back door of her bus and makes quite an entrance. Several of us have to move to stand where the new folks can't get a clear shot at her because their guns have come out when Nat's halfway out of her bus. The looks of shock on their faces is understandable and I think a couple of them may have shit their pants. But when she starts talking? I don't think their mouths can opened any farther. Nat then tells me that I wouldn't be going alone… in no uncertain terms. Then we nonchalantly introduce Nat to Larry, Ben, Eddie and Wendy. It goes easier and faster than even I could ever imagine because the new folks see that none of us are freaked out by her and… I think the major thanks go to some of the kids asking Nat if they can climb on her and them having fun trying to see who can reach the top first, even though Nat's acting like she's trying to shake them loose. Children's laughter is a great way to calm down even the worst situations.

"How uuhhh… how long were you planning on keeping her a secret?" Larry asks me after having a brief greeting with Nat, who continues to play with the kids.

"Not very long, I mean, she's a part of this group too, so…" I say with a shrug.

"Don't get me wrong here but… I'm not saying you were wrong to do it but… Well shit. I can see why you did it this way. The soldiers would love to get their hands on her and most other people would just try to kill her, I get it. You uuhhh… you don't have any more surprises like her around here, do you?" Larry asks and then laughs when Emily slides down one of Nat's legs after almost reaching the top. The pout on her face is just too cute!

"Hey Emily?" I say and she comes over to me and wraps herself around my leg, thumb in her mouth.

"Do you want to know how to make it to the top?" I ask and of course she nods.

"Well then, you need to think like a spider." I say and… the look she gives me. *Damn!*

"Oooo weee! The look she just gave you could peel the paint off a barn!" Ben says with a hearty laugh.

"That's my girl." I say with a laugh and pick her up and give her a hug and a kiss on the cheek, which she wipes off after telling me she wants down, but after returning my hug.

"She's your kid?" Eddie asks in surprise.

"No. She's from Butler. No one has said who her parents are… or were. Either way, I'd take her if I could, but that's just not in the cards right now. But that really hasn't stopped her from adopting me." I say with a fond smile.

"So, you and Nat are going to West Bend. You mind if I tag along?" Ben asks and at his question, Bobby and Lucas volunteer too. Wendy volunteering is a surprise, but not a bad one so now at least I have some back up, but I hope they stay out of the way if I let my darkness out. I'm sure Bobby and Lucas will know the signs. But it's when Emily and the other kids tell Nat that they'll take care of her egg sack for her while she's gone, that… that's a tearjerker for me. I also feel the newcomers shock at the news. But right now, we need to get out of Coffeeville and find a good place to hide for a little while.

By mutual agreement we hit the road and travel east until we find a road right before the no stoplight town of Zimco, right off highway 84. The road is maybe a mile long with three houses within shouting distance of each other on it. The rest of the road is just corn fields and smaller gardens scattered around the houses. If there had been any livestock, they're gone now. None of the houses have been occupied for quite some time and the gardens are full of fresh fruits and vegetables needing to be picked, so this looks like a pretty good place for our immediate needs.

Once everything is checked out and several folks start in on a few projects, those of us heading for West Bend talk it through. We're going to head out around 1am and we all agree that we need to be kind of sneaky as we pass through Coffeeville again. Luckily the bad guys told us that the motel where the meet up will take place should be empty until maybe an hour before the designated time so those of us going all decide to take it easy and maybe catch a nap, if possible. At least right now, if I do take a nap, I don't have to worry about Joe calling me into our place. It sucks that I can't call it anything else since it's his place too but… if I'm up most of the night, I can ignore it if he does call. I think. Oh, and then there's the discussion of what to do with the bad guys. Luckily there's a barn that's empty and that's where we end up stashing them. Nat came up with the idea of just stringing them up but instead, she just made a bunch of tethers to keep them separated but inside. No one objects to this, and it does keep everyone free from actually having to "take care" of them. There's also a really nice workshop next to the barn and we lose my truck in it along with Jalen and Jamal. I really need to get these two in touch with the Brainy Bunch, I know that they'll fit right in with them.

The rest of the afternoon is spent getting to know each other better and Sandra, Marybeth and Liz start canning some of the things that we pick out of the gardens. Then Sandra starts doing something with some of the goop. The guys drift in and out of the kitchen, being put to work occasionally, but they did get to spend a lot of time in the workshop if they weren't helping make a few minor repairs to the houses, other barns and fencing or playing with the kids. I think this new group is getting a really good look at how me and my fam usually operate. Especially when it comes to leaving a place better off than how we found it. Then Jamal and Jalen emerged from the workshop with my truck and the smiles on their faces are huge. Jamal tells me that they've made a few adjustments but when I ask what to expect, he laughs and tells me it's going to be a surprise. Then it's time for me to rest up for a bit after an early dinner of fresh vegetables. At dinner I know everyone is looking at me strange when I tell them that I don't care where they got the meat from, I'm going to pass due to past experiences and not having Willie around to verify things for me. Once I fully fill them in on those stories? I'm sure that they'll understand. *Bwahahaha!*

133

Day 40

I'm woken up by Emily climbing into Nat's bus where I'd decided to stretch out. Nat didn't mind and I didn't want to be in any of the houses. In a tearful voice she says that I need to come back to her then she wipes a few tears on me as she comes in for a hug. Holy Shit! Emily's tears are really potent! I think… no, I know it's not mind control when she… pushes? her power at people. For me… It's more like… it takes away everything that's clogging up my mind. It cuts out the wishy-washy shit, it's also made me drop the useless guard that's been keeping people out. *Well shit.*

Maybe that's why she wasn't taken? I mean, maybe whoever checked her out was never going to believe that a weepy four-year-old little girl could have that much power or even what it could possibly be? I also wonder what would happen if I bottle some of her tears and spit, but that's something to think about… later. Nat gets a hug of her own and a promise from Emily that she's going to read a story to the egg sack. *That's so sweet!*

When the three of us exit the bus we find the rest of the group heading for West Bend, Marybeth and Sandra who take little Emily back into the house, plus an unexpected one standing around waiting on us. Jamal is our newest participant in this excursion but he says he needs to go in case what he and Jalen did to my truck stops working. *Uh huh. Sure?*

Three in the front, three in the back and Nat squished down in the bed with Dos and Tres webbed to the truck bed for safety. I'm glad that Bobby and Wendy are skinny, or I don't think we'd all fit. But then I start the engine and it's super quiet. It's so quiet that even though we can feel the truck vibrating, we can't hear the engine so… Yeah, Jalen and

Jamal need to be with the Brainy Bunch. I can't even imagine some of the wild and crazy shit that they'll probably come up with. *Ha!*

"Wow! I can't hear the engine at all! Is this how we're going to get through town?" Bobby asks excitedly.

"Yeah well, this is certainly going to help." I say with a smirk.

"What? What's that supposed to mean?" Ben asks, looking like he's regretting his choices.

"Well… the rain is going to help with any tire noises but yeah, being super quiet is certainly going to help with stealth mode."

"Stealth mode? Are you kidding me? What? We're going to be making the trip in the dark? The whole trip? How?" Wendy asks, shocked. "Hey! Can you really see through this fog? Or are you just torturing us?" Ben asks while grabbing onto the "oh shit" bar.

"Why can't it be both?" I ask with a cheesy grin.

"I must be out of my fuckin' mind." he grumbles but we can all hear Nat's slightly maniacal laughter coming from the back.

"More than likely, but honestly, I think we all are." Lucas says with a laugh as he thumps Ben on the arm. Going stealth mode all the way through town is interesting. I actually see two spots that might be lookout stations, but I think they're either asleep or we're just that good. Either way, that's something to look into on the way back. And to bring up with the bad guys since they never mentioned them.

It takes us about forty-five minutes to get to the motel, what with the derelict vehicles and only going off roading two times. Even Nat's disgruntled with this last one because it's so bumpy. *Ha!*

The Dew Drop Inn isn't the worst place I've ever seen but it definitely hasn't been taken care of very well. I'm guessing that in the recent past it's only been used by the desperate or those looking for a nooner. It actually has a pretty big lobby area and there used to be a diner attached to it. The diner part is now mostly empty with some recently set up tables and chairs blocking the back and some sad touristy stuff. The recently set up stuff must be for the "interviews". *Fanfuckingtastic!* We must be in the right place. Now... we have too many hours to kill before we get to see any action. This sucks, but oh well, right? After a few minor adjustments to the setup, which includes stashing Dos and Tres under one of the tables, I ask Nat how long it would take her to put up a web across a couple doors.

"You mean like these doors? Maybe a minute, maybe less, why?" Nat asks as we all look over at the clouded glass doors separating the lobby from the diner. Ben, Bobby and Lucas snort a laugh.

"Oh! You want me to let the bad guys in and then booby trap the doors! That's... fucking genius! But that's going to trap them in here with you! I'm not too thrilled with that thought though."

"It might not be ideal, but... can you make it so that your web stuff is razor sharp?" I ask but I know I've got a nasty smile on my face; I can feel it and my darkness is really liking my pseudo plan.

"Holy shit!" is said a few times by a few different people.

"Fuck me! You're wanting them to kill themselves? Ha! I fuckin' love it!" Nat says with a cackling laugh, but as she and the others continue to snicker, I sidle up closer to her and whisper that if she's hungry, she should feel free to take whatever she needs. Nat whispers back that she's planning on spinning a few more webs on a few more doors in case someone makes it that far. I hold up my hand for a high five, which she gives me, but damn! Her toe things are sharp! Everyone else can tell that we're up to something, but I can also tell that none of them are too concerned, yet. *Ha! They'll learn.*

"So, now what?" Jamal asks.

"If you feel like it, try to get a little more rest. When the "new recruits" show up, while we're pretending to be the recruiters, we're going to have to be on our A game in case any of them act up. I'm fairly sure that after they've been gooped, they'll be… if not fine, then certainly more amiable to chat. Don't you think? I mean, I'm sure they're going to have a lot of questions. But… if they're still not willing to talk and only want to fight? Then it's a good thing we have you and Ben here and y'all can just knock them out." I say with a laugh.

"Say what now? Why me? Why do… Hey look, I'm a lover not a fighter!" Ben sputters, but he can't keep a straight face, and we all laugh with him. Then Bobby gets a strange look on his face, so I know that something is brewing in his head. *Aaaand here it comes.*

"Okay, so I have a question. Well actually… what I really want to know is… are we doing the right thing here? I mean, the bad guys are people too, ya know? So… is what we're doing… or planning to do… is it any different than what they're doing?" Bobby asks sheepishly. I try to come up with a good yet polite answer to that but…

"Okay Bobby, let me ask you something. Do you honestly believe, for one second, that if the bad guys ever got their hands on say… me… that they wouldn't try kill me or put me in a cage? Do you believe that they'd let me be free to… interact… with other people? Do you think that I'd be able to leave anytime I wanted? That Lara would? Because I sure as shit don't. The plants that they're using to make people… or whatever… more manageable is not in any way okay in my book and shouldn't be in yours! That's not freedom or even free will. That's… it's nothing but… magical slavery! Now, I kinda get where you're coming from, you know, what with using the bad guys, but… the problem is… well, the problem is that these motherfuckers are bent on world domination or some shit while we're trying to ensure… freedom and maybe… peace? We might be using close to the same methods, but we're after totally different outcomes." Nat says. I think she nailed that answer perfectly and so does Lucas, Ben, Wendy and Jamal since they all stand up and give her a standing ovation.

"Okay, yeah… that I can understand and I'm totally behind it. I mean, I Knew we were doing the right thing, but I was confusing myself, I think, with the… the…" Bobby couldn't seem to find the right words, so I help him out.

"Methodology? Yeah, I get that. I think we all do, but even though our way may seem… harsh? or even cruel? We're really not the ones trying to hurt anyone or anything and we sure as shit don't want to rule the world. Slavery was abolished for a reason, and I personally refuse to let it make a comeback. No one has the right to "own" another sentient being, and we've got a shit ton of them now and they need to be protected."

"Yes! That's it! Right there! Look, we've got Bobby's dogs and they're way smarter than they used to be. We've got Gilligan and now Nat! Oh, and let's not forget about Uno, Dos and Tres! And I know that there's a lot more out there. Lara has a bunch of new beings in her family! So yes… new rules and eventually new laws are going to need to be established." Lucas says while reaching for some paper and a pen. *OMG!* I think he's going to start drafting a new constitution or bill of rights or something. Right now! I really need to get him together with the General. But… I want absolutely no part of that. Nope! No fucking way.

As Lucas gets started on whatever he's doing and the rest of us snicker at him, we all start looking for a place to either sit or stretch out and I just sit on the floor and lean back against the wall and try to meditate. *Ha!* Not to mention that I'm going over some of the worst-case scenarios that could occur here. (It's that overthinker part of me that I can't seem to turn off.) Oh well, since I really can't get into the "zone", I talk to Dos and Tres for a bit. They're really looking forward to taking out the "bad" plants and the bad guys. They even thank me for bringing them along, I think. Seriously, who would've ever thought that this would be how they'd turn out by how they were when I first met them? I still feel a bit sorry for them and I also wonder what will happen when we get more of them together, or if we can get all of the originals together at all. I also wonder how many of the "magically made" ones are around and how many of the originals are left. See? I'm so scattered with my thoughts that I totally miss how the fuck I end up in my weird place! *Holy shitballs!* Luckily Joe isn't around as far as I can tell so I get up and wander around for a bit, looking for whoever it is that's somehow called me in here.

The call actually feels familiar and it's super strong, so I head off in that direction. When I step out of my place I have to immediately step to the left, barely getting missed by some weird acidic spit.

"Nice to see you too Millie." I say with a laugh. If she could blush, she would have, but then she rushes up to me and just about knocks me over with her body checking hug and then she pushes me toward her nest. She's so excited to show me what's in it. Wow! Inside the nest are four beachball sized lavender speckled eggs resting on an odd assortment of ripped sheets and blankets and probably some of Millie and Jasper's old clothes.

"Oh Millie! Congratulations! I'm so happy for you!" I say as I give her another hug. She takes my hand and places it on one of the eggs. It's soft and kind of leathery, and so very warm. I gently touch each of the eggs and I can "feel" her... chicks? They're completely blank slates so the first thing that comes to mind is to tell her to think good thoughts to them, like I'm doing. I also tell her to tell them about her friends and how much she enjoys spending time with them and especially about her new best friend Kathleen. For some reason I feel that these things will help them to develop into PPE's more like their parents. But what the hell do I know? I mean, we're dealing with something completely new here! And magic! I truly hope my suggestions work, otherwise... no. I'm not going there. This will work! Positive thought only! Even from me. I tell her and Jasper again how happy I am for them and to pass on my suggestions to Kathleen, Rosa, Becca and all the Naga that are helping the other two PPE's with their nesting situations. Both Millie and Jasper promise to do as I've suggested, and they both give me another bone crushing hug.

But now it's time to go back and I struggle, a lot, trying to get back into my place. *Oh shit.* But then, with a little bit of help from Millie, Jasper and my darkness, I finally make it. *Pheeeeww!* I can't even imagine how hard of a time I'd have explaining my long absence from my new group if I was unable to make it back, that's for sure. Then I slowly wander back and when I step out? All I get is three guns, a pair of massive pinchers and a scorpion tail immediately aimed in my direction!

"Oh hey! Whoa there! It's just me!" I say with my hands up.

"Holy shit! How the fuck…" and a few other things are said simultaneously.

"Hey look! I'm sorry, okay? I didn't really expect to… go walk-a-bout. It happens sometimes." I say with a blush, like I'd just been caught doing something bad.

"What? Never mind that! Where the fuck did you go?" Lucas demands and Nat slowly lowers her more dangerous extremities.

"Do you remember the big purple guy from the other night?" I ask but I'm aiming my question at him, Jamal and Bobby, who all nod their heads. "Okay, so I was… called?… to visit another one. She's so happy! So thrilled and she wanted to show me her nest, and her eggs. That and she's a bit nervous too." I say, but I know that they don't understand my happy smile.

"Doooo what now? I must be missin' somethin'." Ben says with a grumble, looking between me and the others.

"Sorry. Long story short here. Okay, so Millie is an eighty something year old spinster lady that was under hospice care when the orange fog started. She was magically changed into a One Eyed One Horned

Flying Purple People Eater. Or PPE for short. She and five others were changed and she and Jasper… I guess you could say that they're a mated pair now, well anyway, they're expecting. Rosa and Becca are too but this is Millie's first opportunity to be a mom and she's just so happy! That's why she called and I… went for a quick and… unexpected visit?" I say with a shrug.

"Yeah, no shit! I mean, you were just sitting over there, it looked like you were meditatin' or somethin' and then you were gone!" Ben says.

"How the fuck did you do that?" Nat asks and the others look really interested in my answer.

"Well… it's magic."

"Uh huh. No shit. Are you planning on doing that again any time soon? Oh! Oh! Is that what happened last night?" Nat demands.

"Wait! What?" Bobby and Jamal say at the same time.

"Where is Millie right now?" Lucas asks but I can see that he's onto something, so I hesitate in answering him.

"She and Jasper are in Perla… Arkansas."

"What? Are you fucking serious?" and a bunch of other things are said by everyone but Lucas.

"So, is that how you ended up in Butler? Did someone call you there?" Lucas asks and I can see that he's thinking about the first time he saw me, or at least that's what I'm guessing.

"No. No one from Butler called me. I think I ended up there because that was where I, at one point in time, wanted to go. It's the place my friends and I were looking for and thought that maybe we could settle down there. I wasn't… I wasn't prepared to actually be there." I say but my darkness rushes forward and finishes for both of us with "But since we were obviously needed, we decided to stay and have a little bit of fun." Even I shiver a little but… that statement is pretty much spot on. Oh, and now I can remember smiling at the guys in the garage. Yes, my darkness was in the driver's seat, but now I can remember what we'd done to them. *O. M. G. I really don't think that there's any type of anger management classes or any type of therapy that's ever going to be able to help me with this. Do you?*

"Uuhhh, Lara? Don't take this the wrong way here but… you really weren't kidding when you said that you were a monster too, were you? I mean, I did think you were kinda… insane but… Aww shit. You have no idea how happy I am that I hooked up with you!" Nat says as she bounces up and down. I think that's her happy dance.

"Yeah, well… I'm just glad that you're one of the good guys." Ben says as he and Wendy share a look, but then they smile. Lucas, Bobby and Jamal share a smile too. *Aawww… Group hug!*

"Hey, since we still have a couple of hours until sunrise, and I'm bored now that all the woo woo magic shit is over with… can we take a quick look around? If we stay close?" Bobby asks as the rest of us laugh at his wording, but he's giving me seriously pleading eyes. I shrug because everyone else turns and gives me a similar look.

"Okay, if we stay close and… if you show me what you've got. Magically. Quit being a perv… besides I know you've got something." I say but the look he's giving me seriously reminds me of Casey. And not just because of the eyebrow wiggle. *Jeez, not another one!*

I get that Ben's magic is going to be something somehow physical, maybe, but Lucas and Wendy are more intellectual, as in thinking or just using their heads, and of course Jamal and Jalen are intellectual but with a mechanical twist and will be lumped in with the Brainy Bunch, for sure but Bobby? Bobby is still a mystery… for the moment.

So, we all head out of the motel, and go across the street to a burger joint and the gas station convenience store. The burger joint is easy to check out since it's a burned-out wreck, but the convenience store has a few goodies that seem to have been missed while the place was being picked over and/or just vandalized in the past.

"Hey! There's a ton of stuff back here that hasn't been touched!" Bobby yells from the storage room in the back and Lucas and Wendy say almost the same thing from the walk-in cooler. Ben's amazed at all of the stuff that we're uncovering as we're putting some shelves back in place. I tell him that we've come across this kind of stuff before. It may have been vandalized before someone came in to get supplies and they just didn't think they had enough time to really go through the place. I tell everyone that we've come across a couple Walmart's and other stores that were a mess in the front but the stock in the back was untouched. Jamal and I make our way over to where the store used to make and sell pizzas and with Nat's help we end up where the oven is and we check out the large walk-in freezer back there. I think we've hit the jackpot. I also think that Jamal's mouth is watering almost as much as mine is at the thought of fresh pizza. *Hmmm.*

"Holy shit! We've really hit the jackpot here!" Ben says as he peeks over our shoulders to see all of the pizza supplies, like frozen pizza dough and other essentials neatly lining their shelves. Okay, so Ben might have a little bit of something mental too since he just used the same words I'd been thinking.

"What? No way! Should we… should we make a bunch of pizzas to take back with us when we leave?" Wendy asks.

"Why do that? I mean, why not just take everything… including the oven?" Nat asks. *Damn! I like her style!* After she asks her question, the guys all gather around the oven and start naming off the tools they're going to need and Bobby mentions that he'd seen a big toolbox in the back. We all laugh as he runs to wherever he saw the tools. After Bobby's done dragging in the big toolbox, I grab him and take him outside with me.

"Oh man, pizza." He says almost reverently, and I just laugh and then Nat pops off with how much she misses pizza too. *Oh jeez.* Finally, Bobby's able to drag himself away from the thoughts of pizza and he takes me over to a puddle in the parking lot. He stands by the puddle and hangs his head before telling me that what he can do is nothing special. Nat is staring over my shoulder and I know that she's just as curious as me, so I just look at Bobby, trying to give him courage. He gives us a big sigh then he concentrates on the puddle. After a few seconds several small figures rise up out of the puddle and start to dance. Uuhhh... it's cute but... there's got to be more to it than that. Right?

"Oh! Well... that's nice. But can you do anything else?" Nat asks.

"Like what? I told you it's nothin' special." Bobby says, but he looks so dejected.

"Uumm... have you ever tried to separate the dirt from the water?" I ask.

"What? Do you really think I could do something like that?" he asks, Nat and I nod at him. So, it looks like he's thinking really hard for a few seconds and then the dancing figures get lighter in color, become clearer as the contaminates fall away. He shoots us such a beautiful smile when he realizes that his figures are now nothing more than clean clear water sparkling in the orange moonlight. So, then Nat and I ask him to try a few other things. It's awesome watching him as he makes his figures rise up enough and then he changes them into a tiny rain cloud. With a little more effort, he's got some of the other dirty water to rise up, shedding dirt and stuff before joining with the little cloud making it bigger. I clap when the dirt and stuff falls like hail before the now clean water joins the cloud. I don't think he could've been prouder of himself when his little cloud starts to rain or at the realization that he can do so much more than just making water dance. I already knew that I was going to be proud of him no matter what, but this is great and Nat and I tell him so.

"This is so fucking amazing! I thought all I could do was make little figures and have them dance! I never realized that I could do so much more! What else should I try?" he asks, and I tell him to try whatever he wants to, but he wants examples.

"How the hell should I know? Okay, so how about this… can you… aim the water and make it hit a target? Like a squirt gun?" The mischievous look on his face tells me that most of us are going to be getting wet, a lot, in the near future. Well, I've dodged rocks and dirt, so why not water too, right? And yep! While we're outside dodging getting hosed, and after a bunch of banging and swearing, Lucas, Jamal and Ben come out with most of the dismantled pizza oven and take it over and put it in the bed of our truck. They ask Nat to secure the pieces so that they don't rattle around while the rest of us laugh at the load distribution. Ben's carrying the biggest part with ease.

With the prospect of having pizza sometime soon and after making sure we have everything we could possibly need packed up and/or waiting, we go back to the motel. Bobby says he needs a break because he's used up a ton of power practicing his new gig. Wendy, Lucas, Ben and Jamal take seats at the long table and start playing some card game with the cards that Wendy had taken from the convenience store while Bobby crashes hard and I go back to trying to… not so much get into my place, but to figure out how to do it again, on purpose, on my own. I sit in the same spot and think over what had happened the last time but as I'm sitting here suddenly my crystals give me another look at what's been happening with my family. I think what they're showing me was what happened… yesterday?

It started out in Jones' perspective, again; the whole group was about halfway between Leeland and Indianola. They'd stopped because the road was completely impassable, but I hear the conversation between Jones, Casey, Riley, Lee, David, Doris, Mark, Dozer and Ox. They had asked the coyotes to ghost through Indianola and to report back but the fam wasn't going to clear the road because they noticed that the road was blocked on purpose and they didn't want to piss anyone off, if they didn't have to. It took the coyotes about an hour for half of them to return because they'd picked up several vehicles heading towards my group. Reba let everyone know that she smelled gun oil and was not pleased with the situation. (I laugh at that.) Pit Bull laughed and said something about this being Mississippi, so of course there's going to be gun oil since almost everyone has at least one gun in their vehicles. (I think he's being a little judgmental here, but maybe not.) Then Loretta let it be known that all of the coyotes feel that something isn't right but that was about the time a large group of heavily armed men pulled up and were extremely rude in asking what my group wanted. Alex, in his best peacekeeper persona, requested simple passage through their town, so that they could continue on their way. The other half of the coyotes then started filling in everyone on what they were seeing. They were extremely pissed off when they'd located a large number of new beings... being mistreated. Those in my group that don't look totally human then decided to remain hidden the entire trip through the town. Fast Forward.

Once on the other side of Indianola Casey immediately got on the radio with the General and after he'd heard what the coyotes described to my fam, he was livid! The General then went on to tell everyone to be careful but that they needed to continue to follow our calling then disconnected with a snap. (I'm taking that to mean that he's giving my gang permission to kick some ass.) A few minutes later the General called back, and though he sounded calmer than before he did say that he didn't believe for an instant that I'd sit back and do nothing, but then he asked for everyone to refrain from the scorched earth policy that I'd dropped on Butler. (I think I should be offended at the amount of laughter that followed that statement but even I have to laugh at it.) But when they got going again, they noticed that they had a couple shadows not too far behind them. They had to stop again a couple miles outside of town because they came upon a bunch of traps. Spike strips and other things covered by dirt and other debris. This made it easy to stop again but some were not too thrilled about having to stay hidden because of their shadows. Casey, Riley, Zee, Dozer and Alex got out to check things out and were pissed off for real at the sight of the traps but then they all had a good laugh and everyone then started giving high praise to Orvil for his tire upgrades. (Now I don't feel so bad about having to help swap out so many damn tires when Orvil asked for them, individually, back at the Peachtree's.) Then it looked like maybe an hour had passed in "fast forward" before the shadow cars finally approached to see why my group had stopped for so long. When Alex told them about the traps the guys in the shadow vehicles laughed. (I imagine they laughed because they thought that they had my group at their mercy.) *Idiots!* Then those guys got on a radio and called someone to inform them of my groups predicament. Whoever they talked to apparently gave them permission to help my group out… for a price. The price being an evening with the ladies of our group. *Oh! Holy shit! Bwahahaha!* Oh, and Jones now understands the phrase "almost swallowed my tongue" since he almost did it while trying to contain his laughter at that horror inducing thought. (I did see what he wrote in his journal, and I agree with him.) He wrote "I have absolutely no doubt that the men that spend the evening with the women of my new family will not… enjoy it or… they may not even survive the experience." *Awww, that's so sweet!* Alex, Casey, Ox and Dozer ask the shadow guys for an hour to discuss the issue with the ladies of the group, all of whom had been acting very subservient, when seen. Jones did ask silently if this was going to be a ruse that they were going to be using more of in the future and the ladies of the group made him blush with their response. Tarina toned down her answer and said that this kind of thing is to be expected and reminded him of how the ladies in the hunters house had been treated. (Jones' comment needs to be printed on a t-shirt.) "We're not dealing with very enlightened individuals, are we?" Catherine, Brandi, Lynx, Luna, Melissa and Helen each gave him a mental hug and told him to never change. *Absofuckinglutely!*

The next scenes were in a multitude of different perspectives and it was kind of hard to follow like this so I'll just have to hit the highlights. The sun was setting and four of our rides were full of my female family members, each vehicle being driven by a male that appeared to be the weakest of the bunch. But… in or around each vehicle was someone or something with stealth mode going full blast. There was a large group on foot about half a mile behind them and the PPE's were in the air a little bit farther back. My female family members were dressed a bit on the slutty side and a few of the pieces were straight up armor pieces that Wally had made for me. *Bwahaha!* (At least some of those things were getting worn but not specifically as intended!) Luna said something about at least all their lady parts were being covered, barely. The vehicles stopped at a makeshift checkpoint and after a cursory glance, the guards there had everyone step out and my fam were all subjected to a very invasive pat down. (Even I could feel the growling that was going on from folks too far away to be heard.) When Catherine was jerked around by her arm and James and Radio were knocked down, it was like their silent communications were vibrating in my head.

"That's it! These motherfuckers are dead meat walking!" Parker growled.

"Yeah, yeah, they are but… I say we give the girls first choice." Bulldog grumbled.

"Well now, uuhh… it would be quicker if we did it." Dozer said, trying to calm a few others down but…

"Oh hey! No way! This cock suckin' son of a bitch is mine!" Luna said very heatedly.

"Yeah! Besides, I've always wondered what it would be like to rip some guys nuts off." Lynx said with a catty hiss.

"See? This is why I said that if we did it, it would be quicker." Dozer grumbled again.

"Well, I guess it's a good thing Chance isn't here, because he did that once." Alex said with a chuckle and then there were a lot of questions about that, but Riley started yelling about being on the move again. Casey asked the PPE's to come in and take out the three pissed off looking guards that were left at the checkpoint, and he asked Parker, Ajay and William to take their places. The new caravan continued on for a few minutes but then it made a turn to go to… the airport? *Ha!* Doris isn't happy about that because she said "Fuck me! I thought I quit!" Tarina's answer to her was fantastic when she said, "Now Doris… you know as well as I do that it's not official unless you've turned in your badge." But the lighthearted chatter ended quickly when some of the ladies got a quick glimpse of some new beings behind the big fences surrounding the runways. When Lynx mentioned seeing the dinocows and the fact that they didn't look very good, the growling got louder in my ears. Then the ladies were told to get out and they were frisked roughly again. This time James, Radio, John and Wally were treated cruelly as well. The power trip these assholes were on had them all laughing and they continued to laugh as three heavily armed men marched the ladies towards the airport terminal. Once the ladies were out of sight, David, Perky, Dozer and Zee materialized and beat the ever-living shit out of the assholes that had frisked the girls. James and Radio were able to get in a few good licks of their own while John and Wally stood off to the side, smiling. David had gone over the fence and was trying to get the dinocows to settle down and I'll give him credit, he tried really hard, but they weren't receptive, at all. The dinocows ran David back over the fence and even the coyotes were being rebuffed or repelled.

Then it jumped to inside the airport terminal and the ladies were all silently chatting about how amazed they were at who was in charge of this detestable crew. And then I can see the assholes in charge and I'm as shocked as everyone else. They're nothing but a small group of barely high school kids. Pimply faced teenage boys. How in the fuck did they manage this? Why? Oh, they're another collective, and like so many others, it appears that these little shits are after world domination, in their own narrow-minded way I guess. Then, when they opened their mouths? (Everyone should be extremely grateful that I wasn't there when that happened because there would've been nothing left of those little shits but a smear on the carpet!) And not just because they started whining and were extremely put out by the fact that several of the ladies are old enough to be their mothers. Even though that wasn't going to stop them from "getting it on" with any of them, or so they thought. Even I'm kind of shocked at what some of my friends, no family, were saying in answer to that! It's a good thing that they're all getting really good at using the "they're under control" ruse just like my new group is having to do. Then Lynx and Doris pounce on the boys closest to them with Catherine and Brandi not too far behind. After a couple solid punches and a few scratches, the boys are all lying on the floor, crying like babies, and their guards didn't fare much better. That's when the guys came in and all they could do was stare for a moment then they all burst out laughing at the sight.

I'm sure other interesting things happen after that but all I can hear is Judy saying my name over and over again. I have no idea if I can answer her, but I silently yell her name anyway.

"Judy!"

"Oh! Fantastic! This actually worked!"

"Judy, what the fuck is going on?"

"Oh, sorry. I'll try to keep this short. See, my crystals, and all the others that I've been working with lately have been telling me that I can use them to get in touch with you, so… uummm. Yeah. Oh! I've got a box full of things that I think you really need. I don't know how you're going to get them but I'm going to leave them near the gate to the dinocows paddock. Oh, in case you didn't know, I'm staying here for a little while and uuhhh… I haven't told anyone about all the things that our crystals can do for us. They've asked me to keep most of it a secret, but I know that you've figured a few things out all on your own. I also know that you left Chance's crystal… somewhere? Yeah, somewhere strange and far away? But that's okay, see… all the ones I've been working with lately have been telling me that that's a good thing since it's been… bad? Influenced? Something like that anyway. Sorry that this is sooo nutty and scattered, but… that's me in a nutshell, right? Please, take care of yourself and I miss you." And then she was gone. Wow! Talk about weird. But I think I got pretty much everything she was talking about.

I open my eyes to find my vision full of Nat and she's just finishing up wrapping some type of web around me. *WTF!*

"Uummm…"

"Oh! You're back. Well, you didn't actually "go" anywhere this time, but you certainly weren't here. So, what's happening now?"

"I was… getting caught up on some of the things that my family is or was going through, I think. But… how did you know that something was going on with me? How long was I… not really with it?"

"It couldn't have been very long, less than two minutes I'd guess, but no one noticed anything was wrong until we all felt… something… and Dos and Tres were pointing at you." Wendy says but Lucas has a strange look on his face.

"You've had things like this happen before, I've noticed but… why was this time different?" Lucas asks.

"I don't know how to answer that, but I do know of something that'll help. I just need to go and get it."

"Oh fuck no. You're not going "walk-about" again. Or at least not without me. That's what I was doing, by the way. Making a kind of leash? in case you did disappear again." Nat says pointing at the web that she's wrapped around me. *Hhmmm?*

"Deal, but give me a minute, I think." I say but I'm already touching two of the bigger crystals that I've got as earrings in my left ear. *'Okay gang, y'all record everything, so how do I get into my place?'* I think to them, and they do indeed show me something. Huh, it's not just using power to open a way into my place, there's… emotion and… something else. It might just be "need" but… I already know that it doesn't necessarily have to come from… him, soooo… *Well, that's certainly interesting.* Oh, and I can almost see the way in that Chance has damaged beyond repair, and even though my new way in looks more rickety or risky? I think it's becoming more stable every time it's used, so I "open" the rip? and walk in. I can hear a lot of swearing so I go back out, grab Nat and drag her in. The swearing got louder both inside and out. *Ha!*

"Holy shit! What the fuck? Where are we? Wait! We're still in the diner but… what the hell? Okay so, it's almost like we're in… or on an alternate plane of existence, right?" Nat kind of babbles.

"I have no idea. Really. I just know that this place was made? for me and… someone else. So that we could… be together. But… I think I've explored this place way more and… I'm hoping to avoid running into him. So… Hey! Do you feel any different? Do you sense anything?" I ask.

"Well, this place feels kind of muted? I know that everyone else is still standing where we left them, but they seem almost ghostlike or like they're paused? Can they see or hear us?"

"I'm not sure but… I don't think so. I've interacted with others like this, but… we have a different… no, scratch that, we have a much deeper connection. I don't have anything like that with this bunch. That's one of the things that I need to fix. This trip is to pick up something that might help. So, are you.up for it?"

"You mean wander around in here? Is it safe? Shit, who cares! Let's go!" she says with a laugh and a bounce, so I head off to the left. Even with eight eyes, I don't think she sees very much until we stop walking. Somehow I've stopped on the inside of the dinocows and other things fence and a couple actually approach as we stand quietly. I'm taking that as a really positive sign but that doesn't stop me from sending calm and supportive vibes their way anyway.

"What the fuck are those things? Holeee… are they… are they like me?" she asks in wonder.

"Well, these guys are what we call new beings, and you would definitely fit into that category, but no, they're not like you. They were made… by someone that loved them. He didn't do it to be mean; he just used his imagination and changed them. They didn't mind this because they loved him too, but something happened, and I haven't gotten the whole story yet, only a little bit of what's happened in the last day or so. That's when my group came to this town and started cleaning house." I say as I let the dinocows and a couple emuraptors get close enough to rub up against me. *This is still so weird and so cool!* I still don't know if they can see me or if it's instinct on their part. Then, I start looking around for a box that Judy said that she'd left out here for me. I find it on the other side of the fence but for some reason when I get to it… I can't pick it up? *WTF?* I've been able to move things before while I was in here, so why not now? Shit, I guess I'm going to have to come out of here and into the "real" world. Can I leave Nat, here in my place? Alone? Hell no. Too risky. I think that's going to have to be an experiment for another time and with someone that I don't mind losing. *Ya know what I mean?*

"Well shit. We're going to have to come out of here so that I can get that box. Are you ready?"

"What? Uhhh… yeah? Let's do this." she says and I step out of my place with Nat practically glued to my back. As I'm bending down to pick up the box I hear *"Holy shit! What is that thing?"* and a few other rude comments silently floating around.

"Hey! Watch your language mister!" I yell as I'm trying really hard not to laugh and I'm also trying to get around Nat's large pinchers. Nat has gotten a look at David in his full manticore form and she tells me to stay behind her, but I'm not going to let these two duke it out over nothing, so I ignore her and somehow managed to get in between the two of them. Now, at any other time, standing in between two beings in attack mode Would be on the truly insane side, but there's no way I'm going to let any type of fight happen between these two.

"Aawww. Now come on. The two of you need to chill out." I say after Nat whispers another command for me to stay behind her and that she'll protect me. I know David heard us and he's not budging on his stance, but I can tell that he's not as ready to rumble as before. *Well shit.* knowing Nat isn't going to back down and David is as backed down as he's going to get? I do the only thing I can think of. I reach out and grab ahold of David's big, hairy mane and then I touch Nat on one of her massive claws. *Oooweee! Let me tell you!* That little maneuver causes a massive jolt of magic! Nat and David both jump at it and then stare at me in… wonder? The only thing I can think to do now is to take the magic and shape it how I think it wants to go, since we've already sort of started this little connection. Jones, Casey, Dozer and Willy are all making a bunch of noises while this is going on, but they're smart enough to stay way back. After that, David and Nat settle down as the three of us grow into our new bonds. *Too weird.*

"David, guys, I'd like to introduce you to Natalie. Nat for short. Nat, I'd like to formally introduce you to David. And that's Casey, Jones, Dozer and Willy." I don't know why I bothered because David and Nat are still trying to figure out the bonds, and the other guys are just… pissed off?

"What did you just do?" Jones asks angrily.

"Well, I don't really know but… I'm going to blame this on Ajay and William. I think I just pulled off some sort of Naga woo woo shit."

"How do you figure that?" Dozer asks but Willy didn't care about that since he just came up and starts sniffing us. The big goofball then licks me, and I have to push him away or he'll slobber all over me. Though I do hug him first while he's huffing at me.

"Oh, well, I think I just made a Naga type connection with these two."
I say to Dozer.

"Wait! Do you have a bond with Ajay and Willaim?" Jones asks.

"Uuhhh, yeah?"

"Since when?"

"Uuhhh… since the morning after taking out the J's. I think. Why?"

"You're mated with Ajay and William? And you didn't tell me?" Casey
asks looking shocked and… sad? But then covers that up with an
exaggerated pout. But I'm not buying it.

"What? No. Ewww. No. My bond with those two is more along the
lines of… siblings or something. That's what these two now have by the
way, with me as the parent, I think. Why?" I ask, suddenly suspicious.

"Well Ajay and Kabir have been talking and all of us got to hear most
of it. Then, for some reason Ajay got really pissed off at his dad and told
him to get used to him having a bunch of bonds with different people
and the possibilities of him having a bunch of lovers. Oh, and that once
a bond is made, he's not sure how to break it, and no one strays from a
romantic bond. If you were bonded to them and tried to go elsewhere,
supposedly it wouldn't work, and I thought that maybe that might be
your problem with… him." Jones says. *Oh. If only it were that simple.*

"Well… that's definitely not the issue. In either case." I say but then
Jones comes over and gives me a big hug. I'm not sure he believes me,
but that's okay. Finally, David reverts back to his human self, and I think
he's waiting for Nat to do the same, only that's not going to happen.

"David, Nat can't change back. I know you were with me when I helped
her a little bit and…"

"Oh! So, she's… now like Tammy, Ken and Jones. Well, that's okay with
me. Hello sister, we've sort of met already." He says with a big smile and

then walks up to her and gives her a big hug. I can feel that she's too shocked to do anything, but even if she could move, she wouldn't have. Their bond strengthens some more as they hug. *How awesome is that?*

"So, are you back for good?" Dozer asks as he sneaks in a hug for himself with me.

"No, not right now. I came here to get this box and to take it back to Alabama, to the group that's there. We need the help that's in here but… I'm not sure I can do this on my own." *(You have absolutely no idea how hard it is for me to say that.)*

"Oh?" Casey asks with raised eyebrows. He, at least, knows how hard this is for me. But then, "Wait! What's in the booooox?" he kind of wails, though his mood seems a lot lighter than before, I know it isn't. Even though Dozer, Nat, David and I get the movie reference right away and we all laugh, I can tell he's trying to hide a lot of thing from me. So, I make a show of opening the box and showing off a bunch of crystal jewelry and a few other things, then I notice that Casey's sporting something new himself. I point to his new nose jewelry and give him wide eyes.

"Yeah well, some of this new shit that I've picked up was giving me a headache, so I had to do something about it."

"It's more than that, he's just trying to play it cool." Dozer says with a laugh.

"Oh, believe me, I know all about that. Hence nine earrings and counting." I say with a laugh and a knowing look. He just nods and winks at me.

"So, you need help plugging in your new folks, is that it? Were you going to ask any of us for help or were you going to try it on your own?" Jones asks with his pencil poised over his notebook.

"I'm not… sure. I was thinking about trying it on my own but now that I've got the box in my hands? Yeah, I'm asking for help. You wouldn't happen to know anyone that would be willing to do that, do you?" I ask with a saccharine sweet smile.

"I might know of a few that would be willing to help." Casey says as he narrows his eyes.

"Oh shit! Riley is going to be soooo fuckin' mad!" Dozer says with a big belly laugh and that gets the rest of the guys laughing.

"Why? What's going on with Riley?" I ask.

"It's nothing bad; it's just his turn helping Nate with our newest friends." Jones says as he points at the fence and what's standing up against it, calmly watching us.

"Ha! Yeah! After you were able to get through to them and they let us near them, we found out that there's a bunch of them that are in serious need of medical treatment. We've all spent some time helping Nate, and listening to him bitch and complain, bitterly, about needing help and…" David stopped there because he was laughing so hard. *Yeah, yeah, yeah. We need a vet, badly.* But I know I haven't come across anyone to fit that bill yet, or any other medical personnel at all for that matter.

"Well now, Riley can go if you can wait a day." Jones says.

"Uuhhh, no. We've got something going down in a few hours and uuhhh… it can't wait. Sorry." I say but then I hear Riley calling me a bitch, silently. I just blow him a kiss and shoot him the bird. I know he gets it because everyone there let him "see" it.

"How many of us are you going to need for this op? And to help plug your… no, our new crew in?" Dozer asks but I know that he's already claiming his spot on this op with the other SEAL's.

Nat's so lucky to have so many eyes, because she's got at least one on all of us. Plus, I do believe that she's really enjoying watching how we are with each other and how we operate. Then we see Zee, Lynx, Ox, Garth and Stanley coming towards us. Nat stiffens up at the sight of Stanley, but since none of us seem worried about the seven-foot-tall purple monster landing so close, and David's whispering to her that it's okay, she lets her tail drop back down, but not for long because she stiffens up again when Stanley practically swallows me in a hug. *Yeah, yeah, yeah, it seriously does look like an attack. I know.* But then he moves off and I get hugs from the rest that have shown up and I introduce Nat to them.

"It's like really nice to meet all of you, I think, but... look... I know that I'm a bit... concerned about what we're about to do. What with just the small crew back at the motel and... are you sure that this is going to be enough? I mean, there might be more bad guys than the bad guys said. They've already... lied about a couple other things." Nat says, trying not to cuss, I think.

"Girlfriend, I know that we don't look like much, but we can hold our own." Lynx says with a sunny smile then grows out her claws and fangs. It's impressive.

"So, how are we going to do this?" Jones asks. *Well shit.*

"Uuhhh... Nat? Can you make a bunch more... tethers and attach everyone to me?"

"Ooooo... kinky. I like it!" Casey says as he puts his arms around me and finally gives me a hug. I thump my head on his chest. *Lord, have mercy.* I've actually missed this. And the laughter that follows his pervy comment. While Nat's making the tethers, we all hear "Waaaaiiiitttt!" and see Kabir moving quickly toward us. I'm not sure if this is going to be an Oh? or an Oh shit moment. So, we all wait and wonder, privately.

"Kabir, this is Nat, Nat? Kabir." I say as Nat hooks a tether unceremoniously around Kabir. I'm pleasantly surprised by his almost friendly greeting. Now I know that something's up with him. *Jeez.*

"Quick question. Why the tether?" Zee asks in the meantime. *Damn good question. Shit.*

"Okay, so I'm about to take y'all into a… magical place." Yeah, yeah. Even I have to chuckle when everyone else either snickers or snorts at that. "But this place was "made" for me and… him. I haven't seen anyone else "really" in there and… it doesn't seem to affect the two of us like it did Nat, I think. That being said, I don't know what it would do if someone else was in there on their own. Like I said, it was made for me and… him, so our magic might be what powers it? and if we're not in there, how's the magic going to keep going?"

"You mean it might… like… eat us?" several ask at once.

"I don't believe it would "eat" us per se, but it might absorb some, if not… a lot of our magic, to keep it going until we leave." Jones says with a shrug and a nice save.

"Good to know. So, let's go already." several say. Easier said than done here. Again, I reach up and touch my crystals and "see" how to open the rip, and it does look more like a weird door now, and I think it's getting much easier to get in. I step in with everyone attached to me keeping in step. Once we're all in? the silent chatter is louder than the spoken, so Casey and Jones tell everyone to quiet down. Then I take off to the right. I know what I'm looking for and it doesn't take but a few minutes to get there. Before coming out of my place, I tell everyone that we're here and step out.

Again, I'm face to face with a bunch of guns suddenly pointed at me.

"Shit! Guys! It's just me and Nat!" I say, with my hands up but then, "Well… that's not entirely accurate." Casey and a few others groan and chuckle at my movie line and Ben, Lucas, Bobby and Jamal hear the sounds and relax, just a little.

"So yeah. I've brought a few more friends back with us. So, could y'all back up a bit? And put down your weapons? Please? Most are normal…

looking, but some are a bit different. But! They're my friends… no, they're my family, so I would appreciate it if you didn't shoot any of them." Lucas, Jamal and Bobby put up their guns right away and then Wendy and Ben do just as Casey comes out followed by David, who is directly in front of Jones. Lynx and Ox come out next followed closely by Dozer and Zee, who are all camo'd out. Willy and Garth come out, but no one can see them then Kabir, directly in front of Stanley comes out right before Nat. Lucas, Jamal and Bobby have seen some of my family before, so they aren't as surprised to see Stanley, but Wendy and Ben are going to have to pick their jaws up off the floor. *Ha!*

"Oh wow! I didn't think I would ever see anything like this outside of the pens we were kept in. The new beings? Yeah, the new beings being held in a few pens near ours weren't… mean really, but they weren't… we couldn't reach them enough to actually talk to them. Now I wish we'd tried harder." Wendy says in awe while trying not to stare at Jones and Stanley. Jones steps up to her and asks her to go into further detail while he pulls out his trusty pencil and notebook. Ben, it seems, doesn't know who to stare at more, but Zee and Dozer with their camo actually win. Bobby looks like a kid in a candy store and immediately comes closer to introduce himself to everyone, followed closely by Lucas and Jamal. Jamal just about pees on himself when Willy and Garth materialize next to him and gave him a good sniffing. Of course, they tell me that he smells kind of like Danny, Mike and Ted do when they're together and that I should get him together with the Brainy Bunch as soon as possible. *Huh? Those guys smell different when they're together?* Bobby just laughs and starts petting them as soon as they get close enough to start sniffing him.

"So, it's nice to meet you all and everything but… what's the op?" Zee asks. But before I can start to fill them in Wendy gets a strange look on her face and gasps.

"What's wrong Wendy?" Lucas and I say at the same time.

"I… I don't know! Nothing like this has ever happened before. OH! There's… there's something bad going on where we left everyone else. I can feel Larry and Eddie. There's something really wrong there. Hey, is there any way that we can get back there? Like now?" she asks worriedly. *Huh, looks like I'm really getting in a lot of practice today.*

"Uuhhh, yeah. Sure?"

"Not without me you don't." Casey, David, Dozer and Kabir all say at the same time, Willy and Garth just nod and huff.

"Yes. You all better go with her. You know, in all fairness, I should be going too, being that I'm one of your guards, but I think my time would be better served staying here and getting some of these folks' stories." Jones says while not even looking up from his notebook. A few of us just chuckle at him and shake our heads. *Well, okay then.* So, I reach up and touch my crystals and the rip/door opens for me again. *Seems I'm getting better at this weird shit.* But since Nat had already cut our tethers, we just decide to hold hands, belts or whatever is handy as we enter into my magical place.

"Holy shit! This is amazing! This is where you go? And you can go anywhere from in here?" Wendy asks but then, "I guess I should tell you a bit more about us. I mean, it only seems fair, right? Okay, so the four of us are… see, while we were being kept in the pens, well… we developed some sort of… bond. Not anything like you have with your family, obviously, but… There were more than the four of us being held in that pen, but we're the only ones that bonded. We all took to it almost immediately, but the thing is… For me? I can tell what the others are feeling, and Ben can almost hear our thoughts. I mean, he can't, but his guesses or his own statements are spot on. Larry has an amazing gut instinct and Eddie sort of has a nose for trouble. When it started, we kept it hidden from everyone. See… the problem is, if anyone showed any signs of… having anything out of the ordinary? Then they were taken away and we never saw them again. We didn't want that to happen to us and Eddie kept telling us to wait and Larry kept saying that he'd know when the time was right. Then? We escaped during a big storm. We all felt really bad about leaving so many behind, but..." By the time she finishes that we're at the farm, and we come out behind where everyone is standing, staring at the barn where we'd stashed the bad guys.

"Holy shit! What? How..." quite a few say but then Wendy goes and hugs Larry and Eddie while I get accosted by Emily. I pick her up and introduce her and everyone else to this part of my family and she shyly says "hi" to everyone around her thumb. The coyotes get asked if she can pet them, which they readily accept.

"So, what seems to be the problem here?" Dozer asks while trying to figure out why everyone is standing around the open barn doors.

"Well, we have a problem. The bad guys were tied up in there but... they're gone. And... not in a good way." Larry says while turning pale, again.

"We were woken up by a bunch of screaming, if that tells you anything." Eddie says. *Well shit. I had a few more questions for them.*

"Did you notice anything when you came out?" Dozer asks as my fam and I walk toward the barn but the guys have weapons drawn. Be it gun, claw or fang.

"Like what? The total silence? Hey, you really don't want to go in there." Eddie says with a gulp and I don't think the gulp is just to keep from barfing. He's probably right, but we don't stop. Inside the barn is a splattered mess. It looks like someone had thrown red paint... everywhere. Now I'm pissed. These folks could've given us a few more answers but that's beside the point. They were also in our care, and I think I know who took them. By the looks on my fam's faces, I think they know too. But whoever it is that took them, they aren't "our" regular followers. I come out of the barn and open myself up as wide as

I can. I can sense **THEM**, and **THEY'RE** not too far away, so that's the direction I head off to.

"Alright. Why did **YOU** kill and eat those people?" I ask as I get almost too close.

"Mmmmm? Were they not going to be eaten by something anyway?" a deep growly voice asks.

"Maybe, but then again, maybe not."

"Then why all the fuss?" a more hissy voice asks.

"Because they might have still been useful to us? And they certainly were Not for **YOU** to just take."

"So? They were very useful to US. That is all that matters." *Uh huh.*

"Look, I don't know **YOU** and **YOU** don't know me, so why don't **YOU** just stick to watching and stay the hell out of my business." I say but I know that my darkness is adding her voice to mine.

"Puny human, WE will do as WE please." another growly voice says.

"I suggest that **YOU** reconsider that. Or better yet, talk to our regular followers."

"Why should WE do that?" from the hissy voice.

"Well, I can tell where **YOU** are. Or are **YOU** so stupid that **YOU** missed that fact?" I say but I can feel one of **THEM** trying to come up behind me. I'm so mad that I don't even mind when my darkness takes the controls briefly and I don't even have to touch my earrings this time as "we" open the door and sidestep into my place. *Ha!* My darkness goes back to waiting as we come out behind the one trying to sneak up on me. Then I do the unthinkable. I grab **IT** and drag **IT** into my place and... leave **IT** there after closing the door.

"WHAT HAVE YOU DONE!" the other two yell at me.

"Something pretty Fucking impressive, wouldn't **YOU** say? Now get the fuck away from me and my group!"

"WE will not stand for this!" deep growly voice says.

I just slowly turn my face to where I know the voice is coming from and say "Try me. I dare **YOU**." These two are not very bright because again, I can feel hissy voice coming up from behind me and I pull the same stunt as before, open door-move-grab-close door. Growly voice is so enraged that once I've completed that maneuver again the last one comes at me head on. When **IT** hits me, we fall backwards into my place, and I just hit the ground and roll to the left, and that takes me right on out. I also silently thank Wally for my armor. **THEY'VE** got some nasty claws but… I also got a good look at **THEM**. *Well now, isn't that interesting.*

"Holy shit! What did you just do?" my fam yells almost at the same time as they run up to me as I'm getting to my feet.

I could tell that my smile wasn't a nice one but, "What needed to be done. Sorry. But have any of you noticed that not all of **THEM** are on the same page? I mean, at least a couple of **THEM** have actively tried to kill us a few times and at least a couple have tried to influence some of us. Don't you find that interesting? I mean seriously, if **THEY'RE** truly a hive type mind, shouldn't **THEY** all know what the rest are thinking and doing?"

"Uuhhh, yeah. So?" several say.

"But… ours didn't know anything about the one influencing Riley, right?" David says.

"Could **THEIR** outrage have been a ruse?" Kabir asks.

"No. As far as ours go, I could feel how pissed off **THEY** were. We all could, right? After this last time… I think that our followers are finally starting to realize that **THEY** might be playing by the rules, but a lot of the **OTHERS** are not."

"Holy fuckin' macaroni! What the fu… Babe, was that really the wisest choice? I mean… trapping **THEM** in your… magical place?" Casey asks as he tries to calm himself down but he still looks more concerned than pissed. I know that he's not just worried about my now very apparent anger management issues, or even about our access to my place.

"Oh shit. What if **THEY'RE** waiting for us when we go back in?" Dozer asks wide eyed.

"Well… if **THEY** are, we'll see **THEM** coming at us." I say with a nasty laugh.

"You saw one? You know what **THEY** look like? Oh shit! Okay, spill it." And several other comments come from my fam following my noteworthy comment.

"I'll tell you all about it in a bit but right now, it seems like we're being hailed." I say as I point at Larry and Eddie, who are waving us over. Once we reach them, they ask us what the hell did they just witness, but I'm glad to see that someone has taken the kids back inside.

"Sorry about that but… do you remember me saying that I might feed the bad guys to whatever's been following us?"

"Yeah. But… I thought you were joking." Eddie says looking confused.

"What? Are you serious? We've really got something that's following us?" Sandra asks as she comes back and joins the rest of us.

"Oh yeah, no dude, she wasn't kidding." Ox answers Eddie and Lynx nods her head at Sandra.

"Afraid so. Or at least you… did." Daivd says with a shrug and a smirk.

"What was that we… couldn't see but… we did hear a little of… when you were over there?" Larry asks, still pale.

"But… how long have we been followed? And what was all that?" Sandra asks in wonder at the same time.

"I don't know about how long you've been followed but… that? That was Lara doing the impossible. Nothing new there." Dozer says with a kind of mean laugh.

"This was not the… It still might be… it could still… Oh fuck it. It's done now." Casey says then he laughs after not being able to finish any of his previous thoughts.

"Was that the only reason why you called us back over here?" Kabir asks.

"What? Oh… no. Uhhh, one of those big coyotes? found something in the… mess in the barn." Eddie says while swallowing hard.

"Well shit. Seems Doris, Tarina and Riley are going to miss out on going into another nasty barn. I know how much they love them." Lynx says but she can't keep a straight face for long. Neither can the rest of us. *"Garth, Willy? What have you got?"* David asks silently as we all tromp back into the barn, despite Larry and Eddie looking like they'd rather go anywhere else. If they only knew what we've seen… and smelled, before. The inside of the barn might be slasher film worthy, but it's not the worst, not by a long shot. Garth and Willy are standing near a large blood puddle but that's not what has their attention. On the floor, kind of carved into the dirt is a bunch of writing. We all carefully clear away the straw and other things as we try to figure out what's written there and where it actually starts.

"Hey! Who was tied up over here?" Dozer asks.

"One of the big guys, why?" Eddie says.

"He wrote something, in the dirt." Dozer says and "What?" is asked by a lot of us.

"I think he was trying to tell us something." I say, as Larry, Eddie and Wendy mince their way over to us. Sandra stays by the door, not really wanting to be so immersed in the mess.

"Well? What does he have to say?"

"Well… This part over here says that he sometimes doesn't remember days at a time. What's that all about?" Kabir says.

"According to this part over here, he says that he remembers going to West Bend, but that he's been told several times that he's never been there before. Does that make any sense to anyone?" David asks.

"This part says that he remembers faces and he's never seen the same ones twice in West Bend." Dozer says.

"This says his name is Martin. And a time. 8:00 am." I say.

"Do you think that maybe he wasn't really a bad guy?" Wendy asks. I don't know, and now… we never will. This doesn't mean shit but… I'm sorry Martin. This shouldn't have happened.

"If I had to guess, I'd say that these people were kept on a shorter leash than even they knew. Martin may have been stronger than the rest and that's why he was able to remember more. And… I think he was trying to tell us that his group was supposed to be in West Bend along with the people that they've programmed to be there." Larry says.

"Does this mean that the next group of assholes is going to be expecting these guys to be in West Bend? What's going to happen when they don't show up?" Sandra asks from the doorway.

"That's when they swap out the plants! Didn't they say something about having their plants swapped out? I bet that that's when it happens. And they didn't even realize it?" Wendy says in surprise.

"How twisted of a group are you dealing with here? Really." Ox asks kind of angrily.

"They're more twisted than a barrel of snakes and they're getting worse. I think they might control or have under their thumb a good quarter of the western side of the state… maybe? They have a lot of personnel, and they can keep adding to it because they're kidnapping folks with powers that they think they can use. Their plan, as far as we know, is to take over Birmingham, Montgomery and Tuscaloosa. Oh, and I'm not kidding when I say that they have almost total mind control over everyone that they get their hands on."

"Are they really that powerful?" Kabir asks.

"As far as I can tell? Yes. It's not one person really, but there is one in charge, and he controls, somehow, a bunch of the weird plants that he's using to control everything that he can. Including his own followers. I mean, the leader, Reverend Ansdale, he's bat shit crazy and I'm pretty sure the original plants are what's left of his wife. The newer plants are not as strong or as versatile as the originals. Maybe that's because they're being manufactured? That's one of the first things I was planning to stop. I was also thinking about a jail break, so to speak."

"But with us here now, you've changed your mind, right? You've got a different plan. I can tell. So, what is it? But… you do realize that even now, we don't have enough people to pull off anything on that large a scale, not like what you're talking about. There's no way just of few of us can take care of everything that needs to be handled, right?" Dozer asks.

"How were you even going to start. I know you; you were planning something before you showed up to pick up the box. What was it." Casey asks, staring me dead in the eyes.

"Well, the plan was to free the people and whatever else that shows up that's under compulsion from here. Then take off with every plant that we can get. Next, I was going to find out the exact location of the "camps" and free everything being held in them."

"With just the seven of you? And none of them plugged in yet? How was that even going to work?" Ox asks in wonder.

"The first two parts were going to be the easiest. We were going to pretend to be the bad guys as far as the under-compulsion people and things go. Then when the real bad guys show up, we're going to take their plants and ask them a bunch of questions. I was planning to stash them with the bad guys from here, but that's out of the question now. From that point? I was going to improvise." I say and all the ones from my fam groan at that. Casey just squeezes his eyes closed, like he's in pain. I can't help but to chuckle because damn! I've really missed them.

"I hate to say this. I mean, I really do hate to say this but... that actually sounds... doable. And seriously, with us here, some of your other plans might be... doable too." Casey says, but it's the look on his face that's got me on edge. Oh! I bet you a hundred bucks that he, David and Jones try to pull their "we're your guards" bullshit on me. Well, if they do? I do believe my darkness might enjoy having a little fun with them. *Mwahaha!*

"Well Wendy, are you ready to go back to the motel?" I ask after looking at my watch.

"What? Wait just a minute. You still haven't filled us in on what we didn't actually see but heard some of or how you managed to get here." Larry and Eddie say at the same time.

"You're right, I haven't. Can we table this particular conversation until we're all together again?" I ask with a sigh.

"Oh yeah, guys? This is not something that... no matter how many times you hear it; it doesn't get any better. Believe me, me and Ox... well hell, Dozer and well, a bunch of us have personally experienced several... interactions and... we still don't understand it. But we know for a fact that... Yeah, you need to all be together to hear that story." Lynx says, or tries to say, then she shrugs.

"Even though I'm not too happy with all this secrecy, I get it. Yeah, we can wait. Come back soon, okay? And bring everyone back with you. Then we'll, no, you'll talk, and we'll listen." Larry says as he and Eddie give Wendy hugs, and then they give me a brotherly pat or shoulder bump.

"Are you sure it's safe to go back into your… magical place? Sorry but, even after all this time and seeing some of the things I've seen, that place just about beats them all." Dozer says with a nervous chuckle.

"If any of **THEM** come at us, we'll see **THEM** coming, but I doubt that's going to be a problem. I know I sound cryptic as hell but… Let's just say that I beat Jones to the experimentation thing that I know he's going to bring up. Plus, I felt something when I dropped them off in there. I can't explain it just yet, but when I can, I will." I say but that doesn't stop most of the guys from pulling their guns as I open the now weirdly shaped door to my place.

"Oh, by the way, can any of you see what I see when I open the "door" to this place?" I ask. Even with Casey putting his hands on me, he says he doesn't see anything, but he and the rest of my fam tell me that they can feel… something. The best that they can describe it is that it feels almost like a big cold spot. So, in we all go and in less than a minute, we're back at the motel.

And yet again I come out of my magical place only to be face to face with guns and big assed pinchers, again. At least this time I'm not the only one becoming grouchy because of it. I thought Dozer was going to make Zee eat his gun, from the look on his face. Huh, I think having **THEM** in my place is causing an attitude shift? Are those assholes bringing down my good vibes? Oh hell no! Gonna have to fix that. But while we were in there, I could also feel that my place now has quite a lot more… something… than it had before. Power, for sure, but… atmosphere? maybe? It was certainly quicker getting from one place to another than before as well. I wonder what other changes are going to occur, but that's for another time, right now we're having to fill in everyone that stayed here on what happened near Zelco.

"So, are we still going to stick to our plan, with a few small adjustments? Or do we need to get the hell out of here?" Jamal asks.

"No, we're sticking as close to the plan as possible, but now we know that the bad guys are going to be here earlier than expected and that they're going to be expecting the bad guys from Coffeeville."

"None of us are dressed anything like those guys were, so won't that give us away almost immediately?" Wendy asks.

"From what Martin wrote, there's different people every time, so maybe not? Then again, once they walk through the door, at some point Dos and Tres are going to take out their plant and then everything will be under our or their control."

"Wait, what? Who are Dos and Tres?" David asks. At that question Jamal pulls our plants out from under the table and they both wave at everyone.

"Is there an Uno too? I thought you said that these plants are bad news and that you're wanting to take as many as you can from the... good Rev?" Dozer snorts silently.

"Yes, I did say that the plants are bad news, but... not ours. And yes, there is an Uno. There were three in Butler, and I took them. With a lot of goop and care, they've turned over a new leaf." *Bwahaha! I knew I'd get the opportunity to use that line!* Of course, all my fam laughs, groans or gives me a boo hiss, along with a bit of pushing and shoving. Of course, I just laugh. Everyone else just shakes their heads at us in amusement. "Are they always like this?" Lucas asks Jones as he and the others watch us being silly. Jones just snorts and says that we're actually being on our better behavior, which causes the rest of the new people to smile. Bobby walks over to Dos and Tres and introduces them to David, who's the first one over to check the plants out, Lynx and Ox are right behind him.

"Holy shit! Why, exactly did you take them? I mean, they are kinda pretty and all but…" Lynx asks silently as she actually shakes one of Dos's limbs.

"No! Don't say it!" Daivd says with a laugh and I just smirk at him.

"Well?" the rest ask silently. I guess some of these folks really haven't been around long enough. *Ha!*

"Oh, come on guys. You know why. Besides, I just found out that the plants are more than just magical; they can actually store stolen magic. These guys are the big bad that we need to help Stanley, Oscar, Megan and anyone else! I thought that I'd use my three, at first, but after putting a bunch of goop in with their water, our three really did change. They don't remember much or ever being the Rev's wife, but they do remember pain. Now, the other plants… the ones that have been made from cuttings or something? Now, from what I understand, they're not even remotely redeemable. They've been "made" to serve only one purpose so those are the ones that I'm actually going to use. Also, if we can get the rest of the other originals, then they can be freed from their compulsion and… I think they'll be happy with us. And the best part is that as far as I can tell, even the Rev doesn't know about their little side effect, you know, being a stolen power reservoir. Otherwise, he would never allow them to keep that much magic or ever be out of his sight." I say, but then I notice that everyone is staring at us. I think they're getting the fact that we really can do a lot of different things, including telepathy. The smiles on most faces kind of tell me that they wouldn't mind being able to do this too.

"So, where's the box I brought back from picking up these guys?" I ask Bobby.

"Oh, Nat's got it. Why?" Lucas says and Nat bobs up and down.

"Can I have it, please?"

"Oh, yeah, sure. But… you never did say what's in it."

"You'll just have to see for yourself but… consider them presents." I say as I take the box out of Nat's big pincher. I open it up and I can see a lot of jewelry and a lot of other things in there and I know some of it's for me but there's more than enough for everyone here and in Zelco, plus a lot more. *WTF?* As I run my hand over what's in the box, I pick up a fairly large stone that's calling Nat's name. I have no idea how she's going to wear this, but I'm sure we'll figure something out. "Nat, this is for you." I say as I hold it up for all of her eyes to see. After all of her eyes focus in on the stone, she starts to bob up and down really fast, almost like she's vibrating. Then she starts spinning some type of web and asks me where a good place would be to wrap it around her but she's giggling the entire time. So, with the help of Wendy, Ben, Bobby and Lynx, we wrap the web belt looking thing around the crystal and then we wrap that fairly tight around her thorax. The crystal doesn't dangle, and it really can't be seen, so that should keep it from getting ripped off. Then I go back to the box and pull out an earring and hand it over to Wendy. She looks at it and then her face lights up. As I stick my hand back in the box, I can feel two pieces calling for Ben, so I pull them out. Another earring and a pendant. His face lights up too once his new friends and bling are in his hands. Once all my new friends have their new friends, Lucas asks if this now makes all of them a part of my ever-expanding family. The answer to that is "Yes, of course". But it's Ben that asks if they'll ever be able to do some of the things that he knows we can do but hasn't actually seen yet.

"That's going to have to wait until we get another shitty plant. Then we'll see." I say with a sly smile.

I'm extremely grateful for the piercing gun to have been in the box but I do believe Bobby's mom is going to rip me a new one, not only because of his new fouler language but because he's now gotten his ears pierced. Jamal is enjoying his new eyebrow ring too.

"Are you sure we shouldn't go back and pick up Ginger?" David asks but then Willy and Garth huff and tell us that they're more than capable of doing Ginger's part. Really? Well… that's good to know. I think. While my new folks are getting pierced and getting to know their new friends, Dozer, Zee, Kabir and Stanley have gone out to find a couple more vehicles for us to use after we take care of the shit that's quickly coming up. The guys came back fairly quickly empty handed as far as vehicles go, but they did do a little bit of shopping at a local consignment store. When they present me with a… sexy, yet tasteful business type suit I just about hurt myself laughing. Wendy receives something similar, but she's ecstatic to get hers. Ben and Casey are going to be acting as the muscle, and the guys picked them up a couple sports coats to make them look closer to what the other guys had worn. Ben looks nice in his jeans, T-shirt and sports coat but Casey's trend setting in his cargo pants, snakeskin armor shirt and sports coat. It may sound strange, but it looks really good. Wendy's wearing her new suit like a natural, but I feel like my suit is worse than a cheap costume, though the guys tell that I look nice in it. I really want my cargo pants and t-shirt back.

At least I'm able to keep my kickass steel toed boots on because Wendy and I are seated at the table playing cards with some of the other guys when Willy and Garth let us know that several vehicles are approaching.

"Heads up gang. Willy and Garth are saying that there's a bunch of vehicles approaching so… places everyone!" Zee says as he, Dozer, Stanley and David head for the door. They're going to be outside with the coyotes and they're going to take care of anyone left outside. Kabir, Lynx and Ox are going to be hiding behind the front desk and Jones and Nat are going to be in the hall, ready to close and secure the doors. Lucas, Bobby and Jamal are hiding farther back in the diner, waiting for our signal.

"At least these assholes are on time." I grumble as Wendy and I hide the wrappers and packages of what we've all been stress eating.

You have no idea how hard it is to play it cool when the new group of assholes come strolling in, some of them complaining about having to come all the way out here just to pick up a few "waste of magic" individuals. My darkness really wants to just start ripping heads off. I could also feel my fam and they're pretty much on the same page as my darkness at hearing how cavalier some of these clowns sound at what they're doing. *Ha!* Four men and three women come into the diner and one guy immediately opens a big case that has a plant in it after the first woman snaps her fingers and points at him.

"Report." says the smartly dressed woman but she barely looks at us. She's too busy sneering at this place. My darkness isn't the only one to sneer the word bitch.

"There are five people and possibly two other… things that are expected to show up soon." Wendy says kind of robotically.

"Has no one taught you how to report to us? This is unacceptable. Make them feel pain since they've pissed me off." The smartly dressed bitch says while looking at the plant and pointing to us.

"Oh, fuck this. Dos, Tres, they're all yours." I say as I stand up, then "You know, I get that some of these plants have no redeemable qualities, but I do believe that you assholes are worse."

"How dare you! You'll pay for speaking to us like that!" she and another man say at the same time. But then Dos and Tres hit the assholes… hard… with their magic. It was like they're all hit with an invisible 2x4, then they're all on the ground. The new plant looks like it's trying to crawl under the dirt in its pot.

"Did you guys just do something inside? Because we felt something really strong. Oh, and we're taking out and securing the guys out here." Zee says silently. I guess there's no need for the ruse anymore. "Holy shit! I thought the other guys were bad but… I don't think I have the words to

describe these… people." Lucas practically spits as he, Bobby and Jamal come out from their hiding place.

"Oh, I've got a few but none of them are… nice or polite." Jamal says with a growl. Bobby opens his mouth and Lucas and Jamal both hold up their hands at him, which causes him and us to laugh and that lightens the mood considerably.

"How many did you get out there?" Casey asks.

"Twenty"

"That's a lot of staff just to pick up a few magical people and new beings, especially since they're all under compulsion." Ox says.

"What are you talking about?" Nat asks from the hall.

"Oh, Zee just said that there's twenty other people outside that they've secured." Ox says.

"I didn't hear anything. But you did? That's incredible." Lucas says, looking strangely at Ox and then the rest of us. Oops, that cat is officially out of the bag now.

"Uuhhh, yeah. I did. Look, when you all get plugged in, then you'll be able to hear stuff too." Ox says with a shrug and a small, kind of embarrassed laugh.

"Plugged in? Oh! That's what David was talking about. I don't know about anyone else, but I definitely want to get plugged in, ASAP!" Nat says with a laugh and a bunch of bounces which some of us can see because she's peeking around the diner door.

"Cool your jets, will ya? We'll get to that but first…" David says with a laugh as he points to the folks laying on the ground as he comes in from outside.

"Oh, hey guys? We uuhhh… we can't seem to get near two of the vans or the big transport truck. Something is blocking us? Any idea what could be doing that and how that's possible?" Zee asks.

"Dos? Tres?" I ask and they tell me that there are several more plants out there and that they're just trying to keep themselves safe. *Great!*

"Steer clear for the time being, Dos and Tres are saying there's more plants in them. We'll get them taken care of in a bit." I tell everyone still outside and they all say they're on their way back to the diner. Mostly because I think they're just nosey as hell and want to know what's going on. Lucas is angry when he tells the bad guys to sit in a line against the wall. I'm going to overlook the kick he gave the queen bitch of this group to get her to move faster but I can't hide my smirk. *Sorry, not sorry.* Also, she seems to be fighting the control more than the rest, so I take Dos and place her on the table, right in front of the bitch. *Ha!*

"Let me guess… you have something on your person that's supposed to help keep you immune from these guys. Am I right?" I ask sweetly.

"Yeeesss." she says through gritted teeth.

"Doesn't seem to be working very well, now does it?" Lucas says with a snarl.

"Nooo." she says with a moan.

"Hand it over! You… bitch!" Bobby spits out but I think he stopped himself from saying a few other things. I look at Jamal and he's just as pissed off as the other guys so I'm going to say that they actually know this twatwaffle.

"Oh yes. Please do hand it over. Now!" I say, still trying to hold onto my temper and my darkness. Or my darkness' temper. Whatever. Very reluctantly she pulls something out of her bra, of all places, and hands it over to me. I look at what's now in my hand and I know that it's not a real "seed". The more I hold it the more I think I know what it is, so I ask Dos and Tres to verify it for us. *Holy shit!*

"Well? What is it?" several ask as some just go ahead and crowd me wanting to get a look and checking it out for themselves.

"This is not a "seed". *This is a piece of the Rev's wife's heart. Or part of some other internal organ.*" I say the last part so that only some can hear all of it and no one has anything to say about that for a few silent seconds. Then all hell breaks loose. I can't answer any of the multitude of questions thrown at me, so I hold up my free hand and yell "Enough!"

"Do you know what that thing is?" David asks as he gently moves Lucas over and he proceeds to kick the bitch, but Lucas keeps crowding us to be near the woman.

"No. I was just told that I had to keep it on my person at all times, to make sure that the plants can't control me, but I can control them." she whines but it's still kind of snotty.

"Lucas? Could you take a step back? Please?" I ask but it's Kabir that gently moves him farther away and Lynx and Ox keep him between them.

"Alright. I take it you guys know her. So... who is she?" Casey asks.

"She's a deputy at the sheriff's office in town." Bobby growls. It was good enough that Willy and Garth huff at him as they come in from outside, still invisible.

"She's more than that. She's also the sheriff's wife. We all wondered about them. She and the sheriff were actually some of the first ones to be taken away from Butler." Jamal says while trying really hard to hold onto his composure.

"So, where's your husband?" Kabir asks but she's still trying to fight the compulsion, so Bobby happily brings Tres out and gently plops her down closer to Dos. After that, there's no more fight, but just to make sure…

"By all means, please speak freely." I say but then my darkness comes roaring up and says, "But make sure it's only the truth." Everyone shivers, including me.

"Holy shit." she says with a gulp then, "Weeellll… it's not like you'll be able to Do anything with what I tell you. So, ask your questions." she finishes in a snotty way. She's being entirely too cocky, so I'm guessing she's got another "seed" somewhere, otherwise she wouldn't still be such a bitch, but I'm going to let her think that she's pulling the wool over our eyes. *Mwahaha!*

"Where's Wade? You know, your husband?" Jamal demands.

"He became… too uncontrollable, so… he's in a camp." she says with a shrug.

"And you're okay with your husband being held? In a cage? In some camp?" Ben asks, shocked and disgusted.

"He became uncontrollable! So that's where he needs to be kept!" she says. This woman is unbelievable and delulu to the max because she actually believes this shit. But before I can ask her anything Jones grabs my attention by waving to me.

"The originals look like Dos and Tres, correct? And the ones that you're planning to use are very barrel shaped, right? Then what is this one?" he asks silently. *What?* So I go over and check out the plant that's still trying to hide from us. It looks like a cross between the originals and the newer barrel shaped ones so…

"Tres? What is this? Could this be a first gen? You know, one of the first ones made from you guys?" I whisper as I pull her closer to me and the edge of the table, mainly because I don't want the others to overhear this conversation. She and Dos finally turn their flower heads and "look" at the other plant and are shocked. They answer that yes, this plant is one of the ones that was made directly from them, a first gen. Shocked because they couldn't feel her at first, but now that they can? All they can feel is her pain. *Well shit.* I don't want to be the cause of any more of that. Jones gently picks her up out of her case and puts her on the table, but the bitch and a few others on the floor appear stunned when I check out the plant with my bare hands and nothing happens to me. I walk over to where I'd stashed my bag and pull out one of the new squirt bottles full of Marybeth and Sandra's newly configured goop and use it to spritz her leaves and the soil around her roots. Jones and I then gently rub the goop all over her. We both can feel her relief and… if you ever hear a plant cry? I strongly suggest that you run. That sound really brings out the protective instincts in some. (For example, all of us.) Even Dos and Tres try their best to comfort this new plant. The assholes on the ground just cringe at the sound and try to scoot away from all of us.

"How is it that you're able to touch any of those things without at least gloves on and you didn't even know what a seed was or have one with you?" The guy that had been holding the container that housed her asks but he's not being snotty or anything.

"Because they Like us. Never thought about that, did you" Bobby says as he gives the new plant a gentle limb shake after introducing himself to her. After rubbing her down I can see where she's been smashed when they put her into her container. These folks are not very careful and forget about being nice to her, so I try to fluff that part of her back up, very carefully. It's kind of funny that she's so receptive to us and that was actually before we applied the goop! She's also able to communicate a little better than our three were, at the beginning. I'd even say she's still a little bit better than they are right now.

"Can you tell us about the other plants outside? And how is it that you're so…?" I whisper and David and Casey touch me so that they can see if they can try to hear her answers.

According to her there are eight plants outside and she's able to communicate better because she's been one of the plants that's been in contact with people the most. She's also embarrassed to say that she's partly responsible for subverting the originals. She didn't understand, at first, what she and the others, like her, were doing but once they found out and tried to stop it, they couldn't because there's something about the seeds that forced her and the rest of her kind to... comply. But... there's always a loophole somewhere. The reason she likes us is because she can feel Dos and Tres and knows that they're being treated kindly, not being used to do bad things like all the other plants are, including herself. When I ask her how she knows that she says something along the lines of even though she's afraid of us, she can feel that the originals are... genuinely happy? Then she says something about being a next generation from the originals, she and the others like her got a large dose of something from the originals, something that was very hard to control and was maybe even the reason that the bad guys stopped making them. She's not sure but she thinks the bad guys may have even destroyed a few. Later, because the originals and even the gen 1's are so hard to deal with, someone started making the second generation, but the bad guys were unhappy with how they turned out. Something about how they only kept the gen two's around because they were compliant and useful, in a bad way only. The last batch that was made were completely inert or duds and then the person responsible for making them was killed not long after that.

"Did you guys catch any of that?" I ask silently but the guys just sort of shrug and say they maybe got a few words and some feelings but not the whole thing, so I fill my "plugged-in" guys in.

"So that's what's out in the vans and truck? More plants? Are any of them like yours or even this one?" Zee asks as he introduces himself to her and gently shakes her limb.

"So why do you assholes need so many of these plants?" Dozer asks while flexing his big hands after greeting this new plant after the coyotes give her a good sniffing. They scared the shit out of the folks on the ground when they became visible. *Ha!* Then they body check a few of us as they go back outside. *Rude!*

"Some… things are just too hard to handle by just one plant. Sometimes… even multiple plants have a really hard time handling some… things. So, now we use multiple plants as much as possible. It keeps us safe so we can get whatever it is into a van, truck or cage." the plant's handler says kind of like he's reciting a how-to manual. *That's interesting.*

In the meantime, Jones pulls out a small tablet and after a few finger taps he pulls up a folder that has dozens of pictures of the more recent family units that we've taken on and asks those on the ground if they've come across things like this. Everyone shudders but the bitch and another guy tell us that those are the types of the things that even multiple plants have a hard time handling.

"So, what do you do with them if even the plants can't make them…" David starts but everyone that was close enough to see the pictures are all shaking their heads. *Aahhhh.*

"But you've still caught some and have kept some of them, right? Why?" Casey asks.

"They're used as a threat but mainly as a punishment." the snotty guy says.

"Explain that." Jones demands angrily.

"See, at first, the Good Reverend Ansdale wanted to use them as a strike force or… something to be sent in first to make his point and make whoever's in charge of their town or whatever, surrender quicker. But those things just wouldn't follow orders and killed anything they came across. Now we just keep them in the camps."

"Seriously? Do you hear what you're saying? How is this even remotely something a good Christian, let alone a minister, would do to his fellow man? Or any of God's other creatures?" Jamal demands.

"It's okay, really. You just have to understand that the good Reverend has been chosen to be God's new messenger and his new right hand." one of the other guys says. *Blech*. I think I threw up a little, listening to that shit. But... Okay, so he was picked, just like I was but... he's had way too much of the delulu lemonade and has gone way too far off the deep end if you ask me. Now I'm not saying that some of the things he's been able to do shouldn't be considered pretty impressive, because they are, if you overlook the moral implications, but God's right hand? No fucking way.

"Let's table this part of the conversation for a moment and focus on a few other things." Jones says with a disgusted snort. It's a good thing that he'd stepped in because I was about to tell them a few things that were going to blow their fucked-up minds, but...

"Tell us a little bit more about the family units that you have. You use them as a threat or punishment how?" Jones asks.

"Well... see... if someone or something gets out of line or fights our control, then we have them fight with the... what did you call them? Family units? That's... that's a rather good description of them. I actually know some of the people that make up one of ours. I'll have to remember that. Anyway, yeah, the recalcitrant individuals are placed in with them and if they survive for five minutes, then they're let out, but there's no offer of any medical attention as part of the punishment. The threat is more than enough for most things." the snotty guy says but when the plant handler hears that he start to look a bit sick, like it's finally hitting him that this whole situation is truly fucked up and he's actually a part of it.

"These fuckin' people are freakin' me the fuck out! What is it with them?" Lynx asks silently.

"Yeah! This guy sounds pretty educated, or at least smart enough to know better but..." Ox says.

"Fanatics and compulsion. Not a good combination it appears." Kabir says looking serious. *Ha!*

"I bet if we hit them in the face with irrefutable facts, most of these assholes would probably ignore it because that's not how they Want to see it." Zee says in anger.

"I think all of you are missing a very important part." Jones says and everyone looks at him though the new folks missed out on part of our conversation.

"He said that the Rev was chosen." I say as I point to the man that said it.

"So?" several say.

"Lara was also chosen. We've heard **THEM** *tell us that."* Casey says as he takes my hand.

"Yeah, but she's not..." David starts.

"Nuts?" I ask before David can finish, but I soften that with a wink and a smile.

"I was going to say certifiable... or a megalomaniac or something." He finishes with a smile of his own.

"We all know that you have your... issues, but you don't take them out on just anyone or anything." Casey says silently with a smirk, then a smile and wink of his own. But then he finishes with, "Weelllllll... let's rephrase that and say that that hasn't happened to anyone or thing that doesn't deserve it." *Really? Schmuck.* Then the song "We are Family" starts playing. *Ah! Now isn't that's sweet!* And of course, we all start to chuckle, then laugh, then sing along. Even our new people laugh because how could you not? I'll go so far as to say that we look more

than a bit strange, but… that's just us. The assholes on the floor just stare at us in… contempt? Wonder? Confusion?

"So, can you tell us more about the family units and how you catch them?" Jones turns back to the bad guys on the floor.

"What can we say? They're hard to handle, even with the plants, and there's been too many accidents when it comes to those things. The good Reverend lost quite a few of his top people dealing with them." the zealot answers in a snotty tone.

"I sure hope he isn't planning on stepping into one of the now vacant spots on the Rev's board of directors." Ox says with a snarky laugh. Those of us that heard that comment either snort or laugh and that makes everyone look at us funny. Again.

"So, from your answer, you don't actually know how the catching of the family units is done. Got it. How about the person responsible for making the copies of the plants? Where is he or she?" Jones asks, not even looking up from his notebook.

"How do you know about that?" the bitch asks in surprise.

"Wendel? Oh, he's not with us anymore. He was given the job of trying to see just how many plants and what kind were needed to subdue the… family unit… monsters things and… in the process, he was killed. It was very unfortunate." snotty guy says over whatever else the bitch was going to say. *What a brown-nosing dickhead.*

"Interesting. Now, you wouldn't happen to know how many plants Wendel was able to make before his untimely demise, would you? And what kind?" Jones asks so innocently.

"Over forty in total from what I understand. Apparently the first set were a fairly close match to the originals in power, but they were… way more moody? and hard to control? It's because of them that Reverend Ansdale was able to gain complete control of the originals, but I'm not supposed to know that." Snotty guy says with a very malicious look on his face.

"No. That's not right. The… the originals were still suffering from the original change and… and from being cut up when… when Wendel took two cuttings off of each of them. Oh! That's how he made the first new set! But… yes, you're correct in that they're moody and hard to control. Then later, Wendel … he took three cuttings off of the next set and… made the ones we use the most. He tried taking cuttings from those, but that batch was a complete bust. Nothing but inert plants that stank worse than a sewer. Then… then he was killed by one of those family unit things." another man says with a look of shock on his face. I'm pretty sure that he was compelled to keep the truth about all of that and probably a lot of other things to himself. Jones turns to him and asks more questions, including how it is that he knows so much about what Wendel did and what happened.

"I know because… because I was there! Oh! Oh I… The Reverend is… he's my brother-in-law? Holy shit! I was there! At the very beginning and I was… forced, yes, forced… to watch, forced to stay? I've been… I've been forced … forced to do so many things… for what feels like forever!" the man says so angrily and then he starts to cry. Huge sobs erupt from him. But I think or feel that something is seriously off about that and so does Lucas from the look on his face. Kabir, Lynx and Ox kindly take him out of the diner and into the lobby, though we continue to hear him cry. Some of the folks on the floor seem shocked at his outburst. Some of them are also starting to look a bit sick at what they're hearing, but two show absolutely nothing. *Freaky.*

I walk back to my bag and grab a couple more spray bottles and head for the door. Casey, David and Dozer are practically attached to my back. Zee says he's going to give us a silent play by play while Jones continues with his questioning of the folks on the floor. Lucas, Bobby and Jamal are not far behind us, but I think it's because they don't really want to be in the same room as the Queen bitch.

Once outside we see Stanley sitting on top of one of the cars and Dozer points out the vehicles that he can't get near after telling us that it felt kind of like hitting an invisible wall. Lucas, Bobby and I walk right up to the first van and open the door. Once open, I can see three of the weird containers that these assholes keep the plants in. After taking the containers out of the van, a couple of the guys that are now tied up start to make a fuss. When we open the containers several more start mumbling behind their gags. When we start spraying the plants with goop, and me actually touching another of the first gens, you'd think that some of the guys on the ground were having seizures or something. Dozer tells them all to shut the fuck up and Stanley treats everyone with one of his laughs. Most of us no longer cringe at that sound but then I notice that Jamal is staring at one of the guys on the ground strangely.

"Do you know him?" Dozer asks Jamal as he moves to stand by him.

"What? Oh, yeah, he's my cousin. Damarcus. He's always been a… well, let's just say that he's not allowed in any of our homes anymore, ever. Seems like nothing much has changed for him if he's with this group." Jamal says with a snarl as he turns away from Damarcus, who's yelling something behind his gag. While that's going on I get in a quick introduction to this new Gen 1 and she seems… relieved… is the best way to describe it. Like the other one, she hasn't been taken care of very well. The other two are gen 2's so they just get hosed and closed back up while I take this new Gen 1 out of her case and set her off to the side while we head for the next van and the cases in there. The next van only has three gen 2's, so after hosing them down and closing the cases we head for the big transport truck with its built-in cages. Strapped to the outside of the truck are two cases and once open we see two more originals. *Holy shit!* They look almost dead! Have you ever seen the plants in the garden centers that look so awful and are on sale so cheap because more than likely they're not going to survive being transplanted? Well, that's how these two look, also kind of like they're missing parts of themselves. I take them out of their cases and give them a good spritz with goop but also some just plain water thanks to Bobbys new talent.

While we're messing around with that, Jamal's cousin is causing such a fuss that David gives him a quick jab with his tail. *Ha!* Jamal's surprise at seeing David's tail and jagged toothed grin is understandable but his smile is still huge as he gives him a thumbs up. There's another plus to what David just did, it got the others to chill out, but Lucas and Dozer are still covertly looking at a man and a woman that according to Dozer haven't made peep or put up any protest.

Casey has been going through the vans and comes up with some makeshift cart contraption that we're assuming is used to move the plants around when they're out of their containers and when Jamal sees that he's very unhappy, and we can practically see the wheels in his head turning.

"Oh, hell no! Our girls deserve something much better than that shitty thing. Give me a minute, will ya?" he says as he heads off toward the convenience store across the street. About that time Wendy and Ben come out and even though they look really pissed off, they laugh at what they see of the bad guys and yell for Jamal to wait up so that they can catch up and help him with… they don't know or care really, they just need to get away. Dozer, Casey, David and I can understand why they feel the need to get away since Zee's running commentary has been very informative, but they've been hearing it firsthand, while we're getting a slightly condensed version, liberally laced with cuss words, I might add. I think we're all very impressed with Zee's creativity on a couple occasions.

"In case I haven't said it before, I like this new crew you've picked up." Dozer says with a laugh and Stanley laughs again as well.

"Yeah, they're good people. I really need to get Jamal and Jalen together with the Brainy Bunch though." I say while smiling at the retreating Jamal.

"Oh yeah, by the way, Perky is really pissed off that you took off with some of his party favors. Not so much the theft, but the fact that he wasn't there to judge the blast radius and shrapnel zone." he laughs again. You know, if I could figure out how to get my crystals to give a playback of just those episodes, I could just hand one over so that he could sort of experience the effects for himself, right? *Hmmm...* But then the sounds of heavy chains or something like that hitting the ground draws my attention back to the vans and transport truck. Casey and David are pulling out all sorts of things and Lucas and Bobby are having a hard time holding them but from the looks on all the guys faces, I'm pretty sure I know what they're going to be doing with them. And so do the folks on the ground. Yeah, let's see how they like it. *Bwahaha!* Jamal's cousin is easy to shackle up since he's still unconscious and a few of the others go quietly after David produces his tail again or when Stanley gets too close. The man and woman that Lucas and Dozer have been keeping an eye on still haven't said a word or offered up any trouble, so now I'm curious about them too. But we need to stash these guys somewhere before the first group of compelled folks or whatnot shows up, which will be fairly soon I think. I leave the guys to figure out where they're going to do that and head back inside followed closely by Casey.

Now, I've seen Jones mad before. Several times in fact. Usually he's mad at me, or me and David, but not this time. So, I'm really curious about what he has to say and if he has any recommendations on what to do with the fucktards on the floor, but first...

"Are you through with your questions?" I ask.

"Huh. I now understand the phrase 'you make me sick.' After listening to a few of these... people, I'm actually feeling quite nauseous. The depths of depravity that some of them have witnessed and been an active participant in are completely out of my realm of understanding." Jones says with a massive snort and a head nod.

"You heard a lot of it, so I think we both deserve a fucking vacation *or like a lot of beer...* since we haven't killed anyone yet." Zee growls, doing his first twofer. I don't think he realizes what he's done though or meant us to hear that last part. *Ha!*

"Zee? I think you and Jones deserve more than that, seriously! I'm willing to go so far as to say that the two of you deserve commendations of some sort for not just ripping a few heads off! I've been out here, listening, and I've got to tell you, if I was in there with you guys? There'd be a bunch of body parts flung all over the fucking place. I mean, look, I honestly believed that you, Lara, were certifiable when we first met. Luckily, I've learned differently. But this group of... these fucking people? They're worse than evil!" Nat says from her spot on the ceiling and to the right of the door. *Ha!*

"You people just don't understand! We're doing what a much higher power has decreed for us to do! You can't just go against the will of G..." the guy who thinks the Rev is the second coming starts to say but Zee's boot to his face put a stop to the rest of the bullshit that was about to start flowing from his mouth. *Way to go Zee!* A few of our other folks clap and cheer as well. I calmly walk over and hug Zee, which seems to calm him down a little then I give Jones a hug too. After that I walk over and pick up the "seed" from the table and take it out to show Nat.

"Can you feel this thing?" I ask her in a whisper. Every eye on her head is focused on it and she says that yes, she can.

"Good."

"Why is that a good thing?" she says in disgust. If she could curl up her lip, that's what she'd be doing.

"Because you're going to go in there and start wrapping people up. Starting with the guy with the bloody mouth. If you wrap up anyone else that has one of these things on their person, let me know. Okay?" I whisper but I can tell that my darkness is right at the surface and she's very happy with the plan I'm concocting as I go.

"Fuckin A lady! You are one scary bitch sometimes. D'you know that?" Nat says with a shudder but then she starts to laugh and bounce. *Mwahaha! Of course I know that!* I calmly walk back into the diner and grab a seat while Zee and Jones follow my lead. Nat makes a truly spectacular entrance as she comes in through the door still on the ceiling and does a pretty cool dismount. The gasps and screams are music enough to bring a few more people back inside.

"You! You are in league with the devil!" the zealot screams around his busted lips. Then for some strange reason the refrain from 5FDP's "Wrong Side of Heaven" starts to play quietly.

"What?" I ask with a startled laugh and shoot Casey a surprised look. He shakes his head and looks just as surprised. My darkness giggles. *OMFG.*

"Dude! You're seriously fu… uummm nuts if you think that. She's not in league with the devil." David says with a laugh and a blush as he comes in and stands near me after giving Nat a fond pat on his way past her.

"Come now my good man, if we were in league with anyone evil, would we really care what you think or have treated you much better than you've treated any of the others that you've come across? Think about that for a moment, will you?" Kabir says as he, Lynx and Ox come in, but the look on their faces is telling me that not everything is good with what they've learned either. *Greeaattt.*

"We've stashed our guy in a room." Lynx says silently, but I can feel the disgust rolling off of her.

"You're not afraid he's going to get away?" Dozer asks as he comes in from outside.

"Nope." Ox says with a mean laugh. *Uh oh.*

"What happened?" Jones asks.

"Let's just say that Kabir took the initiative and made sure that he stays put." Lynx says with a mean laugh herself.

"Is he dead?" Casey asks kind of intrigued.

"I'll have you know that I've been practicing with William and Ajay so no, he's not dead. Or at least not yet. I may still need a little more practice." Kabir says with a slight blush staining his face. *Holy shit!* It must be really bad for Kabir to have zapped the guy.

"Where are the folks from outside?" I ask Dozer as we hear a bunch of squeaking coming closer.

"We stashed them in the pool. Luckily, it's been covered and is mostly empty. There might be some new type of lifeform growing in the nasty shit near the drain but…" he says with a laugh. *What? Bwahaha!*

Lucas, Bobby and Jamal come in about that time with Wendy and Ben right behind them, laughing like loons. Jamal has made something out of some shelves from the convenience store and the base of the original cart. The plants getting a ride on that thing seem happy enough, since they aren't all smooshed up in their cases anymore and are able to stretch their limbs a bit. Once Jamal stops the squeaky cart in front of the table and is pulling a can of WD40 out of his pants pocket, Dos and Tres feel the two newest originals and start to cry, which causes the new ones to start crying too. Then the gen 1's start crying once they feel what's going on and then cry harder when they feel each other. It's both a happy and sad sound and a few of the folks with me have to wipe away a tear or two, but most of the bad guys just continued to cringe.

"So, you think that we're evil? Why exactly do you think that? Is it because we've freed these plants from you and now, they seem… happy? I mean, you guys are the ones using them for nefarious reasons, correct? Using them to gain control of others so that you can use them or just kill them? Or is it because we have with us, willingly, some of the new beings that you would just love to get your hands on and force to do your bidding? And we're the evil ones?" I ask as I wipe away a tear. I really don't know what he was going to say next because I think Nat has had enough of him and just snatches him up and starts wrapping him up. *Holy shitballs! She's fast!* I want to ask her if he's still alive, or will be later, but I don't. David walks up to her and checks out the cocoon she's making and even sticks a claw into it and comments on how tough her webbing is. Nat laughs at his cheeky comment. But he's giving me the side eye and asking me who should be next, silently.

"Good question. Jones? Zee? Any recommendations from you guys?"

"The snooty bitch in blue. She's the one that turned in most of her own family, including her kids! and doesn't even know if any of them are okay or even alive anymore." Zee growls after Jones defers to him. Well, that works for me and somehow David passes on to Nat who her next victim? should be. While she was doing her thing with that woman, one of the men was complaining about something to do with the Geneva Convention.

"Uhhh guys? Are you fuckin' kidding me right now? Are you not the same people who came in here wanting to know about the people you planned on kidnapping and holding as prisoners until they complied and probably beyond that? Is that following any type of convention? No? I don't think so. Or is it because she's a woman and we should treat her differently? Why? Do you treat women differently? No, you don't. I should know since I'm one of the ones that escaped from one of your "camps" not too long ago." Wendy says and she's really pissed off by the end. Ben is, I think, holding her back from getting too close but that didn't stop her from spitting at the ones that are left. *You go girl!*

"The woman in pink and the guy in tan, did they have much to say?" I ask silently.

"You mean "Ken" and "Barbie"? No. Jones? Do you remember if they said anything at all? This whole time, they've felt kind of... blank, like there's not much to them. Does that make any sense?" Zee says.

"Yeah, it does. Could it be that too much has been taken from them?" Dozer says as he gets really close to the ones we're talking about. The others lean away from him but not those two, or they don't until they see the others doing it, so then they finally lean away too.

"Are they like… automatons?" Jones asks.

"Or are they clones or something?" David asks.

"Clones? Again?"

"Okay, so not clones exactly, but… if someone can make copies of the plants, who's to say that someone can't make copies of people, right?" Casey says and we all look at those two again. When Nat's done with the woman in blue, she asks who's next. I tell her that it's her pick and the three out of the five that are… animated? They're the ones definitely shaking in their shoes. "Barbie" and "Ken" are just blankly gazing off into space, though still leaning a little. *Jeez, they're really creepy. And the guys did name them pretty well.*

We all know who Lucas, Bobby and Jamal want to be next, but it's Ben and Wendy that raise their hands and suggest it be the "ass kisser" of the group. Before he can voice his protest he's already in Nat's pinchers. Halfway through his top half Nat let me know that there's a seed in his pants pocket. *Awww shit. Why me?* Somedays, I really do miss wearing gloves, especially when touching strangers, but that doesn't stop me from digging around in his pants pockets to retrieve the "seed". The looks of horror on the queen bitch's and plant handler's faces are awesome to see and the looks of glee on my groups faces is a Kodak moment that's not going to be missed thanks to all of our crystals. When I stand in front of those two and hold out my hand, they both pull out a couple more seeds with no comments. *Ha! I knew she had another one. Dumb bitch.*

That's four "seeds", two Gen 1's, two originals and six Gen 2's liberated from just this group. Not too shabby and all without a shot being fired. *Imagine that.*

We've barely finished laughing at their sour and scared faces when the coyotes let us know that there's someone? approaching, so we all try to find a place for everyone. Nat, with help from Kabir, David and Dozer, take the cocooned folks out to stick them to the ceiling farther down in the hall. *Bwahaha!* The other four are taken farther into the diner and stashed back there with Jamal, Lucas and Bobby guarding them, though that isn't really necessary now that I've got all the "seeds" with me, and they're completely enthralled. *Blech.*

The individuals that kind of cautiously come into the motel lobby and then into the diner are a man and his two dogs, or at least that's what he looks like at first glance, but the more I look at him, the more I see that that is totally incorrect. Oh, he's a man with two dogs, no doubt, but if he was to remove his long cowboy duster type coat, I'm betting that his legs will end at the shoulders of his dogs because I really don't see his lower legs and feet at all. Plus, he stinks. I'm not trying to be mean here but… imagine wet dog and B O. *Yikes!* Also, when he comes in through the door, he's either talking to his dogs or cussing them out, in German.

"Is right place. Yes? I vas told to come here and to meet people." he says with a fairly thick accent as he tilts his head back to look at us through his hair but he doesn't remove his cowboy hat. He's a little robotic in his movement but that might be because of how he's having to balance himself. His compulsion must be pretty strong because I doubt he or his dogs are the type to just walk right on into any place without checking it out first, but especially because of what he and his dogs have got going on right now.

"Yes, this is the place. Please, would you have a seat?" Wendy says but I know that she's not paying too much attention to what's going on with him.

"Uuhhh, no." he says.

"Is it even possible for you to sit down?" I ask.

"I can but… is fuckin' difficult, especially getting back up. And don't even get me started on other things." he says with a snort, and I think the dogs laugh at or with him. Wendy and Ben look at me and then look at the guy more seriously, not understanding.

"No worries about that right now. But first, we're going to put something on you and your dogs. It doesn't hurt at all so could y'all hold still for a second, please." I say as I come around the table and dip a finger in a jar of regular goop. I gently rub some of the goop on the dogs' ears and snouts but to get the guy on his face, above his beard, like I've done with Bobby and the others, I have to move away some of the lank dark hair hanging in his face. I also managed to uncover one of his slightly scared blue eyes in the process. Ben has followed Casey's lead, and they're standing on either side of the guy, probably in case he goes for a weapon or something. But what happens is both dogs shake their heads and bodies then they jump, just a little. It's enough to throw the guy way off balance so he's lucky that Casey and Ben are there, they keep him from falling, probably on his face. One of the dogs, the male, starts to growl after seeing how close we all are to him, but I just point my finger at him and tell him to cool it. The female huffs at me and the male dog. The guy looks at those of us that he can see and he goes pale.

"What the fuck? Wer bist du? Was ist los?" he says very confused.

"Hey! Take it easy now." Ben says but the guy is still… very on edge.

"Yeah, you can chill out now. No one here is going to hurt you or anything." Wendy says as she stands up and shows him her empty hands.

"I don't… I don't… the fuck?" and then a whole bunch of stuff in German pours out of his mouth. Surprisingly, Casey answers him and the guy settles down quickly while the dogs continue to watch everyone, but they don't feel worried at all now, just curious and safe?

"Wait! You speak German?" Zee asks as he comes in from the hallway.

"Well, yeaaahh. I mean… there are several Army bases in Germany and I've been stationed at a few. That's where I first met the General, by the way. Besides, how was I supposed to pick up any of the local ladies? Or know what they were saying when they rudely shot me down?" Casey says with a cheeky grin and a laugh.

"Now that I believe." Dozer says as he comes in. The new guy and his dogs just watch us. He doesn't appear to be afraid anymore, but I think he's still trying to hide what's going on with him and his dogs.

"I'm sorry if we startled you but we needed to get you out from under the mind control that you've been experiencing for however long. When did you go to the bookstore?" Wendy asks but he's really not paying attention to her, he's so engrossed with looking at the coyotes that he's taken his hat off and smoothed his hair back so that he can see Willy and Garth better. The two big goobers have strolled in and plopped down beside me. They're actually being pleasant and not trying any of the dominance shit that they like to pull but they are up to something, I can tell. The guys dogs are not exactly playing subservient to them but they're not being pushovers either. This has the guy giving all of us another considering look. Then the coyotes get up and walk away with a jaunty, exaggerated tail wag. At seeing that? I close my eyes, drop my chin to my chest and shake my head. *I wonder… who could they possibly have learned that from? Hmmm?*

"Hey, is there a stool behind the front desk?" I ask silently.

"Yes, do you need us to bring it to you?" Kabir replies.

"That would be great but when you come in with it…. ummm… could y'all be… could you let some of your animal traits out? I think this guy needs to see that… so that he knows that we don't judge… before he's going to be willing to open up to us. I can get most of their story from the dogs but… I think he needs to be the one to decide. Does that make any sense?" I ask. I get back a lot of affirmatives to that so…

As the new guy continues to check us out and my original team kind of ignores him, Kabir comes slithering in with the stool in his hands. Ox and Lynx come in looking like a really good mix of their human and animal selves as well. When the new guy sees them, he tries to hide his shock, but the dogs don't even bother, which is really quite funny to see. It also cements in my mind that his dogs have gained a lot from him but that they're still separate individuals. Maybe, with the help of these crappy gen 2 plants, I'll be able to help them all out. I'm still not sure if the coyotes can pull off Ginger's role, but I'm willing to give it a try whenever they are. *I think.* Bobby, Jamal and Lucas come out from where they've been waiting and pretty much just nod in greetings to the new guy but then they walk on past us and out the door and then out of the building all together. Wendy watches them go then looks at me, then to the back of the diner and heads that way. I really don't think that they've done anything bad to the bad guys, but I do think that they're holding onto their tempers and their good guyness? (*Is that even a word?*) by a very thin thread. Wendy then comes back and shrugs her shoulders at me so I'm taking that to mean that our "prisoners" are still unscathed. Dozer and Zee see our exchange and ask me if they need to go check on our newest recruits and I tell them that I would appreciate it. Kabir kindly offers the new guy the stool and he's able to sit down while leaving the dogs enough space to sit or even lay down without causing any balance issues for the poor guy, which he looks eternally grateful for. We let him and his dogs get settled as we kind of go about our business. We're giving him a little time to slough off his compulsion and to get just a small look at what it's like to hang with us because... you guessed it. I've got a feeling about this guy and from the looks Casey is shooting me, he can feel it too. *Holy shit! Do I really want our connection to be this strong? Fuck No! I'm angry, not crazy. But he might end up crazy by the end of this. Mwahaha!*

"So, what's your name?" I finally ask the guy. He said something so fast in German that I miss it. And from the looks on several of the others faces, they missed it too, so I look at him and ask him to slow it down a bit. He says it again but again; I'm not getting it. I don't think Casey's really getting it either because he and the guy start having a lengthy conversation in German before Casey says "Aahhhh" before turning to me.

"There's something blocking him? from saying his name or just being better understood? Or maybe my German isn't as good as I think it is but… I think his name is Micah. Or at least that's as close as I think we're going to get at the moment." Casey says with a shoulder shrug while Micah looks at us and it's like some type of heavy weight is lifted off his shoulders. After that he and his dogs look even more relaxed. After a few seconds he decides to tell us, in not too broken English, a bit of his story.

"When the orangefarbener nebel started I vas in Georgia helping the polizei with the training of their dogs. I bring mine to show how is done, yes?" he says and we all immediately turn to Casey. He laughs at us and asks us what part didn't we understand. Ben says and David, from out in the hall, yells at pretty much the same time "All of it?" Of course, that has most of us cracking up and even Micah laughs after a couple seconds.

"Hey! I got that he was in Georgia and that he was helping some police with training their dogs. Some of the other stuff was gobbledygook though." I say and after that I hear a bunch of "Oh's" and "Okay's", plus a bunch more laughter.

"Please, continue." I say but I'm trying to hold in my snark and another laugh.

"Ya, I mean yes. Well, ven the nebel start, something big and bad? Yes, bad, well it come after us. I grab my dogs and run. I get lost finding hostel but I find after a day, then I pack a few things and run away again. Have no idee where I go or where I've been? You understand?" he asks. This time most everyone gets it, so I nod for him to continue. Plus,

I think he's getting a little bit better the longer he talks so… I wonder who's helping him out.

"Okay, so who's helping him out here?" I ask silently. At that Willy and Garth materialize slightly behind me and Micah and his dogs all jump. Willy and Garth both move up and give the two dogs a good sniffing, then do some type of whiney/chirpy bark thing before Willy lets me know that he and Garth are actually helping the dogs with their language issues now that the goop is fixing some of their other problems. So, because they're getting help Micah is too? *How freaky is that?* After giving me and the coyotes a very considering look and sharing a look with his dogs, Micah starts again with his tale. He seems totally relaxed now. All three do.

"We run for a long time then meet up with some other people. We stay with them for a few days, always on move, ya? A frau, uuhhh lady? Yes, a lady in the group started having shakes? How you say? Anyway, she shakes then is talking in a strange language. Then everyone starts talking different. I already talk different so is no problem, but after we all got gentrennt? Since then, things have been no good. The next group we meet with keep saying that they don't understand me. So, we leave. The next group was okay until one man walk into trap? We all run off but while running, something happened." He stopped there and put his hands on each of his dogs heads. Even though we want to hear his tale, we all know that we can't push. After a good solid three minutes he and his dogs raise their heads and he continues with his story.

"Dogs can run, ya? Run for long time. I was tired and erschrocken? But Venus and Mars keep forcing me to keep going. We run and run and I don't remember how or when it happens but I pass out sometime and wake up with… no more legs. We all wake up erschruttert. Uhhhh… shocked? Yes. Fucking shocked. It took us two days just to be able to walk again! And I cannot tell you about some of the other fucking problems we have." he says with a blush staining his face. Oh, yeah, I can only imagine. *Ha!* All those that have been able to hear him are pretty much sure of what he's said but there's been quite a few words that are lost on most, but I think I've got it and Casey can fill in the others if he needs to.

"Okay, so I like this guy. Are you going to be able to help him out?" David asks silently.

"Yeah, I think so but... not here. As soon as the last person or thing gets here and we release them from their compulsion, then we need to leave. Put as much distance between us and this place as possible. These assholes seem to be on a schedule or something and once they don't come back, all hell is going to break loose with the Rev and his assholes."

"Should we warn the people who hang out around Coffeeville? You know, tell them what might be coming their way and that they should run?" Ben asks.

"We can try but... while we were sneaking through town earlier, I thought I saw at least two lookout spots that missed us. So, whoever was manning those lookouts will either get into trouble or they might try to follow us."

"Can we hit everyone we come into contact with a little bit of goop, just to help them out in case they're under any of the plants spells?" Nat chimes in from the hall.

"Good question. Maybe? If they get close enough?"

"That's going to leave a lot of folks still under the plants or Rev's spell, as Nat calls it, because we won't be able to get everyone." Zee says as he comes back into the diner.

"Copy that. Oh, and Stanley says that he can see some more people heading this way." Dozer says when he enters.

"How are Bobby, Lucas and Jamal doing?" I ask after nodding about the news of the next group approaching and being body checked as the coyotes head out the door. Micah, Venus and Mars are all wide eyed when after body checking me and several of the others the coyotes simply disappear, but we can all hear their huffing laughter. *Rude! Bad manners!*

"Is that normal for them? To do that? Turn invisible? How? And what type of dogs are they? I have not seen the type before." Micah asks.

"Oh yeah, that's normal for them. Apparently, being rude is also becoming normal for them too." I say with a laugh.

"Oh, they aren't dogs really. They're coyotes. Have you never seen coyotes before?" David asks as he comes in through the door.

"Coyotes? No shit? Huh. The only coyote I ever seen was in a karikatur. You know, the one with the "beep beep" bird?" Micah says with a surprised laugh. I just hang my head when David, Casey and Jones laugh at me. *Hey! We did (sort of) help him change his name. Jeez.* Micah, Ben, Nat and Wendy are lost but I'm sure someone will fill them in, eventually. Right about then Willy lets us know that it's three women and a man approaching. I laugh and tell Ben and Wendy it looks like the tweakers are on their way in. Casey shoots us a look when the three of us laugh but David and the others go back to their hiding places while Jones heads for the back of the diner to take over for Bobby, Lucas and Jamal.

"Hey, do you mind taking off your coat and just have it… uuhhh… draped over your lap? to hide your legs for a bit?" I ask Micah since he, Venus and Mars are at least marginally comfortable for the first time in who knows how long and I'm not going to make him or them get up and move. He and the dogs sigh, I think in relief, and he takes off his duster and does as I ask. *Gak! Oh… holy shit, he needs a bath!*

Within a minute the group that we'd dubbed "the tweakers" comes in the motel doors and walk almost normally into the diner. When they see us, I think a couple of them remember us, or at least they remember

Ben, since he's so large. The looks on their faces are comical, at first. "Haven't we seen you somewhere before?" one woman asks as she points at Ben.

"Uuhh, yeah, you have. Could you all have a seat and answer a few questions for us?" Ben asks and the four new people take a seat and sit almost at attention, like they've been programmed to do it that way. *Crap on a cracker!* That's so hard to watch. Micah, Venus and Mars watch it all with kind of shocked looks on their faces. Ben and Wendy try to hide the fact that this shit is freaking them out too, and after a few seconds they manage to master their emotions and plow on.

"Well… to start with, we uhh… we want you to know that you're under a… magical compulsion. Even if you wanted to lie to us, you can't. Now, by the end of this, we're going to release you from that compulsion, so don't worry, okay?" The four of them just nod their heads. This… I just can't stomach so I get out the goop and go and give them all a smear. Micah and his dogs have been watching intently, and he turns and asks Casey something in German. They have another fairly involved chat while the other group comes out from under their compulsion. They go from looking like living mannequins to scared yet intrigued people. I think, from the way they're looking at us and then at each other, that they get that we could've done just about anything to them, and that we're just not that way.

"Sorry about that but… y'all seem like nice enough people, and I just couldn't take going ahead with the questioning while y'all aren't in control of yourselves. The folks that came here for just that purpose? Yeah, them I don't give two shits about, but it doesn't feel right doing that to good people. Ya know?" I say with a shrug and everyone that I can see all nod their heads. *Ahhh, same page. Gotta love it!*

"While what she said is certainly true, I know that you all have a lot of questions but… could you hold off on that for a moment and give us your names and a brief synopsis of your stories first?" Jones says as he comes from the back. The shocked looks on the new people's faces is understandable of course but when Lynx, Kabir and Ox come in from their hiding places the new folks relax a lot more. I think they've seen a few changed folks and have seen that not all of them are bad.

"Oh, uhhh, yeah sure. I'm Jerry and this is Liane, Amber and Doreen. We all work, or worked, in the same office building, in Atlanta. We were all at work when the fog started. Everyone from my office was there, at the beginning but… once an hour or so had passed, quite a few decided to make a run for their homes." Jerry stopped there to swallow hard.

"They might have been the lucky ones." Liane says as she puts a hand on Jerry's shoulder.

"Oh, come on! Jerry has done a fantastic job of keeping us all safe, well… pretty safe, and fed and everything else for the past who knows how long. If it weren't for him? Yeah, I don't think we would've made it this far." Amber says with heat. I don't know about the others, but I can tell that she likes him. Like… a lot.

"Yes, Jerry has done one hell of a bang-up job making sure that we've been taken care of. I readily admit that. Have admitted that on numerous occasions." Doreen aims all that at Amber then goes on with, "We had a few rough patches in the beginning, but we figured a few things out after a lot of trial and error. We've also been… fucking lucky too many times to count. See… Jerry here can… he can find things that we need. Not want but Need, with a capital N. Liane? She usually can look at someone or something and tell if there's anything sketchy about them. That's also saved our bacon a time or two as well. Amber here can take whatever we find and make practically a gourmet meal out of it. And me? I can see through the bullshit to the truth of things. But… none of us expected to get caught up in whatever the hell it was that screwed up all that we've… come to rely on? Does that make any sense?"

"In a way. How long has everything been… wonky… for you?" Wendy asks.

"A week? Maybe a little more?" Liane says with a shrug.

"Do you know how it started?" Ben asks but before anyone can answer the coyotes and Stanley let us know that something is approaching.

"Something?" Jones asks as my fam and I turn towards the door. Wendy and Ben see what we're doing and look that way too and motion for the new folks to hold on a second. Lucas, Jamal and Bobby come rushing in, pale and frightened so they must have seen… it.

"Well? What's coming this way?" I ask. But before they can answer Dozer and Zee start silently yelling for us to come outside. *Oh shit. This can't be good.* Kabir, Lynx and Ox tell us that they'll stay in the diner until we call for them, which is great because Casey, David, Jones and I are already running for the door. We hit the parking lot and Dozer and Zee are pointing off to the west as something drags itself our way through the tall grass. It's a… it's a… *Fuck if I know!* It's part human but also part crab? Or maybe crawfish? There's some alligator in there and maybe some regular fish? But with the fur and tail I'm going to guess that there might even be some nutria or plain old rat in there too? This person is an absolute mess and I'm not picking up on much besides the animal parts and there's not even much of that. *WTF?*

Casey looks at me and all I can do is shrug while trying to keep the tears from dripping off my face. My guys don't do the big crying thing often, as far as I know but damn, when they see my tears and somehow pick up what I'm feeling, they let theirs run freely down their scruffy faces too. The coyotes set up such a mournful howling that that got Venus and Mars joining in from inside and even Stanley has tears coming out of his overly large blue eye.

"What the actual fuck?"

"If you think this is bad… just watch for a few more seconds." Zee says as he wipes his face on his shirt. *What? Ohhhh shhiiittt.* As we watch… the form of this new being starts to change, again. More legs morph out of it… no, him… and gills grow on his neck and down his back, which goes from furry to scaly. His movements change to more of a scuttling than crawling or even dragging.

"What's wrong with him? Why can't he pick something and stick with it?" David asks.

"That's a damn good question but I don't have an answer just yet." I say sadly. But I think I might know what's wrong with him. This poor guy… he was, at one point, put together enough to meet the bad guys, right? How else would he have known to come here. I bet the compulsion that was put on him screwed something up in him and he's lost his human side almost completely and the other parts are now so lost and confused because there's no one in charge. But I'm guessing here.

"I think that we should ask the… assholes… if they've ever seen anything like this before." Jones says and I turn and look at him in wonder. Yes, I know that he cusses now but this is the first time I've heard it in person.

"I looked this phenomenon up, it's called lalochezia. I've always wondered why so many of you all cuss so much and… now I know. Sometimes… it's the only thing that fits the situation. Obviously, I'm still a novice at this… but I'm working on it." Jones says with a snort and a shrug. I walk over to him and give him a hug because… what else is there to do at a time like this? He snorts again and returns my hug then turns to go back into the motel but he's stopped several times to get a few more hugs and a few manly pats on his way past everyone. The new being has stopped within spitting distance of us and has continued to morph into different amalgamations at an alarming rate but that's all he does, which is depressing to say the least.

"Are you really not getting anything from him?" Casey asks but I just sadly shake my head.

"I don't get it. I mean, he could probably give us a run for our money here. He's got some killer natural weaponry and armor but he's just sitting there, watching us." Zee says but before anyone can comment Jones comes back out of the motel dragging the "bitch" and the "handler" followed closely by almost everyone else. "Barbie" and "Ken" are probably still sitting where they were put and Nat is peaking out of the door from the ceiling. Jerry, Liane, Amber, Doreen, Micha and his dogs stand a bit back from us but they're watching everyone like a hawk. I'm sure they're all wondering what the fuck is going on.

Jones was not kind as he drags the two assholes up and drops them to the ground fairly close to the new being. When they get a look at him, they both cringe and try to scoot away but they have nowhere to go since we're all standing there, blocking their escape.

"Can someone go back and grab Dos or Tres and the Gen 1 that's been talking to us?" I ask silently. David and Dozer head back inside while everyone else stands around, staring and wondering.

"What's that going to prove?" Ox asks.

"Wait! Oh! Holy shit! That's so cruel! Are you really suggesting that the plants could've been used to help him? Holy shit! Could they have?… But no, these assholes aren't interested in helping anyone but themselves." Lynx hisses as anger washes over her face.

"I know you guys are having a nice chat but… care to fill all of us in? Hmmm?" Ben says with a ton of snark. *Ha!* Why did just about everyone shoot looks my way? *Damn! He really is spot on or at least super close!*

The look on Jones' face is a sight to see and thank heavens it's not aimed at me or David in this case. *Oh boy.*

"Have, to your knowledge, any of your people come into contact with anyone or anything like this poor fellow before?" Jones demands. The bitch just turns her head away but…

"I've not seen it personally but... I've heard a couple people from this group talking about encounters with things like this, or at least something similar, I think. I thought they were crazy or pulling my leg about it. Why do you ask?" the handler asks, looking grossed out and scared. He doesn't really look like he wants to hear the answer and maybe he's finally getting that what he and his "leaders" are doing is Not the "right" thing? Tres and our friendly Gen 1 then confirm that the compulsion to stop fighting is probably what's responsible for this poor guy's mental decline.

"Sorry about us not including you earlier but yeah, we've been discussing the fact that, or we're pretty sure that when the other bad guys were talking to him and giving him the compulsion to come here... they probably said something along the lines of "You seem to be struggling with something so just let it go." And this is the outcome. See, the only problem with the compulsion to just let it go or to stop fighting is that he did stop... or whatever, but his main fight was to see who would be... in charge of himself? Now? Even the animals and whatnot that's making up this new being has no one at the controls. His human sense of self was pretty much the only thing holding everything together and now that it's gone? None of the other parts have what it takes to make a coherent entity."

"Are you saying that... that we're responsible for that thing?" the bitch says but the handler looks at her and then back at the new being and he's looking really sick and sad.

"No, that's not exactly what we're saying. What we're saying is that magic is responsible for making him a new being. You assholes are responsible for making it so that he can no longer function. That it's because of you douche bags... that you all have ruined him and undoubtedly countless others. And still... you don't care, do you?" Jamal says in frustration.

"Holy shit! That's almost exactly what they said to us! We were a mess and they told us to relax and let all of our problems go!" Liane says looking sick. So did the other three with her.

"I haven't met any really bad new beings yet, but I've heard a few tales from these kind folks and I've got to say… that none of the bad ones, as far as I'm concerned, are as bad as you and your group are. I'm not making light of some of the things I've been told about, but you and the Rev and the rest of the "soldiers of God" need to be stopped. No, not stopped but… wiped out." Lucas practically spits out.

"What? How can you say that? What we're doing is absolutely necessary. We need to restore a balance. We need to control… all of this madness." the bitch says and she actually believes that shit.

"Oh wow. Now that's one seriously fucked up magical talent you've got there." Ben says with a laugh and that causes all of us to look at him.

"Oh, sorry. See, she's supposed to be only telling the truth, right? Well… she is, in a way. See… I think she's able to… justify? Just about anything? And once she does that, it's her truth. I bet, since she has a police background, that this isn't the first time that she's made something fit her beliefs or made the evidence fit the crime, ya know?" he finishes with a shrug.

"Huh. I was going to say that she's been drinking too much of the delulu lemonade, but that actually makes quite a bit of sense." Lynx says and I think most of us agree with her but I think we all understand where Ben is coming from too. And he's right, that's one fucked up magical ability.

"What are you talking about? Everything I've said is true." the bitch says with a disgruntled look on her face but the "handler" cuts his eyes to her and starts shaking his head. *Huh.* Then he asks if there's anything that we can do for the poor guy who's been just sitting a few feet away from us, constantly morphing his form. I don't know who's been keeping an eye on him the whole time he's been here but I've had to look away several times because some of his morphs are, quite frankly, horrendous. I mean, it's bad but... I refuse to be the first person to toss my cookies, no matter how much saliva keeps gathering in my mouth. Reason one... I'd never be able to live it down and reason two... I can pretty much guarantee that if I do, there will be a chain reaction and I'd never live that down either.

"Are you sure that there's nothing that we can do for this guy? Even with the plants help?" Dozer asks while looking away. I'm almost positive that he's looking for anything to focus on besides this poor guy. Since I'm in the same boat with him and I'll take any help I can get.

"Okay, so let me tell you that there has to be someone or something with enough... sense of self to be able to do anything, and right now? I'm not sure that the crawfish? has what it takes to be in charge of everything else. It's like the more he changes, the less he has of anything... he's losing too much with every shift. Soon he's... he might end up looking like Blobby. Does that make sense?" I answer but I'm still trying to find... something, anything... in him to help me help him. But I can't. *Fuck.* After a few more god-awful morphs and no other suggestions from anyone Kabir steps forward and silently volunteers to do the... euthanasia? *Dammit!* All any of us can do is just give him a grateful nod. This absolutely sucks but we're not really killing him, or them, to be mean or anything like that and it's not even a public service type of thing. It's... mercy? In a worst case scenario? We've spent the past few minutes watching the now much more rapid decline of this new being and it's been so hard to watch.

"Is it me or is he getting worse? I mean, his morphs are becoming really bad, ya know?" Bobby asks while swallowing hard and moving away.

"I think he was looking for help, originally, but he ran into these stupid assholes instead. Yes, I know he was compelled to come here but besides all of that... I think what's left of everything making up this guy wants us to help them... stop. You know what I mean?" Ben says while turning away from the latest mashup that's making a most of us look away while turning green. *Uggg, this is fucking awful.*

"Kabir, if you would, please?" Casey asks sadly and with a gulp big enough that I could see his Adam's apple bob. We all watch silently as Kabir walks up to the rapidly devolving new being. It takes a couple tries to catch something… solid, perhaps a tail, then he gives the poor thing a quick bite. After one final change, the new being collapses and just… stops. We all hang our heads and Jamal offers up a prayer for this poor lost soul, or souls. After a silent moment Dozer and Zee tell us that they had spotted a good place to bury him/them when they were out here earlier. Then David silently snarks that we've got plenty of hands that could dig a big enough hole for him chained up in the pool. *Fanfuckingtastic idea!*

At David's snarky comment there's a whole lot of watery laughter and some of the guys go to the pool and uncover it. Those that didn't hear the comment can tell that something's up and watch quietly as the cover to the pool is pulled back. Even I laugh at the many disgruntled faces looking up at us but when Dozer asks for volunteers the guy and girl that have never caused any issues and a few others readily raise their hands. So, Zee calmly, and with a bit of flair, descends the steps into the pool to unlock those with their hands raised. I think he was trying to look like, maybe, Scarlet O'Hara descending the staircase in "Gone with the Wind" or something. Whatever it was, it was a sight to see, let me tell you. *Ha!* A few of the other prisoners don't seem very amused but that's okay with us, ya know?

Anyway, in total, two women and six men are unshackled and gratefully leave the pool, even knowing that they're only being let out to dig a very large hole to bury… something in. Zee and Dozer grumble a bit about missing having the wormoles here since they could dig that hole in no time flat. Yeah, and they'd have fun doing it too, I'm sure. When someone asks if we should goop the folks that volunteered, the response is a resounding no; but Jones did add in "at least not yet". I think he's learning to be petty along with some of his other new habits. *Ha!*

While Zee, Dozer, Stanley and Kabir take the grave diggers over to the spot that the guys had talked about seeing, Lynx and Ox go and try to find some shovels or something while the rest of us go back inside to finish up or just sit and talk to the new people and more than likely answer a ton of their questions. I'm also wondering what "Barbie" and "Ken" have been up to since we've left them alone the whole time we've all been outside. It wouldn't surprise me if they're still sitting where they were told to sit. *That's beyond creepy if you ask me.*

Once Ben and Casey help Micah and his dogs sit down again and Jerry, Amber, Doreen and Liane drag their chairs closer to us, the whole conversation changes from their stories to what we know and what the hell we're doing. Oh, I know that they all get the part that they were under a magical compulsion to come here but they're not too clear yet on what was supposed to happen to them after that. But before we delve into all of that we're actually waiting on Casey. He finally made the decision to leave the queen bitch secured in the pool with the rest of the bad guys but by mutual agreement we have the plant handler come back inside with us. Even without being gooped he seems more open now and remorseful? Shocked for sure. For what he and the others have been doing? Maybe. I'm also not sure if his own magical talent is trying to reassert itself and that's why he seems really different from some of the others. Either way, he doesn't seem to be too happy with this situation or himself, soooo…

"First off, what's your name and how did you get hooked up with this bunch of shitheads?" I ask after everyone is as settled as they're going to get, including having Barbie and Ken now sitting next to the plant handler on the floor. *What? Someone had to start, right?*

"Well now, that's certainly a classy way to start this off." Casey says and the rest laugh, including myself. But then again what did he really expect from me?

"Oh! My name is Dwight, Dwight Carter, but my friends just call me DC. Uuhhh… I got hooked up in all of this, as you say, because my cousins are involved. As a matter of fact, one of them left here earlier when he broke down? Jim Bob, oh, I mean James, James Carter. Is he okay? Oh, and my other cousin, his sister, is married to Reverend Blake Ansdale."

"Talk about keeping it in the family." David snarks but now I'm wondering just how much this guy knows about his family.

"Which one contacted you first? James or the Rev?" Casey asks.

"A couple days after the fog started, Jim B… uhhh, James came over to see me and some of our other family members. Or I should say the ones that had made it to the house by then. I… I'm trying really hard to remember what we talked about but it's… it's like I'm hitting a wall. It's because I've been compelled, like everyone else here, right? Why would they do that to us?"

"This is just a guess, mind you but… I don't believe the Rev could have anyone working for him or with him that he doesn't have complete control over. If any of you knew the depths of his depravity, you might run away or revolt. He, perhaps, needs to be seen with no opposition to his power base as well. Am I making any sense with this?" Jones asks.

"Yeah, sort of. I mean, maybe the Rev Needs everyone believing that he's totally in charge and that he's the new coming or some shit like that to uhhh… to help his power base or something. I mean, with everyone compelled to back him up, is it just a way to boost his own power or is it an ego boost too?" David says but then he ruins his nice thought with a blush because he cussed. *Ha! He's such a great kid!*

"That's a very interesting hypothesis. He may have been chosen, but that doesn't mean that he can do all of the things he's been doing without some serious consequences or repercussions. He's got to know this, right? There are others out there that have been chosen as well and I don't think all of them are as egotistical or megalomaniacal as he is, you know?" Casey says with a shrug and a sly smile.

"Yes, we do know of at least one other that's been chosen and they're not anything like the Rev is." Jones says with a smile of his own.

"I'm sorry but I really don't understand much of this. I mean, for the past two weeks or so I've been busy helping Jim Bo… James set up some new buildings for Blake. Mainly just making repairs and things like that but when he came and told me that I was going to have to make this trip I uhhh… I didn't understand. When he handed me that seed thing and told me to do whatever Gaylene said, it was like… it was like that's all I could do. I don't think that I even once questioned… anything." he says with a sick look on his face.

"So, being a plant handler isn't your main job?" David asks.

"What? No. I'm a general contractor; I'm more into construction and stuff like that. I've been asked to do makeover shows for TV even." he says with a bit of pride and that makes him seem more animated and natural to me.

"How many buildings have you worked on for the Rev and did you really just say two weeks?" Casey asks.

"Well… I uhhh… I don't know. I remember the last one for sure since he and James came to talk to me while I was working but… you know…" but the more he said, the more he became kind of robotic and shaky, if that makes any sense.

"That's okay. Maybe some other things will come back to you… soon." Casey says and I know that he's seeing this reaction too.

"So, you have no idea of what's going on out here and what you were supposed to be doing besides obeying Gaylene?" Jones asks not seeing anything but his notebook at the moment.

"I uuhhh… I uuhhh." he tries to say but then he starts to shake, again. There must be some other type of compulsion he's under and it's stopping him from either remembering or talking about it. Probably both.

"Hey, hey. It's okay. Let's talk about something else, okay? So, do you know who these two are by any chance?" I say while pointing to "Barbie and Ken", hoping that this is a safer topic.

"I uuhhh… No, actually I don't. I just met them and everyone else the day before yesterday when we got on the road. But… the strange thing is… I may not have ever seen any of these other people before but… I think I've seen the plants before. At first, when they thrust the cases at me, they scared the shit out of me but then I started to feel sorry for a few of them. Don't ask me why." he says and seems to be doing better now that the subject has changed. But Casey and I give each other "a look." Saying that we know that something is really fucked up somewhere.

"So, these two don't look even remotely familiar to you? Would anyone else in your group know who they are?" Jones asks.

"Gaylene might know. I think she knows most everyone with us. I mean, when she bosses us around, she usually uses our names. But for some reason, I don't think I've ever heard her say their names or say much of anything to them at all."

"Anyone want to volunteer to ask the bitch these two's names?" I snark silently and get no takers. Go figure, right?

"Have you ever heard either of them talk?" Jones asks while looking at them and DC shrugs. Jones gets up and gets really close to "Ken" and he asks him his name. Nothing, just a blank look on the guys face. Then

Jones does the same for "Barbie" and gets the same result. Liane pops up out of her chair like she's been goosed and even Doreen is leaning so far forward that it looks like she might tumble out of her chair at any second.

"Liane? Doreen? What's going on with the two of you? What do you sense, or feel from them?"

"That's just it! I don't feel anything from them. It's like they're a… void? Or maybe I should say that they feel more like a vacuum or a… black hole? Does that make any sense to anyone?" Doreen says.

"If my talent is working correctly, again, I'd tell you that I absolutely do not want to be close to those two for any length of time. It feels to me like if you spend too much time with them and they start… copying you? Then they take something from you. Don't ask me what that something is but… I think it might be something that you… need?" Liane says and Lucas comes in about that time and stares hard at the two enigmas. Micah and his dogs then focus their attention on them and the dogs start to growl. So we all look at them.

"These two? Venus, Mars and me are thinking that they are kind of like one of those traps that we've seen? You know, the type that fucks up your natural… uummm, what is word? Rhythmus? Makes everything you do… go off somehow?" he says while pointing.

"Well, that's enough for me; these two have got to go." I mutter.

"What do you mean by that?" Lucas asks as he jerks his head my way.

"What? Oh, no. Nothing nefarious just… Let's stick them in the pool with the others for now. Oh, and if they happen to be shackled on either side of Gaylene, that wouldn't hurt my feelings at all. You know what I'm saying?" I answer with a shrug and a smirk.

"Damn girl! That's petty! I like it." Doreen says with a laugh.

Jones snorts his laugh a few times as he pulls "Ken" to his feet and Lucas and Casey get "Barbie" to hers. They really do follow instructions very well as the guys tell them to walk outside and get into the pool. And yes, some of us can hear the guys laughing as they shackle them on either side of Gaylene. Casey mentions that he can't tell if that bothered her or if it's just the fact that she's in the pool, but apparently, she's got a really sour look on her face. Bobby says that he just doesn't give a fuck as he comes in from outside to join the rest of us. *Ha!* Yep, his mom is going to be incredibly angry with me, especially since I'm the one initiating the high five due to his statement. Lynx and Ox get in on the action too because they're right behind him but once they come in, they just flop down on the floor. But... I can tell that they're not as relaxed as they seem and they're ready for the next thing to happen. *Big sigh.*

"So where's my cousin? Is he alright? What exactly happened to him earlier?" DC asks.

"Oh, he's okay. He uuhhh, he uuhhh had a reaction to coming out from under, at least a little bit, of his compulsion, I think. We uuhhh, we had to give him a type of sedative, to calm him down. He'll probably wake up with a headache fairly soon." Lynx hedges. Shit! We need to get that story.

"Oh, well. I mean, he's my cousin and all but... we're not really close. As a matter of fact, I've always thought he was a..."

"Schmuck?" I ask as I wink at Casey. DC gives me a surprised look and then barks out a really good laugh while Casey pouts then blows me a kiss.

"Ha! That's a whole lot nicer than what I was thinking but yeah, we'll go with that, for now. His sister, on the other hand, now she's a really sweet person. Very quiet and caring and well... if she was married to anyone else, she'd probably be the face of the new Happy Homemaker movement. But because she's married to the Rev, as you call him, it seems to me that she's... I don't know... constantly battling depression?

Maybe? She went from being a fairly shy but very sweet woman to being just a body in the background. She gets kind of lost in his shadow, but… it's strange but I think that she likes being overlooked. Does that make sense?"

"It does actually but you've yet to say her name. Can you tell us her name?" Ben asks.

"You know, I've been trying but… I uuhhh…"

"No! No, it's fine. Just tell us what you can. Without stressing yourself out. Okay?" Wendy says as we all watch him start to shake again. Damn! That's some really strong compulsion. Gooping him might help but I think that he needs time to decompress from the seeds and Gaylene before we totally free him. Call it a hunch. *Mwhahaha!* Casey shoots me a "look" so I now know that he can tell certain things that he's not supposed to or I wish he didn't. Either way… Sucks to be him!

"I've been trying to think of her full name and I can't, I can only think of the name that I've always called her. Her family and even her husband never liked that I've always called her this, but hey! I was just a little kid and she's like thirteen years older than me, when my name for her started. Let's see… I've been calling her this since I was about two, when she used to babysit me from time to time. And… she never seemed to mind. As a matter of fact, we've always had fun with it, so there you go. I've always called her… Norey." he says with a shrug but when Dos, Tres and the two new original plants hear that name, they all start to bob and sway slowly.

"Ladies? Are y'all okay? Do you remember anything?" I ask and they're quiet for a few seconds then let me know that they don't. But… they all do like the way he said that name. It actually made them feel really… happy?

I pass that tidbit on and everyone there that knows who the plants previously were? *Blech. That sounds awful, I know.* Anyway, those that know who the plants really are a part of, are stumped. But… I think I get it. I kind of felt it when they were telling me that hearing that name made them happy. The plants themselves didn't "show" me anything but for some reason I get the impression that the original Norey had really good and fond memories of this guy calling her that name so she, when she was… whole… looked on that name and this guy as a positive thing. Apparently, her life had very few moments that were… positive, and definitely none towards the end. *Holy shit! This poor woman!* The look Casey's shooting me tells me that he's picked up on a lot of what I'm feeling and he's definitely getting a big dose of my darkness's roiling rage at what's been done to Norey. He's squinting like he's got a migraine and someone is shining a flashlight in his face. I try to calm my darkness down but she's not having it and might be the reason for it. It's only when I mention that what we're going through is affecting Casey, and not in a good way, that's when she stops trying to take control of us and go nuclear on anyone that hurt Norey, and I think that… I think that's going to include her own brother. Yeah, I can't see Kabir, Ox and Lynx doing anything to that guy unless they were all kind of… you know… channeling my darkness, if you get my drift. *Oh! Holy shit!* At some point I'm going to have to ask Casey if he's been feeling… incredibly rage filled… recently? *Nahhh.* I just can't imagine having my darkness being contagious, like so many other things seem to be when it comes to my magic and all of the other shit that I end up sharing with everyone that I'm connected to. At that thought my darkness actually perks up then calms down more and… she even laughs. Then she tells me that I'm all hers and she's all mine, but there might be a little bit of something that's bleeding through? She'll look into it. *Gee, thanks?* The new folks shiver and look around for what might be causing that skin crawling sensation. But since none of us act weirdly they just keep watching all of us, soaking up some of our camaraderie and a lot of the things we know about. I think they're enjoying just going along for the ride as we all learn new things as well. Yeah, they're fitting in quite nicely, but before we get the chance to go any further Dozer lets us know that he thinks the hole is big enough now to bury our unfortunate acquaintance.

Casey also looks like he's feeling better as he and Ben get Micah back on his feet because when most of us get up and head for the door, Doreen asks where we're going this time. When the others hear that we're going to the makeshift funeral, all of them want to attend it with us, even DC.

So, here we all are, tromping through the tall grass on the southwest side of the motel's property. Even Nat's with us, but she's kind of hidden behind the tall grass, David, Willy and Garth. When I ask why she's wanting to stay hidden she says that she's afraid that some of the new folks might not be ready for her just yet, but I think she just doesn't want the folks in the pool to see her, I think she feels that someone is going to try something and she's keeping hidden until the perfect moment. *Mwhahaha!*

"Hey guys? Done already? I thought for sure that they'd take their time just so they wouldn't have to go back into the pool too soon, ya know?" Casey says as we all walk up to the new hole and he checks it out. Why? I have no idea, but there you have it.

"Oh, well…. These folks are… they're good. I guess because most of them used to be military. I mean, when you think about it, being in the military taught us early on to get the job done ASAP and it's stuck with us ever since. You know what I'm saying?" Zee says with a laugh. Casey nods in agreement and so does Micah. *Oookay?*

"So, what are you really trying to say here?" Jones asks silently.

"What we're trying to say here is that six of these people don't even know how long they've been under compulsion or even what day it is. Four of them are from an army unit that was doing drills when the fog started and the other two are from the Airforce reserves and the last thing that they can remember is the fog rolling into a building and running. How they ended up with this bunch is a complete mystery to them." Dozer says.

"They told you that? Voluntarily?" Casey asks.

"I know, right? Anyway, our theory on that is that when you told the bitch... I mean Gaylene, and the others to speak only the truth? Well... we're thinking that because she and the others still had their seeds on them, well... maybe because these guys were all "under control" by her? Maybe... that little gem of a command was somehow passed on to them too? Yeah, I know, we're grasping at straws here but... magic, ya know?"

"Oh! And it gets even better here because the two Airforce? They're... dum dum dummmmmm... medics. I think one's actually a PA of some sort but the other is an EMT." Zee says with a laugh. *Hot Damn!* Help for Nate! Now all we need is a vet or two. But hey! Let's be a bit more specific here and ask for veterinarians. Because, when you think about it, these folks are vets, as in military veterans. Right? Magic can be a bit tricky, just ask Doreen, Jerry, Liane and Amber.

"Do you think that everyone in the pool could be like this?" Lynx asks.

"Hey! You guys really need to let us in on what y'all are talking about." Lucas says kind of scoldingly but then he laughs.

"What? What are you talking about?" Doreen asks as she looks around at all of us.

"Well... there's one surefire way to know for sure." I say and everyone can tell by the look on my face that I'm up to something. Even though I ignore the other question, no one seems to mind too much.

"Oh yeah? How's that?" several ask.

"Jamal."

"Jamal?"

"Me?"

"Yeah, you. Look... do you, or can you... ask your cousin about something that you know that he's lied about? If he continues to lie, then we've crossed one scenario off but if he tells the truth? Then we'll know that we're on the right track here." I say while keeping direct eye contact with Jamal. I know that Bobby and Lucas know a lot about that family's drama, so they're all for it and encouraging Jamal to go for it too. The shit-eating grin on Jamal's face is a really nice sight to see.

"Oh yeah. I've got a few things I can ask that mother…"

"Well now, let's go have a chat with him, after we're done with this part, shall we?" I say as I interrupt the tirade I can almost feel brewing in him.

"After you, ma'am." he says with a cheeky grin and an 'after you' bow.

Luckily, when the guys were going through the cars, vans and trucks earlier, they came across several tarps and we use one of them to wrap up our unfortunate new friend and take him over to his new gravesite. Then we perform a quick burial for him. Oh, I know that what we're doing isn't necessary, since there are other things out here that would make quick work of him/them, but I'd already decided, a while ago, that we need to do things like this only when there's enough time or when I or we personally give a shit about the people or whatever. Casey nods at me like he knows what I'm thinking, which he doesn't. We've somehow always been on the same page when it comes to things like this, so there's really no need to worry about that. Pretty much all of my fam is this way when it comes to these kind of things. Then we all seem a bit stuck because, well… what can we say about this poor guy other than we all hope that he's now at peace? Not much since that's pretty much all we can come up with. *Well now, doesn't this just suck?* At least it's a quick service and with all of us helping move the dirt back into the hole, it fills up fast too. Then we're all tromping back toward the pool to have a nice chat with Jamal's cousin. *Bwahaha!*

Most of us end up sitting around the rim of the pool or on the steps waiting for Jamal to get ready, and when he is, he decides to get really close.

"Damarcus! You asshole! Wake up!" he yells and gives Damarcus a rough jostle and an open-handed slap. You know the type that sounds like a gun shot? Yeah. *Ha!*

"Wha... wha... what the fuck? Jamal? What the hell man! What's going on?" Damarcus asks as he tries to keep himself from face planting and while he also tries to find a more comfortable position leaning up against the pool wall after testing his shackled hands and legs.

"I've got just one question for you and you better answer it. What happened to Nana's jewelry?"

"Nana's jewelry? You know what happened to it." Damarcus says with a pout and a tremor.

"Tell me the story again."

"It was... it was stolen." Damarcus says, but he's starting to sweat really badly and shake.

"Right. It was stolen. My question to you is, who stole it?"

"I ahhh, I ahhh..." Damarcus is really starting to shake and it actually looks like he's in a bit of pain. Jamal just stares down at him.

"I ahhh... I ahhh... I stole it." he says through clenched teeth. And then his shaking stops.

"What did you do with it?" Jamal asks but Damarcus starts shaking again and it looks like he's trying to come up with something, anything to not answer the question. Then he just gives in because it looks like he finally realizes that he's not going to be able to come up with anything to get out of answering.

"I gave it to one of my baby mamas. Then I stole it back from her and gave it to someone else that I been tryin' to get with. I've actually done that a couple times now." When Damarcus finishes his statement, it looks like a heavy weight has been lifted from him as he sits up straighter. He also doesn't look at all sorry for what he's done. *What a dick.*

"Oh, hey! Are you asking about what Jalen got arrested for last year?" Bobby asks, looking shocked.

"Unfortunately, yeah. I don't know about how the first part went down but I heard that Gaylene here took the police report about the theft and this asshole pointed her right at Jalen. Then she arrested him with absolutely no proof whatsoever. I do know that when Wade found out about it, he was the one that let Jalen go and had the charges wiped out. Wade even apologized for Gaylene's overzealousness." Lucas says while shaking his head.

"That's right, he did do that, thanks to you. We never really thanked you for steppin' in with all of that. Sorry about that." Jamal says to Lucas as he sticks his hand out for a shake. Lucas doesn't accept the handshake but instead grabs Jamal in a hug. Yeah, that's a whole lot better than just a handshake. While that's going on Damarcus goes back to pouting and so does Gaylene. Here it is, clear proof that she's been wrong and all she can do is pout about it? *What a narcissistic bitch!*

"This twatapatomus must be a democrat. A liberal democrat at that." Doreen snarks. *Bwahahaha!*

"Well gentlemen, it appears that your hypothesis is correct. I suppose now would be a good time to ask a few questions from the rest of these folks so that we can decide what to do with them later," Jones says while nodding at Zee and Dozer but still scribbling away.

"Yeah, well, that's great and all but what should we ask them?" David asks silently. When no one else has any ideas, I look at the newly released folks.

"So, do any of you have any questions that these people might be able to answer for you? We've got a few but we also realize that you guys are the ones that have been… well… in the dark, so to speak, for quite a while now." I say as I watch the couple that are still hanging back and as far as I know still haven't given their story to my guys. The majority of the folks, the military ones, just look like they're trying to come up with the right questions to ask so Casey, Dozer and Zee take them off a little way away to do the military version of the dominance crap on them. I know Casey "heard" what I'm thinking because he looks over his shoulder at me and blows me a kiss and winks. *Schmuck.* So of course I return the favor plus I add in the single digit hand gesture, just for fun.

"And that leaves the two of you. So, what's your story? And please, just tell us. I'm not from around here so I'm neutral on most of this shit. Ya know?" I say. The man and woman stare at me for a few seconds then they both crack a smile as we move a little bit away from the pool and its inhabitants.

"Yeah, we get that. And yes, you're right, we should give you some of our story, at least. Actually, you might be able to answer a question for us. See, we're not really with these guys. The only reason we're with this group is to find our older brother. It's been almost two weeks since we've seen him. We went in search of him and ran into these fools in almost the last place that Martin had last been seen. I can track just about anything and Melinda can sense when me or Martin is close. Which is both good and bad because look what happened to us, right? We got snuck up on and… here we are. Oh, I'm not saying that we didn't run afoul of them plants too. It… it took us a little while… but we've been able to help each other get out from under whatever spell that was put on us. We also realized early on that we couldn't do anything that might give away the fact that we aren't completely under their control. But hey! The plus part of all of this is that you wouldn't believe what some people will say in front of people that they think are nothing more than zombies, ya know?" the guy says with a laugh but all I could think about was the name of their brother. Martin. *Shit. How do I start this shit show? Fuck it.*

"Uhhh… some of us did meet a guy named Martin yesterday. He was acting as muscle for another group that had a plant. They're the ones that compelled some of these folks to come here."

"So you know where he is?" the girl asks, looking so hopeful. *Aaaggggg!*

"Yes and no. I know where he was but he's not there anymore."

"He left? Do you know where he went?"

"Look, I'm so sorry to tell you this but… he was killed earlier this morning."

"What?" she asks and her brother stiffens up.

"He was killed this morning? By you?" he demands.

"What? No! Oh no! We may have had him and the others with him tied up but none of the people with us had anything to do with his death." Wendy says, looking incredibly affronted.

"I know that this isn't what you wanted to hear and this isn't going to make it any better but the ones responsible for your brother's death? Well… it's been… taken care of."

"You're right. This isn't what we wanted to hear and no, it doesn't make us feel any better." the guy spits out as he hugs his sobbing sister and stares at us with murder in his eyes.

"Look, we're really sorry for your loss and all but… it's true, we had nothing to do with it." Wendy says, trying to convey her earnestness.

"Well, in a way… I might… be responsible for them getting killed. But that was never my intention." I say. Even though I'm not under compulsion, there's just no point in lying about any of this."What? What are you saying?" a lot of people ask at the same time. Wendy holds up her hands and tries to get everyone's attention.

"I was there, After it happened. None of us standing here were anywhere close to there when… they were killed. But I did see something and Lara promised us some answers to what some of us heard and saw. But now is not the time and this is Not the place. You understand?" she says while giving me a "what the fuck are you doing" look. Casey and the others are coming back to join us and he's got a strange look on his face as he looks from between me and the brother and sister. I think he's getting the feeling that I'm always getting when I get a hunch. It doesn't hurt or anything like that but it's not the most pleasant feeling. I can't help but to smirk at him.

"Holy macaroni babe! What is that? It's fucking disturbing!" he says silently as he shivers.

"Then quit trying to widen our bond!" I reply. The rest of my fam just look at him and give him smirks and head nods of their own. *Ha!*

"What? Are you really asking us to go with you? After what's happened to our brother? Are you insane?" the sister asks and everyone can hear Nat's maniacal laughter but no one can see her. I just smile in her direction but then face the siblings and give them the 'it's up to you' hand gesture. The sister might not be interested right now but I can tell that the brother reluctantly is.

"Look, let's table this for the moment and see what those left in the pool are all about. While we're doing that, that'll give you a chance to think about it." Lucas says.

Since I really have nothing else to add after Lucas' calm suggestion I turn and walk back to the pool and the people still in it. As far as I'm concerned, Gaylene and Damarcus can rot or have whatever's lurking in the funky sludge at the very bottom of the pool have a nibble. But… the others deserve to be heard out, ya know? And what the hell are we going to do with Barbie and Ken? They're definitely a wild card.

"Gaylene? Do you have any idea who the two chained up on either side of you are?" I ask. She looks like she'd really like to lie but she can't. *Ha!*

"No. They were just given to me and told to do everything that I tell them to do." she huffs.

"Given to you? Really? And you never even thought to ask who they are? Or what they can do?" Lucas asks snidely as he gets close enough to get a look at those still in the pool.

"Do you even know their names?" Bobby asks.

"Of course I know their names." she sneers.

"Then tell us you… you twat!" Doreen says with heat. Damn! She beat me to that! Gaylene turns her sneer at Doreen and then turns up her nose.

"Just tell us already." Jones says exasperated.

"Stacy and Stuart" she grinds out and then huffs again. I suppose to her, telling the truth could be rather annoying and answering to us has got to chafe. *Bitch.*

"And what can they do?" Lucas asks.

"I uhhh… I… I don't know. I don't think anyone told me." she says, now looking rather confused. All I can do is laugh and that gets everyone else laughing. Gaylene doesn't seem to appreciate this but who cares, right?

"What about the rest of you? Are any of you interested in talking to us?" Dozer asks. Only a few more people look at us but the rest just look at Gaylene. Like they're waiting for a sign from her on what they should do. It's a depressing sight. So, Dozer and Zee hop into the pool and unlock the ones that looked at us and escort them out so that we can chat with them. But before we leave, we have a bit of fun when we recover the pool. *Ha!* The three women and two guys all kind of smirk as they watch us do our petty revenge thing.

We all head back into the motel and then the diner and immediately everyone grabs a seat somewhere. Melinda and her brother wander in, in the end and look around. The brother asks where everyone else is as they watch all of us closely. DC laughs and says that the others are hanging around somewhere and not to worry about it. That causes those of us that know that he's not really lying to crack up. I'm glad to see that he really is more like us than his other nutball group. I watch as Kabir wanders away and from the looks Ox and Lynx are giving each other, it's no surprise that they follow him by mere seconds. I guess they're going to go and check on Jim Bob. From the brief glimpse of Dos, Tres and the other two's feelings, I'm just not looking forward to dealing with him. I think a few things are going to come out that's going to send both me and my darkness into scorched earth mode. From the looks I'm getting, it's not just Casey that's getting the feeling that something might set me off because David, Zee, Dozer and Jones get closer to me. Because of that, I'm able to take in a few deep breaths and let the tension go. One thing at a time here. *Jeez.*

"If we're all in here, how are you going to know when someone or something else is coming this way?" the brother asks as he and his sister look around at all of us.

"Stanley, Willy and Garth." Nat pipes up from her hiding spot.

"Who?"

"The big purple guy outside and a couple other group members that you haven't seen yet." I reply and that causes Micha, Venus and Mars to all bark out a laugh. Their laughter causes Doreen, Liane, DC, Jerry, Ben, Wendy and Amber to try valiantly not laugh but… they can't. I'm guessing that our light, fun and snarky nature is what gets the siblings to stop viewing us as being just another group of bad guys because they both crack a smile and seem to relax quite a bit more while finding a place to sit. We can all tell that they're still upset with us, or just me, telling them about Martin's death, but I'm not the only one thinking that they've known for some time that they might not have ever found him again or maybe even that they might've known, or at least suspected that he was gone already. Melinda, being able to find her brothers, might have felt her connection to Martin change, or just disappear. But then again, who knows?

"I feel bad for them and I never even met the guy." Zee says but it's almost like he can't take his eyes off Melinda. *Oh! Well now. Ha!* I think all of us think back to the time when Perky met Brandi, and Zee's acting the exact same way. *Oh boy.*

"I think we're going to have to give Zee just as much shit as we gave Perky. Am I right?" Dozer whispers just loud enough for me and Casey to hear. We both nod and smile. We turn those smiles on a few of the others so that some know that we're up to something and the others know that there's nothing to worry about at the moment.

Over the next ten minutes or so we all relax a bit more as we listen to Jerry and the others of his foursome as they take up their story again and as they go into a bit more detail about Jerry's new gift. With a bit of help and input from Doreen, Liane and Amber, they all tell us that when the fog started everyone in their offices were scared and most of them were practically glued to the windows as they all tried to see what was going on outside. Then a couple of Doreen's coworkers caused a stir when they started to change, in a bad way, so she ran to a different floor. Strange shit started happening on that floor not too long after that so she and Liane, who she'd just met, left and went down two more. Nothing weird happened on floor three for a few hours but some of the people on that floor decided to make a run for their cars and perhaps try to head home. Liane and Doreen kept telling everyone to wait. I believe their talents were coming "online" because they could tell that something was wrong. They all felt and still feel really bad for those who wouldn't listen. Then they met up with Amber and then Jerry and they all felt safe together so they did their damnedest to stay together. Their little group waited over two full days before they left because they were being hunted by something that came from a higher floor. When asked if they saw what it was, they all said no because Doreen and Laine kept making everyone move to different places as soon as it got too close, but they could all feel that something was after them. No, none of them passed out that first day but when they found a really good place for the night, just about everyone slept like the dead, which surprised all of them. I'm taking that to mean that they were growing into their gifts and didn't know it. The next day, after finally waking up, they were constantly on the move for too many hours before Amber said something about needing a way out of the building. Jerry immediately took them on a journey that would have led them to the outside but there was something big and nasty blocking the other side of the door. Liane then said that they needed a "safe" way out of the building and then Jerry had them all on the move again. After quite a while and multiple starts and stops, they made it out with no problems. They also said goodbye to some of the people that they'd picked up along the way because some were determined to go their own way, against advice. Things like that continued to happen to them over the next few days, and during that time they learned that when dealing with Jerry's gift, it had to be a "need" and they had to be very specific about it. Like they needed a car versus they needed a car that would run or could be driven. A route out of the city versus a safe route out of the city. Things like that. After making it out of the city, they started out heading south until they ran out of gas, but that was okay since the roads were an absolute mess. They found some bicycles and turned west do to Amber saying that they needed a safe route to avoid bad people and things. They all agreed to keep what they could do from everyone as well because the first group they met up with outside of their building had some people in it that were not… good, at all. None of them were up for a fight and no one wanted to end up being a slave or anything like that. So, after sneaking away from that group, they kept on the move. They did encounter several other groups of decent people but it was hard staying with a larger group and having to constantly run from things or being ignored when they told others that everyone needed to run. Then they ran into a trap of some kind that screwed their gifts all up. A few days after that they somehow overheard a conversation, something about if anyone goes to Coffeeville, there's supposed to be some people there that can help anyone out with any problems they might be having. That's how and why they ended up in Coffeeville. The people in the Book Nook did help them, as far as that goes, because they got them all to stop being so paranoid and twitchy by telling them to just let it go, like Liane had said earlier, but their gifts were still kind of messed up. Also, last night was the first time that Jerry had been able to find them a marginally nice place to stay for the night that had indoor plumbing and still had some food in the pantry, in well over a week. They even found some much better clothes to wear but none of them could remember where they'd left all of their other belongings and they really aren't in a hurry to find them again, in case the spell or whatever is still on any of that stuff. *Is that even possible? Well duhhh, it's magic.*

Right after that group finishes their story Kabir, Ox, Lynx and a stumbling and groggy Jim Bob, oops, sorry, James come back in. I could feel my darkness' hackles start to rise and from the looks on a few other faces, we're not the only ones having that issue. *Oh, fuck this.* Jim Bob was shown a seat and the two Airforce folks get up and walk over to check him out. Pulse check. Pupils check. Then shrugs all around, mainly because they have no idea exactly what's wrong with him or if there's really anything they can do for him. It's nice to see that they're wanting to help out now even though they haven't been gooped yet.

"I uhhh… I don't know what happened to me or why I feel so shitty right now. Do you think it's because of the plants? Are they… poisoning me or something?" Jim Bob says while rubbing his head and then his neck looking kind of nervous and perhaps… guilty? *Huh?*

"Maybe? You have to understand here that we've been dealing with these plants for only a few days now so how the hell are we supposed to know?" Ox says, but he still looks and sounds pissed off to me.

"Wait! I know we're kinda new to all of this but what's with the plants? I mean, what's with them and how did we end up here?" the female PA asks as she looks at the rest of us.

"The plants can tell if someone or something has magic, which is not really useful when you think about it. I mean, we all have magic now. Even you. What kind? That's up to you to find or to figure out. But from what we've been able to ascertain, the Rev is after folks with big or destructive magic to help him take over the state. How he decides who to keep and what he's looking for is an unknown at this moment. Maybe someone else can help us out with that. Should we ask Gaylene if she knows?" Lucas says.

"What? Wait! So… everyone has magic now? Really? Dammit! I hate knowing that we've missed so much because we've been what? Under a spell? That sounds so weird." the EMT says. At my nod, Wendy and Bobby pull out a jar of goop and give all of our newcomers a good smear. The looks of horror at the noxious colored goop in the jar is funny to see but the smiles from those already gooped are nice and seem to calm everyone's nerves. Everyone's reactions are visible. I mean, even though the plants aren't actively doing anything, maybe the goop is cancelling out some of the leftover stuff? *Who the fuck knows?*

"Oh, I know that's some nasty looking shit there but damn, I haven't felt this good in weeks!" Liane says to the new people with a smile as she points to where we'd gooped her.

"No shit! After I was gooped I felt… lighter somehow. Did that stuff get rid of whatever it was in the trap that basically sent us to Coffeeville?" Doreen asks as she rotates her head and neck then has a bone cracking stretch. We all shrug and tell everyone that the goop does make it so that nothing can interfere with people mentally, so whatever trap they ran into probably messed with their minds maybe even more than their new gifts.

"How do you make it?" Amber asks while getting a better look at what's in the jar. Kind of like she's wanting or needing the recipe.

"Oh, we don't make it. It's… you know what? Let's save that for another time." Zee says with a laugh. That causes those of us in the know to crack up. *Oh yeah, sure. Another time.*

"So, have you remembered anything else that you can tell us about?" Jones asks Jim Bob while looking at his notebook and I think he's trying to stop himself from snorting, and not the good snorting either.

"Well… I remember Blake calling me the day everything started. I think that was the last phone call I've actually gotten since then. Anyway, he called and said that something was going to have to be done with my sister and that I needed to get over to his house, fast. Since that's not anything out of the ordinary, I went. But… I remember walking in and seeing her as she was… in the middle of changing? and… I got jeal… uhh mad. I uhhh, I don't even know why. Maybe… maybe it's because Blake was mad too?"

"What kind of slip was that?" several ask silently but then we all go back to listening.

"I remember that Blake and I yelled at each other and then we yelled at her. Then someone else came over and… and… Oh! Oh my… sometime later we cut her up! Oh! Why would we do that? To her? I love her!" Jim Bob stops talking and starts to wail. At that same time DC stands up and stomps toward him. *Uh oh.*

"Are you fucking kidding me right now? You chopped her up? You did? Why? Why would you do that? Especially to her?" DC says menacingly. Jim Bob continues to cower from DC until Ben and Casey crowd him out and make him go back to his seat.

I've got to say that both of my guys are big but DC is right up there with them, if a lot younger, so I'd hate to see a fight break out between them. Luckily, before I have to do anything, Nat makes her appearance. The new folks are not only shocked at DC's behavior but having Nat come in doing her ceiling maneuver again is quite another thing all together. *Not to mention interesting. Ha!* DC catches sight of her and decides to sit down. Jerry, Doreen, Amber, Liane, Melinda, her brother, the six former military folks and the five other people's jaws drop open and they all tense up and look like they're going to be heading for the nearest exit. *Mwhaha! Too bad she's right in the middle of the only one!* Micha and his dogs just watch Nat and smile. I'm pretty sure that all of them could smell her and have known that she's been close this whole time. If they can do that, yeah, all three of them have been sharing a lot with each other. But somehow I doubt that peeing on trees is one of their newly shared things.

"Nat? You have something you want to add or ask?" I ask in a way to let the others know that she's friendly. *Ha! Most of the time.*

"Yeah, DC, you said Norey is fairly shy right? So how did she get hooked up with the Rev? Or more importantly, why did she do it?"

"Uhhh... I don't know. I was still just a little kid at the time, but ummmm.... I overheard at her wedding a few things that I thought were... odd... at the time. Like her parents telling someone how they managed to talk the Rev into meeting her in the first place and... and that they were so lucky to find someone that would have her since she'd been in trouble a few times. Things like that. But... I don't ever remember hearing anything about her being in any trouble before. There's absolutely no way she's ever been arrested or anything like that. Why exactly are you asking?" he says but he seems very protective of Norey. *Oh shit. Deep breaths. Deep fucking breaths!*

"So, the Rev isn't someone that she would've picked for herself?" Nat asks.

"What? No. No way. If I had to guess... she would've picked a farmer or something. You know, someone low key probably but definitely someone... nice. Why?"

"Because the asskisser was talking about something and I heard him. That's a first for me... by the way. I've never heard anyone like that before." *Holy shit! He's conscience? Uhhhh.*

"You... have any idea what he was talking about? Or more like uhhh... what point he was trying to make?" David asks with a surprised look on his face. Not a happy surprised look either. I think that look goes for a lot of us.

"Yeah, he said something about the Rev, that he's always enjoyed having complete control over people, especially his wife and it was all because of her brother. That part I didn't understand until just... now."

"Can someone please explain that to the rest of us?" Liane asks while giving Nat a look and a nod, like she's come to some conclusion about her.

"Oh! I think I've got this one. See... being in trouble is a euphemism, an old one. I guess being from this part of the deep south, they still use it. It's the part about it being her brothers fault, that's what's got me... well... the ick factor is beyond anything I've ever felt before, if that tells you anything." Doreen says then aims a really nasty look Jim Bob's way.

"Yeah, but as if that wasn't bad enough, asskisser said that he'd heard that the Rev had let... things... continue to happen, as a way to... punish his wife for... whatever reason." Nat says and we all turn our heads to look at Jim Bob. Not a single look was a good one and I think he could tell that he might not survive much longer.

"Wait! That's not how it happened! Look, I love my sister and she... loves me."

"Are you all suggesting what I think you're suggesting? If so... that's... that's more than disgusting!" DC aims our way but then he aims the next at his cousin.

"She's your sister! How could you do that? Why would you do that? Holy shit! You're what? Ten years older than she is?" then he looks back to us and says, "Oh! are you all saying that she's… she's been… pregnant? By this asshole? And her husband let this sick fuck continue to do that… as a punishment? What the fuck kind of family am I a part of? I think I'm going to be sick." I think most of us feel the exact same way.

"I didn't think shit like that still happened. Not nowadays." Wendy says looking sick.

"Oh! You mean you don't ever watch the ID channel? Evil Lives Here? Yeah, that shit still happens. More than we could ever imagine, I think." Doreen says. *I like that channel.*

"DC, I'm sorry but… I think it's way worse than you can ever imagine." I start to say but my darkness finishes. That's because the plants have somehow shown me something and it's breaking what's left of my heart. They may not remember much of anything but when they hear his voice, they get… flashes… and I can see a little bit of them. I see images of a chubby baby boy, then a toddler, then a little boy, then a teen, then an adult. All of the pictures are of DC. I think… I think he's… her son. Casey, Jones, David, Dozer, Kabir and Nat, at David's urging, surround me. The guys know that my darkness is right at the surface. Everyone else can feel something, but my fam knows that I'm about to let the bitch out to fuck Jim Bob up and… We just can't do that. Or at least not just yet.

"Oh, wait! Sorry, but… not sorry… you know what I mean? See… I was afraid to say anything about this before… but now? Yeah well, it seems that I definitely need to get in a bit more practice with this going non-lethal thing. Jim Bob…I'm afraid he's is not going to last much longer. What you're seeing right now is… weeellll… let's just say that he's going to be going downhill very quickly… very soon, so get what information you can out of him before he starts to… melt. From the inside. I think." Kabir says silently with a shrug but he's also got a nasty grin on his face. At

his comment, my darkness and I both return his nasty smile with one of our own. I'm glad that some of the guys are blocking me from being seen by everyone else because they all shudder and they also do a great job of Not stepping away from me, though I can tell it's a close thing.

"Fuck me, lady? If I ever see that smile aimed my way, you can bet your ass that I'm running as fast as my eight legs can take me." Nat whispers.

"Well, like Kabir said, sorry, not sorry." I say to Nat but at that the others are able to step away, knowing that we're all okay… for the moment.

"Holy shitballs babe? Are you sure you're okay?" Casey asks in a concerned whisper.

"Hmmmnnnn… No. But I'm getting there." I whisper back.

"Are you going to tell DC what you mean and about whatever it was that just set you off?"

"Fuck no! Or at least not right now."

"Oh hey! Should we get a DNA sample from the jackass here before he melts?"

"What? What for? Oh! Oh, that's fuuu… that's beyond nasty!" David mutters. *Nice save there.*

"Might as well. Just in case. because once he starts to… melt, I think my poison is going to interfere with… everything." Kabir says with a shrug but he seems a bit chagrined now.

I know that I can't stay in the same room with this sick fucker much longer or my darkness or even just myself might do something… regrettable. Though… looking at a few other members of my fam, I'm not the only one that's going to be getting the hell out of here, and soon. But luckily, it's not any of us that has to leave because Jones kindly takes Jim Bob by the arm and leads him outside, peppering him with questions as they go. DC looks angry about that but I think he's secretly relieved to see him go too.

After watching Jones and Jim Bob leave, we go back to chatting, we answer a few questions from the new folks and actually learn some names. Melinda's brother is Marshall but he prefers Marsh. The PA is Cammy and the EMT is Andrew. The four army guys are Shane, Ryan, Leo and Jay. The last five from the pool are Jeff, Steph, Dido, Erin and Cody. None of these five remember much of anything beyond the fog starting and then being forced into the pool. It's also weird that none of the pool folks and possibly all of the military folks have any idea about what they might be able to do, magic wise. Now that's some super strong compulsion and I guess we'll all learn what they can do… in time.

Once the new folks feel more comfortable with us, Ox and Lynx change back to completely human and that shocks the shit out of all of the new folks. When Micha sees that? He has a very sad and perhaps a longing look on his face.

"Let me ask you guys something. How come you don't have anyone like us in your… former group? You know, the ones that have changed into part something else?" Ox asks after the hubbub settles down a bit.

"I didn't even know that people could do that. You know, change at will like that." Liane says looking amazed.

"Oh well… when me, Ox and a few of our other friends changed, we weren't anywhere near as ummm… put together? As you just saw us. As a matter of fact, we were a fucking mess. And I'm being generous here, and we were stuck that way." Lynx says with a laugh.

"But you can change now! How is that even possible? We've seen and even met a few other people that were ummm…. stuck, like you said you were." Amber asks.

"Really? Now you can change anytime you want to? That's amazing! But..." Cammy says but then she and everyone else turn and look at Kabir as he changes back, not really noticing the scrutiny, but when he does...

"Oh no. I'm not like them. See... when my change happened, I was with my family and we could all change at will from the very beginning. It was only later that we were able to find one more form. It was a form that we could all see and feel but none of us could reach." Kabir says with a shrug. I think the stick in his ass is finally starting to come out because he was very pleasant and not nearly as stuck up about his ability to change like he used to be.

"So how did you get to that new form or how were the rest of you able to make the change... I don't know... work for you?" Andrew asks. That's when Kabir, Ox and Lynx look over at me, Casey and David. Those two goobers step away from me but point in my direction. *Assholes.*

"So, you really have helped others in the past. I didn't doubt you for a second or anything like that but, well... seeing is believing and you sure have been showing us a bunch of new things." Jamal says with a laugh.

"You can fix people that are... stuck? How?" and a few more questions are thrown at me but Casey and David step in and tell everyone that that's something for another time and place. Most seem okay with that answer but a few seem to want more information and that's when Ben and Wendy step up and get a bit more in depth with their story.

"Look... I wasn't, or... we weren't going to mention any of this because, well... we all kind of promised ourselves that we just wouldn't talk about any of this shit, ever again, but I think y'all need to know a few things." Ben starts after looking at Wendy.

"See... for some reason, when we had... I guess you could say that, well... we all had somehow broken free from our compulsion, or just enough... while we were still in the camp. Like we said before, we all hid the fact that we were no longer totally controllable, even from the other people in our… cage. We'd all seen what happened to anyone that acted differently or showed any signs of having any new abilities or that were just different from everyone else. Because of what we'd seen, we knew that we had to act like everyone else, you know, pretty much like zombies. Plus… I think, maybe, a few people and some of the new beings that were housed in our camp… I think some of them might have been hit with something stronger or maybe just different from what happened to us."

"Yeah… some of those poor folks and such are worse than… than coma patients as far as I'm concerned. They just sit or lay where they're dropped. Most can't even feed or take care of themselves and they have absolutely no self-preservation. It was just so sad and hard to even look at most of them. Even now I still feel guilty for not even trying to help any of them." Wendy says, looking like she's about to cry. Ben wraps her in his arms and whispers to her that there was no way that they would've been able to do anything then, but now? Yeah, we need to get to those camps and liberate… everything. *Mwahaha!* I know my fam really wants to wait until I have an army at my back, but I don't think we have that kind of time. Besides, I really think that we can pull off at least a jailbreak or two with what we've got now. But first…

"Well Jerry, if you can really find things that you, or we need, are you willing to do that for us? Right now? Are you up for it?" I ask.

"What? Oh! Really? Yeah sure! Anything you need I can find for you, just tell me what it is." he says with a big smile on his face.

"Okay, so what I, no, let me rephrase that. Hhmmm. Okay, so what we need is… a place that we can keep secure, a place that we can make our own. My family just keeps getting bigger and we're going to need someplace where we can continue to expand, somewhere where we can grow our own food and a place where the kids can see and meet a lot of new people and new beings. But… it has to be somewhere that they can also grow up feeling safe. Being on the road is hard on them. Is that specific enough?" At the mention of kids Jerry and his group along with Micha and his dogs and all of the new people stare at me and my fam like we've lost our minds.

"Kids? You have kids with you? Travelling with you? Are you fucking crazy? There's some really freaky and bad shit out here! Why would you bring your kids with you?" Doreen demands.

"Oh? Are you serious right now? Why in the world would you expect us to keep them at home? Besides, they aren't my kids, or even any of our kids. I personally don't know who they belong to, but until we find out? they're our kids… Now. Some of them are from Butler but we've helped a bunch of others that have lost… everyone. So, because of that? Yeah, they're ours for now." I say.

"Why shouldn't we have any kids with us? How are they supposed to learn about this new world if they never get to see what's in it or what it's like?" David asks, looking confused.

"But… it's so dangerous out here! They could get hurt!" Liane says. David, even though to me, looks like he's maturing nicely; well, he's still just a fourteen-year-old boy… but I can see the much more mature young man that he's becoming when he turns to look at Jerry, Liane, Amber, Doreen, Micha and his dogs, DC and the rest of the new folks. My sweet boy goes for the throat when he turns his sweet boy smile into his jagged toothed grin, then he turns fully into his full manticore self. *Bwahaha!*

"Look… I'm just a kid, and after the first couple of days after the fog started, I was out in this shi… mess, all alone. I was chased away by my brother and his friends because I was changing. I was lost, scared and alone when Lara and some of the others found me. So there I was, out there, on my own for a while and I saw some freaky and scary shhh… stuff, believe me. I had to fight a couple times too and… I was an absolute mess. But this group? When they found me? Well… they took one look at me, immediately accepted me and took me in... with no hesitations. None. And I was one scary lookin' dude! Back then. So yes, we've got kids with us. We've also got another kid that's kinda like I was. Stuck somewhere between... forms, I guess you could say. My new, no, scratch that, my... forever family... helped me out with that and a bunch of other things. I know that I've been extremely lucky because it was them that found me and not someone or something else. Things could've been a whole lot worse... believe me, I know that. But not only did they take me in, they've given me a strong and loving family to belong to, and they've also been teaching me how to be a good person. Oh, I knew how to be that before all of this started but there's a difference now. Ya know? They're teaching me that it's... well shhh... shoot. I don't really know how to explain it." he says with a slump to his shoulders and he starts to blush at his near misses. *Awww, he's just so cute!*

"David, I think I might know what you're trying to say. Because yes, there is a difference, the difference between just being a nice person and being a person that goes out of your way to prove that it's okay to still be nice, to lend a hand, to help out those in need and not expect anything in return." Lucas says with a thoughtful look on his face.

"Yeah well, I think it goes even farther than that. See... I think that when these nice people help... well... anyone, they're spreading the urge to do the same." Ox says and I think he's thinking back to when some of his group first met Catherine and then he and the rest of his group met the rest of us. Unfortunately I couldn't help the smirk that pops up on my face at his wording and a few others just openly laugh. *Twelve-year-old humor at its finest!*

"Okay, so "urge" might not be the correct or the best term to use here, but you get the gist." he says with a smirk and a laugh of his own.

"True, but let's get back to the kids thing, for a second. See, there's just no way that we can forget that we've come across a bunch of kids that were in some seriously shitty situations. Did we find their parents? Or any relative? No, or at least not for all of them, but they're definitely in a better place now. With people that love and care for them as if they were their own flesh and blood. See… to us? It doesn't matter who you are or who you were born to, if you're in our care? That makes you family." Casey says with pride.

"Now, if you want to start spouting off about DNA? Well, fuck that. To us, as far as I'm concerned DNA stands for Do Not Attempt to fuck around with anyone in our family. It also doesn't matter what… species… you are now, to become a full-fledged member of this motley crew. Does that make sense to anyone?" I ask and I know that my darkness has added her voice to mine.

"Absolutely." a bunch of folks reply with a laugh and a knowing look, or just a look of wonder. Not to mention the shudders.

"Okay, so I think all of this is truly amazing. Everything that you all have managed to do and have accomplished so far is absolutely fantastic. That being said… hmmmm… I think the place you need is southeast of here. How far away it is? I can't say, but I know that it's out there. I also have no idea of how we're going to get there but I'm personally going to make sure that you make it there. If you'll let me continue travelling with you, that is." Jerry says with such a hopeful look on his face.

"Jerry, I think you'll be really surprised at how soon we'll all make it there. Lara here has a nifty… trick… but we're not going to use it just yet." Dozer says with a laugh.

"Oh? Yuck it up, asshole." I say silently with a smirk in his direction. Can you believe he had the nerve to laugh and blow me a kiss? He may be built like a bulldozer, but I bet my darkness and I can bring him to his knees in no time flat. I think the look on my face must have said something close to that because he turned a bit pale and moved away from me. Then it was my turn to blow him a kiss. Casey just gives both of us a look and smirks as he turns away. But before anything else

happens Jones calls out to us and let us know that Jim's dead. When those of us that could hear his call all turn and start rushing for the door, Lucas stops us and asks what's going on now.

"Jones just told us that Jim Bob has suddenly passed away." Zee says as he rushes past us and then out the door at a run. Everyone follows the rest of us out and we make another trek out to our unfortunate friends gravesite. Most of us keep everyone from getting too close to where Jones is standing but we do let Cammy and Andrew have a look. The fact that they both turn green and even gag a little is enough to keep most everyone from even wanting to get any closer. *Uggg, it must really be bad.*

"What the hell happened?" DC and a few others ask as they crane their necks.

"I'm not entirely certain. We were talking and he seemed fine and then… he wasn't. I had no idea how to help him and before I could do anything he was… beyond anything I could possibly do." Jones says calmly and shrugs. Not one single word was a lie. *Good for him.*

Cammy stands up from where she's been kneeling and starts to mutter to herself while shaking her head. "I've worked several rotations in a few different morgues over the years and I've never seen anything like this. And somehow, I can tell that there's nothing I or anyone could've done for him medically or at least without some very heavy magical help, if that makes any sense. Oh! Is that my magical gift? I can magically diagnose people?" Cammy asks with a look of wonder on her face.

"Quite possibly. There's only one way to find out. Check all of us and tell us what you get from us." Zee says with a smile. *He's sooo brave being the first volunteer. Ha!*

"What? I can just do that? And you'll just let me?" she asks. When all of us just nod at her, she continues to smile but then takes in a deep breath and puts on her more professional face? Then she checks over Zee and then turns to Andrew and looks him over and says she doesn't sense or feel anything wrong with either of them. Jones is next and watching her eyebrows disappear into her hairline is a funny sight.

"What are you getting from Jones?" Dozer asks.

"Oh, well ummm… if I'm interpreting things right ummm… he's not human. I mean, his body certainly appears to be but he… isn't? What the fuck? I mean… how is that even possible? Seriously, earlier I saw with my own eyes some of you people change from being part animal to back to being completely human again, so I think I need to check you all out before I can wrap my head around this. But other than that, he appears perfectly healthy to me." Cammy says. Ox, Lynx and Kabir step up to her and she looks at all of them. Cammy tells us that those three feel perfectly fine to her but they also feel totally human so she's still a bit confused about Jones. While she was checking out those three Nat had come up and gotten a good look at what was left of Jim Bob and even she shuddered at the sight. Then she asks Cammy to check her out. Stanley steps up and requests through us that she do the same thing to him. Cammy's shocked speechless for a few seconds then tells us that as far as she can tell, Nat and Stanley are healthy but they're not in any way human. So, we now know that Cammy can indeed diagnose or at least verify someone's wellbeing but her gifts can't or won't go any deeper than surface level on the new beings. That's probably going to change in time, especially when she starts dealing with a lot more of them, but I guess we'll just have to see.

"Wait! Cammy, will you check out Barbie and Ken for us? If you don't think that Nat and Stanley are even remotely human, maybe you can tell if those two are something other as well." I say. So, we all turn and start to tromp back to the motel when Marsh asks if we should bury what's left of Jim Bob. Andrew immediately objects and tells everyone that he doesn't think any of us should get too close to the remains. When we ask him why he tells us that for some reason he feels that whatever caused Jim Bob's demise might be caustic or even poisonous and he doesn't want anyone to get hurt or be affected by it. Marsh then asks about some of the other things roaming around out here that like fresh meat and what would happen if any of them get into Jim Bob's remains. *Good question.* Since no one has an answer Andrew refuses to budge until we put up some type of hazmat something or other to keep everything clear of that area. Then Casey and Dozer finally inform him that Willy and Garth have just let us know that they're going to take care of it and their method guarantees that nothing will get too close. Nothing. Andrew asks us what can they possibly do to keep everything away and none of us are able to say a word because we're all too busy laughing. *Oh gross!*

So, apparently, the coyotes peeing on things guarantees that nothing will get close to what they've peed on? Really? Wow! I'm amazed that their nasty habit is actually useful. I know they've peed on things before to warn others away from whatever it was but them doing that actually keeps everything away for good? That's awesome!

"I'm still going to laugh when they do that though." David says silently and Jones adds in that he probably will too. I honestly think we all will. *Thanks, you hairy goobers.*

"Seriously guys, you peeing on whatever ensures that nothing can or will mess with it? Who came up with that fantastic idea?" I ask and those two inform us that due to the inchworm and the mess that it caused, Kenny suggested that they, the coyotes, should be able to do something to ensure everything's safety, after whatever it is dies. With a bit of a bump in power from me, they came up with the peeing on it thing.

"Are you kidding me? Damn, that makes me miss him even more now." David says with a fond smile and the rest of us that can hear this conversation either just smile or nod. Those that can't hear us just look at us but I think they're coming to the conclusion that whatever we're talking about right now is something that we'll let them in on, later. Even Andrew seems satisfied with our not very good or clear explanation, but

I think he and the others can feel that we're not the type to let others… suffer?… due to our lack of due diligence? Either way we all turn to leave the coyotes to do their "business" and head back to the pool, again.

Once we uncover the damn thing again, everyone in it is starting to crowd the steps and staying as far away from the deep end as possible, except for Ken and Barbie, and by default Gaylene. *Ha!* I guess since they no longer have to listen to her and do what she says, they're either lost or asserting themselves? Maybe? Cammy bravely enters the pool to get close enough to them to check them out and the look on her face is beyond puzzled, then she turns and gets out of the pool in a hurry.

"Well? What did you get from them?" Andrew asks as she walks up to him.

"I got… I don't know what I got. They don't feel human at all but they don't feel like the big purple guy or the spider girl either. Those two at least feel… warm blooded? Which is weird because spiders aren't warm blooded, are they? Oh! Is that the human part of her?" she asks as she looks at Nat and then shakes her head as we all walk back toward the motel. Gaylene and Damarcus beg us not to cover the pool again because whatever is in the sludge at the bottom of the pool is scaring the shit out of them, but when asked what does it look like no one can answer, most just tell us that they can feel something touching them. So we leave the pool uncovered because seriously, they're not going to get out because for some reason, I doubt that they'll work together very well and Stanley takes a perch on the top of one of the vans to keep watch.

I've been in contact with whatever it is in the deep end and I know that it's not considering eating anyone but I'm not going to tell those in the pool that. From what I gather, it wouldn't be able to finish off whoever it decides to eat and the leftovers would pollute its water so eating anyone is not what it wants. But… it is sending out feelers to check them out and it's having fun with it. *Mwahaha!* The look Casey shoots my way lets me know that he knows that I've been in contact with it and he wants to know what I know. I think my smirk is going to have to be answer enough for now.

"I'm not sure we're going to be getting any more company. I've been going over the list the other group had, trying to figure out their shorthand or whatever it is and I think I've figured out that the confirmed new "recruits" are Micha and his dogs, Jerry, Liane, Amber and Doreen. Oh! And our friend that didn't make it is only noted as the "fishy guy" as a name. Well now, that's not very nice. Anyway, there seems to be a couple notations about maybe a few other things that were or are wild on it and I think it says that those things are just a maybe at best." Wendy says as she continues to study the paper.

"That's great! Now we can get the hell out of here." DC says with a laugh.

"Yeah, that's great and all but what are we going to do with those left in the pool? Do we just leave them here? If we do that, they're going to get loose then run back to wherever they came from and then send an army out to hunt us down, right?" Andrew asks.

"Well… that's a distinct possibility but… I don't think they're going to make very good time getting back, seeing as how they're going to be on foot. Am I right?" Jamal asks with a shit-eating grin on his face. Well… he's not wrong. I mean, with all of the people we've got now I was definitely planning on taking their rides. All of them.

"He's right. We're taking their rides. If any of you want to come with us, that's great. Or… you're free to go your own way. It's up to you. But for those that want to go with us, there are a few things you need to know. Also, if any of y'all want to go through Coffeeville and hose down anyone you see and then warn them about what might be coming their way, I suggest you do that." I say as I grab up a couple goop spray bottles and offer it up. Cammy takes one and says that she wants a sample to study and David laughs at her and tells her that Dr. Hathaway has a small jar and has been trying to study it since the day we used it on him.

"I have a question,, if that's alright." Leo asks.

"I'm sure you do." Zee says with a laugh.

"Well, it's just that you said that we could just go our own way if we wanted to. My question is… why would you let us do that? This fucked up group that we've been a part of for… however long it's been…" Leo say with a shrug and seems unable to put into words what he wants to say, but me and most of the rest of my fam, both old and new, we get it.

"Leo right? Well, some of us are new to all of this shit too so bear with me a moment as I try to explain to… all of you. Let's see… I'm going to tell you all about what I know, what I've seen and I'll let you draw your own conclusions. From what I understand, no one is ever forced to join this group, no, this family, if you will. I've heard it said multiple times that joining in is on a completely voluntary basis. The same with doing these little forays. I've even surprised myself when I volunteered to come out here and help with this situation. Am I making any sense here?" Lucas says and the rest of my guys just smile at him.

"Yeah, you're making a lot of sense and… because of that… I don't know about the rest of these guys but… I'm willing to join up." Leo says and it looks like a major weight has been lifted from his shoulders.

"Just like that? You'd leave us and join them? Without talking it over with us first?" Shane asks, looking shocked.

"Yeah, I get what he's saying and doing so… I'm in too, if you'll have me." Ryan says and Jay nods his head too. Shane looks at his former comrades and shakes his head like he thinks they're all nuts but then he seems okay with their decision. I'm not too thrilled with this and Casey, Zee and Dozer all cut their eyes in my direction. Then Doreen and Liane look my way. *Jeez! Did all of them get the same sketchy vibe that I just got?*

"My question might be a bit different but… why is it that I still can't remember… well… much of anything?" Jeff asks, totally missing this strange scenario going on, like most of the rest of this rather large group.

"Oh, this I might be able to answer for you, and for everyone else, if that's what's still going on. When I was talking with Jim Bob earlier he said that he couldn't remember certain things either so I'm going to say… that if someone gave you the order to forget something, then you did. It's almost like taking a chapter, or several chapters out of a book, you know something was there but now… it's gone. Completely erased." Jones says while looking at his notes.

"Oh hey! Could that be why when they brought in certain people and other… sorry, new beings, is that why they seemed almost like newborns? Not able to take care of themselves and things like that?" Wendy asks and Ben looks very thoughtful.

"That's a distinct possibility. If someone was to have told them to forget everything that they ever knew? That might do it."

"Holy shit! The plants powers are that strong?" Shane asks and I get the heebie jeebies.

"Yeah, pretty much. But I think everyone needs to remember that it really all has to do with how the commands are worded. Look at our unfortunate "fishy guy". He was told to stop fighting or whatever and he did, but the problem was he was mainly just fighting to stay in control of his new self. He, or the human part of him was the only thing keeping all of his new self together." Jones replies while still checking his notes. Before I get the chance to ask Casey or anyone else if they're really getting the same feeling that I'm getting, Jay starts to twitch and points out in the direction of the pool and then blurts out "Trojan Horse".

"Care to elaborate on that?" Zee asks while rest of us continue to look as surprised as Jay.

"Oh wow, sorry about that. It's just that... I was wondering about Ken and Barbie and then I... I had... I had to say what popped into my head." Jay says with a tremendous amount of blushing.

"So, what you're saying is that your new gift is now telling you that Ken and Barbie are somehow trojan horses? Or at least something similar?" Dozer asks and I think we're all trying to figure out how that works.

"Maybe? How the fuck am I supposed to know?" Jay says kind of pissy. We don't hold that against him because we get that he's missing at least a couple weeks' worth of knowledge. Doreen and Liane get up and approach Jay as he slouches down on himself. I think they'll be able to help him if he's open for it. In the meantime I think Jerry has some work to do.

"So Jerry? Are you ready to head out?"

What? and you are not going anywhere alone! and not without me! and several other things hit me either silently or out loud. All I can do is snicker a little at the looks on the speakers faces.

"Did I say that we were going alone? No, I didn't. So chill out."

"Uhhh... yeah, I'm ready, I guess but like I said earlier, I don't how long it's going to take us to get there. Are you really going to just leave here? Or not do anything with the assholes in the pool first?" Jerry asks.

"No dude, you don't get it, we're not going to be gone that long, I promise you. Just... let me grab Ryan and Leo." Dozer says with a laugh as he motions for the two he'd named. Ben steps up and asks to go and strangely so does Liane. She shrugs and says that she might be able to tell at a glance if there's anything screwy about the place. Stanley lands close and says that he's not comfortable being left to watch over the food in the pool. *Yikes!* Micha and his dogs maneuver over and tell us that they'd like to be included as well. After that Lucas, Bobby and Jamal step up and Nat starts making tethers for the new folks. Kabir, Ox and Lynx tell us that they'll stay here and start to get everything packed up so that we can leave this shithole when we get back from our recon mission after Lynx hands me my bag of goodies, just in case. But we're not leaving before we find a good, secluded place for me to open to door to my place and I need to stop by the pool and ask Gaylene one last very important question.

"Gaylene? When exactly are you due back?"

"The day after tomorrow." she says after a minute of sweating and shaking.

"So that's the earliest that they're expecting you. Got it. So... what if you run into any trouble, with your new "recruits"? How long do you need to be gone before they send out a search and rescue party?" Jones asks after giving me a meaningful look.

"Five days." she grits out.

"So that's at least six days for us to do our thing. Fanfuckingtastic!" Casey says with a laugh.

"But... if we're leaving here, and not taking anyone left in the pool with us... won't they be able to get back way before the six days are up?" Jerry asks.

"Oh uuhhh... I seriously doubt it. According to Stanley, there's not a usable vehicle for miles around this place." David says with a laugh as we all take a few steps away from the pool.

"If they head for Coffeeville, well... we've been through there and I don't remember seeing anything drivable there either, plus it's going to take them more than a day just to get there." Jamal says quietly and with a sly smile.

"Yeah, but also think about this... do you really think that those in the pool are going to work well enough together to get very far? What with being shackled together like they are?" Jones kind of whispers in return. That got a lot more laughter from all of us. Ox then tells us that he,

Lynx and Kabir know of a place that might fit the bill for us if it's a clear space and where no one can see what's about to happen. When David asks why we're doing it this way I smirk and tell him that sometimes a girl likes to appear mysterious. Casey and Dozer immediately start having breathing issues between gales of laughter. *Assholes.*

"What?"

"Oh! Babe, look… at least seventy five percent of the time, your face gives away what you're thinking. So, because of that you… you don't or… you aren't really That mysterious. Sorry." Casey wheezes out between laughs as he puts his arm across my shoulders.

"Oh! Oh! I bet she's probably thinking that you guys are assholes right about now, am I right?" Ben asks with a laugh as I elbow Casey in the ribs as he continues to laugh.

"Ben right? Yeah uuuhhh… don't help us out here. Okay?" Dozer snorts and gives another laugh. That causes some of the others to crack up. *Damn!* Ben really is pretty spot on. Most of the new folks laugh nervously because I don't think they know what else to do. If they stick around? That'll change, quickly.

So Jerry, Casey, Jones, David, Stanley, Nat, Dozer, Ryan, Leo, Ben, Lucas, Bobby, Jamal, Liane, DC, Micha and his dogs and the coyotes still in stealth mode go with me into my magical place. Those that haven't been in here before are asked to quiet down but I don't think Jerry is even paying that much attention to his new surroundings as he immediately turns to the southeast and heads off in that direction. In less than five minutes Jerry stops walking and shakes his head while looking confused.

"Is this the place?"

"Uhhhh… yes and no. I mean, this is the place but it feels different somehow." Jerry shrugs.

"Well then, let's change your perspective." I say as I open the door to let us all out. Poor Jerry jumps like someone has goosed him when his feet hit the "normal" ground.

"Oh! Now this feels right to me. Oh, wait! How far have we actually gone? I think I missed something while we were on our way here." Jerry says, looking perplexed. I'm stumped as to how to answer him and I don't think even Jones will be able to come up with anything so no one says anything and we all kind of shrug. *Magic is weird.* But then I really look around at where we all are and all I can do is point and laugh. We're all standing in the middle of a road and directly in front of us, a little to the right is a set of road signs. Mystic Springs Road and Worley Road. Jaws drop for most but Stanley immediately does a running leap and takes to the air and the coyotes ghost off to check things out.

"You have got to be shitting me. Mystic Springs Road? We're standing on Mystic Springs Road? What the fuck." Casey says in bafflement.

"Well, uuhhh, since we're now a bunch of magical people and new beings, what better place to come to?" I ask with a straight face. But keeping that straight face is taking everything I've got and even a little help from my darkness since even she thinks the name is hilarious too. "Jerry? Can you tell how far we are from where we were?" Liane asks but a giggle slips out.

"Oh! Uuhhh, well… if the roads were clear and traffic was light… I'd say we were about an hour and a half away, give or take a few minutes. Or about a hundred miles or so. Why?"

"Jerry! We made that trip in just a few minutes! Were you not paying any attention at all?" Liane asks in shock.

"Uhhh… what? Really! Damn! That's incredible!"

"Jerry? What were you feeling or sensing while we were on our way here?"

"Well… it was like I was feeling A Lot of people that Need things. Oh! And a bunch of… of paths? To get to them. Does that make any sense?" Jerry says with a look of bewilderment.

"Maybe not to anyone else but I get you. Thanks Jerry." I say as I pat his shoulder.

"Well? Where should we start? Oh! And do you sense anything?" Casey asks, still looking around in wonder.

"I would suggest the City Hall, which appears to be that way. They'll have maps and other things that we'll need." Jones says as he heads off in that direction.

"Yeah, not to mention a town name. Mystic Springs Road huh?" DC says with a laugh as he follows Jones.

"I have a feeling that no matter what this town's name really is, it's about to change." David barks out while laughing. So down Worley Road we walk and I tell Casey and everyone that's paying attention that all I feel are critters and a few new beings. Nothing seems aggressive or sinister or anything like that, so far, mainly curious.

"Worley Road huh? I had an aunt and uncle and their last name was Worley. I still have three cousins, or I did. Saying that we aren't close is an understatement.." I say as we steadily make our way up to the city hall/police department building. The inside of the building smells a bit musty but other than that everything seems like people just got up and left. Jones and DC have already disappeared into one office while Dozer takes Ryan and Leo to check out the police station side.

"Hey! According to this, the name of this section Is Mystic Springs. It's mainly due to the springs and the camp site directly south of us but we're also a part of McDavid. Wow! We're in Florida!" DC yells.

"You know, I think my… birth mom… said that we have a bit of Irish in our family tree." David says casually then smirks and laughs and dodges getting swatted by a few of us.

"Hey! There's no way to get into the computers here but Jones just ripped the top off of a filing cabinet and we've found some more interesting info. We're in Escambia County and the population of this place is, oh ooops, was 1602. This is a mainly rural community bordered on the east with some protected land and the Escambia River." DC says as he comes out of an office reading a bunch of papers to join the rest of us.

"If we're in Florida, how far are we from the beach?" Nat asks as most of us head back outside to check out some of the other buildings.

"I'm going to guess not that far." Micah says.

"What makes you say that?" Jamal asks.

"Because of the pelicans and seagulls on the roof over there?" Lucas asks.

"The seagulls? No. I've seen them nasty suckers way inland before but the pelicans always stay close to the water's edge." Dozer says as he, Ryan and Leo come out of the police station side.

"You find anything interesting in there?" Casey asks.

"Not really. It's small, obviously. A few desks, two cells, empty armory." Leo says then looks up at the rest of us like he's about to get into trouble for speaking out of turn but we all just smile or nod at him. He relaxes a little more after that.

"I don't know about anyone else but… I'm liking the feel of this place. So, how are we going to get everyone here? Your magic highway?" Ben asks with a laugh.

"I have a question." Ryan says.

"Go ahead." Casey answers.

"Well, it does appear that everyone just up and left here. Coffee still in cups, sitting on desks. No blood or bodies that we've seen so far, right?"

"Yeah, so what's your question." Dozer asks.

"Well… what if, after you or we? move in… what if the original owners show back up and want their stuff back?"

"Well then, if they can prove what's theirs, it's theirs again. Of course there's going to be some type of deal that's going to have to be made in exchange for all of the repairs and stuff that's going to happen when, yes we, if you want, move in."

"Really? You're going to let us move in here, with you? You'll just let them have their stuff back if they come back?" Leo and Ryan say practically at the same time.

"Well yeah. If we need more housing, we'll just go and look for some prefab homes. A bunch of us know how to set all that stuff up. We've recently had a lot of experience with it." David says with a laugh.

"Oh! I think I can do even better than that. See… back in February I went to a conference and got to see and work with something new that's coming out of China, I think. It's a 3D printer but it makes houses and buildings. All you need is some rebar and cement. I also saw the way a bunch of newer prefabs were put together that can be shipped and all you have to do is open them up and hook them up. Now those things were super cool. The best part is, I… I'm pretty sure I know how to make all of that stuff!" DC says with his face shining with excitement.

"Look, we might be in pretty close quarters for a little bit, but then we're going to be able to spread out as time goes on. We'll make do, don't you worry." Dozer snorts out.

"You know, this almost sounds too good to be true but… I believe you. I don't really feel anything wrong with this place except for it being so empty. At the moment." Liane says after spending most of her time here just looking off into the distance in different directions.

About that time Stanley lands and tells us that to the west is a four-lane highway and past that is a lot of open land. There's a lot of open land to the north but everything ends in water not too far to the south. Quite a few empty homes, barns, businesses and a school. Some of the homes and businesses have quite a bit of structural damage but it looks maybe storm related and a few wandering cows and things but he didn't see any people on his search. Not even any bodies. *Shit!* I know that he's hungry and I don't want to freak all of our new people out. But then he goes on to say that there's a place to the north that feels kind of familiar to him. *Huh?* When Jones asks him what he meant by that he can't or doesn't have an answer, just that it feels familiar but he knows that he's never been to Florida before. Then the coyotes return and say that they really like this place but that Stanley's not the only one to feel something familiar because they found that same spot north of us. A new mystery? Damn, it's not like we don't have enough of those already, right?

"Well... what do y'all think? Should we get ready to move everyone that wants to come out here?"

"I don't know about everyone else but... I'm okay with not being on the road all the time. Even if manual labor is in my near future, I know that I'm going to be making something for us and myself. You know what I mean?" Dozer says and I see a lot of other people thinking really hard about this.

"Lara... you need to know something." Casey says all serious.

"What?" I ask, but I'm not liking that he looks like he's about to drop something really heavy on me. My darkness is in complete agreement with me on this.

"Well... it's just that... we had to abandon your tractors and stuff, when we left Lake Village. I think the stoners were planning on expanding their plots." he says so morosely. The only thing I could think to do was try to swat him but he just takes off running, laughing the whole way. Our antics get everyone else laughing but it gets worse when David pops off with "Oh shiiii… shoot! I forgot all about that!" So I take off after him too. Once we're done with that I think everyone really starts making lists in their heads about what we're going to need. It's a good thing Jerry wants to stay with us because I think he's going to be very busy for a while.

"You said something about the springs and a campsite, right?"

"Uhhh yeah, why?"

"Well… let's check that area out next. It might serve as a great place to get people here and to unload some stuff. Plus I'd like to see how high the river is and just get a general idea of what we're going to be working with. RV hookups are going to come in handy if there are any and the same with any cabins. If we're only within walking distance of the camp, then yeah, that's a great place to unload." Casey says while I can practically feel the gears in his head grinding. So we head back up Worley to Mystic Springs Road and turn left. We pass Gunner Road on the right and Dozer, Leo and Ryan laugh. Then Dozer says that that's the perfect place for Perky to set up his shop. A little farther down there's a driveway into the Mystic Springs Cove campgrounds and there's an airstream park, so that's great news. We check the area out briefly and the water is definitely up, but the majority of the flooding is on the other side of the river. From what DC reads off from some of his papers, the river should only be about 14 feet wide here but everyone can tell that it's much wider than that. I'd be willing to bet that it's more than triple that.

"If you look closely here at this dock, it's still solid, like there's been no extreme flooding or anything. Which is weird because look at the other side." DC says as he does a pretty thorough inspection of the main boat launch and dock.

"So all the flooding is only on the other side? That's so bizarre." Leo says while scratching his head. Most of us laugh and David tells him that we've seen some really bizarre stuff recently and that he just needs to open himself up to the fact that magic is here and it's just plain weird. We finish checking out the campsite part and go back to Mystic Springs Road and turn right to check out where the road ends. There's a nice loop to the road and a lot of space for things and us to roam around. DC goes back to reading some of his papers and tells us that everything around here is protect land and that works for us. I'm sure there's plenty of other places around here to build up without messing with the ecosystem. *Not that that hasn't been fucked around with enough thanks to this whole mess. Ya know?*

"Liane? Do you see anything around here that's going to be an issue for us?" Casey asks.

"Maybe something coming out of the water or from across the water but I don't see that being that big of a problem, at least not right now. Actually, I think this place is great and quite frankly I'm tired of the road and running. I really want to rest, for a bit." she says with a laugh and a sigh.

"Anyone else have any objections?" Casey asks and no one says a thing. *Fanfuckintastic! Mystic Springs, here we come!*

"I have no objections but I do have a question." Nat says kind of shyly.

"Alright sister, let's hear it." David says as he leans against one of her legs.

"Well, I mean… is it really alright if I live here, with all of you? I mean, where will I live, ya know?"

"Oh, now that's the beauty of this place; you can pick anywhere you want. You can hang out in any attic or barn around here. Or hang out in the woods, like you were before or find a place near wherever I pick, the options are pretty limitless right now." David says kindly.

"Wait! She's his sister?" Ryan whispers to Dozer and those of us that can hear it all crack up!

"Ha! No, not through any biology that I know of or even blood. They just met… today! But… because they went through a… magical bonding… they're now the next best thing to true siblings, as I understand it." Jones says with a snort.

"No shit? Nat! That's awesome! Now… aren't you glad you came with us?" Bobby says happily as he walks up and gives her a hug. I think she would've blushed if she could have at all of the attention and congratulations that she's getting from everyone here and the camaraderie just keeps getting better as we turn and start walking back to Worley Road. I feel another bond forming but I'm not saying shit about it.

"So how are we going to do this? I mean, how are we going to get everyone here? If we continue on like we're doing, it's going to take us at least a few weeks… or longer, even if we ignore our calling to help out who or whatever's on the way to get here, by road. Bridges have already proven to be an issue and who knows what else we're going to run into. Maybe even some of the Rev's crew." Dozer says while looking around with a happy yet thoughtful expression on his face. Well shit, he's not wrong.

"You're right. This is going to be a logistical nightmare. Even if we move everyone just a few at a time, there's all of our stuff to contend with. Plus hitting the Rev's camps before he even knows about us or… those in the pool if they actually manage to get into contact with some of their people." Casey says looking thoughtful.

"How big can you make your openings? Would it be possible to drive through?" Jones asks, pen poised over his trusty notebook.

"You want to do experiments? Now?" David asks with a laugh.

"Of course. See, the way I see it, she's already started. That reminds me, where are the ones you've somehow trapped in your magical place? I mean, no one has run into any of **THEM** and some of you have been in and out of there at least twice since the incident."

"Well, I don't know how big I can make an opening but as far as I can tell, it closes on its own after I'm in there and step away. I don't know if I can keep a door open without being there and I sure as shit can't… no… I won't ask… him… for help."

"That's as it should be, but… can we, or you try to open a door and have Nat make a web or something to keep it open?" Ben asks, even though he has absolutely no idea about some of what we're talking about. For some reason, that strikes several of us funny, though it's not. Not really. But it certainly is thinking outside of the box.

"How about it sister? You up for a little experimenting?" David says with an eyebrow wiggle; but damn, he made it sound so… nasty. I'm absolutely positive that he's been spending way too much time with a few of the SEAL's because even Casey looks shocked. Dozer looks like he swallowed a bug or something as well. That leaves Sonny and Zee. My money is on Sonny. He may look wholesome and intellectual, maybe even the silver spoon type but some of us have learned better while working with him making gizmos. (*It wouldn't surprise me if he has a Fifty Shades of Grey thing going on.*) Nat must've thought it sounded nasty too because she gives him a swat, knocking him over.

"Brother? That sounded more like you were propositioning me for a fuck than trying to figure out how we're going to get people here in a timely fashion." She tells him with a sharp claw pointed at him. All I can do is laugh and thank my lucky stars that I'm not the one putting him in his place. He's really a good kid and I'm afraid that I might come across… too harsh. Dozer leans over and whispers that he'll have a man to man talk with him but he's trying not to chuckle. *Uncle Dozer to the rescue!* Casey leans in and whispers that we need to tell Sonny that he needs to tone it down a bit, while trying to contain his own laughter.

Nat turns to me and asks if we should give it a try anyway and all I can do is shrug while trying not to laugh at the look on David's face. Then she asks what kind of web should we try and Jones asks her if she can put a web just around the edges of the opening.

"You know, I probably could if I could see the fuckin' thing." she huffs. Yeah, that's a problem.

"Well, that was a good idea but I think we're all going to have to think a little harder on this one. In the meantime, I think we should head back." Casey says still looking thoughtful.

"Oh! Yes, but along the way, could you show us the last place you saw your… unwanted visitors?" Jones says.

I shrug and say sure as I open the door or whatever it is and take us all back into my magical space. I know the way to go but Jerry immediately takes the lead and we stop only a few yards from where I last saw one of **THEM**.

"How did you know to come to this place?" I ask, surprised.

"What? Oh, are we here? This is just too weird. Were you actually needing to find something here?" he asks, kind of dazed. *Maybe?*

Everyone stays clumped together as I make a circuit around them and then I stumble over something. I can't really see what it is but it does kind of remind me a recently filled hole. You know what I'm talking about, the humped-up earth? When I bend down and put my hand on it I know immediately what's under the hump. It's one of **THEM**.

"Is that…? Holy fuckin' macaroni! This place… ate one? Really?" Casey asks in shock. I think I'm in shock too because I really didn't think that this place Could eat anyone. The hump is smooth, not lumpy like it should've been if dirt had been shoveled over a body and it wasn't as big as it should've been either. **THEY** are over 7 feet tall and have a tail. *WTF?*

"Well… apparently so. Huh. Now you did say that your travel experience was quicker, correct? It appears that this place has not exactly… eaten this one but… it seems to have, maybe, absorbed it? What about the other two? Are they close by?" Jones asks while writing away in his notebook after kneeling down next to the… not grave but maybe **IT'S** new prison?

"Uhhh… I think the other two are more over that way." I point in the direction I think might be the spots so we all slowly walk that way. Liane finds the next one, by stumbling over it, and it's just like the last, weirdly smooth and really only the size of a large manhole cover? *Holy shit!* Were **THEY** absorbed standing up? Jerry finds the third one and just stands by it, looking dazed. Jones comes over and studies this one just like the last two.

"If **THEY** have been absorbed, there really shouldn't be anything left but… this appears to me like **THEY'RE** being used as perhaps… some type of batteries?" Jones says.

"Wait, wait, wait! What are you guys talking about?" Lucas asks.

"Wait! Wendy told me that you said something about something following you and that's what killed those four in the barn. Is that who you're talking about? The things that were following you, uuhhh us?" Ben asks.

"Yes, that's what we're talking about." David says staring at the hump in wonder.

"When was the first time that you noticed that you were being followed by this new bunch. Was it in Butler?" Jones asks.

"No, not in Butler. The first one I felt was as we were leaving the grocery store in Gilbertown, so that one might've... latched on... when we stopped for gas right after that."

"So, our followers were right when **THEY** told us that you'd been spotted in Alabama but not where."

"**THEY** spoke to you?" I ask.

"Oh yeah, a couple times. At first **THEY** were pissed that you were missing. Then **THEY** uuuhhh... **THEY** asked us to tell **THEM** if we ever find out where you are. Oh shit! **THEY'RE** going to be pissed off again when we go back because no one said anything to **THEM**. I mean, we just left!" David says and he didn't even blush at his blunder.

"When was the last time you were contacted?"

"A couple days ago, I think. Why?" Casey asks.

"I've been followed for a couple days now and as you can tell... the new ones aren't anything like ours."

"And this means what?"

"Well... think about this for a minute. We've had several directly interfere with us and supposedly that's a big fucking no-no, right? Once... when we met John, Judy and Wally at Judy's place. I think that... some of **THEM** were trying to keep us from taking and making friends with our crystals. Then one started messing with Riley. I know our regulars flat out told the **OTHERS** that that is not allowed. But... another one messed with Chance and his crystal right after that. Or maybe that started before, who the fuck knows. But look... if **THEY'RE** truly a hive type mind and everything is shared and everything is known by each other, then why have there been so many attempts to fuck us over or flat out kill us?"

"You've mentioned this before. You don't think that all of **THEM** are on the same page or… playing by the same rules; the rules that **THEY** made."

"Exactly. Something is really wrong somehow with **THEM** and… we're getting the brunt of it… I think. Look… with the three in here, I'm going to say that these are… more of the rogue element, like some of the **OTHERS** we've run into have been. I think these rogues are the ones that want humanity to fail. The question is, why?"

"So you're saying that you think the game is rigged? So to speak?" Ben asks.

"Yeah. And the problem with that is, how do we convince our followers that I think that even **THEY** are being used."

"Well… it has been pointed out before." Casey says looking concerned.

"True but… did **THEY** take heed?" Jones answers before I can.

"Let's get back to your… new batteries… for just a moment. Just for the sake of argument here, and not really understanding all of this but… if **THEY** are in constant contact, as a collective, wouldn't there be a shit ton of **THEM** all over the place looking for the ones that have now gone missing?" Lucas asks.

"Ahhh. That's another very good point." I say and some of the newer folks and all of my long-time family start nodding their heads.

"Uhh, sorry but… since some of us have absolutely no idea what you all are talking about, can I make an observation?" Ryan asks.

"Sure, go right ahead." Dozer says.

"Okay… I'll start out by calling us the… home team and the other side… just… the opposition. Makes it easier that way, right? Okay so… you have some followers that are on or are perhaps rooting for the home team, right?" Ryan says.

"Well, we do have some followers and I'd like to think that **THEY'RE** rooting for us. But... sorry, go on." I say.

"So, what exactly is it that you'll win? Or I should say... what's the game about?" *Well shit.*

"The game in a nutshell is... the survival of the human race... as a whole." Jones says. I think he's shocked the shit out of all the newcomers.

"What?" is said or yelled multiple times by all of them.

"Long story short here. **THEY** are responsible for the orange fog and for magic being... reintroduced?... into the world. I'm pretty sure that the magic is a natural byproduct of **THEIR** reemergence. Anyway, I was told early on that I would have to Impress **THEM** enough or the human race was or is going to be wiped out. But... I'm not the only one that has to impress **THEM**. **THEY** have chosen other people and things to... I guess give it their best shot."

"Are you serious? That's... that's..." Liane says.

"Look, we've recently learned that the Rev has also been chosen and... I'm not sure what all of that means but I'm getting the feeling that he's also got a few of the **OTHERS**, or in this case, the opposition, on his side and I think that **THEY'RE** some of the ones not playing by the rules." Casey says.

"Now that I believe. Don't ask me why but... yeah. He's able to do too many things and... The fucker is cheating! Of course he is!" DC says exasperated.

"But you said that your followers are playing by the rules so... the opposition has a type of home field advantage or more likely has the referees in their pocket or something, right? So... are we losing?" Ryan asks.

"Fair question. Now let me ask you one. But wait... I want all of you to think about this but I need Ryan to answer. Do you feel like a loser?

Yes, I know that you've Lost a lot of things in the past almost forty days but, do you feel like you've lost… everything? The better question is, are you the type that's willing to just give up… on everything? See… I guess what I really want to know is… are you willing to just sit on the sidelines or are you going to get in the game with the rest of us?" Dozer says. *Hot damn!* I'm glad my crystals and Jones with his notebook caught all of that! That was one fanfuckingtastic mini speech. Or is it more of a convoluted pep talk? Either way, it's great!

"Hey! I'm no benchwarmer. I'm in." Ryan says with conviction. Leo, Liane, Micha, Lucas, Jamal, Bobby, DC and Nat all echo Ryan's declaration almost immediately. *Sweet!*

"Holy shit! Is this what you're going to be talking to us about when you get us all together again later today? Wendy said you told Larry and Eddie that you'd fill them in on something. And this is that something? That's… I mean… Holy shit! But you know what? I'm in too." Ben says. All I can do is shrug and laugh at him. Dozer claps him on the shoulder and Casey just grins. Then I look at Jerry to see what he has to say about all of this but he's just looking off into the distance.

"Jerry? Are you okay?"

"What? Yeah, maybe. This place is… what is this place?"

"I don't really know. What I do know that it was made for me and… someone… by my girls and Chance, as a way for us to be together. Actually, I think it's worked better than my girls or Chance ever thought it could. I also know that it's changed, a lot, over the past couple weeks. Even more so after Chance tried to fuck things up for me and especially now that it has a new set of "batteries". Does any of that help answer your question?"

"Not really, but then again, I don't think I really know how to ask the right question." he says with a shrug and a smile.

Jones has been on bended knee for a minute or two trying something but then he stands up.

"So, you can feel that **THEY'RE** here, right? Are **THEY** still alive?" Jones asks.

"Well yeah. This one here is… quiet, like **IT'S** asleep or something. Or more like **IT'S** gone back into hibernation or something. Why?"

"Bear with me here but would you check the other two for me?"

"Sure." I say as I walk over to another one. I put my hand down and I can't control the snort that slips out.

"What? Is this one different?" Casey ask and pulls his gun, then shrugs.

"Yeah, you could definitely say that. This one isn't quiet at all. Actually, **IT'S** pissed."

"What are you getting from **IT**?" Jones asks.

"Oh, a bunch of stuff. Some of it isn't even words but feelings, I think."

"Can you talk to **IT**?" he asks and I shrug but the look on my face has my long-time fam and even a couple of the newer folks suddenly shifting like their getting ready to run or tackle me or something. *Well shit. I guess I'm really not all that mysterious after all. Ha!*

"Hey there, you dumb fucker. How's it hangin'?" I ask with a darkness infused laugh. I guess everyone could feel the sinister or malevolent vibe or… maybe just the cloud of hate? that came out of the ground at my question because they all back up, some more than others. "Ha! So **YOU** assholes Are responsible for the bad vibes feeling that's invaded my magical place. But that's okay, we're going to change that, don't **YOU** worry."

"You will release US! Now!" a deep growly voice says.

"I don't think so. Besides, I don't even know how it is that **YOU'RE** trapped in here."

"What do you mean, you don't know! You did this! You will fix this! Now!"

"Apparently I did name **YOU** correctly. **YOU** are one dumb fucker. Like I said before… I don't know how to release **YOU**. But even if I did, I don't think I'd be doing it just yet."

"WE will kill you when WE get out of here!"

"Well… it certainly won't be the first time some of **YOU** have tried that. Jones, do you really want to ask this dumb fucker some questions?"

"WE will not answer!"

"That's fine by me but… think about this for a moment will **YOU**? We've figured out that not all of **YOU** are connected to the collective or whatever it's called at all times, otherwise… there'd be a shit ton of **YOU** all over the place looking for **YOU** three, correct? So… who even knows that **YOU'RE** missing?" Jones says with a snort while scribbling away in his notebook.

"Damn Jones! Not only are you cussing and using the words correctly but that was an amazingly petty jibe." I say as I walk up to him and give him a hug. Sometimes he gets flustered when we praise him and this is one of those occasions. It's hard to believe that he can blush but his happy thoughts and ours go a long way in helping to clear the air and replace some of the bad vibes with good ones. *How fucking amazing is that?*

"It appears that I'm… learning from the best." Jones snarks and the rest of us laugh. *Fanfuckingtastic!*

"Are we done in here or in this place and do we need to come out and inform the crew that's here that they need to start packing up?" Ben asks after giving Jones a high five.

"We're almost done in here I think but I would like to try the last one, just to see if that one will answer. I'd like to have as many answers as I can so that we can give our followers something to think over before attacking us. If that's what **THEY'LL** do. But quite honestly, I think Lara should be the one talking to our followers since **THEY** do listen to her more than us." Jones replies and then heads back in the direction of the last one of **THEM** that's trapped in here. Smart thinking but he's also throwing me under the fucking bus. Well… I guess it's a good thing I've always got armor on nowadays. *Ha!*

"So… are **YOU** willing to talk or should we just leave **YOU** here with the rest?" I ask after we find the last one and stand in a circle around **IT**. The miasma that comes up out of the ground isn't near as potent as the last one.

"You will let US out of here!" hissy voice says.

"In case you missed it, I already told the last one that I can't do that because I don't even know how it is that **YOU'RE** stuck in here." I say but my darkness has a question of her own. "Hey! Are **YOU** willing to concede that this is pretty fucking impressive?" she asks. That question was on the tip of my tongue but I wasn't really going to piss hissy voice off quite that much, just yet, but now that the cat's out of the bag, so to speak, yeah, an answer to that would be appreciated.

"WE will kill you!"

"Not if **YOU** can't get out."

"What do you want from US?" hissy voice says but I think there's a lot of… fear… in that question.

"**YOUR** story would be a good start but we're really not expecting that. No, my first question is what happened when **YOU** first entered here?"

"That answer is much too technical and you would not understand it."

"We are not stupid! But maybe it would help to… dumb it down for us." my darkness growls.

"Fine. This place, at first, felt like it's made up of the same… magic… that WE use to coexist in this world, but it does not act like it and it has done something to US that WE cannot… figure out. In order to protect US WE have tried to put a protective cover around US, but even that is not working well since this place continues to… leach… from US. Now WE are trapped here. If WE open the protective barrier, just to move, more is sucked out of US. When too much is taken, WE lose certain abilities."

"Is that what happened to the one that's not… conscience… anymore?"

"The first of US in here tried many things and now you can see the result of those efforts." hissy voice says with anger and fear mixed in with the arrogance.

"Well, **YOU** are correct in that we don't understand but then again, we don't understand most of this magic bullshit and the learning curve is majorly screwed up, but we'll figure something out. Eventually. But I get the feeling that **YOU** don't have that much time." Casey says with a mean smile and chuckle.

"The last statement appears correct if something is not done… quickly." hissy voice says with menace. Well… since none of us have a clue in how to get these fuckers out of my magical place, I think **THEY'RE** screwed. From the looks on everyone else faces, they're feeling the exact same way that I am. Quite frankly, I'm okay with that. But first…

"How is it that some of **YOU** can separate from the rest? I know that it's not a permanent thing since **YOU** knew to look for me and passed on at least part of my location. Can **YOU** just turn it on and off at will? And why exactly would **YOU** do that? Isn't that against the rules of engagement or something? I mean… the three of **YOU** weren't attached to the… whole? … of the **OTHERS** before and even now **YOU'RE** not even connected to each **OTHER**, are **YOU**?" I ask.

"Now that is one colossal mistake. No oversight, which might be part of the problem but that also means no backup and no rescue either. I take that to mean that we were never meant to even come close to winning or impressing **YOU** enough to let the human race continue. So… why the ruse? Was it just to study us?" Jones asks, his pen poised over his notebook.

*"**WE** do not know the reason for some of what is happening now. **WE** have been here since the beginning of this planet's… ability to sustain life. **WE** have been… integral in its development. When **WE** emerge it is mainly so that **WE** can make adjustments then go back to slumber. Some of **US**, over multiple millennia, have remained… awake… to ensure what changes have been made continue to progress. Those of **US** that stayed awake for long periods obviously became… separate. **THEY** passed on the knowledge of how to do that to Others when **THEY** would emerge to check on the progress of certain experiments. Most of **US** do not see the advantages of that or want to participate in those activities so those of **US** that are able to separate do so and are not interfered with."* hissy voice says and I think a lot of us here have picked up on a few things that this one has inadvertently revealed. Yeah, we are not stupid.

"Does this thing think we're really that stupid?" Dozer grumbles silently. A few of the other folks with us look like they want to say something but I hold up my hand and motion for them to keep it quiet for the time being. *"If I'm getting this correctly, I think **IT**'s saying that **THEY** are not from here, originally but… are **THEY**… tera formers of some kind? Either way, **IT** really didn't answer the questions the way I thought **IT** would. I also don't think that we should discuss anything further where **IT** can hear us."* Jones says silently.

"Let's get out of here and tell Larry, Eddie and everyone else that they need to start packing up so that we can get the hell out of here before the Rev and his assholes or even more of these assholes find us." Ben says with a strange look on his face.

"Damn! You did say his guesses are pretty spot on but holy shit balls!" Casey says with a laugh.

At that I turn and walk closer to the barn area with everyone following behind and when I open the door to let us out something comes streaking in causing quite a few folks to pull weapons and such. My little buddy hits me square in the chest them holds on while he chitters away at me in a scolding manner.

"What the fuck is that?" several ask. I just laugh and try to get Gilly to settle down.

"This is Gilligan, my little buddy." I get a couple groans and a few guffaws as I shrug then say, "I guess he's missed me or something because he's not worried, just mad." I finish with a laugh as Gilly finally settles down enough to sit on my finger while giving me really good eye contact.

"Is that what's been zipping around out in the "normal" for the past few minutes?" David asks with a laugh as he tries to get a better look at Gilly. Other folks gather around to see him too and Gilly fluffs up his feathers and kind of preens at them.

"What… what is he?" Leo asks looking shocked and I think impressed.

"Well, he's part hummingbird part lizard of some kind, probably anole and some type of bug."

"He's so cute! Like a mini dragon or something." Liane says and he wiggles his antennae at her. *OMG. Why am I always surrounded by flirts?*

"So he knew you were here, or at least close by? And he's able to come in here on his own? Once you opened a door?" Jones asks while turning to a clean page in his notebook.

"He can see your doorway? Hey! Maybe he can help Nat with that, you know, so that she can make sure the door doesn't close?" David says while giving Gilly a gentle chin scratch with one of his claws. Dozer opens his mouth to say something then just shakes his head and chuckles. *Hey! He's finally learning!*

"Well… we can give that a try in a bit and a little farther away from **THEM**. I don't want to get anyone's hopes up or having **THEM** try to make a mad dash for the exit, you know what I'm saying?"

"Point taken." Dozer says and a lot of other folks nod. As we step out of my place Larry, Eddie, Marybeth, Henry and Jalen all come out from behind their cover and lower their weapons.

"Have you been around here for a little bit?" Larry asks and we all nod.

"Your little buddy there has been going crazy, zooming around the place, so we figured that it might be you." Eddie says with a relieved smile.

"Either that or we were about to be getting more company of some kind. He makes a pretty good first warning system." Marybeth says with a laugh and everyone else comes out of the house and more introductions are made. Most of the newest folks were truly shocked to see so many kids but that didn't stop them from getting in on the nice to meet you hugs from most of them. Emily on the other hand attached herself to me as soon as she came out of the house.

"As you can see we've picked up a bunch of new people and the best part is, is that we've found a really good place to call our own. If you want to that is." Ben says while looking at Eddie and Larry. I think the look on his face was enough for them because they both nod their heads and smile.

"You found a place? Is it near here?" several ask at the same time.

"Let me rephrase that. Jerry here, he found us a really good place and no, it's not around here. So, if you want to go there I guess y'all better get everything packed up and we'll get you there pretty quickly." Ben finishes with a cheeky grin in my direction.

"Have you been having any problems or seen anything suspicious?" Dozer asks.

"What? Oh, you mean because of the guns? No, not from people, we still haven't seen any of those but we have seen a few uuhhhh new beings, heading south. A bunch of them cut right through here." Henry says with a smirk then a laugh.

"Oh yeah? What'd you see?" several ask.

"I don't know really. I mean… there was some deer in there mixed with some raccoon and armadillo and possibly something else. I'm just not sure but there was like a herd of them and each one was just a little bit different from the rest but, I mean they didn't bother us at all. Scared the shit out of us at first but… They just looked around a bit and then went on their way through the yard." Henry says with wonder and a rueful smile on his face.

"They were probably looking for Lara. All the critters look for her and some even ask about her." David says with a fond smile of his own. All the new folks here turn and look at me.

"What? Okay so my new calling started out as a Dr. Doolittle type of thing. Then it kind of morphed into… well… a lot of things." I say with a shrug. *Could word of mouth made it this far? How cool is that!*

"Wait! You mean things have continued to change? Even after the first few days?" Liane asks in surprise.

"Well… yes."

"Things are constantly changing… for us… it seems." Casey says with a smirk and he shoots a look in my direction.

"Uuhhh… I have a question." Ryan says and all of us motion for him to spill it.

"So uuhhh… what happens if you don't like what you get? I mean, what if you uuhhh…" Ryan asks looking lost as how to finish his question but Bobby steps up and tells him that he didn't like what he'd gotten until Nat and I made him think outside of the box. Now he couldn't be happier. I think that summed it up nicely and got a few of the others thinking about that as well. But seriously, I think if anyone gets something that's awful or maybe even damaging and can't control it, maybe, just maybe the plants can help with that too? Maybe that will help them realize that their gifts are good and needed? And maybe that'll help them heal more in the process? It's definitely something to think about. But right now we've got to get this shit show on the move. I'm still feeling that we need to get a move on.

"How soon can y'all have everything packed up?" I ask. By the amount of smiles and laughter going on I think that everything that we've got is already in the buses and everyone here is just waiting on those of us that are on this op and the new folks. *Fanfuckingtastic!* "We're just waiting on you sweetheart." Marybeth says with a cheeky grin.

"Sweet! But uh… which bus has Nat's sack in it?" I ask and everyone points at the second bus.

"So, I hope everything in the first bus isn't too essential in case this goes sideways." I mutter. Those closest to me try to hide their smirks.

"So, what are you thinking?" Lucas asks.

"I'm thinking that if I open a door and we push this bad boy through, then push it out the other side, that'll at least give everyone the bus and everything that's on it when they get there?"

"If that works, then moving the other bus should be easier. Hey! I said should be. I'm not making the same mistake that Tarina's made in the past." Dozer laughs. *Smartass.*

"If this works, I'm going to have to get on the horn to the General." Casey says and I agree with him but I really hope that the General doesn't try to rope us in to becoming a moving service to go along with all of the other shit he's gotten us to do. I don't think he'll like how I make my refusal to that known. My darkness giggles in the background and the guys look over at me.

"That is some freaky shit right there. You know that, right?" Zee asks and shudders.

"What ahhh… what was that all about?" Casey asks.

"Oh, you know, thinking about your upcoming chat with the General and in the past all of the shit he's roped us into doing."

"You've caught on to that, have you? Well, just so you know, according to him, you can't get into too much mischief if you're busy. But… I really don't think that that applies to us… anymore." Casey says with a laugh.

"Oh? No matter how busy we are, somehow… some of us still manage to find mischief, or more to the point… mischief finds us. Right?" Jones says then snorts.

"That sums it up nicely, right there." Dozer says with a laugh.

"Alrighty then, let's see if this'll work. But uhhh… this bus is going to be heavy, you realize that, right?" Larry says.

"Yeah, it is, but… it's a good thing we've got lots of guys with big muscles all around us. Right?" Marybeth says with a laugh. Nat laughs even while she's making a bunch of tethers for everyone else so I guess it's time to see if this is going to work.

I stand in front of the bus and then I step up onto the first step after I open a door. Jalen's brave enough to volunteer to be the "driver" and already has it in neutral. He's got such a maniacal grin on his face so even if this goes wonky, I'm pretty sure he's up for whatever. The door is big enough, I think, and then the bus starts moving. Everyone on foot is tethered up to at least someone that's tethered to the guys pushing. I wonder if I should've had Emily up here with me. Her power boost might've made this a little easier, but then again… Maybe we'll give that a try… later.

The bus and everyone behind it makes it into my special place and I can hear some of the chatter even over the bus's idling engine. I also can hear a couple of the guys bragging about how smooth this is going. I quietly ask Jalen to tap the breaks. He holds up and hand then laughs and disappears under the steering wheel and comes up with a fuse. Then we hear the guys pushing start complaining to whoever said something that they spoke too soon. *Ha! He took the break light fuse out! Bwahaha!* Gilly comes zooming in about a couple minutes later and I get out of the bus and walk the last few dozen yards on foot then open another door to let us out. Gilly beats the coyotes out by a hairs breath. I guess they're off to check things out while the rest of the group emerges from my magical path. I've got the bus facing west but almost at the end of Worley Road, the city hall and everything else is now in front of us.

"Oh my! This looks just wonderful!" Sandra says while looking around. Larry, Eddie, Marybeth and Henry are all smiles and the kids look excited to explore or just play.

"Pick a place that can house everyone for a few days. Let's stick together for a while longer as we clean this place up and settle in. We're going to be bringing in more people in a little bit." Zee and Dozer tell everyone at the same time and Leo and Ryan jump in to help the Butler group with which buildings would work the best for our immediate needs. It's good to see them being so gung-ho and eagerly helping out.

"Sorry guys but we're going to need your muscles getting the other bus here but once it is, y'all can stay and help out if you'd like or come back to the motel with us. The choice is yours." I say with a smirk at their sudden downtrodden faces.

"Jalen, you ready to do this again?" I ask with a wink and he gives me a thumbs up and a very mischievous smile. *Ha!*

So some of us go back into my magical place but before the door closes Gilly comes zipping back in, very excited. I ask which place he likes better, Mystic Springs or my magical place and he lands on my shoulder and lets me know that both are good with him. Within a couple minutes we're back to get the other bus and Nat's egg sack but in the time we were gone a large group of critters had wandered up and are milling around the bus.

"Holy shit! Would you look at that?" Ben says in wonder. Everyone else is just as awed by the sight. These must be what Henry and the others had been talking about. It's a… herd? of regular and new beings that have deer, raccoon, possum, and who knows what else mixed in but some are also mashed together. The blends seem to be working really well. Everything moves naturally and except for some of the teeth, yeah, these new beings look… not exactly harmless but…

"Can I help you with something?" I ask as I approach one of the ones with big antlers or horns. It, no she steps forward and asks if we're going to be staying here or at least close by. I tell them that we're just passing through and that made quite a few of them look sad.

"Are you being hunted or threatened here? If so, you're more than welcome to come and check out the place we're claiming as our own territory. There's plenty of room." I say and several of the new folks just stare. She asks if where we're claiming our territory is near here and I tell he no, it's quite a distance away. She then tells me that her herd is not in any distress at this time but she does know through others of several different kinds of things that are afraid where they are. I ask her if the ones that are afraid can come here and she tells me that she feels that they're too far away. Well this sucks. But then I remember Sophia's message to me. That I'll be saving a lot of people and other things by using my new path.

"Can you give me a direction or a location in which to find any of them?" I ask and she steps closer and I put my hand on her muzzle. And somehow she shows me a little of several locations. *How awesome is that?* Then I ask her if she's able to pass on the message that we're going to be coming for them but we don't know when yet. There's a few other things that need to be taken care of first. Then Willy and Garth materialize out of nowhere it seems and they sit calmly by me but I can tell that they're doing a serious amount of sniffing.

"What are you guys up too?" I ask them. They tell me that somewhere in the herd are several females that have some type of canine in them and that they're in heat. *Oh shit!* I just turn my head up to the heavens and close my eyes as both of the coyotes stand up and let their willies drop down. There's a bunch of gasps and other noises from everyone here. Nat comes closer to me and asks what is going on.

"Well, apparently, there's a few females in that herd that are in heat at the moment and the boys are showing them their goods. You know, in hopes of getting some action." I say with a shrug.

"Are you fucking kidding me?" Nat barks out with a laugh. I roll my head her way and I can't answer her because I'm too busy laughing too. Everyone else is having no problems displaying their shock at this new development.

"Boys, if you manage to get lucky, you know your way back to the motel, right? If you take too long, we'll swing back this way later to pick you up." I say as I turn away because I've already seen Willy's goods and once is enough for me. Casey catches up with me almost immediately and we both try really hard not to continue to laugh. Everyone else quickly follows us to Nat's nursery bus and the looks on their faces is too much. *Bwahaha!* Several people open their mouths to ask something but I hold up my hand and tell them that if their question has anything to do with Willy and Garth, or their not so wee willies, I'm not going to answer it. Most mouths close with a snap. Nat just continues to cackle as she gets on the bus and checks out her egg sack. Jalen tries to contain his mirth but a few snorts slip out while he starts the bus and pulls the taillight fuse again. Even I'm having a hard time of it when I open a new door to my new path and I know that most of the guys pushing the bus are struggling because we can hear them. Then I hear David asking Nat how heavy her egg sack is because being weak from laughter or not, this bus is heavier than the last one. Jalen continues to snort at that. *Bwahaha!*

Maybe it was our laughter or maybe it was just that there's so many of us that are feeling something, anything other than rage or hate, but my place feels a whole lot lighter at the moment and we get to Mystic Springs quicker than the last time. Even with Jalen riding the brakes almost the whole way. *Ha!* I get out and manage to open the door with enough space behind the first bus so that when Jalen stops this one, there's still room to maneuver. I can hear the guys panting and complaining that they all need a break and probably a beer or two. Everyone who'd stayed behind appears as if by magic with water and beers for all.

Then Casey reaches for his radio. But before he places his call I ask him to wait a minute because the box with the crystals in it is making such a racket that I have to find out what's going on with it. As soon as I touch it names are being called out so I ask for everyone to gather around. I pick up the first crystal I touch and call out Jalen's name. He takes the crystal pendant with a shrug but then his face lights up with the biggest smile I've ever seen from him. Once everyone sees that, when their names are called, everyone eagerly steps forward to get their new friend and bling. After everyone has their new friends and are getting to know them then I motion for Casey to continue. He doesn't look too happy. Casey grabs a beer and chugs it while getting out his radio and calling the General.

"Casey? Has there been any word?"

"Yes sir, there has. As a matter of fact, we know where she is and what she's up to. Plus… I know what she wants to do… very soon." Casey replies while giving me a considering look.

"Ah. That's certainly good news."

"I would hold off on that until you hear her plan." Zee snarks.

"Well don't keep me in suspense."

"Well sir, there's a group that she's run afoul of and I'm in complete agreement that they need to be taken care of… immediately and harshly. Her plan, as of a couple hours ago is to hit their recruitment and training camps."

"Hmmm… I don't know about that. That's a lot of collateral damage to have to deal with and the ramifications could be huge."

"Not necessarily. She's not the one planning on wiping them out. She's going to let the newly freed hostages do that." Casey says while giving me a thumbs up.

"Explain." That one word… said that way somehow gets under my skin and my darkness doesn't like it either. But… it appears I'm not the only one feeling that way from the look on a lot of faces.

"It appears that all of the hostages and even the soldiers are under a compulsion… to obey. I've met a few of both and the ones that we've released from the compulsion are angry and rightfully so. And that's just the people. I can only imagine what the new beings are going to be thinking once released." Casey says with a nasty smile on his face.

"Wait, what? You've met some on the newly released? How? Did she… send them to you?"

"Uuuhhh… yes sir. I've personally met some of the former soldiers and some of the soon to be hostages. As to how? Well… She showed up and some of us accompanied her to be in on this op."

"WHAT? How is...? Where are you presently?" the General barks. Casey pinches the bridge of his nose while contemplating what to say next, I think.

"Well sir, one of the people that was under compulsion is... what would best be describe as a... locator. He was asked to locate her a place that we could call our own. And he came through... brilliantly, I might add. So the exact location is now going to be called Mystic Springs." "Casey... that's all well and good but you didn't answer my question. Where are you." the General asks with a growl and Casey holds out his hand for another beer, silently lamenting the fact that it's not something stronger. I hand him another already opened can and he chugs it, just like the last one.

"Some of us are here in Mystic Springs... Florida." Casey says and unkeys the mike to let out a burp and hang his head while waiting for the explosion that he knows is coming.

"WHAT? Did you just say Florida? How the fuck did you end up there? You were just in Mississippi! I'm not that bad at geography I'll have you know. I also know that there's NO WAY that you could've made it to Florida in less than ten hours. Not with the roads like they are." the General ends with another barking growl. Dozer, Zee and Casey all stand straighter because of that sound but then Jones snorts and that's it. We all crack up and the guys lose their former rigid stance.

"Yes sir, you are correct. There's no normal way to get from Mississippi to here." Casey says, trying valiantly to keep his snicker from being heard.

"Casey... what the fuck is going on?"

"Well... you know that we've had some suspicion that she's been going places... without us. What we didn't realize was where and... how far she can go. Or even how she's doing it. Now... some of us have experienced this new phenomenon." Casey tries to hedge.

"Why are you dancing around this?"

"Because there have been some difficulties with this and there's still a very monumental learning curve going on. Plus, it's her business." Casey says while looking at me and shrugging.

"Explain." the General demands. *Oh hell no.* I take the radio from Casey and hand it to Lucas and ask him to continue to listen in while I grab Casey, Dozer, Zee, David, Nat and Jones and I motion them to go back into my new place with me.

"Are we going to go visit the General?" David asks excitedly. I grabbed him because I know that he's wanted to meet the General since right after we first adopted him. Dozer and Zee because they're SEAL's so military and Nat… for a bit of shock and awe. *Mwahaha!*

"Why are we going with you for this? I mean, I get that he's been helping us out with things and that we're sort of following his orders and all but…" Zee says.

"No. That's just it. We're not following his orders. He does not give us orders. He asks us to do things and sometimes we agree, but we do not follow his orders. I made that perfectly clear when I left Y City. Parker and Riley are with me on this. We're no longer under anyone's command. We don't operate that way. Haven't you noticed this?" Casey asks surprised.

"He may make suggestions and we may talk to him every day but he has no authority or control over us. I do know that he supports us 100% because when he was told of what we were doing when we first made it to Y City, that intrigued him, and well… he adopted his role in our affairs and we let him. Mainly because of his experience. But it was us, the group from Fort Smith that started this whole… movement." Jones says proudly.

"Really? Wow! Okay, so why are we going to Y City now?" Dozer asks.

"Well, think of it this way... we're putting our foot down on certain things and the General needs to understand it. He doesn't have to accept it right away and we know he's not going to like it, but he does have to adhere to it. Besides, I think I know why he's all of a sudden becoming so overbearing and this should give him something else to think about." I say with a smirk.

We reach Y City in about five minutes or so and we come out behind the General. We can hear the conversation that he's having with Lucas and I think Lucas is putting the General in his place quite nicely when he says...

"I understand where you're coming from but I think that you need to understand that what you're wanting is fine and all but it's not going to happen the way you want it to. You're going to have to let go of the past and the old ways of doing things and adapt to this new world. Look... I'll admit that this is something that even I'm having a hard time with but...I was recently released from the compulsion that they were talking about earlier. I know what it's like to not be in full control of myself. In the past few days I've seen and experienced a lot of new things. Some things and people that I could never have imagined. Also... I'm not the only one from Butler or other places to think that we've been incredibly lucky after being incredibly unlucky for so long. Do you get what I'm saying?"

"Yes, I do understand where you're coming from but they need to listen to me and do what I tell them to do."

"Heya Chuck? Slow your roll there and keep your shell on. Your way might not be the best way or even a viable option since you don't or haven't experienced this kind of shit before." I say but my darkness has added her two cents worth in too. Casey shoots me such a look of horror at how I'd just addressed his friend and former commander. Jones snorts, David and Nat giggle and Dozer and Zee are just kind of awestruck at their first sight of the General then try to disappear.

General Charles Levin Williams jumps about a foot off the ground and turns around as fast as he can to stare at us. (I didn't know that tortoises could jump.)

"What? How? Who are you? Holy shit! Casey? Explain yourself!" the General demands. Casey just shrugs and points to me. David has a huge gnarly toothed smile on his face and gives the General a wave and Nat waves one of her legs. Jones snorts again and does a polite old timey bow. Zee and Dozer immediately fade farther into the background thanks to their camo.

"Hiya Chuck... look, I know that you don't know Lucas from Adam but at some point soon I'm going to get the two of you together to work on a few things. I think Lucas was starting to draft a new set of laws or constitutions or something. Either way, y'all really need to put your heads together on this."

"Fuck all of that! How did you get here? And why are you calling me Chuck?" the General says with menace.

"Oh, do you prefer Charles? Or maybe Levin?" I ask sweetly. The General turns to Casey and gives him such a nasty look. Casey again shrugs his shoulders and points to me again.

"No. Casey didn't tell me your full name. I'm pretty sure that he's only known about the L and not that your middle name is Levin. I found that out a few days ago, when I stopped by here, briefly. So, I know a lot of things. Now let that sink in for a minute. Plus... I might be able to help you out with your size problem but not right this minute." The General doesn't say anything for a few seconds then he kind of sags. Like a weight has been lifted.

"Okay fine. I'm sure you have a lot to tell me but I think you also don't have that much time right now. So this little stunt was to what?" the General asks and I look at Casey so he stands up straighter.

"Sir. We've run into a few problems recently. Oh hell, who am I kidding. Since this whole fucking mess started, we've all run into a multitude of problems. Some can still be fixed using our tried-and-true methods but some? We need... or you need... to start thinking outside the box. Do you see these two men here? That's Dozer and Zee. Navy SEAL's. They're slowly learning to embrace this new method of thinking." Zee and Dozer manage a sloppy salute after smirking at Casey. "Jones you already know but as you can see, he's changed... A Lot... since he was last here. You've heard us mention and even talked to David before. He's a big fan of yours but now you're getting the chance to finally meet him in person and his... new sister Natalie. Nat and David have become siblings through uhhh... uhhh."

"The Naga's woo woo shit. Is that the term you're looking for?" I ask sweetly.

"Yeah, anyway I uuhhh... I guess..."

"Smooth, so smooth." I aim that comment at Casey, then face the General again. "Look, what I think Casey is trying to say is that the box, or our Old box... is too small now. I've got some new shit going on and there's no way that any of it will ever fit into that small box, ever again. Just to give you a visual, imagine trying to put yourself, as you are right now, into a VW Bug. That's kind of what's going on now. You can still think the way you do, that's fine but you also need to think... bigger or instead of a square or circle, think dodecahedron or dodecagon." I finish with a shrug.

"I'm an old man and I'm pretty set in my ways so it's going to take me a bit to get on board with this new way you're demanding of me. But... I do get you and... I really have no alternative but to try, do I?"

"Oh yeah, you're so old you fart dust. Give me a fuckin' break. If you can accept yourself and everyone around you that's now different, this shouldn't be too hard for you." Nat says. *Bwahaha!*

"Oh, well yes. I suppose so." He says while trying to hide his shock then, "Was this the reason behind this visit? To get me to start uhhhh… looking for solutions… outside the box?"

"Partly. And once you get the hang of it, you might want to share your results with Jack. But Nadja would be the better bet there." Casey says with a snicker.

"The other parts are number one… to let you kind of experience this new thing for yourself so that you won't be nagging the shit out of us with questions and whatever that we have no answers for at the moment. The second part is to make sure you're prepared." I finish with a shrug. The shocked and hopeful look on his face is actually nice to see.

"Really? And Prepared for what?"

"You might be getting an influx of people and new beings that want a safe place to stay for a while."

"I'll talk to all of the safe zone leaders as soon as I can and let them know but uhhh… what about that other thing you said. About experiencing this new thing you have going on."

"I hope you find it interesting. But seriously, you might as well save your questions because I really don't have a lot of answers so…" I say as I motion for him to start moving forward with Nat and David beside him, urging him on.

Once everyone is in and the door closes I don't take us very far. Well, it's far for him but the Peachtree's are at least still in Arkansas. We come out on the far side of the new chicken run and Hexy immediately approaches the fence to say hello to those of us that she knows. I'm not sure if she even cared about Nat and the General at all but she and a few of the other critters are happy to see us. Jasper makes a nosedive at us until he realizes who most of us are and then he lands. Of course he freaks Nat and the General out with his overly aggressive approach and when he hugs me. Jones, Casey, Zee, Dozer and David are having to hold Nat and the General off from attacking Jasper.

"Hey Jasper, it's nice to see you too. Look, I'd like to introduce you to someone that you've heard over the radio. This is the General and this is our new friend Nat." I say and Jasper looks up at the General then over at Nat. Jasper makes a courtly bow to them and then David heads in for a hug for himself while Jones holds out his hand for a shake. Hexy and a few other things in the run hum a nice soothing sound in the background as they crowd the fence line.

"Pictures are worth a thousand words but seeing in person is far better." the General says in embarrassment and then awe. About then Orvil and Reggie come around the corner to see what's up and of course they get introduced and more hugs are doled out. Nat's still freaked out but I honestly think at this point it's because no one has really even batted an eye at her or the General.

"Hey fella's, there might be a bunch of new beings and/or people about to be coming your way, can you handle that?"

"Oh hell yes. You just send them here if'n they're needin' some old fashioned lovin' and support. We got ya." Orvil says with a smile. Reggie says he'll inform the women folk and then run for the hills before he's roped into cleaning something and Orvil seconds that statement with a laugh. After that the rest of us say goodbye to everyone and thing that we know here and I open a door to take the General back to Y City. On the way back there I ask him what he feels.

"Honestly? On the way to the Peachtree's I was too busy looking around, trying to figure out what was going on. I didn't even realize that we'd gone anywhere. Now that I'm looking around? I still don't see much but... everything feels... muted? What is this place? Wait, I know, stop with the questions, but... This is how you got to Y City and is this how you're going to be transporting people to me and to the others?

That's fantastic! This'll also make relocating others easier too! I'll have to mention this." he says with a laugh.

"Oh no you don't. Fuck that. We're doing enough as it is. We're not going to become your new moving service." Casey says as he beats me to the punch. I think he's afraid of what I might say and do and well… he's got good reason.

"Becoming the new moving service is not what you want to do, right? I mean, I know I don't."

"Like you said, fuck that. But seriously, no. And thanks for speaking up, I'm not sure what would've come out of my mouth." Jones and David shudder at the thought, I think.

"Whatever it was, it wasn't going to be anywhere as nice and polite as what Casey said, that's for sure." Zee snarks silently. Nat and the General know that we're all up to something because we're all laughing.

"You guys need to stop that shit or at least plug me in so that I can get in on the jokes." Nat says with consternation.

"Wait, what? Plugged in? What's that?"

"We'll have to get back to you on that, and a few other things but… as you can see, things are off the charts when it comes to weird shit. But I do want to let you in on something really important. You know about **THEM**, right?"

"Yes, Jones takes wonderful notes."

"Thank you sir but I intentionally leave out quite a few things because of their sensitive nature."

"That's ahhh… well, that's to be expected, I believe. So what is it that you want me to know about **THEM**."

"We've gotten confirmation that not all of **THEM** are playing by the rules given to us." Jones says.

"What? How is that possible? I thought that…" the General starts but I hold up my hand for him to stop.

"We have proof positive that some are able to… disconnect? from the rest and it's the rogue element that's causing some of the issues. If we can get our followers to realize that things are really off about this, then things might change. But then again, who the hell knows? Either way, we still might end up being screwed but in the meantime, I don't plan on giving up. How about you?"

"Absolutely Not. And I do believe that none of the rest of us, I mean those in our care or a part of our ever-expanding communities, feel that way either. But just to be on the safe side, I'll keep that little tidbit to myself."

"Well, we're back where we started here. How'd you like your first mini tour?" I ask as we all come out of my magical place. I guess someone had noticed that the General was missing so as we're coming out a bunch of people are coming in, weapons hot. *Oooopsy.*

"HOLD! Weapons down! It's just Casey and Lara with a few other friends." the General yells as Casey and I follow him out. Zee and Dozer are directly behind us then Jones and at seeing them most have their weapons already put away but when David and Nat come out, the guns reappear as if by magic. *Yeah, yeah. I know I use that line a lot. Ha!* David steps in front of Nat and so do Dozer and Zee but David goes one better as he morphs out to become his full Manticore self. Jaws drop and hands shake as the General yells at his people to drop their weapons again. It's also the first time he's seen Davids other form. Even his jaw drops at the sight of it.

"Holy shit son! I knew that you could change but… but you look amazing! Truly." the General says and that seems to take the wind out of his guards or whatever they are sails.

"Thank you sir but I just want you, all of you, to know that I would Not let any of you hurt my sister. Even if that meant that I was going to hurt some of you." *Awww, that's so sweet!*

"David? Let me extend my apologies for this and you may be on to something here. Harper, Anderson, Jacoby you've been here since the beginning, so I think it's time that you guys and everyone else gets a firsthand experience with what it's like outside of Y City. If it's okay with Casey and Lara, I'm going to have you all make up a rotation of some kind and all of you are going to be joining the trailblazers for a bit. I'm coming to realize that even though you all have been crucial to the success of this place, you've all become… I don't want to say sheltered, but… it seems to be the only thing that fits at the moment." While that's going on Nat has picked up David in her big claws and turned him around to face her.

"Look here pipsqueak, I can take care of myself." Nat tells David while he hangs a good three feet off the ground.

"Yeah well, I'm bulletproof and as your brother it's my job to protect you." he says with a shrug. Everyone is staring at them and I think the new guys are a little intimidated.

"Uhh, yes sir but uuhhh… I have a question. For Casey." a guy says and Casey nods for him to continue.

"Will uuhhh… will we be running into a lot of new beings… like these two?" he asks.

"Oh, these two are mild compared to what we usually run into. Plus, I think they're trying to be on they're better behavior. Seriously though, some of the other new beings we've run across have tried to kill us." Casey says with a laugh. Whoever he is, he turns a bit pale but then nods his head.

"I'm taking a page out of your book and not sugar coating anything." Casey says silently as he shoots a look my way. I nod in acknowledgement.

"While your guys are doing that, we've got other places to go and things to do so we'll be back for them, later." I say.

"Wait! I uuhh… I'm…" (his shell slumps again.) "Thank you for stopping by and giving me a run down on your activities and sharing with me a few things. I'll uuhhh… I'll be thinking about that and looking into some of the things you've shared with me." the General finally gets out.

"Not a problem, Chuck." I say as I make a door and everyone gets ready to follow me in.

"Do Not call me Chuck!" is the last thing we hear, after several sputters, gasps and cuss words as we disappear into my magical place. I hope he can't hear our laughter.

"Where to next?" David asks. That's a damn good question and I stop to think about it for a minute. As I'm standing there I get a hint of where to go coming from Wakinyan because she's just started calling for me. So we turn to the northwest and head off in that direction. In less than four minutes we're close enough that I slow down and open a door still on the move. That was not a good idea.

"Holy shit! Walter! What the fuck? Are you trying to roast us?" I yell and everyone behind me yells and hops to the right as we come out really close to a raging fire.

"What the fuck? Jeeeez woman! You scared the shit out of me!" Walter yells as he clutches his chest and Wakinyan and the mustangs gather around my group and we all get buffeted, sniffed then rubbed on. It's good to see the mustangs and Wakinyan filling out and looking so well. The folks with me may have been startled at first but they just let themselves be checked out just like I'm doing. I'm pretty sure they can all feel the curiosity and acceptance emanating from the mustangs and thunderbird. We also hear a bunch of rounds being chambered but I doubt anyone can see us through the milling crowd. After my exchange with Walter the milling doesn't stop until after several cries of pain can be heard, then the mustangs stop and stand with and around us in a semi-circle facing Walter.

"Are uhhh… are you wearing anything under that hand towel around your waist?" Zee asks trying to keep his chuckle from popping out.

"It's called a breechclout." Walter huffs as he crosses his arms.

"Well, it still looks like a pretty decorative hand towel to me." Dozer snarks. Walter huffs again then gives me a really good once over.

"Hey girl. It's good to see you and all but… it seems your caliber of companions has dropped. Speaking of dropped… how'd you just happen to drop in here? I mean, Wakinyan and the others asked us to do a dance to call you in but… I mean… shit. I really didn't think it was going to work. Or at least not this quick. Ya know?" Walter says with a sheepish smile on his face.

"Oh, I get it, believe me. But the main reason I'm here is to let you know that we've found a place to make our own and any time you want to, you're more than welcome. The second thing is, how far are we from Tulsa?"

"Really? That's amazing! Oh, and Tulsa is about fifty miles or so, why?"

"I have some other people who are on their way there or maybe they've made it by now. Either way, could you check it out for me? The leader's name is Becki and her right-hand man is Jim. You can't miss them; he's got white feathers for hair and she's got nice long dreads. If you find them they'll probably be in or near Sam's club or Costco. I think." But I've barely gotten that out of my mouth when Wakinyan and two mustangs take off.

"Oh, well thanks Wakinyan and …" I bust out laughing. "Rusty and Forge? Really?" I laugh again.

"Yeah, well… they were tired of searching for names and settled on those for the time being." Walter says with a laugh.

"But seriously, the gang has been telling me for a few days now that something is coming and that they're going to be with you when it hits you're new place. Any idea what they're talking about?"

"Maybe. See, we've run into a group that kidnaps people and new beings that have a lot of power and they're putting them under a compulsion to obey. Think a lot of cannon fodder here for the not so powerful. The leader of this bunch of nuts is a preacher but think uuhhh… the Jim Jones type. Anyway, his immediate objective is the entire state of Alabama but world domination is probably his main goal. We're going to be trying to get some of the folks and whatever else he's got in at least one of his "training" camps free from his influence and maybe even hit one of his internment camps. But yeah, I think it's his group that's going to be coming for us. Eventually."

"Holy shit! How's he doing all of this? Is he that powerful?" Walter and several folks from his group asks.

"He's got power but he's also got unexpected help. We can't say much more than that." "Ahhh… got you. Anything else we need to know?"

"Watch your back and, well… you know the drill." I say with a laugh.

"Yeah, we know the drill. It's really great seeing you again and we'll be on our way soon." Walter says as he envelopes me in a hug but he whispers in my ear that he knows a little bit about **THEM** and he also knows that there are spies for a lot of different groups and things all over the place. Wakinyan and the mustangs are keeping him filled in? That's fanfuckingtastic!

"It's great seeing you and knowing that y'all are doing so well. I'll try to keep y'all in the loop from now on." I whisper back to Walter and Casey smiles at him as he hands him a radio that Zee had handed to him. After that we disappear back into my magical place and the guys immediately start peppering me with questions.

"What was that? Who was that and what were those new beings?" everyone asks at about the same time.

"That's Walter Runninghorse. His wife's magic is what brought Wakinyan, the thunderbird and the mustangs to "life" during the first few days of the orange fog. We met not long after that and helped them all out with their problem with some guy that had some compulsion thing going on. He wasn't anywhere near as good as some we've seen. Anyway, Wakinyan and the others used to be metal works of art but as you saw, they're fleshing out really well. I think that's because Walter's wife not only wished them to life but also gave a bit of herself to them in the process. They're also the first new beings that I know of that are made from inanimate objects. Now, think about this… can you imagine… Toy Story on a global scale?" most of the guys mouths hang open in shock. *Ha! My original thought was Puppet Master.*

"My… birth dad's stepmom has a room full of dolls. I avoided that room like the plague." David says with a shiver.

"If you think that's bad, my granny has a room full of clown dolls." Nat says in horror.

"Nope! Stop now! Ewww. Nope. Fuck. Don't say another word." Zee says with a shudder and the rest of us go along with that suggestion with no problems. *Can you imagine? Yikes!* "Anyway, thanks for giving Walter your radio and he whispered to me that he knows a little bit about **THEM**. Wakinyan and the rest must be able to sense **THEM** or something."

"Well… he seems like a pretty stand-up guy, no matter what he's wearing." Dozer says with a laugh. The rest of us gave a chuckle too. "So where to next?" Nat asks after cackling at Dozers comment.

"I'm not sure but I'm wondering if Jerry can find people like he can find other things that we need."

"Why's that?"

"Well, this is going to sound bad but the last I heard from my mom she was with my sister and nephews and they were taking shelter with a bunch of religious survivalists. I was thinking about finding them and seeing if they wanted to join us. If he can find them then he could maybe find anyone that you guys are wondering about." I say but right about then we all feel a… something. It feels kind of like a ping?

"What the fuck is that?" most ask at the same time.

"I don't know! But… let's find out." I say with a shrug and we all start walking southeast again but for some reason I think the ping is something that Jerry usually feels. Within a couple minutes I stop in front of a house that has a bunch of cars parked in the driveway and the street is crowded with other vehicles getting packed up. All I can do is stare in wonder then I see a familiar person come out of the garage and I laugh.

"What's this?"

"Well… this is my street, my house and that's my friend Teresa. Looks like she's going to be part of a caravan." I say as we all get closer to her and listen in on her conversation with herself. She's pissed off about something and just wants to get on the road already. Being around a lot of strangers is getting on her nerves. I open a door behind her and we all come out silently.

"If they're bothering you this much, I might have a different job for you." I say conversationally. She jumps about a foot.

"Gawd damnit woman! You just scared the shit out of me. I could've shot you!" Teresa says with heat but then notices that none of her guns were pointed anywhere near any of us. She's shocked by that and then she gets a good look at my companions. *Ha!* She cracks a smile and then her guns completely disappear.

"So what are you supposed to be? The newest version of Anne Oakley?" I ask as I give her a hug.

"You know, that might be exactly right! Well, except for the fuckin' camo. Everything I put on, no matter what it is, changes to camo somehow. But wait! Enough about that! I thought you were in Mississippi or something. How the hell are you and who are your… friends?" Teresa asks with a laugh.

"I'm… there have been moments, you know what I mean? I'm still trying to work some of this shit out and I don't think we have enough time for the rest." I say with a laugh and she laughs with me but we all hear raised voices coming from my house.

"Yeah. Leave it to you to have a bunch of freaky shit going on. Ha! But hey! You said that you might have something for me? Besides babysitting this bunch of idiots? I'll take it! Anything! I just can't deal with some of these fuckin' people. My dad, Rita and James can handle them. They're already afraid that I might shoot a couple of them as it is." Teresa laughs again.

"Okay yes, I have something for you, if you're up for it. Now, the last I heard, my mom, sister and nephews were going to some compound on the Missouri Kansas border to stay with some Bible thumping survivalists. Do you think you could go and find them for me?"

"Oh shit! Your mom? Hell yes, girl! Besides, I bet she's ready to chew her own arm off if she's been stuck with that kind of group for this long." Teresa says with a hearty laugh. *Exactly!* "Let me tell my dad what's going on and I'll be heading out today!" Teresa says as she heads back into my house. *Too weird.*

"This is really your house? It's nice!" David says and I think the guys want a tour but we can hear a bunch more shouting and stuff coming from inside so there's no way I'm going in there. So I walk over to the corner of the garage where the walkway to the front door is and I point and I'm looking at Nat when I tell everyone that this is where I killed Charlotte, my spider lady neighbor that had preyed on and killed a lot of my neighbors in the first few days of the fog. I think Nat thought I was joking when I first told her that. The really weird part is that there's a spider plant growing in that exact spot now. *That's really creepy.*

"No shit? Well… I'm not doubting you ever again. I've learned my lesson." Nat says with a laugh.

"Are you done here? Because if not, I think we're about to have a whole bunch of people coming out of your house. Do you need to talk to any more of them?" Zee says, looking kind of nervous. *Nope.*

"Will your friend be mad that you aren't here anymore." Dozer asks as we all hightail it into my place and I practically slam the door closed.

"I doubt it. Plus she's got a radio now." I say with another laugh.

"Is that what you put in the orange Jeep? Sneaky."

"So where to next?" Casey asks as we start walking east-southeast. I don't have an answer just yet and I'm wondering if something else might catch my attention until Nat comes to a stop.

"Are we… are we heading back to… Mystic Springs?" Nat asks.

"Uuhhh, yeah, why?"

"Well, I recognize this path. I mean, I don't really see anything other than a blur when we're moving but I know that I've been this way before. It feels familiar and maybe… maybe the ground is a different color or something?"

"Hey! I think you might be right! I mean, this path does feel familiar and I'm not sure about the ground being an actual different color but maybe it's just lighter?" David says while looking around.

"No. Not exactly lighter either, more like lighted. I think it's got a slight glow to it. Or at least the part I recognize does." Jones says after getting on his knees to check it out. Everyone turns to look at me. All I can do is shrug. *Freaky!* We follow Jones as he takes us right to the spot that I've opened a couple doors and stops. Yep. At least I know Jones and the rest of these guys won't get lost in here. We step out and again I'm hit in the chest by Gilly. He's not angry, just excited. He fills us in on some of the progress that's been made and then the kids come running up, laughing and claiming that he's just too fast for them. I guess he's been keeping the kids occupied by having them chase him. *Ha!* Then everyone else comes up and from the looks on Lucas, Eddie, Sandra, Marybeth and Larry's faces, there's something up.

Larry starts it off by saying, "Not to sound ungrateful for our pretty rocks and all but while you were gone a lot of us have gotten to know our… new friends? Ben filled us in on a few other things too but…" he stops there because I don't think any of them know exactly what to ask.

"Well… you're welcome for you new friends and we'll explain more when we get back with some of the other folks we left at the motel in West Bend. Then we're going to try something that might… if not answer all of your questions, then it might at least answer a few or give you a little more insight to what's going on. Sound fair?" Everyone nods at that. *Yay.*

"I tried to get everyone to wait but since you do seem to have a lot of answers, they thought you would just start spilling things. I told them that that's not how it works. Even if you had all the answers, I'm not sure that everyone would be happy with most of them. You know what I mean?" Ben huffs.

"Holy shit! I was just thinking something like that!" Dozer says silently and Zee, Casey, Jones and David all nod while looking at me.

"What? I was thinking something like that too. The only suggestion I'm going to make is… don't ever play poker with him." I say with a shrug and smirk. Unfortunately, I'm being serious. Ben just kind of glares at us. *Ha!*

"Alright. So, everyone that came from West Bend, we need to be heading back. If you don't want to, that's fine but we're going to have to let whoever you were with know the reason. There's no way we're going to let folks think that something bad happened to you, you know what I mean?" Zee says while a lot of faces start to look glum at the thought of going back. Liane steps forward and tells us that she doesn't think that's going to be necessary. Doreen and a couple of the other folks will know that they're all okay and pass that on to whoever needs to hear it. She's absolutely right! *Fanfuckingtastic!*

With last longing looks at Mystic Springs and a wave to Liane, since she's staying, the rest of us gather around at the corner of Worley Road then I open a new door. Gilly smacks into me before I make it through the door. Looks like he's coming with us. I take us back to just down the road from the motel and we come out and all of our spirits sink. *Shit.*

"Why'd we come out way out here?" Leo asks as we trudge up the road. Me, Dozer, Zee, Casey, David and Jones just give him a look.

"Oh! I get it. Sorry." he says sheepishly.

"Ah, the art of misdirection. Yes?" Micha asks.

"Yep. Damn! I didn't realize how gloomy this place is. It's like all of our good and happy feelings are being sucked out of us." David says.

"That does appear to be the case. I think it might be coming from one of the newly released. But I'm just guessing at this point." Jones says as he gets out his trusty notebook.

"You think so? Fuck, and I thought my new talent was bad. At first." Bobby says with a sigh.

"But that's just it. It could still be a pretty cool talent if it's used the right way. I mean, if whoever has it could focus it on just the surroundings then that would make a pretty good barrier or something to keep people away from his place or even just to keep things away from a dangerous area." I say. A lot of the others start nodding at that and even Zee and Dozer seem to be thinking about this rather seriously. Casey sees this and gives me a smirk and a wink. Jones is jotting it down in his notebook.

"Yeah, stop thinking small, duffus." Nat says as she gives Bobby a strong nudge.

"First we've got to figure out who has it. But what I'm wondering is… is this natural for them or is it because of this situation." Zee says.

"You know, this is close to what we were feeling after a trap? Yes. This is close." Micha says as he and his dogs finish sniffing the air. Really? *Good grief.*

We approach the motel from the west, like the soldiers had and as we get closer we see a lot of activity. Kabir, Lynx and Ox meet us in the parking lot and fill us in on what's been going on but some of the new people start peppering us with questions.

"Hey guys, you were only gone what, five hours or so? Whatever you were looking for can't be too far away." Shane says with a very calculating look. I'm not the only one to get the heebie jeebies from his statement or his look. Those that went with me all cut just their eyes my way.

"Just doing a little recon." Dozer says casually.

"Oh, I thought you were looking for some place specific. My bad." Shane says then walks away.

"I bet you that that creepy fucker is a mole or something. Or maybe he's bought into the Rev's plan and still believes all of that shit even after being treated like everyone else." Nat grumbles. At first, Leo and Ryan seem like they want to stick up for their buddy but after just a few seconds they both come to the conclusion that Nat's probably right. It's hard to watch the looks on their faces but it's great to see that they can accept it and get past it so quickly.

"This fuckin' sucks man." Leo says as he watches Shane move farther away from us and Ryan nods.

"I know." Casey says and Leo and Ryan turn on him and open their mouths but Casey holds up his hand and starts again with, "I know. I Do Know. It's happened to me. Some of my own company changed, and not for the better, back in the beginning. I didn't want to believe it either. One of the guys, one of my former friends, we had to kill him to get him to stop. It's hard losing a brother in arms, I know this. But it has absolutely nothing to do with you."

"You can't do anything to make him see beyond himself and his own wants. He wants power, I can almost feel it." Ben says.

"See, you guys have it easier in one way and harder in another. Me, Zee, Sonny and Perky lost the rest of our team but we weren't there when it happened. We did get a little bit from Casey when he told us that they'd found a couple of our mates. There's still a couple missing but if they'd been able to make it back, they would have." Dozer says.

"The hard part's going to be keeping everything you've seen and learned from him. If he knows anything that we do, that's going to put the rest of us, including those kids, in danger much quicker than we'd like. You understand that, right?" Zee asks. Both guys nod but they've got very serious looks on their faces. I do believe that they'll be okay, in time. The conversation turns more mundane as we continue back to the motel and finish listening to Lynx as she tells us that there's no way any of them wanted to pack up any of the mattresses from the motel but they did take all of the unused sheets, blankets and towels and ran them through the washing process, twice, and then packed them up for just in case. Along with all of the cleaning supplies that they could find. Smart thinking but I think Lynx has been spending too much time with Doris. *But, I'll never say that out loud. Nope.*

Once back in the motel Nat goes off to check on her uhhh… snacks? But then she starts yelling for us. David, Casey, Jones and I get to her first and she tells us that the "ass kisser" is talking again and wants to know if we can hear him. After shooing away the rest she unsticks him from the ceiling. We stand around his cocoon and everyone places a hand on it and yes, then we can hear him. He kind of gloats about the fact that even if we do leave everyone else here or locked up or whatever he thinks we've done, that soon, some of the spies and whatnot that they have in Coffeeville will follow their compulsion and come here and if no one is here, they'll head for the next outpost and report.

"Do your spies need to talk to anyone from your group or will seeing some of you be enough?"

"I don't know. I would assume that seeing us would be enough but then I don't know if they'll need to be… reprogrammed with new instructions?" he says, sounding confused and uncertain for the first time.

"Well shit. What should we do now? I know you're not going to want to open a doorway to your new magical path place where everyone can see." Zee grumbles silently. But I've got an idea. The look on my face gave me away because everyone that can see it groans. *Bwahaha!*

"Holy shitballs babe. Let's hear it." Casey says with a resigned sigh.

"How about a car chase?"

"A what? Huh. No shit. Really? That… that might actually work." Dozer says while it looks like he's working out the logistics in his head. Casey and Zee have the same expression so I'll let them figure out the best way to go about it.

"If we can get a volunteer or two to ride in the cages, that might make it even more believable." I say while looking at David. His full Manticore form would definitely be something that this bunch of assholes would be interested in. David gets it and grins in my direction. *That's my boy.*

Jones sees the look and snorts which gets a few of the others looking at us. Some snort like Jones but most smile or laugh.

"The rest of us are going to be playing the part of these asshats, right? Yeah, I can see that working. It's just too bad that we can't hose everyone down with goop before we leave." Ox says.

"It might be safer for them if they're left alone. We can't have everyone in the town to just up and vanish. That for sure would raise a bunch of red flags and then they'd be hunted down." Lynx says.

"But what are we going to do with or about Shane?" Leo asks.

"This is going to sound really bad but I can… zap him and we can stick him with the rest of the people in the pool. I don't think they'll drag him around so they're going to have to wait until he wakes up and then it'll be getting close to dark." David says with a grin and a really nasty laugh. *Oh yeah, I really love this kid. Mwahaha!*

"Zapping him isn't going to hurt him, is it?"

"Well, not permanently. It's just going to knock him out and he'll wake up with a headache. Look at Demarcus, he's fine." David says with a shrug.

"I'm okay with this plan and I'm going to talk to Jay about it. If he hasn't seen or felt what we have then me and Ryan are just going to have to get him to trust us. We've known Jay longer than Shane anyway."

"Make it quick okay? We really need to get this shit show on the road." Zee says. At that comment everyone else heads off in different directions to check on one thing or another leaving me, Casey, David and Jones with Nat and her snacks.

"We can take them with us if you want to." I say as I point at the ceiling and the other cocoons plastered to it."

"Well… the chick, you know, the one Zee pointed out? Well… she's uuhhh… she's…" Nat tries to say and if she could blush she'd probably be beet red.

"Oh! Okay, well uummm…Is there enough of her left to uhhh… to help Stanley out with his hunger issues?" I ask. *I know, I know! That's fucked up but… waste not want not, ya know?*

"Well uuhhh… if he doesn't mind beef jerky?" *Oh gross!*

We ask and Stanely tells us that he isn't picky. He's actually very appreciative of Nat's offer and when he shows up the rest of us look for somewhere else to go. Fast! *Gag! Gak! Erp!*

While Stanley's finishing up the bitchy woman in blue Nat takes down the other one and places both at the end of the hall for David and Jones to grab and stash in the bed of my redneck special. Everyone else that's unchained meets in the parking lot and we discuss the next steps. "Are we really leaving now? What about those in the pool?" Amber asks. Jerry and Doreen have a brief whisper conference with her and then she smiles a really nice big smile. *Ha!*

"So, those of us that don't want to go with you can just leave, right?" the snotty woman Steph asks.

"Absolutely. But if you don't want to go with us, you're on your own but just so you know, we can't spare any of the vehicles. Your best bet is to head south from here because Coffeeville is going to be hip deep in soldiers fairly soon." Lynx says with a saccharine sweet smile. Oh boy, what'd we miss there?

"Uhhhh…" several of us start.

"There's just something about her that's not right. She's the type that has to have her way or she throws a fit. The worst part is that her fits are over practically nothing. She's thrown two so far and… I kinda feel sorry for Jeff but since he lets her get away with that shit, that's all on him."

"So those two aren't coming? Got it. Who else?" Zee asks.

"Well, personal opinion only here but... I don't want that Shane guy anywhere near me." Kabir says and that surprises us and I think we surprise him with our plan with dealing with Shane.

"What about the other three that came out of the pool with them?" Zee asks.

"Dido, Erin and Cody are pretty much like us and want to continue on with us. Oh! Did you guys feel anything when you were coming in?"

"Yeah. Some major keep away or just downer vibes. You know who's doing it?" Dozer asks.

"Yeah, that's Cody. He didn't even know he was doing it so me and Kabir took him for a walk and showed him, I don't know... where to aim his new thing at? Turned out pretty good, right?" Ox says and he and Kabir look really proud of themselves. Smart thinking.

"We want to hear all about it but fill us in while we're on the road." Casey says silently but the others can tell we're up to something.

"So, have you given those not going enough supplies to last them for a few days?" Zee asks.

"Yep. All kitted up and ready to leave I believe." Lynx snarks.

"Okay, so what about the rest? I mean, how are we going to do this?" DC asks.

"Well, we're going to need a volunteer or two to ride in the cages in the trucks. Stanley and David are two but we need probably two more. But the gist of this plan is to make it seem we're all in a car chase as we go through Coffeeville." A lot of people seem shocked by this then we all break out in laughter.

"That's... that's pretty genius and devious at the same time. I love it." Doreen snorts.

"Who wants to volunteer?" Jones asks and Micha raises his hand but then looks down at himself and his dogs.

"How the fuck can we get us into cage?" he asks. Stanley lands next to him and looks down then puts his big, clawed hands under Micha's arms and lifts. Of course Venus and Mars start freaking out because they're not used to being picked up so Kabir and Ben grab the dogs and everyone kind of crab walks over to a truck with an empty cage in the bed. After Micha and the dogs are on solid ground again Micha starts laughing like a loon. The dogs appear slightly startled and embarrassed but then settle down quickly. Stanley calmly climbs into the second cage and gives us a big grin.

"How's everyone we see in Coffeeville supposed to know who's who?" Amber asks and several point at the silly armbands some are still wearing. The fact that they haven't taken them off appears to be either another compulsion that's so mild that it's been overlooked or someone else's power. Those with the armbands and a few others appear surprised to see the damn things. Yeah, that's an interesting power. Then there's a kind of scramble to see who's going to sit where. Steph and Jeff stand to the side and if I'm not mistaken, another fit is coming. Aaaannd yep!

"What do you mean you're taking all of the cars and stuff. What about us?" Steph says as she comes up and stomps her foot at us. *Seriously?*

"Yes, we're going to be using all of the rides that are here. Since you don't want to go with us, then you can walk. Also, like we said earlier, you're not going to make it very far before dark so you might as well wait until morning to start out." Kabir tells her with a lot of his old attitude.

"Well that's just not going to work for me. You need to leave something for us." she says with a lot of attitude as she gets up in his face.

"No." he says as he turns his head into his snaky Naga head. She backs up fast and calls all of us freaks. *Mwahaha!* During that hubbub David had snuck up behind Shane and zapped him. Then he went invisible and with Zee and Dozer's help, drug him to the pool and shackled him with the rest of the folks in there and I don't think anyone even noticed. *Bwahaha!*

DC and Jamal come out of the motel with all of our new, much happier plants along with Dos and Tres on Jamal's cart and some of us hear DC apologizing to them and telling them that they won't be kept in those awful containers for very long. When they went past us I could feel that they were very accepting of this and very happy to have DC and Jamal taking such good care of them.

"Babe, I know that we've run into some freaky and fucked up shit in the past but… those plants, that woman? I really feel bad for… them, you know?" Casey says.

"Yeah, I know and I've just got to throw this out here. At least now the ones we have are free and happy."

"That's as it should be." Jones says as he walks by us on his way to another truck and hoists himself up into another cage. David's laughing and being silly as he gets into the other cage next to Jones'.

Casey, Zee, Dozer, Ben, Lucas, Nat and I stop by the pool long enough to pull the cover way back. The dozen or so people still in it are a sad sight. I'm still unsure about leaving Barbie and Ken with them but I just don't want those types of wildcards too close to us. The rest of those folks, well… it's a shame. They could do so many things for the good but they just don't want to and that's fucking sad. Or it could be that they're the type to always follow the crowd or bow down to peer pressure but that's neither here nor there. They have a choice and they had their chance with us. Nat takes the keys for the shackles and attaches a web to them and then she climbs the motel exterior and hooks them way up high, laughing like a loon the whole time. If they can figure out how to get the keys down, then they're free to go running back to the Rev. Good luck with that. Or maybe they can talk Jeff and Steph into helping them out. I don't know and I don't care. Now it's time to get this shitshow on the road.

I hop in the redneck special with the crew I came here with and Casey, Zee, Dozer and DC get in the first super snazzy Escalade. *Of course.* Next is one of the vans and one of the trucks with the cages in it. Nat's maniacal laughter can be heard above the buzz from those in the truck with me. As we all pull away from the Dew Drop Inn, in my rearview mirror I see Steph stomping her foot again and Jeff watching us leave with a look of longing on his face. "I hope everyone went to the bathroom before we left. I'm going to be hitting a few bumps and shit like that to make this appear as real as possible." I say silently and aloud for those in my ride. Nat starts to grumble about the last time we came this way and how bumpy it had been then so I tell everyone in the truck with me to yell "Weeeeee" every time we hit something. At first everyone just stared at me then they all crack up. Gotta make fun where you can, right?

"I seriously didn't expect this to go as smoothly as it did. Or that we'd end up with so many new people. This is great and all and don't get me wrong here but… there's one guy that I just don't feel right about." Wendy says.

"Everyone was gooped, right?" I ask.

"Well yeah but…" Wendy says.

"If it's Shane you're worried about, don't be. He's not with us." Nat says with an evil chuckle through the back window.

"What? I mean yeah, there's something just not right about him but how do you know that he's not with us?"

"You're not the only one that found something off about him and it was decided that he wouldn't be coming with us but it was also decided that it would be a covert action so as not to cause an issue." I hedge. "Do his army buddies know about this?" Lucas asks.

"Oh yeah, they know."

"But what happened to him?"

"He's in the pool with the other bad guys."

"What?" Wendy says with a laugh.

"Let me ask you something about him. What was it that made you uuhhhh… uncomfortable?"

"He reminded me of someone in the camp. One of the guards. He wasn't mean or anything but he…" Wendy says then shrugs because I don't think she can articulate what she felt.

"Oh yeah! I remember that guy. He was super nosey and… I always thought that he was uhhh… power hungry?" Ben says with a thoughtful look on his face.

"Well… that's pretty much what several of us got from Shane too. He's not the type of person that we want or need in our ever expanding group. He's the type of person that only looks out for his own interests first. We really need much better people than this guy." I say.

"I know we're being kinda hard on him and he's not even here to defend himself but… I also know that you're right. He's just another version of that asshole Todd." Bobby says thoughtfully. *Yep!*

"You know, I kinda thought that after being gooped that maybe that Jeff guy would run for the hills but apparently he's okay with being with someone like that Steph woman." Lucas says with a laugh and shudder.

"Well… she's also not the type of person or whatever that we're looking for or need." I snort.

"I thought I heard that she was a college professor or something." Bobby says.

"You really want the kids or even yourself to be taught anything by someone like that?" Nat asks with a whooping laugh as I take us off road for a bit. Everyone else in the trucks does the same thing.

I don't know about anyone else but I feel like I'm in an action movie or even just on one of those car chase shows. I mean, between Lucas, Ben, Jamal and Bobby giving me hilarious instructions, I think we did a damn good job of making everything look pretty realistic. David and Jones silently complained a bit about all the bouncing and Casey, Dozer and Zee were really whooping it up a few times but then we're finally through town. We keep going and only slow down a mile or so from where we have to turn onto the road where some of us have stayed before. After the last vehicle pulls into the driveway and everyone gets out then a mini celebration happens. I don't think even Cody's new thing can put a damper on us but I know that Marsh and Melinda are going to crash, hard, when we show them where their brother met his untimely end.

I gather Marsh and Melinda up and Casey, Dozer, Zee and Wendy go with us into the barn. The siblings look around a bit and take a few minutes to read what their brother wrote. After a few tears and hugs they ask us what happened. Since none of us really know it's hard but we do reiterate that his killers are in **THEIR** own type of prison at the moment.

"So what's next? I know that this isn't the place that you're planning on staying." Marsh says sadly. We tell him that we're going to take everyone to our new place.

"Are you sure you still want to go with us? I mean, we'll give you one of the cars if you just want to go home.

Maybe tell your family what you found." Zee says but we can all see his heart's in his eyes as he looks at Melinda. *Aawwww.*

"There's no one left at home, just… just too many memories. So no, we want to go with you, if that's okay." Marsh says as he continues to hug Melinda and she nods her head at us.

"So are we going to do this the same way as last time?" Zee asks but I'm wondering if he's wanting to show off his muscles or something. The look Casey shoots me tells me that he might have picked up on a little of that so I just smile at him. *Let him wonder.*

"I suppose so. I mean, it should be easier since the vehicles are lighter than the buses." I say with a smirk.

"Well okay then, let's get this shit show going already." Dozer grumbles.

"Jamal? Would you hop in and put the redneck special in neutral for me? Everyone else needs to get back in their rides and do the same thing, we're about to go on an adventure." I say.

"You mean another but stranger adventure, right?" Ben snarks. *Yeah, exactly.* Everyone gets into their rides and I open a door right in front of the redneck special. Casey and Dozer start pushing it into my magical place as soon as I point at them. It doesn't take us very long to get to Mystic Springs and I make it so that my truck is practically at the corner of Worley Road and Mystic Springs Road, in case we need it for something later on. Everyone in it bails out and Lucas says that if I bring in all the other things right behind my truck it'll be easier for everyone. So Dozer, Casey, Nat and I head back. Once we come out we see everyone still in their rides but they're not paying any attention to us, they're all staring at the herd of new beings and Willy and Garth.

"Wow! Are you guys done with whatever it was that you were up too?" I ask and the two fuzzballs snort at me but then tell us that a few of the smaller new beings and things want to come with us because the herd moves too fast for them sometimes.

"Hey, this is going to take forever if we're only moving one vehicle at a time so how about I string a web between all the other cars and trucks?

That way we'll all be hooked together and get everyone there faster, right?" Nat states. That sounds good to me and the guys agree as well so Nat gets started on that while the new beings and a few of the regular critters that are going with us mill around us. David and Jones hop out of their cages and offer them up to whatever feels comfortable riding in the bed of that truck. All of our new people stare in wonder as Jones, David, Casey, Dozer and I pick up and place a bunch of these new, sometimes scary looking critters into the now empty cages. Stanley gives his cage up but even though Micah would like to, he, Venus and Mars are more than willing to share theirs.

"I never would have imagined anything like some of these things. Not in a million years. Are they really here so that they can go with us?" Dido asks in awe. I just smile and nod to her on my way to the front of the line. I'm going to have to get to know her better because… you guessed it. I get back to the front of the line and open a door and the guys start pushing. Nat's webs pull tight and the next car in line starts slowly moving forward. *Heh, this might just be the ticket here!* It's slow going but it does work as we finally reach Mystic Springs via my magical new path as David jokes. When we come out we're met by everyone already here and most point to where to park. Marsh and Melinda seem shocked by all the happy faces and the rest of our brand new folks are equally shocked. Those that have been here for the past few hours, including the kids are absolutely thrilled to see all of the new folks and critters. But I think they all realize that these new critters aren't for petting or even getting too close to. Thank you Wally for the gloves or we wouldn't have been able to get the porcupine, armadillo, some type of bird combo into the bed of one of the trucks. Poor thing can't fly but he seems okay with that. He and most of the others that we brought with us happily wander off as the new folks get introduced to everyone else.

"I'm sorry to interrupt this nice get together and all but how in the hell did we get here and where the hell are we?" Andrew asks as stares around in wonder and he maneuvers himself away from Marybeth and Eddie's rather warm welcome. *Ha!*

"You got here by magic and this is Mystic Springs." Larry says with a laugh.

"Oh Andrew! This is truly amazing! Can't you feel it?" Cammy says as she gives Andrew a shove.

"I definitely feel something." Andrew says as he looks at the woman named Erin and then blushes.

"Holy shit! This guy better watch it, especially once he's plugged in or we're all going to end up hearing things we'd rather not!" Kabir says silently with a laugh. *Halleluiah! I think the stick up his butt has finally been dislodged!* The rest of my fam stops what they're doing and all look at me. What? I did not broadcast that and neither did my darkness. So I just smile and shrug.

"Well, on that note… look, it's getting late and unfortunately we need to get back fairly soon. The we includes you too since you really need to talk to our followers about a few things." Casey stops there and holds up his hand to stop me from speaking and continues with, "So, are we going to wait to try to plug everyone in until you get back here and have Ginger with you or are you willing to let Willy and Garth prove that they're capable of doing her part?" I know Nat wants to be plugged in now and from the looks on a few other faces I really don't want to let anyone down after making so many promises. Fuck it. Let's do this. "If they're sure that they can do it, let's go for it. But only with those that absolutely want it right now. I'm pretty sure some of the folks from today are too overwhelmed for more magical bullshit thrown at them." I say and I can tell that everyone knows I'm standing firm on this.

"Volunteers only, right?" Ben says with a laugh. Exactly!

"So what do we need to do?" Larry asks.

"Make sure you have your crystal on you and we'll take care of the rest." David says with a laugh as we turn and go to the vans and truck that have the plants in them. Jamal and DC have already gotten our originals and gen 1's out but it's the gen 2's that I'm after. The guys figure it out quickly so they start opening cases so that I can pick my target. I need one that has a crap ton of power but not too much. This is going to suck; I just know it. I find the one that I think will be just about right for this and take it out of it's case. Everyone else moves back from me and they're all in a kind of semicircle going from one side of the street to the other. Dozer, Ox, Lynx, Kabir, Casey, Zee, David and Jones are talking to everyone while Willy and Garth stand close by me in the middle of the street.

You know, sometimes I forget that I'm wearing a sword and from the looks on a lot of faces, others forget that I have it too. Magic is just plain weird. So, I take out my sword and internally apologize to this gen 2 for what's about to happen then cut it in half. The power, the stolen magic that it contains comes out and into me in a tidal wave. If Willy and Garth hadn't been behind me I think I would have been thrown back several feet. As it is they're having to dig their claws into the concrete just to stay put. Maybe it's because they aren't Ginger or maybe it's because they're so rough and tumble but that's how the power, the magic feels. Jones, David, Casey, Kabir, Lynx, Ox, Dozer and Zee come up and try to help stabilize me. I know they're talking but I can't hear shit at the moment because it sounds of wind or maybe water is rushing in my ears. After a little bit things settle down and I'm able to hear again but holy shit, this is awful.

"Babe? Can you hear me?" Casey asks while panting.

"Mom? If you can hear us, say or do something!" David says sounding frantic. This is the part I'm not really fond of but I hold out my left arm and David sighs as he makes his nails into claws and cuts my hand. Then I point at Stanley. My big purple friend comes up and stands directly in front of me. No fear. No hesitation. I reach out and put my bloody hand up to his face and paint his purple lips with my blood. Then I place my other hand on his chest. We stand there silently for a moment and then the other guys start calmly telling him to remember what he used to look like and to think about that. My big purple friend licks his lips and it feels like it takes him forever to get his thoughts in order. When he finally does then he starts to get smaller and paler until a middle aged skinny man stands naked in front of us. It took so much to get him to this point that we're both panting. Kabir rips off his shirt and places it around Stanley's skinny waist but Stanley hasn't taken his still glowing eyes off of me. I can hear a lot of gasps and other comments from the onlookers.

"Hi Stanley." I say silently and the rest of the old-timers chime in.

"Hhhh mmm… hi." he says after clearing his throat a couple times.

"Hey man, how do you feel?" Ox asks with a smile and a huge sigh of relief.

"I feel… I feel different. I've been a PPE for so long that this form feels… unfinished or something." he says with a thoughtful expression on his face.

"Well… you do realize that you can change back at any time you want to now, right?" David asks with a smile.

"I can? Really?" Stanley asks.

"Sure you can. Give it a try." Lynx says. With a couple stops and starts and more power pushed at him, Stanley is able to change completely back to his big purple self and back a couple times and the look of wonder and joy on his face is fantastic to see. He stays human for a minute and then after rewrapping Kabir's shirt around himself he steps off to the side and motions for Micha to come up. With a bit of reluctance Micha, Venus and Mars step up to me. His smile is more of a grimace than a real smile so I ask him if he really wants to be separate from his canine companions. All three immediately say yes but I still feel some reluctance from all of them so I ask them if I can show them something. All three shrug and that causes all of them to teeter and I reach out and grab Micah's arm. Then a I smear my blood on Venus, Mars and Micah's mouths right before I pour magic into him. He and his dogs become separate entities once again but there's something about that separation that feels wrong somehow. The dogs eagerly run around for a moment, happy that they're able to move whichever way they want to and Micah looks down at his feet and wiggles his toes, but again, something feels off so I ask them a question.

"Can the three of you work well enough together to become something different? Even more different than you were before? If I can do this for you, I think the way y'all are feeling right now will stop. But... It's completely up to you." Micah looks at Venus and Mars and they look at him and then all turn their heads back to me and nod. Well... here goes nothing. I take the magic and push a lot more at him and his dogs and I think to myself Greek mythology. The three of them start to change again but this time instead of three bodies, there's only one. Only one body but with three heads! Oh! and he's as big as the coyotes are! Even my guys gasp at the sight.

"So, what do you think, Cerberus?" I ask silently and all three of them look down at themselves, have a whole body shake and then answer with a joyous howl. The middle head, Micah, then tells me that this is beyond anything that they could ever have dreamt of. But then they all want to know if they can still be separate at times. The answer is "of course" so with the help of my OG's and a lot more power pushed at them they give it a try. They change back and forth a couple times then they finally stop. Dozer takes off his shirt and hands it to Micah to wrap around his waist and all three of them laugh and howl again. So of course the rest of us howl with them. Our howling gets everyone else doing it and even the new and local wildlife join in. *How awesome is this?* There's still a lot of power left and it's turbulent but then Nat steps up and says "I almost wish you could do that for me but... I know that you can't and... that's okay. We're... no... I'm going to be just fine. Yeah, I'm okay with this, now." I reach out and wipe some blood on her face then I give her the best hug I can. While I'm doing that I push magic into her, to help her

where she needs it the most and then plug her in. She pushes me back and gives herself such a huge whole body shiver.

David steps up and gives her a hug and asks, *"So how do you feel?"*

"This? This is being plugged in? This is absofuckinglutely fanfuckingtastic!" she says aloud then, *"Oh yeah, now I get it, I think. Wow! I mean, holy shit! This is fantastic!"* silently. The rest of us chuckle at her and we all welcome her and Stanley and Micah into our ever expanding family.

"Babe, I know you have more left so what's next?" Casey asks and I just say Butler. Everyone from Butler is called to step up and after touching all of the adults, they're now plugged in after a strong push of magic. The kids, the kids aren't plugged in like the rest, there's no way I'd do that to them but their crystals are plugged in enough so that we can still communicate silently with them if we need to. Nothing more. Their crystals are going to protect them from the more unsavory aspects of this shit. And quite frankly, I think that's a very good thing. They've seen enough and are going to see more than they should but it can't be helped. Someday this might be the norm but I want them to stay kids and innocent for as long as possible.

"Billy, I need you to take the rest of the kids inside and you need to stay there. Got it?" Ten year old Billy jumps like he's been goosed but then nods his head.

"Yes, I mean you too Emily." She pouts at me and puts her thumb back in her mouth but she goes off with the other kids.

"You plugged them in but you didn't. I would not have thought of that. Wise decision." Jones says while jotting this down in his notebook.

"Holy shit! I didn't even consider the ramifications of that." Lynx says and then laughs. "Damn, that's really smart thinking there. So, who's next?" Ox asks and I say Coffeeville. So Larry, Eddie, Wendy, Ben, Jerry, Liane, Amber and Doreen step forward. They look incredibly nervous but exited so I hold out my hand and each one puts their hand on top of mine, like we're about to have "go team" moment. Then I push power out of my hand into them. They all get plugged in with what feels like a snap.

"What the fuck was that?" Larry says as he stumbles back and tries to suck in some much needed oxygen.

"Well... what did it feel like?" Ox says silently with a laugh.

"It felt like I was punched in the gut, through my hand! Oh, wait! Your lips didn't move, but I heard you." Larry says in wonder.

"So this is how you do it? Holy shit! This is soooo cool!" Ben says silently and the rest of us laugh. *"Welcome aboard the crazy train."* Lynx says with a laugh. Wendy just smiles at us with tears in her eyes while Jerry, Doreen, Amber, Eddie and Liane look on at us in wonder.

"You still have more in you, don't you?" Jones asks and I nod. I think I know what I want to try but I need something first.

"David, where's the box with the crystals?" I ask.

"Oh! I'll get it!" he yells as he takes off running. While we're waiting on him I decide to push a little bit of the magic into my sword before I wipe it off and put it away. For some reason I feel that me giving my sword a boost will make up for the fact that I've been kind of misusing it, a lot, lately. I'm done making amends with my sword and it seems very happy by the time David gets back with the box. Our newest people are just standing around watching everyone and I think they're trying to figure out what's going on. Well... seeing is believing and all that jazz, right?

I ask the rest of the folks to come up and reach into the box and pick up whatever it is that calls their name. They all look at me like I'm crazy. *I wonder if that will always be my theme here. Ha!* The others from my fam all nod and get them to come up. Each person reaches into the box like they're expecting to get bitten but when they finally pull their hands out, it's nothing but smiles. An earring here, a pendant there, rings, bracelets, all sorts of crystal bling slowly comes out of the box but there's still plenty left in it after everyone has at least one piece.

"Look, I know that this isn't the best time for this because y'all are still coming to terms with what's happened to you recently but just talk to everyone here. What I'm about to do might just help you as well… now that you've all gotten a new friend or two." I say but I'm struggling here, I've got to get more of this power out of me.

"Lady, uuhh Lara, you've already helped us way more than we'll probably ever know and definitely more than we can ever repay. Whatever you need me to do, just ask." DC says and Leo, Ryan and Jay step up beside him. The rest follow by a few seconds and none of us feel any hesitation from any of them. *Hot Damn!* I touch each one, just like I've done with everyone else here and push more power out and plug all of these really new people in. At first it looks like they're all getting hit with a cattle prod, what with all the twitching and shaking going on but after they all manage to get back on their feet, their smiles seem to radiate hope and happiness. It's the first time from some of them, I think. Marsh and Melinda especially.

Unfortunately, I've still got power and I need to get it out so I walk over to the corner of Worley Road and Mystic Springs Road and off to the left I open a big fuckin' door. From the looks on everyone's faces no one notices what I've done. No one but Gilly that is. Gilly comes up and lands ON the door frame and he finally shows me what type of insect he has in him. He touches his abdomen to the perimeter of my door and that interesting green glow outlines the opening where his body is touching it.

"Lightening bug? You're part lightening bug? Really?" I ask with a laugh. He just wiggles his antenna at me in response. So then I touch my little buddy's face and smear a drop of blood on it. He wiggles like he's being tickled and then the whole door frame is outlined in his neon glow.

"What the fuck is this?" Dozer and a few others ask.

"Babe, is… did he just outline a door?" Casey asks in awe.

"That's so cool! Oh hey! I get it! We talked about something like this earlier, right? Hey Nat? Now that you can see it, can you put a bunch of webs around the opening to uuhhh… keep it open?" David asks as a bunch of people come over and check out the doorway that they all can now see.

"Well uuhhh… I can certainly give it a try." Nat says and she approaches the weirdly shaped opening. It's bigger than the ones that I've made for the buses so maybe one of our RV's or something can make it through.

"Oh hey, do we really want a door here? I mean, are we going to have to post guards or something in case something tries to come out?" Zee asks. Oh, well uuhhh, let's just check and make sure that **THEY** can't get out. I think Casey, David and Jones figure out what I'm thinking because they rush in behind me, along with Larry, Ben, Micah, his dogs and Bobby as Nat starts spinning a strange looking web around the opening.

"Now don't do anything rash here and for fuck's sake, don't burn yourself out. You need to get rid of a lot more of that magic stuff. It's burning you up 'cause I can feel the heat from here." Ben says and I know that he's partially right. I kneel down and place my bloody hand on the ground and release a little bit of the power, the magic onto the path that's slightly glowing under our feet. Huh! That actually made it brighter. I also pour in a bit more to make sure that our unwanted guests will never be able to leave without my help. No unwanted or uninvited guests of that nature at all, if we're going to be getting particular. Then I get another idea. There's no telling if this'll work but… David still has the box so I walk over and look into it and…

"Shit. I can't just reach into the box. I feel that if I touch certain ones it might hurt the crystals." I say with my hand hovering near the box.

"Can we… can we poor them out on the ground so that you can pick what you're after that way?" Bobby asks with an unsure look on his face.

"Uhhh no. I wouldn't advise doing that until you know what this place will do to them." Jones says immediately. Then Micah offers up the shirt around his waist and I laugh and thank him kindly. Seriously, I really don't want to see what he's got especially since I'm going to be kneeling down and that'll be right in my face. *Nope! No way. Not happening.* Nice thought though. I think he gets it and blushes beet red but then Casey takes his shirt off, with a flourish, lays it down, and smooths it out. *Of course he does.* Zee and Ben do the same. *Big sigh.* But hey! At least now there's plenty of room to spread the crystals and jewelry out.

"Are you looking for something specific?" Larry asks as he helps the other guys spread out the box's contents. I spot one thing right off the bat and pick it up. The guys didn't see what it was and they start peppering me with questions.

"Look, this one is for me." I say but then I drop it down the front of my shirt. Nosey Nellies, the whole lot of them. I see a bunch of loose crystals, some are extremely pale and I think I know how to use and help them so I ask Nat, who's just about done with the door frame if she can make a few Jacob's ladder webs about 8 inches long.

"What do I look like? A novice? Of course I can. How many?" she says with a laugh.

"Four." Within a minute she hands them over to Larry and he lays them out on a clear section of shirt. Now, how to make this work. Hmmm.

"Nat? I need a little bit of really sticky web put at certain spots, to hold the crystals in place. Is that possible?"

"Well, I guess so. I mean, just point to where you want it." she huffs at me. So I point out a few spots and when she puts a very small liquid looking drop on those spots. Casey, Jones, Ben and Micha place the crystals that I point out on the liquid web stuff.

"Wow! Check it out! Nat's making her own version of super glue." Bobby says with a smile and a laugh. Nat grabs the back of Bobby's shirt in one pincher and picks him up off the ground so that he's dangling a foot off the ground.

"Well now… think of it this way, this is definitely using my talents outside of the box. But just so you know, this shit's better than any type of super glue." He just smiles at her as she puts him back down.

"Not that I'm not happy to be helping you with this arts and crafts shit but what's this all about? And… are you doing okay? I know you're not done yet." Casey says and I just smile at him as I palm another piece of jewelry while he's not looking. After I stand back up David asks if I'm done with the crystals and I shrug because I just don't know. Either way, he folds the shirts up enough to pour what's left back into the box and hands the shirts back to their owners. Can you guess who didn't put his back on?

"Look, I know that I pester you a lot with wanting to experiment but… with what you're now exhibiting, I think that this is the perfect opportunity to do a couple things while you still have power." Jones says and then we hear Jay bark out "Jerry needs to come!" We all look out of my now glowing door and Jay's standing there with a blush staining his face. Jerry looks at Jay and then us and tells us that he's okay with whatever we're doing. I think he's just more interested in coming back into my magical place but hey, why not? But Jay gets to come too. *Ha!*

"Alright professor Jones, what do you suggest first." I ask but I'm not feeling very good.

"First we need to see how far away you can get from the doorway and see if Nat's webs do work." Jones says. A good plan so far but I go one step further with putting my still bleeding hand on the glowing opening and webs. My blood almost instantly disappears and I'm not the only one that feel a quick zing in my magical place. My old-timers look at each other and they immediately start to do the same thing. The zing of magic is felt by all but then Casey sees my hand and he's shocked by the amount of blood that's still dripping from it.

"Shit babe! Oh man. This isn't good. You've got to heal yourself before we go any further." he says.

"Why didn't you say anything?" Jones demands, angry at me.

"You want to experiment." I say but I'm finally feeling a bit lightheaded.

"Yeah but not at your expense. We can still do things but you've got to finish the… you've got to finish this part first." Jones says as he comes over and walks me out of my magical place. Everyone standing around looks kind of shocked.

"Don't forget to give them a heads up." I say with a slurring laugh. Casey stands in front of me and turns my face up to his.

"Fuck. I know how we usually do this but… I don't want to do it that way. Not again, Not anymore. I don't want you to think about him. Do you understand me?" Casey says urgently as he looks into my eyes.

"Well shit." is said multiple times by multiple people. Then I see a bunch of movement but can't seem to focus on what's going on.

"Not going to be a problem, but just so you know, my imagination only goes so far." I say, still slurring.

"What's that supposed to mean?" Casey asks, looking confused

"Just do it already!" Jones and David say at the same time. So Casey looks into my eyes and tells me to heal myself and then he kisses me. But this time it's nothing like he's done in the past. Not hard and forceful, like he's angry. This time it's with a soft touch. The moment his lips touch mine the power that's left in me comes out turbulent at first then mellows out. What happens to everyone here isn't mellow but it's a whole lot better than it could've been. *Ha!* It's so strong that no one is left standing but at least they weren't thrown off their feet.

I'm smooshed between Jones and Casey in such a way that when I start to giggle, they both complain about the bouncing and that makes me giggle even more. Other people hear me giggling and some of them start doing it too before others start asking what the fuck just happened. Ben sits up with a groan and gives a big belly laugh after getting a good look at everyone laying or just sprawled out on the ground. Lynx and Ox sit up and tell everyone that they should be thankful that no one was driving or working with anything sharp, then they both bust out laughing. *Assholes!*

"Does this happen a lot?" Andrew asks as he sits up and groans, then chuckles.

"Yeah, but only when big magic is used. When she has to heal herself." Dozer answers with a straight face, then he ruins it as he starts to laugh.

"Damn, that's one hell of a side effect!" Larry says as he sits up.

"It definitely has its moments." Zee says as he helps Melinda sit up. Of course he'd make his way over to her for this.

"As embarrassing as all of this is, I rather enjoyed it." Dido says as Lucas helps her sit up from being plastered to his chest. Both are blushing. *Well… would you look at that.*

Casey finally raises up enough to roll off of me and Jones and I roll off the other side so Jones can get up. Once he's up he says that what just happened isn't the only side effect as he politely offers me a hand and helps me to my feet. Cammy asks about the other side effect. He in return asks everyone how they feel. Everyone is silent for a few seconds and then they all start talking about how something or other doesn't hurt anymore. The song "Sexual Healing" by Marvin Gaye starts playing and I just laugh and shake my head at Casey, who has a big goofy grin on his face. Then a radio starts squawking and we all hear Riley yelling at us and asking us what we hell did we just do. *Ooops?* Can the door still being open have made the rest of my fam go through this too? *Holy shit!* Riley says that everyone felt something. Apparently, it wasn't a full blown episode, like usual. *Phew.* Then he tells us that he's done working with Nate and he wants to join the party. Dozer asks him if he'd like to reconsider his request after filling him in on what we're planning on doing. His answer is a resounding "I'm in." After a fairly lengthy conversation and him saying that he's going to fill the rest of the fam in we sign off.

"I'm sorry Jones but it looks like we don't have a lot of time to be doing experiments." I say. "That's okay, I know that we'll get to some, very soon." He says with a smile.

"Well, I guess it's official. Y'all are all now a part of our family. Welcome aboard." David says with a laugh.

"That's right. All are welcome. Now… who wants to go poke a bear or two and stir a bunch of shit up?"

330